PRAISE FOR

*The Last Interview*

"In Eshkol Nevo's extraordinary *The Last Interview*, a writer
reflects on that which sustains and troubles the human heart,
including the fragility of love, the friability of truth, the constancy
of friendship, and the certainty of loss. Through engaging prose,
poignant storytelling, and the sorrowful yet irresistible voice of
Nevo's unforgettable narrator, we are asked to consider the question: How should we be in the world? Always heartfelt and often
heartbreaking, *The Last Interview* is ultimately a balm for those
of us living in these troubled times."

—Judith Claire Mitchell, author of *A Reunion of Ghosts*

"Like J. M. Coetzee's *Elizabeth Costello*, Eshkol Nevo tells us
one writer's views of the world as he answers a series of questions posed in an online interview. His unflinchingly honest
responses—on work, marriage, children, friendship, envy, guilt,
and even the soul of Israel itself—make for an affecting portrait
of a modern Israeli man looking for the truths of his life. The
narrator reaches deep within my heart as he asks the ultimate
question: How can we love, knowing there will be loss?"

—Elayne Klasson, author of *Love Is a Rebellious Bird*

ok a notebook to Ras Burka and every once in a while I u
ills and write about the world beneath the water and the o
its decided to move from Jerusalem to Haifa. I wrote a feu
ove, but as usual with protest poems, it didn't help. After
ad an end-of-year show and Tali Leshem played the flute.
s much as possible in the hope that she would notice me, bu
ng or dance or play a musical instrument. So I volunteerec
ings in the show. In the army, I wrote Tali letters. I though
om me every day, she wouldn't leave me for someone who c
outh America, after the army, I wrote letters to Dikla. Sor
ings that happened on the trip and sometimes I made up t
noticed that I enjoyed writing the made-up things more. D
re I joined my first writing workshop, after I'd graduated f
ord that came out of me there, maybe even ever since, was
oace created by her absence. A year later, Dikla and I got
few choices in my life: marriage, kids, a mortgage. Life m
ow path, and writing was the only thing outside it. The life
orked for a few years, numbed the longing a bit, but then
way to boarding school. And Dikla no longer delighted in
ing of one of those times. A crisis, I think it's called. I figur
w months, but I was wrong. People on the outside don't se
nd I know that now I write to survive. For the last year, I
ar, a trench war in every sense, against dysthymia: an act
rized by a chronic, low grade feeling of depression. In simp
ake up happy and now I wake up sad. I'm not sure I knou
o shake it off, and I don't know how much longer Dikla ca
ie feeling that she's keeping her distance from me. Maybe s
nyway — my morning always begins with strenuous physic

# THE LAST INTERVIEW

### Eshkol Nevo

*Translated from the Hebrew*
*by Sondra Silverston*

OTHER PRESS / NEW YORK

*Production editor: Yvonne E. Cárdenas*
*Text designer: Jennifer Daddio*
*This book was set in Horley by*
*Alpha Design & Composition*
*of Pittsfield, NH*

1  2  3  4  5  6  7  8  9  10

Library of Congress Cataloging-
in-Publication Data

Names: Nevo, Eshkol, author. |
Silverston, Sondra, translator.
Title: The last interview / Eshkol Nevo ; translated
from the Hebrew by Sondra Silverston.
Other titles: Re'ayon ha-aḥaron. English
Description: New York : Other Press, [2020] | First
published in Israel as Ha-Re'ayon Ha-Acharon by
Kinneret Zmora-Bitan, Tel Aviv, in 2018.
Identifiers: LCCN 2020003973 (print) |
LCCN 2020003974 (ebook) | ISBN 9781635429879
(paperback) | ISBN 9781635429886 (ebook)
Classification: LCC PJ5055.35.E92 R4313 2020
(print) | LCC PJ5055.35.E92 (ebook) |
DDC 892.43/7—dc23
LC record available at https://lccn.loc.gov/
2020003973
LC ebook record available at
https://lccn.loc.gov/2020003974

THE LAST INTERVIEW

*Did you always know you would be a writer?*

No. But at some point in my adolescence, I realized
that my masturbation fantasies were much more detailed
than those of my close friends. With them it was always
as bare bones as a mug shot. With me there were obstacles, conflicts, rounded-out characters. If I wanted to be
aroused by my fantasies, I had to believe them, so I constructed them in great detail. I remember a night we spent
in sleeping bags in the basement of Hagai Carmeli's house,
four close friends, and each one talked about his fantasies.
I was the last one to speak, and by the time I finished,
everyone was fast asleep, except Ari. Before zipping up his
sleeping bag for the night, he said in a drowsy voice: Bro, I
think you're going to be a writer. But you have to learn to
cut it down a little.

*What motivates you to write?*

A teacher of mine once told me to keep a journal
during the Passover vacation. I took a notebook to Ras
Burqa and every once in a while I would take it up into the
hills and write about the world beneath the water and the
one above it.

Then my parents decided to move from Jerusalem to Haifa. I wrote a few protest poems against the move, but as usual with protest poems, it didn't help.

After that, in twelfth grade, we had an end-of-year show and Tali Leshem played the flute. I wanted to be around her as much as possible in the hope that she would notice me, but I had no talent—I didn't sing or dance or play a musical instrument. So I volunteered to write the lyrics for the songs in the show.

In the army, I wrote Tali letters. I thought that if she received a letter from me every day, she wouldn't leave me for someone who came home more often.

In South America, after the army, I wrote letters to Dikla. Sometimes I wrote her about things that happened on the trip and sometimes I made up things that didn't happen. I noticed that I enjoyed writing the made-up things more.

Dikla and I split right before I joined my first writing workshop, after I'd graduated from university, and every word that came out of me there, maybe even ever since, was an attempt to fill the huge space created by her absence.

A year later, Dikla and I got back together.

Then I made a few choices in my life: marriage, kids, a mortgage.

Life moved onto a much too narrow path, and writing was the only thing outside it.

The life I couldn't live—I wrote. It worked for a few years, numbed the longing a bit, but then Ari got sick and

Shira went away to boarding school. And Dikla no longer delighted in me.

That was the beginning of one of those times. A crisis, I think it's called. I figured it would be over in a few months, but I was wrong.

People on the outside don't see it, but I know I'm sinking. And I know that now I write to survive.

### What does your workday actually look like?

For the last year, I've been waging an ongoing war, a trench war in every sense, against dysthymia: an acute mood disorder characterized by a chronic, low-grade feeling of depression. In simpler terms: Once I used to wake up happy and now I wake up sad. I'm not sure I know why, I have no idea how to shake it off, and I don't know how much longer Dikla can take it. Lately I've had the feeling that she's keeping her distance from me. Maybe she's afraid she'll catch it.

Anyway—my morning always begins with strenuous physical activity, running or bike riding, which is supposed to release mood-enhancing substances into my bloodstream. Then I call Ari and we talk about Hapoel Jerusalem basketball, the nurses in the department, the chance that the Shabak S rappers will reunite—anything but his illness. Though the conversation is meant to cheer him up, it cheers me up too and takes the edge off my intense feeling of loneliness. Then I doze off for a while, wake up, drink two cups of coffee one after the other, eat an entire bar of milk chocolate, and turn on my computer like someone who seriously intends to write his next novel. I sit in front of the blank screen. A few minutes later, I wander over to this interview, which was sent to me by an Internet site editor who collected surfers' questions for me. I answer one or two of them. Three at the most. Now it's one thirty already, my middle child is home from school, and the racket she makes in the living room is so distracting that there's no point in continuing. So I turn off the computer and go to make lunch. We sit down to eat together. She's been really prickly this last year, and I, with my dysthymia, find it a little hard to take. Nevertheless, I still try to get to her through the tangle of thorns that has suddenly shot up around her, but that's so tiring that after lunch, I have to take a nap. I set the alarm so I won't be late to pick up my sweet little son from day care. When he sees me come in, he laughs with joy and runs to me, and for a moment as brief as a song, it seems that everything will be fine.

### How autobiographical are your books?

Once, I knew how to answer that question. I mean I knew that I would always respond with blatant lies to protect myself and the people close to me. But I also knew the truth, which is that there are and always were bits of autobiography in my fiction, usually in the female characters. To throw readers off the track.

As time passed, things grew more complicated. Because, for example, what can you do with a book that predicted what actually happened in your life? You think you've created a far-out plot, something really bizarre. Then a year after the book comes out, the plot becomes reality. Is that autobiography?

And what about all the "behind-the-scenes" stories I tell the readers at those meet-the-author evenings, stories that are supposed to reveal the personal experiences that led me to write my books? From constant telling, those stories have become so polished and refined that I'm not sure anymore that they actually happened.

Not to mention the habitual tale-telling that has slowly trickled into my personal, nonliterary life.

For example, when I visit Ari in the hospital.

Before we went on our big trip together, my grandmother asked me: Who are you going with? When I said, With Ari, she sighed and said, Very good, he'll take care of you.

Now his strong, sinewy arms have shriveled. And his once full cheeks are sunken.

He asks me to get him a glass of water from the cooler, and when I come back, we begin to talk.

Once, I used to tell him what was going on with me. Today, I tell him well-constructed anecdotes. And I see in his chemotherapy eyes that he knows I'm telling him a well-constructed anecdote, and he wants, he needs me to tell him one unpolished thing, something that has no beginning, middle, or point.

But I can't tell anything but stories anymore. Everything that happens in my real life, from the moment it happens, is adapted into a good story I can tell sometime. When I meet with my readers. In interviews. In my hospital conversations with Ari, who closes his eyes while I'm speaking, takes my hand, and says: Let's shut up for a minute.

***What are you working on right now?***

The truth is that I'm still recovering from the previous book, or more precisely, from the endless emptiness that comes after I publish a book. That's when I invest most of my energy in trying not to fall in love. The year after publishing a book is dangerous. You walk around with such a powerful inner hunger that people can see it from the outside. And the easiest way to satisfy that hunger is to fall hopelessly in love. Let's say with a Slovakian documentary film director with a scar on her left cheek that looks like a dimple who you meet at the Haifa film festival. A passion that takes you a year to recover from. So it's better to stay home. Withdraw from the world. Seal off your heart. To prevent any crack from forming that would allow a woman other than your wife to enter. That's what I'm working on now.

***As a man, how do you manage to write female characters?***

No one notices, but all the female characters in my books are actually variations on the same three:

My wife.

The fictitious woman who is the negative image of my wife, the woman I had to give up any possibility of being with when I decided to get married.

The woman who is me.

I'm embarrassed to admit that it's the third woman I'm most attracted to.

### How do you deal with the exposure involved in publishing a book?

I googled myself once. What a mistake. I spent all night reading things people wrote about me. Once, during a school trip, I pretended to be asleep and heard two kids talking. About me. This time, there were a lot more than two. Maybe a thousand. Maybe two. On one site, they even posted a picture of the sunspots I have on my cheeks and demonstrated how to photoshop them out. I finally went to sleep at four in the morning. The nasty retorts kept rising in my throat. I spooned myself against Dikla's back. Once, when I did that, she would take my hand and put it on her heart. Not lately. Lately, I'm no longer sure she loves me. Nevertheless, I matched the rhythm of my breathing to hers and whispered to myself: I have a home. I have a home. I have a home. I didn't sleep a wink that night, and I suddenly began thinking about—of all people—a neighbor we'd had years ago. An elderly woman—you might even call her old— who once gave me a ride to the sea and, on the way, told me she belonged to a nudist group. And I, only nineteen, loved the idea and asked if I could join. To expose myself.

Dawn was already visible through the shutters. My wife was still breathing the even breaths of sleep.

Everything is foreseen, but there is freedom of choice.

***What kind of kid were you?***

Too much like the crying kid whose picture hung on the wall of the medical clinic. While we waited our turn to see Dr. Schneidtesher, the other kids would point alternately at him and at me.

I delighted in imagining. Not reading but constantly imagining.

And I fell in love. Head over heels. With a different girl each time. But I never said anything to her. And I felt a persistent sense of longing. I remember myself, from an early age, always longing for what was gone. No one had died yet, but we kept moving house. I'd say goodbye to my old friends every summer, and every autumn I was supposed to find new ones. It's not clear, by the way, that that's the reason I felt a permanent sense of longing. Maybe that's just how it is, some kids zigzag their way forward through life and others are steeped in longing for the past.

I try to isolate a concrete moment among all those emotional words. That's what I ask my students to do, be concrete. Dismantle the feeling into specific pictures. But with all the pictures, I don't know what—

I was six, maybe seven, and Grandpa Itzhak took me to an amusement park. He was pretty old already and didn't have the strength or desire to go on the rides. So he just walked from ride to ride with me and occasionally convinced me to drink water from the army flask he'd brought with him. It was fine with me that he didn't join me on the rides. Being alone didn't frighten me then. I got on the roller coaster alone, happily, and didn't scream at all, not even on the steep descents. I found the ghost train to be mostly amusing. The Ferris wheel was an opportunity to look down at the entire city from above. Not even a shadow of fear passed through me—until I reached the hall of mirrors.

A seemingly innocent attraction—so innocent that I don't think it exists today.

All you had to do was find the right path from the entrance to the exit in a hall lined with mirrors.

It started out fine. I took the first and second turns in the labyrinth quite confidently, but then I became trapped inside my own reflections. I remember the moment: I was surrounded by many distorted images that did and didn't look like me. Some of them had a large head and skinny legs, others the opposite, fat legs and the head of an alien. I felt slightly dizzy and had a strong feeling I'd never had before of no way out. I tried to keep walking, but wherever I turned, I encountered my distorted self. Again and again. In the end, I collapsed, defeated, into a sitting position, my back against a wall, and thought, there's no point in calling for help because Grandpa doesn't hear well without his hearing aid. And I thought, I will never get out of here.

Now I suddenly realize how similar that is to the nightmare Dikla woke up from in terror during our first years together. She would jolt upright and pound her chest as if she were choking. Then she would look at me with wide-open eyes, not knowing who I was, and when she suddenly recognized me, she'd ask me to hug her. I didn't have to ask her what happened, I knew that she'd once again been trapped in the classroom and couldn't get out because the terrorists were guarding the door, and she tried to open the window so she could get away and couldn't do it. (In life, not in nightmares, the tragedy in Ma'alot happened when her mother was pregnant with her. The ninth month. They lived right next to the school the terrorists had invaded, and when her mother heard the children's screams, she ran into her neighbor's house, where she knew they had a hunting rifle.)

It's amazing, I think, that two people whose worst nightmare is to be trapped between four walls had managed, somehow, to build a home together.

### Where do you write?

For years I wanted a studio. I wanted to say things like, "I'm coming from the studio." "I'll call you from the studio." But it seemed to be the sort of thing that happened to other people, not to the ones who grew up in a port city and were taught not to spend a penny unless they really had to. Who needs a studio anyway, I convinced myself. Amos Oz wrote in the toilet.

Nevertheless, whenever someone, a colleague, told me he was going to his studio, my heart constricted, as if it had been encircled by a tight elastic band. And involuntarily, the word rolled around in my mouth. The tip of my tongue tapped lightly on the roof of my mouth with the first two syllables and the third spread my lips: stu-di-o.

More than a year ago, I rented a studio in the moshav Givat Chen. I had no choice. I swear by everything dear to me.

The building next to ours was being renovated, and the horrendous noise of the drills and hammers kept me from concentrating. Also, my eldest daughter—before she left for boarding school at Sde Boker—didn't really go to school, and to drown out the racket coming from outside, she played Enrique Iglesias at full volume every morning in her room. Slowly, the walls began to close in on me. A feeling of unease settled in between my stomach and chest and refused to move. I think that was when my dysthymia began, even though I still didn't know that there was such a thing as dysthymia. So I thought, I need a change of scene, and took my laptop to the office of a psychologist who worked mainly in the evening. I agreed to all the demands she said were preconditions, asking only that, in the contract, we change the definition from "office" to "studio."

After moving my laptop to the studio, I added a few books, for atmosphere. I hung a painting I'd received as a gift from a Holocaust survivor, which Dikla said was too sad to hang in the living room, and placed Mayan's picture on the shelf. Walking distance from the studio was a grocery store that sold fresh, salty bagels. And olives. I like olives when I'm writing. There was an orange tree outside the studio and the landlady said I could pick the fruit. In the studio itself, there was a coffee corner with instant coffee, Turkish coffee, and a fridge with milk in it.

Everything was ready.

Givat Chen—so I learned from the sign at the entrance
I passed every morning—was named after the poet Chaim
Nachman Bialik. No one talks about it, it's not very nice
to tarnish the image of our national poet, but Bialik hardly
wrote anything after immigrating to Israel. Apparently, as
he once wrote, his little twig had fallen, leaving him without
bud or flower, fruit or leaf, and for ten years, he produced
only nine poems, which are not among his best. Was the
house they built for him in Tel Aviv too beautiful? Too
comfortable? Did people's adoration rob him of the freedom
every artist needs? And perhaps all his literary activities,
the journals and book publishing, left him no time to stare
into space, and without that, without allowing empty space
to be empty, how can you replenish yourself? Or maybe it
was the opposite. Maybe he took on more and more literary
activities to avoid being alone with his unable-to-write self?
I picture him telling his wife, Manya, before going to sleep
that another day had passed without his having produced a
poem worthy of the name, and the weary look in her eyes as
she listens to him: Really, Chaim Nachman—she thinks but
doesn't say—how long can I listen to the same song?

He waits, eyes open to the darkness until she falls asleep,
and then leaves the house to walk the few blocks to Ira
Jan. She's a passionate woman, an artist who is still im-
pressed by him, and after they have sex, he waits with eyes
open to the darkness until Ira Jan falls asleep, then goes to
another woman, the third—we can assume he had a third

woman—to lay his bald head on her lap so she can stroke
it as she sings to him in Yiddish. But all that bed-hopping
in Tel Aviv is no help at all, it changes nothing, because the
page waiting for him on his desk the next morning is blanker
than usual.

I spent long months in my studio in Givat Chen. I read
my students' texts. I spoke on the phone. I answered e-mails.
I went to the grocery store and came back with olives. I
picked oranges and squeezed them. I stared at the picture of
Mayan, the girl who was killed on Death Road and in whose
backpack my book was found. I listened to entire David
Bowie albums on YouTube. I read medical articles about
dysthymia. I told people, "I'll call you from the studio."
"Let's meet at my studio." I even tried to do yoga on the
psychologist's yoga mat and threw my back out. Maybe it's
the dysthymia that has nailed me so firmly to reality. Maybe
other forces have been at work here.

In the end, I decided to go back home.

Go back home.

The tip of my tongue waited patiently to tap lightly
on the roof of my mouth as my lips alternately opened and
closed around those three words.

***Do you think about your reading public when you write?***

Me? Are you kidding? Absolutely not. It's irrelevant.
And I have no time for it. My mind is so filled with the characters' vacillations and the plot twists that there's no room
for extraneous thoughts. I categorically deny—

Only sometimes, like a streaker dashing onto the field in the middle of a soccer game, a powerful sense of anxiety about money bursts into my mind: What if they don't like it? What if they don't buy it? How will I make a living? For long moments, that anxiety manages to evade the guards of my self-confidence until they finally catch up to it, grab it a bit too hard by the elbows, and escort it off the field.

**Do you imagine a specific reader when you're writing?**

For years, I imagined Dikla. I would picture myself reading the manuscript to her in bed. Reading a page and dropping it to the floor. Reading another page and dropping it to the floor. And she would listen and look at me with the same warm, supportive expression tinged with amusement she'd had before we kissed the first time in the apartment on HaRamban Street.

Recently, it hasn't been working for me. Imagining Dikla as I write. I think the problem stems from the way she's been looking at me since Shira left for boarding school. Her expression is no longer warm and supportive, and it's tinged with criticism.

Do you remember that I'm flying to Colombia on Sunday? I asked her last week.

Yes, she said.

Once, that "yes" held the anticipation of yearning for me. Once her "yes" said: I'll miss you.

This time, her "yes" said: It's actually a good thing you're going away for a while. To tell the truth, I've become tired of you.

I'm not a child. I know that, ultimately, the energy between two people is destined to change its shape. It's a law of physics. I've seen it happen with other couples, and in fact, I knew that it would happen to us sometime.

I just never thought it would happen to her first.

————

A few days later, I sorrowfully packed a bag. Underwear, socks. Copies of my books and students' manuscripts.

Usually, I look forward to traveling.

Usually, when the plane begins to soar, so does my spirit.

*How do you live with the way people interpret and analyze your books?*

I take it in stride. Really. That's the beauty of literature, with every reading, the book is somehow rewritten, right? And that's fine with me. Besides, what can I do? Follow everyone who buys my book from the bookstore to his home, then get into bed with him and make sure he understands?

Simply speaking: Everyone is invited to read my books however they want to.

Except for a certain academic type.

Usually from the literature faculty.

Sometimes you can find them in the cultural criticism or gender studies departments. They're people who have been indoctrinated by the twisted promotion and tenure mechanisms of the university to focus on a very specific niche. Again and again, they publish articles that examine the same research question. And they compel their students to feed on the same square meter of pasture. They've been doing it for so many years that they can read a book only through the narrow prism of their research.

I was once invited to one of those academics-with-theories conferences.

I was happy about the invitation, I must admit. Artists need recognition the way scientists need proof. I even snapped a picture of the poster with my name on it at the entrance to the liberal arts building and sent it to my parents, to make them proud.

But later, at the conference itself, people with advanced degrees took the stage one after the other and imposed overly methodical readings on my book, speaking in authoritative, omniscient tones that made me feel like an ignoramus. I hunched over in the first-row seat that had been reserved for me, and with every knowledgeable sentence spoken on the stage, I withdrew further and further into myself. I put my head in my hands, pressed my elbows against my chest, felt my chest stick to my stomach, until I finally disappeared entirely and the presenter apologized in my name, explaining that personal reasons had kept me from attending the conference.

*Can you make a living as a writer?*

I always fumble for an answer to that question.

I explain that it's a small market. Mention that I also run a workshop. Point out that Dikla is the business development manager of a large firm.

Sometimes I have no choice and I also tell the well-known story of Hershel of Ostropol, whose mother sent him to the grocery store for milk. When he left the store, he was suddenly struck by the fear that the milk was spoiled, so he took a healthy swig before continuing on his way. But then he was struck once again by the fear that the milk had spoiled during his walk. And drank again. Just to make sure. And so he continued walking and stopping to take a drink, until he reached home, and was sent to buy milk again.

As far as I know, there is no such story about Hershel of Ostropol. It's a Yiddish tall tale that makes everyone smile in understanding when it's finished even though the moral of the story is not exactly clear to them.

That's how I dance around a simple truth: We're fine.

———

When I left the ad agency to focus on writing, I said to Dikla, Listen, we'll have to cut back.

She was pregnant with our first child, Shira, not the best time for such a conversation.

Nonetheless, she immediately said, So we'll cut back.

I remember every word of what we said. I remember where we were sitting: in the small kitchen of our rented apartment on Yeldei Teheran Street. On folding chairs.

I remember what she was wearing: A white maternity top with buttons and a ribbon that tied under her breasts. And black leggings.

I even remember what was on the plate that sat on the table between us. Sunflower seeds. From the beginning of that pregnancy, she had a powerful craving for sunflower seeds, and the entire house filled up with small mounds of shells.

Are you sure? I asked.

I'd like to remind you that you didn't marry some princess from a mansion in Savyon, she replied, and that has some advantages. Besides, I'm sure your book will sell and everything will work out.

And if not?

We'll manage. Hello, I'm here too, you know. And that's the dream you've been talking about since we met. To write.

Okay. Should I run down to the kiosk and get you some more seeds?

Later, she said, and pointed to the bedroom.

Again? I sighed. As if I didn't want to.

It's not me, she said apologetically. It's the hormones.

———

The list of things that attracted me to Dikla is very long. Among them are some small, seemingly unimportant things such as the smell of her shampoo or the fact that she knew by heart the plots of David Bowie music videos from the eighties. There were larger things as well, like the fact that she wasn't a flirt and didn't form opinions based on what she read in the weekend papers, and she looked away during extra-violent scenes in TV series.

But I think that the hidden element, what drew me most profoundly to her, was that she didn't have a critical bone in her body. She accepted me and believed in me from the first moment. No undermining or attempts to fix me. She showed her love for me exactly the way her father showed his love for her at the family dinners in Ma'alot. With the warmth in his eyes whenever he looked at her. With the softness in his voice when he called her "my little girl." With the eggplant-and-tahini salad he made especially for her. With the quiet but clear excitement for her every achievement, no matter how small.

That's how Dikla loved me then. Without reservation.

It never occurred to me that, twenty years later, I would call her again and again from Madrid before boarding the connecting flight to Colombia, and she wouldn't answer.

### *How do you deal with criticism?*

My parents are very critical people. Not to your face, of course. But they're both academics, which means that they painstakingly examine everything taking place in their immediate radius in an effort to prove it fundamentally erroneous. For example, for years they've been coming to our place every Monday to babysit their grandchildren. Many things have changed during those years: Every time they arrive, they're a bit more stooped. And they tend to get emotional much more often. My father has developed a chronic cough and my mother doesn't hear very well anymore. Shira, the apple of their eye, has gone off to boarding school. And still, after every visit, they give us feedback. My father in a long text that includes clauses and subclauses; my mother in a phone conversation that begins in an empathetic tone and continues with a detailed description of all the mistakes we're making as parents.

Take a look at yourself, I want to say. But don't. Because I don't want to be disrespectful. Because of the effort they make to come here every Monday.

In any case, when you grow up in that kind of environment, the need to criticize seeps into you, becomes part of you. It flows in your blood like another sort of cell: white blood cells, red blood cells, critical blood cells.

All that discouraged me for many years, and even now, sometimes flings me backward and downward (the movement is always backward and downward). But it also immunized me. After all, the harshest criticism is written in my mind even before the book is published. Now too, as I write, I take a potshot at myself: Are you crazy? Answering an Internet interview honestly? Now it'll be available for years to anyone who googles you.

**Did you ever have writer's block?**

Are you kidding? I have writer's block every morning. This whole interview—to confess the truth—is an attempt to deal with writer's block in a different text.

**What is most challenging about writing?**

The minute I start writing, I have an urge so strong that I can't ignore it, the urge to eat. I go into the kitchen after every page. No, after every paragraph.

But that physical hunger is something I can deal with.

The real problem is a different kind of hunger.

**Your books are very Israeli. Don't they lose something in translation?**

I wish I knew. The truth is that I have no idea. At a dinner with my publishers in Turkey, for example, they told me that they had to cut several erotic scenes from the book because the Erdoğan regime had recently begun to harass publishers who weren't careful enough. I sat there as if nothing had happened, nonchalantly ordered *sütlaç* for dessert, and thought: Who knows how many times this has been done, in other languages, in other countries, without anyone bothering to tell me.

Generally speaking, there is something fictitious in the whole business of translations. You go to a foreign country. They invite journalists to your hotel. It's a two-star hotel, so there's no lobby to speak of, just a small corner with an uncomfortable couch. You sit on that uncomfortable couch for three days. And are interviewed. Some of the journalists represent publications with names like *Quinoa Chic*, *Unshaved Men*, or *Dogs and Sleds*, and they seem a bit too friendly with the publisher's PR woman. You can also see, or think you see, slight physical similarities between them and her, and you begin to suspect that these interviews have been prearranged: All the PR woman's relatives have been recruited to give you the feeling that there's enormous media interest in your book. Even though that week, in the country you're visiting, a new book by Axel Wolff was published.

Your suspicion grows stronger when you suddenly realize—how did you not notice it before?—that even after years of work trips abroad, you have never actually seen someone reading a translated copy of your book. Not in cafés. Not in the subway. Not on trains. For years you walked through train cars, ostensibly to get the kinks out of your lower back but actually in the hope you would see someone, on the left or on the right, with your book. One reader would be enough to restore your confidence in the reality of your existence. But on the right and on the left, in the standard cars, the first-class cars, and the reserved-seat cars, everyone's reading the new Axel Wolff.

Conspiracy theories begin to sprout in your mind, maybe some convoluted plot has been hatched behind your back by Udi, your devious agent, the Israeli Foreign Affairs office, and the publisher that's hosting you. They all know it's just a facade, they all make an easy profit from the fact that your book has been published but not distributed, and you, the only Truman in *The Truman Show*, keep traveling abroad, still believing that this time it's happening, this is your breakthrough.

The last trip was to Colombia, and something in the combination of the huge quantities of rum, the terminally

run-down hotel whose only occupants, apart from you, were
Japanese, and the streets full of totally nonliterary beggars
blurs the line between reality and simulation. It makes you
feel untethered, like an astronaut outside his spaceship,
repairing a glitch, whose cable suddenly disconnects.

After the series of interviews, you spend the free time
you have left in Bogotá making the rounds of the bookstores
that are open late. Axel Wolff's new novel in Spanish translation appears in all the windows. You go inside and look
for your book on the central display tables. You search the
eye-level shelves, then the lower ones. Your book is not on
any shelf, not in any store. In one of them, you swallow your
embarrassment and go over to the counter to ask. The clerk
checks the computer and says they don't have any in stock.
But he can order it for you if you wish. When you go out into
the street, you hit the lamppost just to see whether it hurts.

After the sixth tequila, in a bar where all the patrons
look like extras hired for a bar scene, you pay the bartender
and begin walking to your hotel. You remember that when
you were a kid in the fourth or fifth grade, your social life
improved miraculously in only a few months. In the time
between Hanukkah and Passover, you went from being shut
out to being sought out, and the shift was so sharp that you
suspected your parents had set it up. That they had bribed
everyone, boys and girls, so they would be nice to you.
For an entire year, you walked around with that suspicion,
looking for signs to reinforce it. And now, thirty years later,
you're right back there.

You want to call home. Speak to your wife. Hear a familiar voice. Grab on to something before you finally lose your balance. But the time difference. And the expense. Besides, whenever you've called her from abroad recently, she hasn't answered, and if she has, there was no indication in her voice that she missed you. And there are other signs: She stifles yawns when you insist on foreplay, she doesn't notice your haircut, when you tell her about an argument you've had with someone, she automatically takes his side. But of all those signs, which have become more numerous this year, her I-don't-really-miss-you voice on the phone is the most upsetting.

So you don't call home, to avoid feeling hurt, but the next day you have no choice, and in order to be sure you exist, you come on to a Colombian journalist who looks like Gabriela Sabatini, the tennis player. You flirt with her during the interview and ask for her e-mail address so you can send her some poems by Yehuda Amichai in Spanish translation. You send her the poems along with an invitation for dinner, but there's still a cloud hanging over the meal: Maybe she's an extra too? But when you kiss, the cloud disperses. She kisses hard and well, and you hail a taxi and go to your hotel. You walk past dozens of Japanese in that lobby, and you feel as if you exist. You fuck, and suddenly, you don't care whether people abroad read your book or not. Later, she looks for her large earrings, which she took off before she undressed. She wants to go, but you touch her arm and ask her not to leave you, and all night, you sing Shlomo Artzi songs in Hebrew into her ear and fuck her. You fuck her and sing Shlomo Artzi songs. Over and over again. She's divorced with a kid, and in the town she comes from, everyone knows everything about everyone, so she hasn't been with a man for two years to keep them from gossiping about her in the local *churrascaria*, and she has a poem by Cavafy tattooed on her lower back, right near her buttocks, not "Ithaka," something less well known. She doesn't write fiction, only poems, and not for publication, and every time she comes, it sounds as if she's having a serious asthma attack and might die.

She puts the large earrings on in the morning and goes off to interview other writers who have come to the festival, and you fly back to Israel.

You arrive in the middle of the night, carry your suitcase up the stairs to your apartment, and feel like Odysseus returning to Ithaca. Your wife is sleeping, buried deeply in the blanket, and you wake her with a kiss and tell her everything. There has always been complete honesty between you, and after you started becoming a professional liar, it became stronger, the need for one person to whom you can tell the truth and only the truth. But it's not just that. You want her to truly wake up. To open her eyes.

The more you tell her, the straighter she sits up in bed. Shoves another pillow under her head. Moves from lying down to a full sitting position. Her eyes open wide. She can't find words.

Talk to me, Diki, you plead. Say something.

She shakes her head. Slowly. Her eyes are shining.

I was lonely, you say, I was very, very lonely.

Lonely? she asks. There is disgust in her voice, but you ignore the caution sign and continue—

I wasn't lonely just in Colombia, but before then too.

What are you saying, she says, and now her tone is blatantly sarcastic. Distant.

You try to take her hand. To keep her from dropping away from you.

Don't touch me, she says. And says, I was lonely too. And says, But it didn't make me sleep with someone else.

After the last sentence, she stands up, her long hair tangled, brown snakes climbing over each other, one hand clenched into a fist, the other spread like a STOP sign on the road.

She asks you to leave the house.

She doesn't care that it's the middle of the night. Or that the neighbors can hear you begging for your life. Since the dysthymia, it's been impossible to live with you anyway, she says, she's been close to the edge because of all your trips, and Colombia—Colombia is just the last straw as far as she's concerned. She pushes you out, actually puts her hands on your chest and pushes you out, and you stand outside your front door at five thirty in the morning, one foot on the morning newspaper, the other on the doormat, and you don't know where to go. The last time something like this happened to you, you found shelter at your grandmother's place. But she's dead. Until a year ago, you could drive to Ari's, because you had an unwritten agreement that, no matter what, you would always be there for each other. But Ari is dying in the hospital now. And they're very strict there when it comes to visiting hours. Anyway, this isn't the right time to dump this whole story on him. So you get on your bicycle and pedal to the studio. You're no longer a partner in it, you left a few weeks ago because you couldn't write even a short story there, but you remember that the lock on one of the windows is broken. When you arrive, you open that window, climb inside, and go to sleep on the psychologist's yoga mat. In your clothes. Without a blanket.

In the morning, you buy toothpaste and a toothbrush in the grocery store, brush in the sink that's in the coffee corner and wash your feet in the same sink. While you're lowering your feet back onto the floor, your lower back goes out again, so you hobble to the yoga mat and lie down.

At nine in the morning, there's a knock on the door.

You're still on the mat. And you can't get up to open it.

You shout, "Come in!"

A messenger enters and hands you an envelope.

You sign for it, lying down, to confirm that you've received it.

The messenger looks at you and says, I don't believe it!

On second glance, you recognize him. A few years ago, he was in your workshop. And he was pretty talented too. He wrote an inflammatory story about euthanasia, about someone known as "the Angel" who went from hospital to hospital in Israel between two and four in the morning to help people die. You remember that this student standing in front

27

of you now used to go out to smoke during breaks, and at the tenth and last meeting, he raised his hand and said defiantly: We've talked about a lot of things in this workshop, but we've ignored the most important question—why write at all?

Now he asks, Does your back hurt?

Along with other things, you say.

He suggests you phone a house-call doctor to give you an epidural.

You say, I've taken enough painkillers.

He says, Okay, but why suffer?

You promise to consider it.

After he leaves, you open the envelope, find the forms, and read them. Several seconds pass before you understand that you're reading divorce papers.

The director asks the cameraman to do a close-up of you.

You don't see a director. Or a cameraman. But suspect they're there. Part of the convoluted scheme, the big, ingenious translation scam.

You think about your kids, who still don't know—

And start to cry.

For the camera.

And then it slowly turns into real weeping.


***Does the line between truth and lies sometimes become blurred for you?***

They took us for a polygraph test, all the cadets in the course for field security officers, they wanted us to learn about it up close, understand how it works. They put a small group of us, along with our commanders, into a room that contained a lot of instruments and a bearded researcher in civilian clothes. The bearded researcher asked for a volunteer to demonstrate. Without too much thought, I raised my hand. Just to stand out. He sat me on a chair and connected a few tubes and wires to my stomach and arms. Then he said, I'll ask you several technical questions. He asked my name, my age, and my address. I answered succinctly, and then suddenly he asked me whether I'd ever used drugs. I said no. Without blinking an eye. The researcher didn't blink either, and continued to ask me more questions that I don't remember anymore. At the end, he thanked me, asked everyone to approach his Formica table, and explained how to read the graph. My heart was pounding and drops of sweat rolled down from the back of my neck along the length of my spine. The researcher said, Our volunteer spoke the truth all the way through, and he showed us how the various measurements the polygraph had recorded indicated that the responses of my body, even if there were big jumps in the lines, were still within the normal range. Later there were some questions, I think, and then we left the room and another group entered. We went to the canteen to wait until the bus took us back to the base. I bought a Coke, I remember, and when I opened it, the gas burst out all at once and sprayed everyone standing next to me.

For years, I hoped I'd accidentally bump into that bearded researcher again, on the train, on the street, in my family doctor's waiting room, and ask him what really happened there: Did I manage to fool the polygraph machine? Or for some reason, did he decide to lie and save me from being thrown out of the course? But time is going by and the image of him is getting so fuzzy in my memory that sometimes I suspect I might have made up the whole story.

**When you start writing, do you know how the story will end?**

No, but I know how I will end. I always knew that the men in my family die young. Based on the family average, I'll have my first heart attack in two years. It's all about genes. But recently, since Ari got sick, it's been having a real effect on me. The feeling I had in my twenties and thirties that nothing's urgent has now become a feeling that everything's urgent. Among other things, the crucial question of whether I want to spend what's left of my life on earth writing. Whether finishing another book is the most important thing to do before the chest pains begin. Maybe, instead, I want to spend more time with Dikla and the kids? Maybe I want to go into politics? For a short time, is what I mean. Until the heart attack. Or live in Australia for a year or two? Or travel around the world looking more seriously for my childhood friend who disappeared on me after the army, and then have the attack knowing that, at least, I did what I could to find him?

I usually begin to see the end of my books—the way you see land from a sinking ship—close to the end.

I keep on swimming a while longer in the sea of infinite possibilities. Then I emerge from it in sorrow and relief.

*How do you choose the names of your characters?*

Ari's mother came to take her shift at his bedside.

Usually, we exchange only a few words in Spanish and I leave. But there was something in the way she came into the room. The way she walked, heavier, wearier than usual, made me decide to stay a while longer. I didn't have a home to go back to anyway. Just a yoga mat. So I offered her my chair and dragged one in from another room.

Ari was sleeping. From the way he was breathing, it was a deep sleep.

I brought a few empanadas, she said, taking a plastic container out of her bag.

She looked a bit like Mercedes Sosa. That thought flashed through my mind every time we met. Something Indian in her eyes. And, in fact, in her son's eyes as well.

*Gracias*, I said, and took one.

Your friend, he's very strong.

I know.

*Finalmente*, he will conquer this disease.

What are the chances, I didn't say.

When he was two—she said, and stopped.

I looked at her. She was silent. I took another empanada.

He was . . . very naughty, your friend, she began again. We ran around the house after him to keep him from breaking things.

That sounds just like him.

When he was only a year old, he refused to take his afternoon nap. All the children in preschool went into the room with the small mattresses and went to sleep, and he would drive the teachers crazy. But they loved him. Because he did everything with that smile of his.

I can picture that.

And one evening—she said and closed the box of empanadas—I was in the kitchen. Marcello, my husband, was at work. I usually picked up the pieces of Lego after Ari finished playing, but I forgot. It just happened. I forgot. I was with him all afternoon and I was tired. He didn't tell you this story?

No.

All of a sudden, all I heard was silence. I was in the kitchen and I heard a bad silence coming from the living room. I ran there. He'd swallowed a Lego piece.

Uh-oh.

A big piece. Four quarters.

Oh no.

I tried to get it out, I slapped his back. It didn't come out. I called an ambulance. Meanwhile, he didn't have any air. He couldn't even cry because he had no air. The ambulance came fast. On the way to the hospital, he actually died. *Muerte clínica*. How do you say that in Hebrew? He was clinically dead? But in intensive care, they brought him back. And he was like that for a few days, between life and death.

Wow.

Then we changed his name to Ari.

What do you mean, changed it?

He never told you he had another name?

No.

*Bueno*, maybe he forgot.

What was his other name?

Enrico. That was the name of Marcello's brother, he was one of the *desaparecidos*, the ones that the junta disappeared.

I didn't know that—

You see, Marcello, instead of blaming me for being so stupid to leave the boy alone with the Lego, the way any man would, he blamed himself for giving him a bad name, an unlucky name.

Why unlucky?

You heard about the Madres de Plaza de Maya?

Yes, of course.

So Marcello's mother was one of them. Her son Enrico, Marcello's brother, went to work at the printing house one morning and never came back. She demonstrated with the mothers in the plaza every Thursday until the junta fell. But even after the junta fell, the government didn't give any information about Enrico.

Bastards.

They say some of the disappeared were thrown out of airplanes.

Really?

And that's why Marcello came to Israel. He didn't want to stay there anymore.

What a story.

And the doctor in the hospital said, Your son fought like a lion, an *ari*. He fought like an *ari* for his life. So Marcello went to the Ministry of the Interior and changed his name to Ari.

And it helped?

Only God knows. And I don't believe in God at all. But yes, Ari opened his eyes and started breathing again, and the doctor said—I will never forget his words—"The deciding factor in cases like this isn't only the death force but also the life-force. And your son has a very strong life-force."

That's true.

And that's why I tell you that he will win this time too.

I hope so.

You really didn't know anything about this whole story?

Not a thing.

Okay, you know what they say—you learn something new every day.

That's right.

Now you can go, you were a good friend long enough today.

Don't be silly, Mrs.—

Carmela—

Carmela.

And take the empanadas with you. You look hungry. Everything is okay with you, *corazón*?

———

My characters' names are inspired by people close to me, to commemorate them or to get my juices flowing. But sometimes the fate of the character changes as the story moves forward, so there's a burning need for a different name.

***If you could invite three writers, dead or alive, for dinner, who would they be?***

If we're already talking about a dream dinner, I wouldn't waste it on colleagues.

Writers, dead or alive, tend to be focused on themselves in a way that turns them into the most frustrating conversation partners. Furthermore, there's always a suspicion that an intimate anecdote you relate at a dinner with writers will become raw material for any one of them. After all, most of the supposedly biographical details in this interview are supposedly taken from a conversation I had two years ago with a supposedly Scandinavian writer in a Jerusalem restaurant. Supposedly. Axel Wolff's thrillers were phenomenally successful all over the world, but nonetheless his shoulders were stooped, his eyes dull, and his blond hair lackluster. I asked him a lot of questions in an empathetic tone, trying to understand how he could possibly be so popular everywhere and not be happy about it. That's how I learned, among other things, that what happens in Colombia doesn't always stay in Colombia, that a girl can break her father's heart, and that the dysthymia makes you feel as if your body is covered by a layer of ice: Tiny fish of happiness swim beneath it, but you can't reach them because the ice is so rock-solid that you can never break through it.

In any case, I would invite three childhood friends to that dinner. We've been friends since high school, but lately, we haven't had a chance to see each other. We made too many children. We took on too many mortgages. And Ari is hospitalized in Tel Hashomer.

I would pick up Yermi and Hagai Carmeli from their mortgaged houses and we'd drive to see Ari. We would disconnect him from all the machines, dress him in his old twelfth-grade sweatshirt (because of his illness, he's lost all the weight he gained since then), and sneak him out of oncology to the pub in Kfar Azar. Maybe it still exists, that pub, with its long wooden tables. We'd drink shandies and munch pretzels from a little glass bowl, in memory of the old days, and talk about everything but the fact that Ari might die. Hagai Carmeli would definitely start crying at some point, he always cried when he drank too much, and Yermi would constantly look at his phone and come on to the waitresses, even though at our age, it's pathetic.

When the check came, we'd all pay our share and, as usual, realize that we'd paid too little, and everyone would have to add something. Except for Ari, whose share we'd pay.

| | |

My friends never think of me as a writer, and never will. At the most, they think it's funny that I've become a person who gets interviewed.

They saw me copying during the Bible final exam; they saw me come home from basic training in the Armored Corps broken and humiliated; they saw me in love with Tali Leshem for four years, a love that everyone but me was sure would end in tears; they scraped me off the floor after she married someone else; they sat shivah for my grandmother with me and know that I'm still mourning for her; they helped me walk after my slipped disk; they helped me move apartments, even when we'd already reached the age when you hire movers to do the job; they call me at the studio now twice a day to make sure I'm still alive.

They know very well that I don't have answers for anything. And that if I had the courage, I'd reply to all the questions people ask me in interviews the same way: I don't know. I have no idea. Ask someone who understands.

———

After we managed to pay the check, we'd return Ari to the hospital, take off his sweatshirt, dress him in his open-backed gown, cover him with a blanket, and sing him songs from the first Knisiat Hasechel album until he fell asleep.

Yermi would definitely try to flirt with one of the nurses in the department.

And Hagai Carmeli and I would wait patiently until he finished. Like we had so many times in the past.

Then we'd all go out together to the huge parking lot.

On the way, Hagai Carmeli would definitely say: Maybe that was the last supper. He always had the tendency to say things there was no need to say but that sounded nice.

After a long silence that might have embarrassed other people, we would get into the car and I'd drop each of them off at his house and say, Regards to the wife, and then drive to the studio, alone, slower than usual, thinking that if Ari really dies, it'll be a sign that an era in my life has ended. And a new, totally different era is beginning.

**What is your favorite word?**

Scandalmonger.

**What word do you hate the most?**

Terminal.

Such a two-faced word. It can be the place where you begin a journey, filled with the promise of exotic lands and new experiences.

Or it can be the end, the very end. Of everything.

**If you weren't a writer, what would you be?**

A deejay. That's my standard reply. It sounds good and it's not a complete lie.

But the truth is that if I weren't a writer who ran workshops and acted as my kids' chauffeur, I would spend more time and energy looking for Hagai Carmeli. In high school, we were a threesome: Ari, Hagai Carmeli, and me. Ari and I trusted and supported each other totally. Hagai Carmeli, you could only trust him as far as you could throw him. But I've never had the kind of soul-searching talks I had with him in his basement with anyone else. Not even later, with the women I loved, did I have conversations like that. We would play chess until midnight to the sounds of Pink Floyd, and then get into our sleeping bags and talk till morning. To the sounds of Pink Floyd. There was an old grandfather clock in the living room that used to chime really loudly on the hour, and that's how we knew time was passing. At six in the morning, light would come in through the curtainless only window in the basement, and that's how we knew that the night had ended. When I close my eyes now, I can hear Hagai Carmeli's voice drifting over to me in the darkness of the basement, always a bit hoarse, the slow lilt of his speech a soft buffer against the very sharp things he sometimes said. "Tell me, man, don't you feel . . . a little stupid when we sing 'Wish You Were Here'? Everyone we know is pretty much here, right? So who's left to miss?"

An intimate conversation with someone you're close to is one of the greatest pleasures life has to offer. But for such a conversation to take place, you need a partner who knows how to listen and also how to confess. How to seek the truth without being hurtful. Unpredictable but not threatening. And of course, you need time. So that both sides can dig deep. And you need a place where all that can happen. In short, we're talking about a miracle that takes place only rarely. And that miracle happened to me with Hagai Carmeli over and over again—before he disappeared.

It's tempting to blame the army for the way his life got turned around. It adds an ideological layer to the story. And yes, the army really did screw him up. A series of unfortunate incidents possibly caused by his big mouth and his slowness, but also by the stupidity of the system, led to the most intelligent person I know ending up as a base maintenance worker. He transported gravel from one place to another in a wheelbarrow, swept sidewalks with a witch's broom, and, as he walked the paths of the base, contemplated the unbearable heaviness of being. I used to visit him on the Saturdays he was confined to base for one reason or another, and we would sit in the sentry booth all night—his cocked weapon hanging across his short body, his curly red hair sprouting from under his helmet—and listen to Pink Floyd, cooking up schemes to help him transfer to another platoon, to a job that would truly enable him to contribute. Occasionally, we would go out for a slow walk, a very slow walk, around the booth so he wouldn't fall asleep, and when he fell asleep anyway, I kept watch so his commander wouldn't surprise us, ready to elbow him in the ribs to wake him, listening to the random words he muttered in his sleep, "No," "Normandy," "Twenty-two," trying in vain to squeeze some meaning out of them.

He was finally discharged due to psychological problems.

But it wasn't just the army that unhinged him. There was also that business about his little sister Danya. They were too close, almost joined at the hip. He never said it in so many words, but apparently, when they were teenagers, that closeness spilled over into forbidden territory. Or maybe it was just in his head, maybe he just fantasized a spill over, which in itself was forbidden. I'm not sure. That was the only subject he was silent about in our conversations. But I remember something he once said to me, in the basement (he spoke the kind of language that wasn't ashamed to be beautiful, which also got him into trouble in the army), "I need to get as far away from her as possible. There are people who simply weren't meant to live together in the same house."

In the end, he left the country. Not because of her. And not because of the army. He got involved with the wrong people. After his early discharge, he became obsessed with making as much money as he could. He opened a café and closed it. He imported and exported. He bought and sold. When I asked what, he said, "You're better off not knowing."

With me, he only talked about what he would do with the money, a different grandiose plan every time: establish an NGO that would help soldiers in emotional distress, establish a museum of the Hebrew language, buy all the land adjoining Ga'ash Beach so no one could ever build there.

Then one night, when he was twenty-five, he pulled a vanishing act. It seems that he owed a lot of money to a lot of people and loan-shark thugs came by his apartment twice and broke windows.

He didn't get in touch with me before he disappeared. Or after. I thought it was his way of protecting himself and was sure he'd come back. I give him a year, two at most, I told Ari. But three years later, there was still no sign of him on the horizon. And what was more upsetting: There was no sign of life. And even more upsetting: I was the only one who cared.

His father had died in the Yom Kippur War—Hagai was two then—and his mother developed Alzheimer's at a relatively young age, and when I called her, she didn't even remember who Hagai was.

So I called Danya. His sister.

A year earlier, by chance, I was sitting in a café where she was waitressing, and now I went back to that café. She was still working there, and she dashed around the tables with amazing speed. So different from the pensive way her brother ambled through life. When I told her I wanted to speak to her, she said, "Not now," and wrote her number on a piece of paper.

She answered after one ring.

I said: It makes no sense that in the twenty-first century, a person can fade away without leaving a trace. I suggested we raise some money and form a search party. Or that we hire the services of a well-known missing persons site.

You can't laugh in someone's face over the phone, but that was my feeling, Danya laughed in my face. A search party? To look for Hagai? First of all, if he doesn't want to be found, you won't find him. Believe me. My résumé includes hundreds of hours of playing hide-and-seek with him in the backyard. Besides, exactly who would you ask to contribute? All the people he owes money to? Do you know that your friend went through all the money I saved up in a year of waitressing? He asked me to lend him money right before he disappeared. Said he'd pay back everything in a week. You think you know him? You don't know a thing about Hagai.

But I miss him, our conversations, finally I have someone to think about when I hear "Wish You Were Here"—I wanted to tell her, but didn't. Maybe because it suddenly occurred to me that the bitterness in her voice had something to do with what had spilled over between them.

Ari didn't think it was such a great idea either. You know what I think of Hagai, he said. A brilliant guy, but bottom line, the only thing he cares about is himself. You think he'd organize a search party for you if you disappeared?

And so it happened that the search party formed to find Hagai Carmeli consisted of only one person. Me.

I developed a ritual I follow on every trip I take. Right after checking in at the hotel, I drop my luggage in the room and check the schedule left for me on the desk to make sure there's no interview planned for the next hour or two. I'm considered a minor, if not unsuccessful, writer in most of the countries I visit, that's the bitter truth, but it has its advantages—the schedule they leave for me on the desk has enough holes in it to be insulting, so I can leave immediately to wander around the city. Without a map.

Those rambles have two purposes: The obvious one—to get lost. And the hidden one—to find Hagai Carmeli.

———

Two years ago, in Istanbul, I momentarily thought I'd succeeded.

There are chestnut vendors on the streets.

And one of them—it's hard to explain.

Something in the way he moved his hands. His protruding elbows.

I moved closer to him.

I listened to him speaking with a customer. The voice—slightly hoarse. The cadence—slow. He could have dyed his red hair black. He could have surgically altered his face. That's what you do when you want to disappear.

I went over to him and asked for some chestnuts. I tried to catch his eye. But he treated me as if I were just another customer. Picked up a handful of chestnuts with an iron scoop, dropped them in a brown bag, and turned to the next person in line.

I decided to take a chance. I walked about ten meters, leaned on the fence of Gezi Park and shouted: Hagai!

It's instinctive to respond when your name is called.

I didn't think he would look at me, but I studied his face for the slightest movement. The smallest twitch.

Nada.

A few birds, frightened by my shout, flew into the park, and the chestnut vendor continued serving his customers.

But the next morning, he wasn't there. I told the story
to my hosts from the publishing company, who explained to
me that all of Istanbul knows that chestnut vendors are actually undercover agents for Erdoğan. They have been keeping
an eye on the goings-on in Gezi Park since the attempted
coup five years ago. That's why they change their posts so
frequently.

That explanation didn't convince me and I kept searching for him in Istanbul. And, in fact, in every place I've been
to during the last few years.

When I meet with people, during newspaper interviews,
on the subway, in taxis, on the streets—I never stop searching for Hagai Carmeli.

In an act of desperation, I made him a character in one of
my books. Under another name, of course. He also disap-
pears in the book, and there are all sorts of rumors about
him, but in the end, at the moment of truth, he returns. I'd
hoped he would somehow get ahold of the book. I pictured
him arriving at a meeting with readers—at first I wouldn't
notice him because he's short and hidden by the crowd.
Only later would his red hair pop up, and at the end of the
meeting, he would wait patiently for the last person who
approached to ask questions to leave, and only then would he
come up to me, my book in his hand, and smile that mini-
malistic smile of his at me.

Even in my answers to these questions—which I promised myself would be totally honest and open—I mentioned
him as a genuine friend who played an active part in my life

and included him in the last supper with Ari (it's so easy to learn what didn't happen in a writer's life from the books he wrote, but most readers still insist on doing the opposite).

I also returned Yermi from the abyss of oblivion to that supper, even though I have no idea what's happening with him today. In fact, even though I've been writing about circles of friends for years and lecture about friendship as a major value of Israeli society—

I've had only three good friends.

Only one is left.

And soon, maybe he . . .

Then what?

Where will I take my secrets? Who will I tell that I haven't been sleeping at home for two weeks now and that when Dikla and I talk on the phone about which of us will go to the parent-teacher meeting and who will take care of the car insurance, her voice is colder than Jerusalem in winter? Who will I be my real self with? Can a person live without any friends at all?

*How do you manage to deal with the loneliness that's part of writing?*

I don't.

*Who is your first reader?*

I circle around Dikla on the days she's reading my manuscript, waiting for her to say something. Waiting for her to fall asleep so I can see how much she's read. And if she wrote any comments. Bottom line, I can't do anything without thinking about what she will say.

The most difficult time was during my exile to the studio. She didn't really send a messenger with divorce papers for me there after I returned from Colombia. She's not that kind of person. She just asked me not to come home for a few days, or weeks, it was hard for her to know. She needed time to digest it all and decide what she would do. She also asked me not to call. So she wouldn't have to not answer.

That was a dark time. I could barely move from the yoga mat because of my back pain.

I canceled all my writing workshops. And all my meetings. I didn't tell anyone, at first. She asked me not to. And I didn't know what to tell them. The situation was unclear.

The tone of her voice in our last conversation led me to believe that there was a real possibility I might lose her.

———

On our fifth date, she said that since she read *The World According to Garp*, she'd been dreaming of marrying a writer. That was the most personal thing she'd said to me until that moment. Most of the time she was silent, listening, and every now and then, she offered mature, astute opinions on a variety of social issues. It seemed to me that she was hiding a wound under all those adamant opinions. She majored in philosophy and business administration, an unusual combination, and she'd come back from London a few months before we met. She'd gone there on a trip, met a rich twenty-year-old Brit, and moved in with him. A year later, they had a bad breakup. She didn't want to tell me any more than that. But whenever she mentioned him, there was more anger than hurt in her eyes. Maybe that's why she's so cautious with me, I thought, but never dared to ask. She wore tailored clothes. Restrained. Not Israeli. Not student-ish. She was my height without heels, and taller than me with them. It lent her an aristocratic look. Distant. Sufficient unto herself. But the way she moved her hands was remarkably impassioned and sensual. She had long, thin arms, and her hands opened so slowly that they seemed to be caressing, inviting.

It was like that for almost a month. Her body said, Don't you dare come close to me, but her hands said, Come here now. I didn't know what to do with that double message, and more than anything, I didn't want to make a mistake, because from the first moment Ari and Meital introduced us at that club in Kibbutz Cabri, I'd had a sense of destiny. As if something very important was about to be decided. Or, in fact, had already been decided.

We went out four times, and at the end of each date, I didn't know if there would be another one.

That's how bad I was at reading her.

Then I told her that I write. Sometimes.

And she said those words, that she had always dreamed of marrying a writer, adding a flirtatious smile, the first flirtatious smile. She leaned slightly toward me, revealing her spectacular collarbone.

———

After we slept together, we lay beside each other in bed.

I remember that I said: Wow

And that she said: Wow.

I remember that I stroked her and said: You have a dancer's body.

The truth is, she said, that I danced in the Ma'alot Hora group. And she giggled. They thought I'd turn out to be something.

And . . . you didn't? I asked gently.

I didn't pass the academy tests, she said. Truthfully, it was pretty humiliating.

I waited silently for the story, which did not come.

I still didn't know that that's what I'd always get, it was all her pride would allow: quick glances into the wounded area. And there would be something terribly frustrating and, at the same time, seductive about that.

———

I was twenty-four that night, an age when it's still possible to have new dreams.

I can't say that I became a writer to win Dikla's heart, but I can assume that with another, less stimulating woman, I wouldn't be writing.

When I left on a trek to South America a few months after we met, she was in the middle of the academic year, and she wasn't the type to change plans for anyone.

One of us suggested that maybe we should see other people while I was away.

The same one, waiting in Amsterdam for his connecting flight, changed a bill for some coins to drop into the pay phone, and said, I take it back, I don't want to lose you, you're the love of my life, it doesn't matter how long this trip takes, I'm yours. Yours alone.

I kept my word.

I wrote her long letters while I was away. Very long. Dozens of crowded pages. There were days when that was all I did: write to her. Ari showed exemplary patience. I remember a particular roof in a town called Tumbes in Peru that had straw chairs and a footstool on it, along with an ugly view of buildings. I didn't come down from that roof for two days, and every time Ari came up to ask what was going on with me and when were we finally going to move on to another place, I said, Just a sec, bro, I'm in the middle of a letter.

In fact, everything I've written since then, eight books, is one very long letter addressed to her.

I never let anyone else get as close to me as she did. Her name alone engulfed me with softness.

I can't fall asleep without her, wake up without her, fall without her, find my way in the hall of mirrors without her.

In the end, I'll probably show her this interview too.

————

She called me after I'd been sleeping in the studio for two weeks.

Said the kids missed me.

That she doesn't know what to tell them.

That she's sick and tired of having to take care of everything herself.

I said, Does that mean I can come back?

Yes, she replied, but—

I said, I'd like to remind you that all the men in my family die young.

And she didn't play her part and laugh.

We haven't slept together since then. After the kids fall asleep, I go to the couch in the living room, and before they wake up, I fold the sheet and blanket, drink a cup of Turkish coffee, and make their sandwiches: cream cheese for Yanai, cream cheese and olives for Noam. I also make a third sandwich, with cream cheese, olives, and cherry tomatoes— for Shira. Then I remember that she doesn't live at home anymore. So I eat it myself.

————

Yesterday, I asked Dikla if she would mind reading something new I was working on. Of course, I waited for the right moment. I waited for her to come back from her evening run. Ten kilometers. I waited for her to finish showering. Shampoo, conditioner, body lotion. I waited for her to put on the sweat suit she wears at home and the thick woolen socks she bought in London when she was there with that twenty-something guy. I waited for her to brew her homeopathic tea, spread her long legs on the couch and sip it. I waited for her cheeks to redden from the heat of the tea and her eyes to become shiny, as if she were crying.

Then I asked her.

She said she didn't have time for it. She's in the middle of another book, a thriller, by that Scandinavian writer, Wolff? You know, the one who looks like a Viking?

I persisted. I asked again.

She shook her head and said that, the Viking aside, it was just too soon for her to read something of mine. That until now, she could always separate the story from the writer, my fantasies from the reality of our life, but she wasn't sure she could do that now.

A wave of coldness flooded my body. Like the one I'd felt at the edge of the abyss on Death Road in Bolivia.

I went into the kitchen to load the dishwasher and said to myself, It won't be easy, but that's my mission: to do everything to make her believe once again that everything except her is and always will be only a story.

### What kind of music do you listen to?

Damn that song. Even when our love was very much alive, there was something stressful about listening to it on the radio when we were driving together. Even when the drive could end in our turning onto a dirt road to undress each other, right then, because we couldn't wait—those lyrics sounded like an ominous prophecy that would come true in the end, because even we, whether we wanted to or not, would follow the herd of mumbling souls—

Now, a week after returning home from my exile in the studio, we're driving to the wedding of one of her employees. And there's a traffic jam on the highway.

We'll be late, Dikla thinks.

Of course, I think. It took you so long to get ready.

I'm getting old, it takes time to camouflage it, Dikla thinks.

You just get more attractive with the years, I think.

Colombia, she thinks.

Not a word is spoken.

And then that song that Ariel Horowitz wrote for his wife, Tamar Giladi (how does a woman feel when a man writes a song for her called "Love Is Dead"?)—

And both of us, at the same moment, reach for the dial to change the station.


*All of your books are written in the same style. Have you ever thought of writing something completely different? Maybe science fiction? Fantasy?*

So let's say I wrote something about a different planet. And let's say that planet had two suns. And three moons, one of which was the planet's Siberia, where people were sent for punishment. And let's say that every new person you met on that new planet wasn't really new to you, because a few seconds before the encounter, all the intimate information the Web had collected on him was transmitted into your brain. And let's say there was an underground of people who wanted to disconnect from the Web so they wouldn't know everything. People who believed that life without secrets was not worth living. And let's say that the authorities on the planet persecuted those people in the underground. Or the idea of democracy didn't yet exist, and the council of representatives of various giant Web corporations ran things. And let's say that the leader of the underground was a woman with a dark secret in her past. Really dark. Which was revealed to every new person who met her. And let's say she was sick of it, which is why she had the need to conceal, to leave the past behind and turn over a new leaf. And let's say she knew a hacker named Tristan Carmeli, who fell in love with her despite her dark secret, or maybe because of it. And Tristan Carmeli managed to find a way to hide her and all the underground people somewhere inside the Web. Not outside the Web—because that's where the authorities would search for them—but inside it. Very deep inside it. Intra-Web. Like an air bubble in bread. And let's say that Tristan Carmeli lived deep inside that intra-Web hiding place and wrote poems about the world that he and the other underground people would have liked to live in. And let's say that his poems had to be short, shorter than

haiku, so he could conceal them in code. And let's say that
one of the poems was:

*I will wait here*
*Until the first leaf*
*Falls*

And the other poem was:

*Once*
*To travel*
*Without destination*

And let's say that, in the end, he couldn't control
himself and wrote a longer poem, maybe even a story, to
the leader of the underground, confessing that he thought
her dark secret, the secret she tried so hard to hide from
the world, was beautiful. And let's say that because of that
overlong poem, the underground was exposed and all its
members received the harshest punishment of all: a full
Wikipedia entry loaded with links. And banishment to the
third, Siberian moon. And let's say there was an iRobot
with a sense of humor in the story. And a forest where the
trees could run. And cars that turned into jet fighters with
the click of a button. And an app that enabled you to see
the dream you had last night, along with possible interpretations, on your phone display.

What difference does it make.

In any case, it would turn out that once again, I wrote about an impossible love.

**Have you written any stories you would never publish?**

### MAYAN'S PICTURE

So listen. I lost your picture when we moved. And I really tried to make sure nothing happened to it. I put it into a plastic sleeve, an entire plastic sleeve for one small picture. I have no idea how it happened. I still hope I'll find it, there are two or three cartons we haven't had time to unpack yet, but chances are I won't. And it's breaking my heart, you know? I kept it with me all the time, I want you to know that. Since your mother came over and handed it to me after the lecture in Ganei Tikva and told me that they found a book in your backpack, which returned on the plane along with you.

Look, this is Mayan, she said, pointing to you in the picture.

Even before she pointed, I knew it was you. Something in your expression. If I had been your age and traveled to South America and we met in some ramshackle hostel for trekkers—I would have fallen in love with you, Mayan. I have no doubt at all. I'm a powder keg of emotion just waiting for a match, and the way you're standing on the sand, your right foot slightly forward, your left hand on your waist—even

though it's a still, I can guess how you walk, Mayan.
Your steps are like a dance, and you tilt your head a
bit to the right when you approach people, right?

I kept the picture in my hand even after the taxi
picked me up and looked at it for a long time: four
girls in bathing suits. One of them, not you, was
holding a surfboard. I liked the picture because,
contrary to what I would expect from a trek picture,
there was no pretense in it. It looked as if someone
sneaked up on you and took your picture before any
of you were ready. None of the girls but you looks
especially happy. To be honest, you all look beat.
People don't talk about it when they come back, but
wandering is exhausting, and there are so many moments of extreme loneliness on a trek, aren't there?

At home, I propped your picture up against the
books on the shelf in my den. It was so small that it
fell a few times before I understood how to position
it on Yehuda Amichai's *Achziv, Caesarea and One
Love*—do you know it?—which jutted out a bit from
the other books. But even then, I would occasionally
find that, when I was out, a gust of wind had blown
the picture onto the floor. I would pick it up and put
it back on Amichai. Gently.

It was obvious to me that people who entered
the room would have something to say about that
picture. A man who keeps a picture of four girls
in bikinis in his den—how could they not make

remarks and give me a conspiratorial pat on the back. But I never gave them an explanation. I never told anyone the story behind that picture. Even a story monger like me has his red lines. They can all go fuck themselves, I thought, it's something that has to stay between you and me.

What I did do sometimes—can I admit it?—was look at you before I started to write. It helped light a fire under me and made me remember that there was someone on the other side.

To be honest, it's become a ritual lately, standing in front of your picture before I start to write. Like a moment of silence on Memorial Day, except without the siren. (Tell me, Mayan, did you raise your head and look at other people's bowed heads during the moment of silence at school? I suspect you did. In the picture, too, you're standing slightly apart from your friends, not completely a part of the group, sort of watching from the sidelines.)

In any case, when we moved, your picture disappeared. As if there were a hidden abyss between the apartments into which only the most important things dropped. Maybe that's what I'm trying to tell you in this letter, Mayan. That you have become someone important in my life. Without ever having met. Without ever having spoken. Without ever having written to each other. Somehow, it happened. I've become attached to you. I began wondering what you would say about certain stories. Then I began consulting with you before making decisions about things that had nothing to do with my stories. One look into your green eyes, and suddenly it became absolutely clear to me what I should do. I told you—not out loud, I'm not crazy, at least I wasn't until recently—about things that were happening in my life. About becoming my own jailer. About the fact that I dream about tunnels. About how it feels to be unloved in your own home. And about how your picture got lost—I really hope it hasn't, and as soon I finish this letter, I'll have to unpack those three cartons, and I pray I'll find it there, but if the picture is really lost, I can't see how I can go on from here. I mean, first of all, I can't see how I can continue to write. If I don't write, I have nowhere to put my memories, and that's dangerous. I have a problem. I don't forget anything. My forgetting mechanism is completely screwed up. All the partings, the deaths, the unexploited opportunities. They are all trapped in my body, and writing is the only way to release them. Like a passenger arriving at the check-in counter only to find that his suitcase weighs too much—I write because if I don't occasionally unburden myself of the weight of some of those memories, I won't be able to breathe. No air will enter my body. Or leave it.

I'm not exaggerating. It's a matter of life and death for me. It always has been.

Sometimes I imagine your last trip, from La Paz to Coroico. If I close my eyes and really concentrate, it's as if I'm with you and your friends in the van. I'm sitting beside you. Fear is making you sweat, and I smell the sweet scent. You're wearing fisherman's pants tied with a string, and your legs are pressed against each other. Our knees are almost touching. And on the turns, they do touch. Did you know that I once traveled on that hellish road too? When your mother came over to me with the picture after my lecture in Ganei Tikva, I didn't tell her. I didn't want to hurt her with the fact that I survived. But I'd also been warned about that road, twenty years before you were, and I didn't pay any attention either. When you're twenty-something, warnings are like flies you shoo away with your hand. But I remember that during the first hour of the ride, I realized I was in real danger. The lane was terrifyingly narrow and three days of constant rain had softened the shoulders, turning them into mud. Every time a van came from the opposite direction, our driver executed some frightening and risky maneuvers in reverse: In order to let the other van pass us, he had to pull back so that the rear end of our van was almost hanging over the ravine, but not completely, because then the center of gravity might move too far back.

At some point I closed my eyes. I couldn't keep looking into the chasm that opened beneath us without getting seriously dizzy. Did you close your eyes too? Or maybe you opened them when the drop began? Whenever I picture that precise moment of your final trek, I suddenly feel a powerful desire—idiotic but powerful—to save you. After all, I took a medic's course in the army. If I had reached you in time, and not twenty-four hours later, like those useless Bolivians, maybe I could have saved you. I don't know whether you had a normal life, and even if you did, after a five-hundred-meter drop in a van that turned over at least six times before it stopped at the bottom of the wadi—but maybe, who knows, who can know . . .

I kept my eyes closed almost all the way to Coro-ico, opening them only when there were potholes and the van juddered.

The two Germans who were with me didn't speak, either. I remember that one of them had a book. He held it open as if he were calm enough to read, but he didn't turn a page for a long time.

Suddenly it turned very cold.

Each of us huddled into his poncho.

The German with the book closed it and pushed it under his thigh.

A list of things I still hadn't done passed through my mind: becoming a father, publishing a book, learning to scuba dive. Silently, I recited the haftora from my bar mitzvah from beginning to end three times. I shoved my hands under my thighs to keep them from shaking. I wanted so much to live then. I mean—

I think I already knew then that life brings pain. Of course I knew. But the proportions were different: There were more desires. The pain was duller.

Over this past year, because of the dysthymia, I sometimes wake up in the morning with a pain in my other heart, not the one that pumps blood but the one behind it that feels fear and anxiety, and the pain is so strong that I have to ask the question, THE question—

But until now, I always had a clear answer.

I would go over to your picture.

There's a hint of a smile in the corner of your mouth. Not an actual smile. Definitely not laughter. More an inclination of the mouth that hints at an inclination of the soul toward goodness.

Do you understand? This entire year—maybe it's even longer? It's hard to know exactly when the deterioration began, or why, maybe Ari's illness was the trigger, or Shira's departure for Sde Boker. In any case, this last year I've been a musician who's lost the rhythm of the piece he's playing, in the middle of a performance, in front of hundreds of people. All the other musicians are waiting for him to get back in step. The audience is already whispering. But he can't manage to do it. Every time I looked at your smile this last year, it reminded me that I haven't always been like this. Which means that maybe this dysthymia thing is just a tunnel I have to pass through. Then I'll reach the light.

I still have three cartons to unpack. We put them in my den temporarily, and they've been here, piled one on the other like blocks in a kindergarten. I've postponed opening them for a few days already, each time with a different excuse.

Actually, this whole letter is an attempt to postpone opening them for another few hours. To leave us a chance, even a small one.

### Were you ever in therapy?

I decided to surprise Dikla at the Watsu pool. Once every two weeks, she took off early from work, went there to do Watsu, aquatic shiatsu, and came home a different person. More radiant.

I thought, We'll go out to eat after her treatment. It could be a propitious time.

I arrived a few minutes before two thirty. There's a kind of waiting space there with cushions and poufs. And a pleasant breeze. A thin partition separated it from the pool.

At first, music came from the direction of the pool. Just music. And then the music stopped and I heard Dikla say something. Her therapist, Gaia, replied. Then there was the kind of trickling sound of someone coming out of the water. Then some more trickling, similar but different. Now they were both standing close to the partition and I heard Dikla say, "In any case, before the bat mitzvah, I don't plan to make any deci—"

In the middle of the word, they moved the partition and came out together.

Dikla is tall and narrow-shouldered. Gaia is short and broad-shouldered.

A thought ran through my mind: I wonder how they look when they're in the water.

Dikla completed the word—"sion"—before she realized it was me, sitting on the pouf. She stopped talking.

In the tenth of a second it took for her to dredge up a reasonable response to my being there, I understood that she wasn't happy to see me and they had apparently been talking about me. About us.

Hi, I said.

Hi, Dikla said and kissed me on the cheek. Not on the mouth.

I have a free hour, I said. I thought we could go to Goferman's for something to eat.

They've closed, Gaia said.

And I have to drive Gaia home, Dikla said.

Right, I said, and casually took a step back.

But we can have coffee at Aroma, near the house, Dikla said.

Okay, I said, see you there. Then I said to Gaia, I want you to know that I'm really jealous of Dikla. The way she looks when she comes home from here makes me think that Watsu therapy is just what I need.

You're always welcome, Gaia said, her tone reserved.

———

We didn't have coffee at Aroma. Dikla got stuck in traffic on the way back from Gaia's and then it was time to pick up Yanai from day care.

But I did go for Watsu therapy. A week later. Not at the same pool Dikla goes to, so as to not invade her territory (that's how I felt, like an unwanted invader).

On the way to Safed to give a lecture, I stopped at Amuka. There's a therapeutic pool there too. From the outside, it looks like a greenhouse, and inside—water and a wooden deck, a small dressing room, and robes for men.

I don't remember the name of the therapist who greeted me. Fifty-something, long hair gathered into a ponytail with a rubber band, soft eyes.

The water was hot, but not too hot.

I leaned on the rim of the pool and asked her, How exactly does this work?

You'll see in a minute, the therapist said with a smile, and asked, How are you?

How am I?

Yes, how are you?

So many people have asked me how I am these last few weeks, I thought, but no one asked like that. With simple curiosity. Not prying. In a way that required an honest answer.

I hurt, I said.

Where?

In my posterior heart.

Your posterior heart?

Not the one that pumps blood, the one that's afraid of losing people.

Where exactly is it located, this posterior heart.

In my back, between my shoulders. That's where I feel it.

Is there someone in particular that you . . . are afraid of losing?

The truth is that I'm afraid of losing a few . . . someones.

Okay, she said, and instead of asking me about my childhood and my relationship with my parents, she leaned forward and put floaties around my ankles, took hold of my fingers, and in a slow, continuous movement, cradled me into her body and began to slide me through the water. Gently, at first, like a paper boat, and then slightly faster. I closed my eyes, but a series of practical concerns kept me from abandoning myself to it: I hadn't asked her how long the session lasted. I still had to drive to Safed, a minimum of twenty minutes away. Do they accept credit cards? And if not, where the hell would I find an ATM in this out-of-the-way place?

Slowly, the water separated me from my thoughts. Of all the images that came into my mind during that session in Amuka, I remember only two—

The first very brief, really only a flash—Shira walking into the boarding school at Sde Boker, her curls bouncing on her back, dragging two suitcases, one in each hand, as I wondered whether she would turn around for a last look.

The second slightly longer—Dikla and I cutting and running out of the Arad music festival because it was too crowded for her and going down to the Dead Sea. We found an unpopulated beach and went into the water. Before that, I had never been able to float in the Dead Sea. I always thought it was something that happened to other people. But that evening, Dikla and I found a position: her legs on my shoulders, my legs on her shoulders. We held hands and floated, looking at each other and talking. Balance was very precarious. One wrong movement, one wrong word, and we both might lose our equilibrium.

Other images followed. I might have fallen asleep for a few minutes. At some point, the therapist massaged a few shiatsu pressure points between my shoulders, where my posterior heart is, then hummed a song I didn't try to identify.

In talk therapy, you can tell the session is about to end when your therapist takes a quick glance at his watch or when he begins to prepare you verbally for the separation.

In Watsu, it's more like music: Something in the melody of the gliding signaled me.

The therapist returned me to the edge of the pool, still grasping my fingers, and then released them, one by one, until my hand was left floating on the water.

I dove. Resurfaced. Opened my eyes and said, Thank you.

You're welcome, she said, and asked, What sign are you?

Pisces.

I could tell, she said, adding, you're welcome to shower. I have to get moving, but I'll leave you some tea and dates on the table.

———

I drank the tea and thought, Body therapy works much better for me than talk therapy. The body can't lie.

After the lecture in Safed, I drove to Haifa, to that store in Hadar, and found a rare David Bowie CD for Dikla. It had only Bowie's voice singing the whole *Ziggy Stardust* album a capella, clean, exposed, no embellishment, no arrangement. I put it on the passenger seat. I touched the bag occasionally, thinking that Noam's bat mitzvah was still a few months away and maybe all was not lost.

**What question that you have never been asked would you like to be asked?**

What do you think about when a German actor stands on a stage in Munich and reads a forty-minute passage from one of your books? No, really. You pretend you're listening to him. You have to pretend. There are people in the audience. Not many, but there they are. Well-dressed. The Holocaust is always in the background of every event in Germany, lending it an air of gravity. And yes, for the first minute, you're still looking for Hagai Carmeli in the sparse audience, but then you have another thirty-nine minutes, and you can't really spend thirty-nine minutes listening to a text you don't understand a word of. So where do your thoughts wander? How many of them are devoted to Ari, who is dying the hospital? How many to your wife, who continues to be cold and distant? How many to women who aren't your wife? How many to your daughter, who left for boarding school and doesn't want to speak to you? How many to guessing which of the silver-haired people in the hall were in the SS? How many to what the exchange rate of the euro is? And could it be that right then, as your thoughts wander freely and your body is relaxed, free of any obligation, the seed of your next book is born?

*Could you write in a language that isn't Hebrew?*
  No way.

*In your opinion, what role should the Jews of the Diaspora play in relation to Israel?*
  They should come to meetings with Israeli writers.
  Because no one else does anymore.
  Except for BDS members, who stand up and leave the hall together, in open protest, as soon as you begin to speak, leaving you alone with the presenter and the interpreter. And the two girls from the publishing house who are constantly checking messages on their cell phones.

*Obviously, former Israelis come to hear your lectures
abroad. How do those encounters make you feel?*

She comes into the hall a bit late. She was always a bit late
for our dates. I would wait for her on the bench in the park
near her parents' house on Harufeh Street and build up my
expectations. I recognize her immediately, even though it's
been nine years since I saw her last, during Book Week, when
the event still took place in Yarkon Park. We used to meet
there, as if by accident; she worked for Steimatzky, the book
distributor, and I was autographing books at a stand, knowing that at some point, she'd come to see me, and, sitting so
close to each other that our chairs almost touched, we'd talk.
Rather, she would talk, and I would mainly listen. As usual.
And when I caught a whiff of the scent of her hair, something
inside me was aroused. An echo of something. After we'd
exchanged kisses on the cheek and she'd left, people, I mean
men, would come up to me and ask about that woman I'd sat
with for so long. I'd answer proudly, My first girlfriend, sometimes adding: For four years, from the middle of my senior
year in high school until I was discharged from the army.

During one of those Book Week conversations, she told
me that she was getting married. Even though I didn't want
to marry her, I was jealous. She had a beautiful coffee-colored
birthmark to the left of her navel, and I loved to linger there,
my lips on it, until moving farther down. And she had this
gesture—running her fingers under her curls and shifting
them, all at once, from left to right. And she played the flute
very well, but not well enough for the army orchestra. She

loved to tease me, didn't get along with my mother, and unintentionally—sometimes intentionally—insulted the few girlfriends she had in high school by making tactless remarks. She sent me perfumed letters when I was in basic training and then the officer training course, and traveled from Haifa all the way south to Mitzpe Ramon on the Saturdays I stayed on the base, just to sleep with me and then go back. She was discharged a year before me, and went to work as a security checker at the airport. She sprayed a bit of perfume on herself at four in the morning, when she heard the short beep of the cab that had come to pick her up for work. But she quit that job after two months because she didn't get along with the shift manager. She had to earn a living doing something, so she babysat for, among others, my older sister. Until the incident.

She didn't want to go to the annual Arad music festival with me, a week after the incident, and didn't answer when I asked if that was the reason. When I came back from Arad, she said hi, without moving her eyes from the TV screen. For weeks, she didn't want to sleep with me, or she slept with me without any desire and without coming. She started going out to salsa nights without me, and came home later and later, her clothes smelling of cigarettes. She didn't try to stop me when I began putting my clothes into large garbage bags, and she didn't say: Don't go, I love you. She didn't come to my grandmother's house in Holon to ask me to come back, and didn't send messages through mutual friends, and when I went to the apartment to collect the few things I'd left behind, she made sure not to be there.

She canceled her wedding a week before the date. Mutual acquaintances who had received invitations told me. I wasn't surprised. It was just like her. Later, I heard from those acquaintances that she met someone else, a guy who came in second in a national high-jump competition, married him a month later, and moved with him to the United States, to a town in the Midwest. Because of some job offer he'd received. Or a sports grant.

The Midwest is far away and not on the way to anywhere. Our mutual acquaintances broke off contact with her and I didn't hear any gossip about her for years. I had almost completely stopped having dreams of running hand in hand with her, escaping from something, and it had been a long time since I took her letters out of the shoe box I kept them in to check whether they still gave off the scent of her perfume.

And now here she is. In the third row on the right. The lecture I prepared is over, and now people are asking questions, too many questions, and I answer, Yes, Hebrew is assimilated by other languages, but is that necessarily a bad thing? And someone asks, Would you be a writer if you weren't born in Israel? I offer my ready answer, constantly stealing glances at her, trying to figure out how I can skip out on the kosher dinner, another kosher dinner, that the Jewish community organized for after the event—

In the end, I tell the organizers the truth. Listen, I see a childhood friend here, and this is the last night, we won't have another chance to talk, I hope it's all right with you—

Look, they say, we've already reserved the restaurant—

She's waiting on the side, as if embarrassed, but not really, biting the nail on her pinkie, a gesture I know very well, and crossing one leg over the other as she stands there, another gesture I know very well.

I don't say anything, don't back down, I know for certain that what I'm doing is not polite, but it's obvious to me that I'm doing the right thing.

They look at me, look at her, and something apparently becomes clear to them, because they retreat, only reminding me that they will pick me up at seven tomorrow morning to take me to the airport.

We go outside and begin walking the downtown streets. I'm a bit cold, but she seems to be okay, so I don't say anything about it. We walk in our regular positions, she on the left, I on the right, and I wonder if she notices this as well. She's wearing tight jeans and a button-down denim shirt, and I remember the way her army shirt was tucked into her uniform pants, which were always a few sizes too big for her. I remember that, although she was a natural chatterbox, she always needed someone else to begin the conversation.

You look great, I say.

How can you tell? she teased me. It's dark!

No, really, I say, smiling.

You, on the other hand, look older, she says. Then she caresses the back of my neck briefly—or simply lets her hand linger on it, depending on how you interpret it—then adds, What's with all those white hairs?

I'm silent, admitting my guilt.

And since when did you become such a big lecturer? she adds. You used to be so shy.

Inside, I'm still shy.

You hide it very well.

Did you enjoy the lecture?

It was terrific, even though ...

Even though what?

Never mind, we haven't seen each other for nine years, and I'm already putting you down ...

You started already, so go on—

You ... fake it. You're not really there. It feels like you're giving a speech. Even the jokes you tell—it's like you know they'll work because they did in the past.

I guess you're right.

But people enjoyed it, don't worry. I'm the only one who noticed that you weren't totally there.

I wasn't there at all because of you, funny girl. The minute you came in, all I wanted was for the lecture to end, I think, but don't say.

We reach the small lake—really just a puddle—in the middle of the little park. We sit down on a bench, which is slightly damp. The water in the puddle glistens like eyes.

So tell me, do you ever get used to this quiet? I ask.

You get addicted to it, she says.

You live close by? I ask, pointing in the general direction of the city.

No, we live in Cincinnati now. We moved not too long ago.

No kidding. So it was just my luck that you're here?

No, you idiot, I came especially to see you. A two-hour drive.

Then she turned to me. Face-to-face. And immediately looked away.

———

It took time for me to work up the courage to kiss her. Back then, in Haifa.

We used to walk around the Carmel Center, somehow always arriving at the end of the Panorama Promenade that overlooks the refineries and the bay. On the one hand, the kiss was in the air, but on the other, her sarcasm undermined the already shaky self-confidence I had then. Before every date, I would decide, that's it, this time it'll happen, but the minute we exchanged our first words, I would decide to postpone leaning toward her until it was really the right moment. And then one night she said, in her usual cool tone, If you don't want us to end up just friends, then you really should kiss me—

———

I don't feel like going back to Israel, I confess.

Don't I know it, she says, and looks at me. She's wearing blue mascara. Like she used to back then. And there are small wrinkles under her eyes. Not like back then.

I wonder whether to tell her that the David Bowie CD didn't soften Dikla, that she wouldn't open her arms when I come home. And maybe she wouldn't take her eyes off the TV. But I don't want to sound desperate. So I say: This is the first time it's happened to me, you know? I enjoy my trips, but I'm always glad to go home.

Of course, she says, and shifts her glance to the darkness. What I don't understand is how people live in Israel with all the tension there.

Yes, I say.

A war every summer, she goes on, and if not in summer, then on the holidays—it's not normal.

It's not, I agree.

How can children grow up there without having a few screws loose?

I agree.

Sometimes I log on to Ynet—and it's enough for me to see the name Yoram Sirkin in the headlines to remember how much I don't miss any of it.

But still—I think but don't say—you log on to Ynet.

My father died two years ago, she says. I flew there for the funeral.

Her father—I remember. A large man. A crane operator in the port. Came home from work wrecked, barely spoke, didn't interfere when her mother harassed her at dinner but looked at her with compassion. And he'd pass her the salt a minute before she asked for it. Only once during the four years I was his daughter's boyfriend did we talk. She was in the shower when I arrived to take her to the movies. Her mother wasn't home. Her elder brother was in the army.

There's something that . . . he began a sentence, but didn't finish it—and pointed to the living room. We sat on the black leather couch. The TV was on, a soccer game. He was silent. He seemed to still be trying to choose his words. I almost said, It's okay, don't worry, she takes birth control pills. But I wasn't sure that was the issue.

Be careful with her, okay? he finally said.

Okay.

She's . . . much more sensitive than what she . . . he said, then stopped again.

I nodded.

And that was it. The shortest man-to-man conversation in history came to an end. His eyes and his body turned to the TV, and so did mine. The game being broadcast, I remember, was between two Haifa teams, Hapoel in red and Maccabi in green. Since I'm color blind, I couldn't tell the difference between them, so I just pretended to be watching, while I was actually only waiting for his daughter to finish her shower.

———

I'm sorry for your loss, I say now.

Thank you, she says, no one's said that to me for a long time. People stop saying that at some point, even though the loss still hurts.

That's true, I agree, and almost tell her that Ari is dying. But I don't want my own sorrow to encroach on hers.

I counted the minutes until the shivah would be over, she says. All those pastries, and the never-ending conversational loops. And the picture albums being passed around. I was the only one—the only one who wouldn't look at them, the only one who remembered all the family trips, which were actually nightmares. And my mother, you know, she can't be around me more than a few minutes without saying something nasty. I don't get insulted anymore, you know, but I won't keep quiet either.

———

Back then—she would feel hurt, come to my room in the middle of the night. Two knocks on the door of the separate entrance, and I would open it, in my sweats. She would take a small step inside, say, Hug me, and stay with me the rest of the night. In the morning, we'd walk hand in hand to school and French kiss in the corridor before she went into her class and I into mine.

———

When I went into the army, I sent her at least one letter a day from the base. So there would be something to keep her from going out with all the guys who were constantly after her. We always laughed, saying that the military censor who opened those letters definitely looked forward to reading them.

During my last year in the army, my parents went on a sabbatical to Boston, so the apartment she shared with her roommates on Hess Street became home for me. That's where I went on weekends. That's where I moved the few items of non-army clothing I had, my CD collection, and the Hapoel Jerusalem scarf.

Until one night—

She was babysitting for my older sister in Ramat Gan. And I was given a rare twenty-four-hour pass in the middle of the first intifada nightmare.

Hug me, I asked after she closed the door behind me, and as she hugged me, she opened the belt of my army pants and pulled me inside. We made love on the living-room couch for a long time, while Danielle, my sister's two-and-a-half-year-old daughter, should have been sound asleep in her room. She had an afternoon nap every day, Danielle. Between one and three. Regular as clockwork. Today I know that there's a moment when little kids stop taking afternoon naps, all at once, without warning. Every kid and their particular moment. But then—

———

Now she suggests we start walking again. There's a kind of observation point she wants to show me.

It's clear to me that as soon as we get up from the bench, she'll notice that my lower back is slightly out of joint, and she'll definitely say something about it.

But she doesn't comment on it. Instead, she intertwines her fingers with mine.

I calm myself: It's okay, you're in the Midwest, no one knows you here.

And I think, It's been so long since anyone touched me tenderly.

We walk hand in hand, in our regular positions, until we reach the observation point, which reminds me a bit of Atarim Square in Tel Aviv. A large, charmless concrete surface.

We lean against the railing, and then turn to each other and kiss. A brief kiss. Her lips are dry.

Hug me, she says.

And I hug her.

The feel of her body is both familiar and unfamiliar.

She caresses the back of my neck and I make my way through her curls to the back of her neck and draw circles on it with my fingers the way I remember she used to love.

We kiss again, a longer kiss. But still not with total abandonment.

My hotel . . . if you want . . . I mumble, not sure what I'm suggesting. She moves back slightly—we are still embracing but no longer pressed up against each other—and shakes her head, no.

But it's only a story, I tell her.

She shakes her head, a bit more slowly this time, and strokes my chest with an open hand the way she knows I love, the way no one but she had ever stroked me, and says, We were lucky, you know? True love at such a young age. How many people have that?

And says, still caressing my chest, You hurt me so much. Leaving the way you did.

And says, You didn't realize either that Danielle had left the house. You fell asleep, too. But you let your family blame it all on me.

And says, I still dream about it sometimes, you know? And in the dream there are no neighbors to come to the rescue at the last minute, it's just me running out to the street, but my legs are heavy, too heavy, and the car hits her before I—

Tali, I—

I try to tell her something, but she puts a finger on my lips and says—

How does it help me now if you're sorry.

And says, The only time I got out of bed for six months after we split up was when you came to collect your stuff.

And says, Since then, I have never let anyone hurt me like that.

And takes her finger off my lips and her hand off my chest and says, It's important, the way we end things. You need to know that. And says, Don't turn around. This time I'm the one who leaves, and you, don't turn around.

So I don't.

I don't turn around. I hug myself against the spreading cold.

I look at the darkening skyscrapers of downtown.

At dawn, I walk slowly through the wide, empty streets to the hotel and check out.

**Aren't you afraid sometimes that, that's it, you've run out of ideas, you've lost it?**

I'm afraid of losing it. I'm afraid of losing Dikla. I'm afraid of losing the kids if I lose Dikla. I'm afraid of losing Ari. I'm afraid of having a heart attack in another three years, at the age my father had his. I'm afraid that, unlike him, I won't survive. I'm afraid that this plane taking me from the Midwest to the Middle East will plunge into the Mediterranean Sea. I'm afraid that something will happen to Shira at Sde Boker and I won't be there to protect her. I'm afraid that Shira won't ever come back from Sde Boker. I'm afraid of an economic collapse. I'm afraid of a systems collapse. I'm afraid of a knock on the door, and on the other side is a policeman with a baton. I'm afraid of how easily things in Israel deteriorate into violence. I'm afraid there'll be a war. I'm afraid I'll be called to reserve duty. I'm afraid that the war will be a civil war.

**What did you do in the army?**

They picked me up at the train station in Phoenix. Or Minneapolis. I don't remember anymore. All platforms look alike everywhere. She had moderately short hair, and he had long hair, slicked back with oil.

She said she lectured in the law department of a local college. He said he was in business and gave no details.

She drove, and he occasionally gave her instructions. Signal. Slow down. Be careful. Outside, snowflakes swirled, and she said we'd probably have a storm that night.

They spoke the heavily accented Hebrew of people who had been in America many years, and every now and then, they used a word that made me think they had left Israel at the end of the seventies or, at the latest, the early eighties.

———

I don't remember how we came to speak about their son. But it happened pretty fast. Five, ten minutes after we set off. I think that at that point, I already felt the tension between them. It's hard to explain how. Little things. Maybe it was because they didn't smile at all. Not even when they met me at the station. Maybe it was her clenched, bitten lips. And the words seeming to flee from her mouth.

Our Benjamin is considering joining the IDF, she said.

Why did you say "considering," honey. Benjy has already decided.

Maybe you've already decided, honey, she said.

I'm his father, he said in a voice trembling with controlled rage. I have the fucking right to offer my opinion, honey. Even if someone doesn't like that opinion.

Was Benjamin born in Israel? I asked quickly, in the hope that a concrete question would prevent the argument from escalating.

No, she said. He was born after we moved.

So why would he want...? I asked.

Birthright, he replied. What do you call it, *taglit*? He toured Israel for ten days with a group of Jewish kids and felt at home. Now he wants, and rightly so, to join the army because he feels it's part of his identity.

And I'm worried, she said, looking at me in the rearview mirror as if I were the arbitrator who was supposed to pass judgment on the matter. I'm not sure he understands what it means to be a soldier and how different it is from his life here.

Stop treating him as if he were a little boy, he said.

He's not a little boy anymore, but he's still my child, she said.

He's my child too, mind you, he said. And his hand, lying next to the hand brake, clenched into a fist.

When is he supposed to make his... final decision? I asked.

The deadline for the forms is next week, he said. But he's already decided. You're not listening, buddy.

What do you think, what would you advise him to do? she asked, giving me another quick glance.

What do I think? I repeated the question. Slowly. To gain some time. Maybe we'd suddenly arrive at the motel.

I shifted from where I was sitting. Until that moment, I'd been more behind her than behind him, and now I moved to a spot right in the middle, between the seats. The place my sister and I used to fight over during family trips.

Look, there are positive things to be said about both sides, I said. On the one hand—

Oh, come on, man, he said and punched the glove compartment. That's what I can't stand about your books too. There are so many points of view and voices, there's no way of knowing what you really think. What do you bohemians call that, postmodern? Postmodern my ass. Sometimes you have to pick a side. That's all there is to it. Come on. Choose.

Listen, it's a complicated issue—

Just tell us what you think, man. Bottom line!

———

He pissed me off, that guy. His tone, and the fact that he called me buddy. And his patronizing comments to his wife about her driving—why don't you drive yourself, you shit?—and I was also on edge because I hadn't been able to fall asleep on the plane and that trip to the States was turning out to be a total professional flop. Just like the ones that preceded it.

What do I think? I fired back. I think there are ways to unite with your Israeli identity other than joining the army.

That's exactly what I say, the woman said.

Don't misunderstand me, I qualified my words. I'm not sorry I served in the army. It's part of being a citizen in my country. It's an obligation. But to join the army of your own free will? As an "experience"? Sorry, there are experiences that can contribute in much more positive ways to the development of an eighteen-year-old boy than shooting rubber bullets at children or standing at checkpoints.

Stop the car, the man told his wife in English.

There's no place to stop here, she replied in Hebrew.

Stop the fucking car, he shouted. And closed his hand around the brake. As if he were planning to stop the car himself if she didn't.

Okay, Effi, another minute! she said. And signaled. And looked at her side mirror. And looked at the mirror on the passenger side.

———

I was sure they were going to throw me out of the car. That happened to me once, with Ari. Before going into the army, we were invited to his uncle's house in Eilat, and somehow, the conversation at dinner turned to politics. The next morning, we were politely asked to leave.

Why the hell don't I learn from my mistakes?

My leg muscles were poised for movement. I even managed to wind my scarf around my neck. But when the car pulled over to the side of the road, he was the one who opened his door and stepped out into the raging snowstorm.

The slam of the door shook the chassis.

The woman and I stayed where we were.

It's okay, she turned to me and said. He'll come back in another few minutes.

You're sure? It's pretty stormy out there . . .

That's what they taught him to do in the anger management course. A second before he loses control completely, he has to try to cut off contact. Simply move away from the situation. It usually helps.

And in the meantime...?

We wait. It's only a few minutes, really. Want a piece of spearmint gum?

I said yes, even though I can't stand spearmint. She handed me the pack and said, He's really a bookworm, Effi. I want you to know that. He gets a shipment of books from Israel every week and devours them all in one weekend. He's the one who insisted on bringing you to the Jewish Community Center.

Lightning flashed across the sky from one end to the other, like the terrifying lightning bolt on the cover of the Dire Straits' album *Love Over Gold*. I've never seen lightning like that in Israel. It was followed by a tremendous clap of thunder.

Isn't it a little...dangerous for him to be outside? I asked again.

There's nothing to worry about, he'll be right back, she said.

So when...in fact...did you leave Israel? I asked. So she would have something to answer.

In eighty-five, she said.

Wow, I said.

After the Lebanon War.

I understand.

Effi was . . . he was in the building that collapsed in Tyre.

I didn't know there were any survivors in the Tyre disaster.

Very few.

Tell me, does he have a phone or something? Sorry for nagging you, but . . .

He left his phone here—she pointed to the phone in the coffee-cup holder—but this isn't . . . this isn't the first time he's done this. And he always comes back in the end. Another piece of gum?

No thanks.

When we were in Israel, he used to write letters to the editor, you know, demanding that the government set up a national commission of inquiry.

For what?

He's sure that it was a car bomb that destroyed the head-quarters in Tyre. He saw it arrive.

But they said it was a gas tank, no?

He claims that the CID report was one big whitewash. That, with his own eyes, he saw a Peugeot drive into the area. And there was no explosion until after that.

You don't say.

He sent letters to the editors of different newspapers every week.

Wow.

It wasn't until we arrived here that he stopped that craziness.

Tell me . . . Maybe we should drive around to try and find him? It's been . . . quite a while.

She looked at her watch. Then at the side mirror. And then she took a deep breath and said: We'll wait another two or three minutes. I don't want him to come back and not find us here.

Of course, I said. I looked at her face in the rearview mirror. Nothing I saw indicated that she was worried or upset. She was only very pale. But I didn't know her well enough to decide whether that was unusual.

You're probably dying to get to the hotel already, she said, looking at me matter-of-factly. I'm really sorry we're holding you up . . . Effi is going through a sensitive period now because of the business with Benjy—

It's okay, I said. I'm in no hurry. But I have to say that something here . . . is not clear to me. If Effi . . . I mean, if that's the experience he had in the army, then why—

The door opened suddenly and Effi stepped into the car, soaked to the bone. Snowflakes stuck to his greasy hair. His teeth chattered.

She shifted gears and began to drive.

Slowly, at first, as if she wanted to be sure he wouldn't leap out again, and then at normal speed.

———

We were silent all the way to the hotel.

He looked too embarrassed to speak.

She looked like someone whose major concern was that everything would at least look normal again.

And I was afraid that anything I might say would stir up trouble again. At some point, I remember, she turned on the radio to make the silence less awkward, and of all the songs in the world, the Dolly Parton–Kenny Rogers duet filled the air.

*Islands in the stream, that is what we are . . . Sail away with me to another world—*

The third time Parton and Rogers sang the chorus, he reached out, pressed a button, and turned them off.

I really understood how he felt.

———

We reached the hotel parking bay. She turned half her body to me and said: Effi and I will pick you up at a quarter to seven. Is that okay with you? Wait for us at the entrance?

Her tone was forced. American. Dolly Parton–ish.

Thank you, that would be just great, I said with the same contagious inflection.

———

Effi didn't come with her to pick me up at a quarter to seven. Instead, their Benjy was sitting in the backseat.

I looked at him through the mirror. Children are usually a fascinating combination of their parents, but that boy looked like he wasn't part of them or of this place. I realized why he felt at home in Israel.

Effi sends his apologies for not joining us, she said. I think he's caught a cold. What a winter we're having this year, right Benjy?

Oh my God, totally. What's it like in Israel now? Benjy asked.

Sunny, I admitted.

It's never really cold in Israel, right?

———

Someone has to tell him, I said to myself. Someone has to tell him something, at least—so, unlike me, he'll go into the army a bit more prepared.

I'd actually tried to prepare then. A week in Gadna, the pre-army field course. Lectures in school by army officers. Long talks with my father, who fought in the Six-Day War, and with Uncle Albert, a veteran of the Yom Kippur War. But I think that all the people in charge of smoothing my entry into army life had conspired together. None of them told me how difficult, how impossible it was to turn someone into a soldier overnight. None of them put a hand on my shoulder and warned me simply: For the next three years, your soul, not only your body, will be in danger.

———

On the way to the Jewish Community Center, we talked about the weather, Benjy and I. A little about the nightclubs in Tel Aviv. But every time I was about to break my silence, I pictured him screaming in response: Stop the car. And leaping out alone into the storm, which, through the window, looked even wilder now than it had in the afternoon. More dangerous.

His mother didn't intervene in our idle conversation, only stole a quick, almost pleading glance at me every now and then. Her jaw was clenched.

———

The lecture itself was as embarrassing as all its predecessors on this Jewish American tour. I mean, the hall wasn't completely empty. The amplifier worked. I read passages from my books. They asked questions. They even laughed once—except for Benjy's mother, whose face remained impassive. But, as always in America, I had the feeling that there was some basic misunderstanding between me and the audience. A bottomless pit of expectations I could never meet. As if I didn't conform to the image of an Israeli they had in their minds—or even worse, the Israel I described in my books didn't resemble the one they wanted to see in their mind's eye: the Israel of oranges, folk dancing, and Operation Entebbe. The only one who listened to me with yearning eyes, and even nodded occasionally in solidarity, was Benjy.

I've lost the audience anyway, I thought, so at least I can do something for the boy—

There was a copy of one of my books on the podium. I opened it, riffled through it for a few moments, and stopped on a random page.

It was in Nablus—I read straight from memory because I had never managed to write about that night—and they woke us up at two in the morning to clean slogans off the walls. There was this policy at the time of the first intifada: During the day, Palestinian kids sprayed anti-Israeli slogans on the walls of the Palestinian camp, and at night, Israeli soldiers went into the houses, pulled people out of their beds, and made them wipe away the slogans with their own hands.

We knocked on the door—or more accurately, banged on it—and an unshaven grandfather leaning on a cane opened it. We could see the trappings of an entire life behind him: couches, a TV, a sideboard, mattresses on which the family members slept. Alon, the commander of our platoon, ordered the grandfather, in Hebrew, to go out of the house. The grandfather said something, maybe he asked if he could change his clothes. But Alon said no, grabbed him by the arm, and frog-marched him a few dozen meters to the wall sprayed with slogans.

We watched them as we secured the periphery, and when we reached the wall, Alon asked the old man: Who did this? The old man replied, *La'aerif.* I don't know. From the way he spoke, it was clear that he really didn't know.

This was repeated four or five times. Alon asked more loudly each time, and the old man replied more weakly each time, close to tears.

Meanwhile, someone else came out of the house with a pail and a rag. A younger man. And stood beside the old man. Leave my father alone, please, he said to Alon in solid Hebrew. I'll clean it off. Alon ignored him and asked the old man again: Who did this? Don't lie to me that you don't know! And the old man said, more accurately sobbed, *La'aerif.* And then, to our great shock, Alon slapped him. Hard. Almost punched him.

The old man, who, until that moment, had been leaning on his cane, lost his balance and collapsed onto the sidewalk. The cane fell out of his hand and rolled away, and his body, which had folded into itself, looked suddenly very small, like a child's. His son yelled in Hebrew, What are you doing? What do you want from him? And moved a step forward. But Alon promptly aimed his rifle at him and shouted that he'd better start cleaning, or he'd get a bullet in the head. The son gave him a defiant look, but bit his lips, picked up the pail, and dipped the rag in it. A minute or two later, the father stood up, with great effort, and joined his son. Moving swiftly, they washed off the slogan, and when the last letter had disappeared, Alon signaled with a movement of his rifle barrel that they could go back inside. The father obeyed the order immediately, but the son stayed a moment longer, put his hand on the wall where the slogan had been, and only then joined his father. Alon followed them with his loaded rifle until they disappeared into the house.

We watched them and secured the periphery.

———

At the end of every week of the officer training course, we had a summarizing discussion with the platoon commander. Before the discussion following the incident with the old man, we spoke among ourselves in the tent and decided that if Alon didn't bring it up, we would.

Toward the end of the discussion, when we realized that he planned to ignore what had happened, we signaled each other with our eyes. Dror, the huge navy guy, spoke first, followed by Amit, from the medical corps, and then me. We all said more or less the same thing: that we didn't understand why he had to slap the old man. We chose our words carefully. We said we really wanted to understand. To have it explained to us. We were all new at this business in the territories. And he, Alon, had a lot of experience.

In response, his face turned redder than his beret, and it seemed that, in another minute, he'd aim his rifle at us.

He said: You want an explanation?

He said: Should I tell you about Rudner from my platoon who had a refrigerator dropped on his head from a roof in Jenin and has been in rehabilitation for a year already? Or do you prefer to hear about Samama, whose face was burned by a Molotov cocktail they threw into his jeep?

He said: This is war here, in case you didn't realize it. We're at war.

He said all that—but didn't dare to touch any other Palestinian during our patrols in the alleyways of the camps. As soon as he realized that he wasn't getting any support from us—that we wouldn't secure the periphery for incidents like that—he took a step back.

And began to abuse us.

Until the end of the course, he took every opportunity to make our lives a misery. There was no mistaking the look in his eyes when he sent us running all over the base for no good reason, confined us to quarters on Saturdays, and looked for excuses to throw us out of the course: He despised us.

My army service can be divided into two parts: before that night in Nablus, and after it.

Something inside me broke that night, but something began to grow as well.

I closed the book and gestured to the audience that that was it, I had finished reading and the meeting was over. I thanked them in English. Then in Hebrew.

There was a light sprinkling of applause.

People put on their coats and spoke together in hushed voices as they made their way out.

Of my dozens of books, only two copies were bought at the improvised table-stand.

One by Benjy.

He asked if I would write a dedication to him in Hebrew.

His mother approached, put a gentle hand on his shoulder, offered me a pen, and said quietly, and quite genuinely, "Thank you." Her face remained frozen. Expressionless. But it seemed to me that I could see the thin trail of a tear running down her cheek. Or maybe it was just a wrinkle.

I took the pen—and it remained in the air for several long seconds. I couldn't decide between a few seemingly personal but actually generic dedications I use in such cases, but then a Meir Ariel song began to play in my head, "It's Been a Rough

Night on Our Forces at the Suez." Go figure how our minds work. In retrospect, I think it was because the first words are, "I'm reading *Islands in the Stream* by Ernest Hemingway, in a beautiful translation by Aharon Amir"—and "Islands in the Stream" by Dolly Parton and Kenny Rogers was still stuck in my inner music player. In any case, at the end of Meir Ariel's song, there are a few lines in English:

> *Hey nice Jewish boy*
> *What are you doing here?*
> *Hey nice Jewish boy*
> *Nothing for you here, go home.*
> *Hey nice Jewish boy*
> *You go see some nice Jewish girl.*
> *Hey nice Jewish boy*
> *Go home.*

It had never been clear to me who Meir Ariel was singing those lines to. An American soldier, a new immigrant come to relieve him on watch? Himself?

And when I wrote them in the dedication, in Hebrew letters, I wasn't sure who I was writing to: Benjy? Myself? Both?

———

I saw him a week ago, the boy. At the Binyamina train station. There's that moment when the doors open, and the people on the platform wait until the flow of disembarking passengers stops.

He was the last one off, wearing a uniform and red paratrooper boots and carrying a rifle, holding his cell to his ear and speaking.

He looked like he belonged.

### Did you ever do anything you're ashamed of?

The first intifada broke out when I was in the officer training course. They sent my company to the territories and returned us to base, then sent us to the territories again and returned us again. That went on for thirty-five days, during which we never saw home. Even worse, I never saw Tali Leshem. I'd pursued her for the entire last two years of high school, and she'd finally let me catch her only a few months before I went into the army.

Which is what caused the first year of my army service to consist mainly of finding ways to go home so I could see her.

The moment when this story takes place, I felt—as I do now, with Dikla—that Tali was going to leave me.

Something in her voice was clouded over (we spoke on pay phones, there was no WhatsApp or texting).

Her letters kept getting shorter.

When I asked her if she was tired of waiting, she said no, but her tone said, Yes, I am.

In short, I felt that I had to see her, or else I would lose her.

But we had no leaves. For thirty-five days. And I felt I would go crazy. Go fucking AWOL. Nothing else mattered.

And then, on a Thursday, the platoon commander issued an order. Three members of the platoon, chosen by a lottery run by his current aide, could go home.

The aide was Dror, a career soldier from the navy who slept in the bunk above me. He was a few years older than us. Someone you could trust.

He waited until we were in the personnel carrier that would take us to field training, sat down in the seat closest to the driver, facing us, and asked each of us to write his name on a slip of paper and hand it to him. Then he put all the slips of paper in a hat and mixed them up.

I've never won a lottery. For years, my sister used to buy me scratch cards, and the only time I won—I won a free scratch card.

I had no expectations from that lottery. If anything, I had a feeling of defeat foretold.

And then Dror chose the first slip of paper and read out my name.

I was so happy. I could have jumped with happiness. I hadn't felt such a sense of freedom and relief very often in my life.

The minute we got out of the van, Dror started walking toward me, and then took advantage of a moment when we were far away from the others and said: So, are you happy?

You bet I am, I said.

Great, he said. Thanks to me.

I turned pale. What do you mean, thanks to you?

When I folded the pieces of paper, I folded yours so it would be larger than the others. That way I could find it more easily.

But why?

I heard you talking to Sabo the other day about your girl-friend. I thought you needed this leave more than anyone else.

Thanks, I said. But I felt a heaviness in my heart. Because in terms of the officer training course, he had committed an offense, and had made me, against my will, an accomplice.

In the officer training course, only three things are important to your commanders: Trustworthiness. Trustworthiness. Trustworthiness.

Not only in the course. My father—I had never heard him lie or scheme.

The whole business ran counter to who I am.

What should I do?

During the night between Thursday and Friday, the guys from the platoon teased me about my good luck. After lights-out, Sabo came to my bunk and asked if I could take a letter he wrote to his mother, who was hospitalized. His brother would come to pick it up. I said, Yes, bro, sure. And I couldn't fall asleep all night. Should I expose the deceit and get Dror into trouble, or should I go home at the expense of one of my friends? That is, go along with the deceit?

Friday morning I got up, dressed, and went home.

I wanted so much to go home.

But then, when I reached Haifa, the pressure apparently got the better of me and I just broke down. All that Saturday, I got out of bed only to eat. I ate very little and hurried back to bed. My parents understood that something had happened, but didn't dare ask me. Tali Leshem came to visit me. I told her about the lottery and she didn't understand what the big deal was. At her post in the administrative office, dirty pool was par for the course, she said. Later we had sex, but she didn't come and got up quickly to shower. Then she hurried back to her parents' house. And didn't kiss me goodbye. She called Saturday night, sounding distant, and didn't suggest we meet.

On Sunday, I went back to the base. Dror was the only one in our room. Wearing his navy whites.

I was drinking a can of orange soda and I felt like spilling the entire contents on that uniform.

So how was your Saturday? he asked, and patted my shoulder.

Just another Saturday, I replied.

What do you mean? Did you see your girlfriend? Did you calm down?

Sure, I said.

And no thanks for Dror, who set it up for you? He gave me a small punch on the shoulder.

Thanks, bro—I raised my hand to my temple and saluted him—I'll never forget it.

*Do you ever dream about your characters?*

I'll get to that in a minute. It's just that . . . I'm still thinking about the previous question. I keep remembering more and more things I'm ashamed of, and all of a sudden, I think that the story about Dror and the lottery was actually meant to conceal other stories, darker ones—

We left Oren, from Hadera, sick in Peru. In a small, ugly city on the shore of Lake Titicaca. I don't remember the name. Maybe I'll google it later. In any case, he was burning up with fever, almost 104 degrees. Maybe if it had passed the 104 mark, we would have stayed. Maybe not. We had a plan for our trek and we wanted to follow it. Bolivia. Then Brazil. Although Ari had agreed back in Israel that if he met a girl—not one just for the night, someone he really liked— all options were open, anything was possible and no hard feelings. But Oren was a guy. An Israeli. From Hadera. He had a good smile and big, happy eyes. We met him in Cusco at one of those Mama Africa parties and hit it off right away. I mean, he always told boring jokes like the ones that start with "A Christian, a Muslim, and a Jew get on a plane," and there wasn't a day when he didn't get into a noisy, almost violent argument when he bargained with a street vendor, but the trio—Ari, Oren, and I—worked well together. He injected some new energy at the point in the trek when Ari and I needed it. When he asked if he could join us to Titicaca, we looked at each other and said together: Sure, great idea.

———

When I re-create the events in my mind, it doesn't seem as if there were early signs of his illness. On the contrary, he looked like a pretty strong guy. Energetic.

An hour after the bus left, he vomited the first time. Into a bag. Then he turned very pale, and half an hour later, he vomited again. And that's how it continued, every half hour. After each time, he said he was sorry.

No "sorry" necessary, we said. We got more bags from other passengers. We poured him tea from the thermos we bought from a street vendor on one of the stops. We said to him, Try to close your eyes, sleep a little.

When he finally fell asleep, Ari covered him with his poncho, put a hand on his forehead, and said, Wow, he's burning up.

After a ten-hour ride on the bus, we arrived at our destination. Ari climbed on the roof and took down our three backpacks. Down below, I supported a wobbly Oren to keep him from falling and said, Don't worry, we'll be at the hostel in a minute and you can rest in the room.

When we reached the hostel, it turned out that they didn't have a room for three. We pretended to be disappointed, but honestly, we were relieved. We didn't want to catch whatever he had. Ari carried the backpack up to his room and said we'd meet at breakfast the next day, and that we'd get him something from the pharmacy to settle his stomach. When he didn't come down for breakfast, we knocked on his door and asked whether we should bring him something to eat, and from the other side of the door, he said he was dead tired and maybe he would join us later. We went out in search of a pharmacy in the town, described by *Lonely Planet* as picturesque, but which in reality reminded both of us of the northern Egyptian town of Rafah: Ruins instead of houses. Sewage running in the streets. Rebellion in the eyes of the residents.

We looked at each other and said in unison, "Weren't we here already?"—our code on the trek for "It's time to take off from this place or these people"—and went to the port to find out when we could catch the ferry to Isla del Sol in Bolivia. It turned out that in the off-season, it only sailed twice a week, but luckily, one of those times was the next day. At seven in the morning. We also found the town's only pharmacy next to the port. But it was closed. And according to the sign hanging on the door, it wouldn't open until eight the next morning. Neither of us mentioned Oren as we walked back to the hostel, but it was clear that we were thinking about him, and when we reached the room, Ari said, Let's at least bring him some tea and toast. We went downstairs to the grungy lobby, and while Ari made Oren some tea, I went to the restaurant across the street and asked for *tostada, con nada*. We went back up to our floor with the tea and toast and knocked on the door. At first, there was no answer. Ari said, I think he died, and I said, Not funny. But I laughed. We knocked harder, and then heard a weak voice say: It's open. We went inside and found Oren in bed. Watching a soccer game on the tiny TV with its rabbit-ear antenna that stood on the small cabinet across from his bed. His face was very pale. His eyes were glistening, as if he were crying. Who's playing? Ari asked and sat down a safe distance from him. Who the hell knows, Oren said. Hapoel Cusco versus Beitar Lima. How do you feel? I asked, and sat down too. Lousy, Oren said. I took his temperature. Almost 104.

Fucking shit, Ari said.

Did you find a pharmacy? Oren asked.

There is one here, I said, but it doesn't open until tomorrow.

It's a lucky thing you guys are with me, Oren said.

We looked at each other and didn't speak.

Then Ari said, The truth is that, for the time being, you're not missing anything, bro. This town is disgusting.

It is? Oren said. Because *Lonely Planet* says—

*Lonely Planet* also says that the ferry to Bolivia leaves the port twice a day.

And what's the truth?

Twice a week. Sunday and Thursday.

What day is today? I'm totally out of it.

Wednesday.

Wow. Excuse me a sec, I need the bathroom.

———

When he came back, we didn't talk about the ferry anymore.

We watched Hapoel Cusco versus Beitar Lima. I think I've never seen a game in my life with so many red cards. At least seven. Every few minutes, the referee sent a player off the field, and they refused to leave each time, until their teammates pushed them off so the game could continue.

———

Take the ferry tomorrow, Oren said when the game ended.

We'll see how you feel, I said.

Listen to this joke, Oren said. A straight guy, a homo, and a trans get on a train—

Ari and I give each other a "not again" look.

But Oren broke off in the middle of the joke and said, I'll be right back. And rushed off to the bathroom again.

When he came back, Ari had already taken out a deck of cards and we played Yaniv on the bed until Oren said he was wiped out, but we could keep playing without him.

Ari collected the cards and I smoothed the sheet, which had become wrinkled when we sat on it.

We stood at the door.

Oren coughed lightly and said, Take the ferry tomorrow, guys. Don't wait for me.

This time, I didn't say anything.

Ari said, We're in room four, bro, if you need something.

———

We had a huge alarm clock we'd bought in the thieves' market in Quito. It rang so loudly that you couldn't argue with it. We set it for six in the morning. The sun hadn't risen yet and we got organized quickly. Literally, without making a sound. As if Oren were with us in the room and we were afraid he'd wake up. Neither of us mentioned him until we boarded the ferry. Only after we had moved away from the coast and the sunrise began to glitter on the water did Ari ask: You think we should have stayed with him? And before I could reply, he answered his own question, And then what? We'd have been stuck in Rafah until Sunday? Hello, this is a trek here, not punishment.

———

The ferry got stuck in the middle of the lake. One of the motors broke down. We waited half a day for another ferry to arrive, and we boarded it. In Isla del Sol, on the steps leading from the port to the hostel, Ari slipped and sprained his ankle. But only a week later, when we realized that someone had stolen our backpacks, with all our equipment in them, from the roof of the bus we had taken to La Paz, Ari declared the existence of the "Oren from Hadera curse" for the first time. We should have stayed with that Oren guy, he said. Fever almost 104, bro. Not a joke.

———

The Oren from Hadera curse pursued us for the next few weeks: We set out on a mountain trek and had to go back because of a snowstorm. When we got back, it turned out that all the rooms in the recommended hostel were taken and we had to go to a different hostel that was hideously depressing. No hot water in the shower. For a minute, I thought our luck had changed, because it was in that depressing hostel that Ari met Clara from Canada, the only girl he really liked in South America. But then we found out she had a boyfriend.

———

When we returned to La Paz, Ari dragged me to the Witches' Market. To remove the curse.

We wandered around among the stalls until we found an old lady who supposedly understood English. We told her the story and she nodded and said, Very bad, very bad. Then she gave us two bottles filled with a yellow liquid and told us to drink them in one swallow at exactly midnight. We followed her instructions. An hour later, it turned out that the yellow liquid caused a huge, painful erection that lasted until morning, and two days later, in the middle of the street, someone grabbed my pouch, which contained four hundred dollars in cash.

We have to find Oren from Hadera, Ari said.

And fast, I said.

A long silence followed because neither of us had the slightest idea how to do it. There was no Facebook then. No cell phones. Nothing.

In Uyuni, a small city considered the entrance to Salar, the Bolivian salt flats, we met a group of eight Israelis looking for a minyan, not for prayer, but two people to fill the empty seats in their ten-seater van and join them on their trek. During the drive through the salt flats, they began talking about the antimalarial drug Lariam, and the sick dreams the people who take it have, although, if that's true, a girl said, no matter how scary that drug is, it's even scarier to stop taking it. Just last week the consulate flew an Israeli trekker from Peru to Israel after he caught malaria. Wow, really? Ari and I asked together, our voices too loud. Yes, she went on, the people he was traveling with left him behind and took off as if nothing had happened. The guy sitting next to her said, He was probably traveling with Germans, Israelis never leave the wounded behind. Never, Ari echoed his words. He looked at me. And lowered his eyes.

But then there was something else. In Brazil, on the beach in Fortaleza, we met a broad-shouldered Dutch girl who grimaced when we told her we were from Israel. Israeli men are bad news, she said, refusing to elaborate. It wasn't until that night, after a few beers, that she agreed to tell us that a week earlier, in Rio, she met an Israeli guy named Oren. He always told her unfunny jokes, she said, but she was extremely lonely and hadn't had sex for six months already, so she invited him to her room. But then, in the middle of getting it on, she said, out of nowhere, he slapped me. What the fuck? the Dutch girl asked, as if we were the ones who had slapped her. What a nutcase, I said. According to the law, that's assault, Ari said. And the Dutch girl said he told her it was because of some trauma he had in the army. That he couldn't control it. Bullshit, she said, slapping her open hand down on the bar. Fucking bullshit.

So . . . what does he look like, that guy? Ari asked. The Dutch girl almost broke the bottle over his head. Come on, man, that's what you care about? After everything I told you, that's what you're interested in? What he looks like? If you describe him to us, Ari persisted, we can slap him when we see him. You would really do that? she asked, looking at him hopefully. Ari nodded. So she described the guy, who sounded as if he looked like our Oren: A receding hairline, like a forty-year-old. A kid's smile. Happy eyes. Bargains like a crazy man with the street vendors.

I would have liked to say that when we came back to Israel we went to Hadera to look for Oren. Or that we at least went to the newspaper archives in Beit Ariela to check whether, while we were in South America, there had been a report about an Israeli trekker urgently flown home from Peru because he'd caught malaria. But the truth is that we left the story behind us. Just like we left Oren behind us.

He didn't appear in our photo album of the trip. Or in the letters from the trip. I was ashamed to talk about him to Dikla when we came back, and I was ashamed to write about him when I wrote about South America.

Over the years, the shame faded. Because it's the way of shame to fade. Only the curse was left. Ari and I still blame it for every bad thing that happens to either of us:

The engine died on the way up to Jerusalem? The Oren from Hadera curse.

Hapoel lost right at the final buzzer? The Oren from Hadera curse.

Ari has pancreatic cancer? The Oren from Hadera curse. (That's what he said when he called to tell me about his tests. I didn't respond. I didn't know what a person says in such a situation. And he said: The Oren from Hadera curse strikes again, bro.)

**Do you dream about your characters?**

Wait a minute, there's one last thing I have to get out of my system. But I just can't write it. You know, in the first person. There's a limit to honesty. Even in this interview. So I'll do what I usually do.

## HARASSMENT

It takes him a few seconds to recognize her. And even then, he isn't sure she recognizes him. Whether she recognized him earlier from his name or only when he came into the room. Or maybe she's embarrassed. You can't tell anything from looking at her. She doesn't blush. Doesn't stammer. She continues asking him questions and typing as he replies.

She had been one of his soldiers. He was an officer, a first lieutenant. A small unit in the Intelligence Corps. Four huts. A tile path connecting them. A broken drink machine, long lunch breaks, long nights of work during operations.

On one of those nights, he thought he saw a flash of invitation in her eyes. Or maybe there really had been a flash of invitation in her eyes. What difference does it make—

Now the look in her eyes is all business.

She asks: It says here that you're studying for your master's. You haven't completed it yet?

He replies: I've already submitted my thesis. Now I'm only waiting for official approval.

Where do you live? she asks. What's that zero four area code?

Binyamina. It's less than half an hour away from here by train, he replies.

She nods slowly. As if his answers are unsatisfactory.

———

He began to drive her home on Fridays, to Beit Hanan. Told her it was on his way, but both of them knew it wasn't. On the drive, they spoke in a totally different tone from the one they used the rest of the week on the base. She told him that she wrote poems and short stories, but she didn't think she wanted to be a writer. It was such an egotistical profession. He told her that since his mother died, they no longer had Friday-night dinners at home, and his father had become addicted, really addicted, to Coca-Cola. The time in the car passed quickly, too quickly, and when they arrived at her house, she would linger in the car another few seconds, as if she were waiting for something to happen, and then she touched his arm lightly and said, Wait a minute, and disappeared. When she came back, she held a bag of blood oranges from their orchard. Food for the road.

———

She still has long hair, even if some of it is silver now. But she no longer winds the strands around her finger when she stops to think.

Your age, she says, are you aware that it's a disadvantage? Most of the marketing staff is in their thirties. And I should prepare you for the fact that we almost never take on people over fifty. It hardly ever happens.

Her inflection—he thinks—is almost the same.

There are also advantages to my age, he tries.

She touches the bridge of her glasses, pushes them back into place, and doesn't ask him to list them.

Besides, I'm young at heart, he says.

She doesn't smile.

———

She was nineteen and he was twenty-one. A two-year difference, that was all. But he was the chief officer of the section and she was just an ordinary soldier. There were no roll calls in their unit, she didn't have to salute him, but the hierarchy was most definitely there, in small things. Who ate in the officers' canteen and who didn't. Who had his own computer and who didn't. Who participated in pre-operation discussions and who only prepared the documents, made appointments, and swept the office floor at the end of the day, moving as if she were dancing.

She's typing something on her computer now. Apparently filling out a standard form. Does it make sense that she doesn't recognize him? Yes, he's bald. And has a potbelly. And started wearing glasses a year ago. And his name isn't exactly uncommon. When he and Nirit got married, they decided to blend their surnames, so from Gonter, his name, and Oren, hers, they created Goren. But even so, how is it possible that she doesn't remember anything, while he watches her type with those long fingers of hers and remembers everything. The entire scene appears before his eyes.

———

One Friday, when they started their drive, he told her that they had to stop off in the apartment he and his roommates shared in Tel Aviv. He had forgotten to take his bag of laundry, he said. And he would be happy if she would help him carry it because there was a ton of it. They went into the apartment and he immediately asked her how many

sugars he should put in her coffee. She said, No
thanks. He asked if the no thanks was about the
sugar or about the coffee. Both, she said, and remained standing. Why are you standing, make yourself at home, he said, and touched her for the first
time, placing a hand on her shoulder and leading her
toward the blue couch, thinking: Exactly the way I
pictured it, it's happening exactly the way I pictured
it. Then he went into the kitchen and made himself
coffee, twice, because he was so excited, he put two
spoonfuls of salt in the first cup.

When he returned, he sat down very close to her,
his leg almost touching hers, sipped his coffee, and
asked: Are you sure you don't want any? She shook
her head, and he leaned over to put his cup on the
small table. Then, with a pounding heart, he leaned
his elbow on the back of the couch, stretched out
his arm and trapped a strand of hair with two of his
fingers.

———

What's your family situation? she suddenly says.
I forgot to ask.

Happily married plus three fantastic girls, he
says.

How old are your daughters? she asks.

Twelve, fourteen, and eighteen. The oldest is
starting the army on Sunday.

Where will she serve? A spark of interest ignites in her voice. Or is he just imagining it?

Intelligence, he says with a smile. He's thinking that if even the tiniest muscle in her face moves now, it's a sign.

But her face is frozen. Her body is frozen. Only her fingers continue to type. How much can she possibly have to type?

———

Then, too, she froze. But he continued to twist a strand of hair around his fingers, finding it difficult to part from the fantasy he had spun for so many months. Then he moved his fingers down her neck, as he had in the fantasy, to her beautiful collarbone, slightly lowering the Dacron collar so he could move along her collarbone to her shoulder, and a long moment later, he stopped. He asked her if it felt good. She moved her head slowly but clearly. To the right and then to the left. He touched her hair one last time and returned his hand to his lap. And that was that. He didn't press up against her. Didn't kiss her on the mouth. Didn't tear off her uniform. On the contrary, he moved back and drank his now cool coffee as she rearranged her collar, and they sat beside each other in silence for another few moments. Along with the bitter disappointment and the desire to get on his knees and ask her forgiveness, anger began to grow inside him. All those light, seemingly random touches throughout the week in the office. All the times she leaned over his desk to show him documents, her long hair whipping his face, and the small dance of her sweeping the floor at the end of the day that seemed meant to emphasize her narrow waist. And the brief lingering a moment before she got out of his car in Beit Hanan, the lingering he was convinced meant: Kiss me.

———

Now he says: Excuse me—can I add something?

She straightens her glasses on her nose and says: I'm listening.

I'll be as straight as I can with you, he says. When I left my last job, I never imagined it would be so hard to find work in this field. You saw my CV. You will agree with me that it's not . . . sparse. Nevertheless, I've been going from interview to interview for six months now, and they give me the feeling that, because of my age, I'm not . . . current enough. Which is ridiculous. In marketing, it's not age that counts, it's hunger. Only hunger counts. Don't you think so, Rotem?

Her lips tremble slightly when he says her name, and for the first time, he suspects that her behavior at this meeting is one big sham. But she quickly overcomes the trembling, goes back to typing, and says impassively, It doesn't really matter what I think. There is an entire staff here that will make the decision.

But you have some influence, right? he persists.

Yes, I have some influence, she confirms.

So maybe you could pass on the message—he asks, his voice sounding too high in his ears, too pleading—that I am prepared to work hard. That if you give me the green light, I'll get results.

I promise to pass on the message, she says with a small smile, a tiny smile, which he thought was more like a smirk. Then she looks at her watch. More accurately, she lifts her arm with the watch on it so he can see that she's looking at her watch.

He gets the hint and asks, So what now, don't call us, we'll call you?

You'll receive an e-mail, she explains as she stands up. Within a week, two weeks at the most.

He stands up, too, and she accompanies him to the door. A moment before he leaves, he considers saying something about what happened back then. But he still isn't sure that she has made the connection and is afraid to hurt his chances—small as they might be—he needs the job. So, behind his glasses, his eyes look straight into her eyes behind her glasses and he says, Thank you for . . . your time.

What could he actually have said to her? he justifies himself in the elevator. That he's sorry?

That he apologizes? After all, what really happened there? Confusion. That's all. Misinterpreted signs. He was only twenty-one at the time. He'd barely had a girlfriend before then, and it hadn't been serious. He didn't understand anything about anything. Even now, if God forbid Nirit were to leave him and he had to start all over again, he'd be just as lost. Clueless and clumsy.

When he leaves the parking lot, he thinks about his last drive to Beit Hanan.

After some silence, she asked, in a barely audible voice, if he could drive her home. Is it okay if I finish my coffee first? he asked. She nodded and eased her body away from him, a few centimeters to the left. He deliberately sipped his coffee slowly, and thought, What a mistake. She can file a complaint about me.

All the way to Beit Hanan, they didn't exchange a word. She sat pressed up against the window and he clutched the wheel as if it were a lifesaver. There was a stop-and-go traffic jam on the coastal highway, and his leg hurt from so much pressing on and releasing of the clutch. On the radio, someone was translating love songs from English: "Mary Jane," "Woe Is Me," "Better Off Dead," "Oh Carol," "My Destiny," "You're Are My Happiness." A bit before Netanya, he thought she was crying, but when he turned his head, he saw that she was only blowing her nose. There are more tissues in the glove compartment if you need them, he said, and she said, No thanks.

When they finally reached Beit Hanan, she opened the door quickly, pulled her backpack out of the backseat in a single movement, making do with one strap instead of two, walked to her parents' house, and didn't come back with blood oranges from the orchard.

———

Back at the base on Sunday, they both acted as if nothing had happened. He didn't take it out on her after the incident. Didn't order her to do meaningless tasks, didn't make her wait to go on leave after the others had already gone, didn't toss sarcastic remarks at her in the presence of other soldiers. Just the opposite, he was careful around her. Thought twice before asking her to do something for him, careful to sound as if he were making a request, not issuing an order. But the rides to Beit Hanan stopped. He didn't offer anymore and she didn't ask. And when they passed each other on the tiled paths connecting the huts, he would avert his eyes. So did she. Sometimes he really wanted to say something to her, but he didn't know what.

After a few weeks, to his amazement, she asked for a transfer to a different section. He had no idea what reason she gave the unit commander. No one said a word to him, neither good nor bad. No one summoned him for a talk, put him on trial, or asked to hear their separate versions of the incident. One morning, she simply wasn't there anymore.

———

He comes to the late conclusion that there was no way she didn't recognize him. She recognized me, all right, but didn't want to show me that she did. Bottom line, even though I'm right for the job, better than anyone else, there's no way I'll get an e-mail from the company within a week, two at the most. There's no chance I'll receive an e-mail as long as she's their human resources manager.

———

Late Saturday night, an e-mail lands in his in-box. From her private address. The domain name wasn't the company's.

The subject: To Eli from Rotem—personal.

Right after he reads the first words, "Of course I recognized you," he closes his laptop and makes his "shoe rounds." Picks up all the scattered shoes and returns each pair to its owner's room. His eldest daughter is still on the phone with a friend, and he reminds her that tomorrow's a big day, so she shouldn't go to sleep too late. Okay, Daddy, she says, and goes back to her phone conversation.

Then he takes a pack of cigarettes and a lighter out of his wife's bag, returns to the study, and opens his laptop.

———

The next morning they take their daughter to the army recruiting office, the words from Rotem's e-mail still echoing in his mind. Her side of the story was so different from the way he had imagined it.

They're five in the car now, and it's very noisy. In honor of the event, the new recruit is given the right to choose the soundtrack for the drive and she plays Enrique Iglesias songs on her phone. Nirit sheds a tear and the girls laugh at her for getting so emotional about every little thing. When they reach the recruiting office, it turns out that the younger girls had filled a bag with presents that will help their older sister get through her first night, and now they give it to her. The three of them cry and hug, and he and Nirit glow with pleasure as they watch from the sidelines. A moment before their daughter boards the bus, he finally manages to catch her alone for a few seconds. Take care of yourself, he says, putting a hand on her shoulder. Dad, I'm going into the Signal Corps, she says and laughs, what can possibly happen to me? An Arabic–Hebrew dictionary will fall on my head? No, really—he hugs her suddenly, too hard—take care of yourself, little girl. Okay, Daddy, she says, barely able to move out of his embrace, then adds with a smile, on the condition that you do too!

———

A week later, the official letter arrives. From her official e-mail address.

*To Mr. Eli Goren,*

*We would like to thank you for applying to our company.*

*Unfortunately, after a careful evaluation of your CV and the information provided during your personal interview, we believe your profile does not suit our needs.*

*We wish you success in your future undertakings.*
*Sincerely,*
*Rotem Ashkenazi*
*Human Resources Manager*

**Do you dream about your characters?**

There was a time when I did.

Today I dream that the members of BDS rise up as a single entity during my reading, climb onto the stage one by one, and murder me with a fountain pen while I desperately try to convince them that I have always been against the occupation and that the essence of my writing is an attempt to give a voice to the other.

*Are you in favor of two countries for two peoples?*

I don't want to answer that question. I wrote books,
I want to talk about my books. But I'm not naïve, I know
how things work. It's clear to me that the title of this
interview will most likely be taken from my response to
this question and not from my responses to other questions related to my books. I don't understand why writers
always have to be asked their opinion on political issues.
Even after they've had a sleepless night because the wife
came home late, very late, disturbingly late, from a night
out with a friend, and also because recently, they have more
question marks than exclamation points about everything
related to current events, and most other things as well.
But not all of us are Amos Oz. Not all of us are always fully
prepared with a perfectly formulated reply to every question. Which doesn't mean I won't answer that question in
the end, my way. Of course I'll answer. Because more than
I don't feel like answering it, I don't want people to think
I'm avoiding the question.


*Do you find yourself dealing with criticism when you're
abroad because you're Israeli?*

My father warned me. I can't say he didn't. I wrote to
him from Singapore that the festival had sent a guy to escort
me everywhere, and he replied: From my experience, he
might be an agent with their secret police.

I wrote back: Don't be silly. He's a mild kind of guy.
Nerdy. He writes poetry for his own pleasure.

And he replied: Maybe everything he says about himself is true. And maybe it isn't.

———

My father worked in Singapore in the eighties. He advised the only university there on how to improve their screening processes, and was expelled from the country in disgrace after, in a private conversation, he expressed support for Singapore's only opposition politician.

"In any case, I advise you to weigh your words carefully," he wrote in the last text he sent me. But I—

I was intoxicated with the compliments I received there as an Israeli.

Usually, I shrivel when confronted with accusations. Admit to injustices. Watch sadly as BDS members leave the hall in open protest as I begin my talk. And suddenly—

Start-up nation. Jewish innovation. Nobel Prize sensation.

And the food. So many new tastes on my tongue! They have small open markets with food stands that sell only one dish each, but what a dish! And the liquor. They pour you something called a Singapore Sling, and after a few glasses you just—

———

Maybe it was because of the Singapore Sling that I spoke to my escort about democracy. Until then, I'd been careful about what I said, even when he himself complained about the regime (the price of cars, he kept saying, the price of cars), but after my fourth glass, I said: There's no start-up nation without democracy. Every teacher who wants to encourage creativity and originality in his students knows that the first rule is to create an atmosphere of openness, tolerance, attentiveness in class, and, most important of all, zero awe.

You understand, I pontificated—

(Oh, the *hubris*.)

You can send a delegation to Israel and bring Israeli experts to advise you, that's all well and good, but as long as you have only one party here, and one newspaper, you'll never be able to be truly original. Do you understand? For creativity to exist, you need liberty.

———

That night, more specifically, at four thirty in the morning—

The door of my hotel room was flung open and two guys burst in with a large gun.

They were polite in the scariest way possible. According to them, they were there only to take me to my flight.

But gentlemen, I protested, my flight is in another two days! (How serious can the protest of a man in pajamas be?)

Your flight has been moved forward, said the taller one, who was still a head shorter than me, but he was the one with the gun, and I had six-year-old Shira and two-year-old Noam waiting for me at home.

So I did what they said.

Pack, they said. I packed.

(I remember throwing all my clothes haphazardly into my suitcase, and I felt they were contemptuous of me for it.)

Check to see that you haven't left anything behind, they told me. I checked.

(I remember that my toothbrush was in the bathroom, in the soap holder. I took it.)

Please give us your passport, they said. I gave it to them.

(I remember sweat rolling down the back of my neck and being absorbed by my shirt.)

We walked through the hotel lobby—I carrying my suitcase and one of them on either side of me. The reception clerk buried his head in his keyboard. The doorman at the entrance held the door open long before we reached it.

I remember the drive to the airport. The silence in the car. I usually get people to talk. I always get people to talk. This time, there was clearly no chance. The car, which looked like a normal Hyundai, sailed through the roads of the city. We passed the botanic gardens and the tall skyscrapers that are joined together by a walkway that looks like a ship. An Israeli architect designed those breathtaking towers. Safdie. And everyone I met in Singapore mentioned Safdie's aerial ship as another example of the creativity of the Jewish people.

Apart from my two companions, whose silence was anything but companionable.

They also remained silent as we skipped check-in and skirted security.

The first and last time they opened their mouths was at the passport check.

The tall one handed me my passport.

The short one took a piece of paper out of his shirt pocket, unfolded it, and read: "The Republic of Singapore thanks you for your visit and your contribution to our cultural enrichment and the breakthrough to new ways of thinking. Nonetheless, we wish it to be clear that any additional visit to our country by you or any member of your family is unwelcome and will be treated as such."

(That was the first time anyone had hinted that the government had made the connection between me and my father. That, in fact, I had been marked from the first minute and someone had been assigned to follow me. But it took me a while to think about that. At that moment, all I wanted was to board the plane. Never in my life had I wanted so much to board a plane.)

———

Three hours after takeoff, my heart was still racing. The last time my heart had pounded that way was when Shira banged her head on the corner of the table and lost consciousness for a few seconds.

There were many Hebrew speakers on the plane, but I didn't tell any of them the story of my expulsion. I think I temporarily lost my faith in people.

That escort, provided by the festival, was so open. Ostensibly.

He showed me his poems.

Poems about unrequited love. To a girl who left him for his best friend.

And several other poems, more original ones, in which he speaks on the phone with his dead father.

I don't remember specifically, but I do remember the idea: Every year, on the son's birthday, the father calls from the place of his death to say happy birthday and hear how he is. Every conversation has its own poem, and every poem reveals to us the changes that have occurred in the son's life that year. And how, with time, he is becoming more like his father. Almost against his will.

You see, my escort had explained to me while we were still reading his notebook of poems, in our culture, the dividing line between life and death is more indistinct. Sometimes, it doesn't even exist.

———

Damn it, I thought on the plane, how easy it is to put one over on me.

I took two sleeping pills and slept until we landed.

———

The first person I spoke to (I remember myself standing at the gift shop in the arrivals hall and putting the phone to my ear) was my father.

I warned you, he said.

You did.

So why did you rile them?

I didn't think I was riling them, Dad. That guy, my escort—

Nerdy, writes poetry. I remember.

I never suspected for a single minute that—

Those are the people they choose for jobs like that, people who inspire trust.

Okay, the main thing is that I'm here, right Dad?

Right.

You know, all of a sudden I value the freedom of expression we have here.

Yes.

The fact that we can criticize freely, without fear.

For the time being.

Why "for the time being"?

Never mind. Should I come to pick you up, son?

No, it's okay, I'll take a taxi.

Call your mother after you've gotten organized, okay? But don't tell her about the incident. Her heart is weak enough as it is.

The incident in Singapore occurred ten years ago, and I decided that I would never write or tell anyone about it. And so it remained banished from my life as if it were a leper.

But it isn't only people who change with time. So do countries. I had a conversation a few hours ago. The literature teacher in the Itzhak Rabin High School in Ness Ziona called me. He began with compliments. Told me how excited the students were about the meeting with me the next day. Said they had prepared questions that he would print out for me. And then, after explaining where the best place to park was, he said, in a slightly tenser voice, Look, I have a request. More accurately, it's a request from the administration that I ask you, if possible, to please not speak about controversial subjects. Politics, I mean. It's better for all of us if you remain in the area code of literature. Family, love, childhood. You know. And you can save your criticism for more suitable opportunities. This is a rather sensitive time, you see. We've just asked the Ministry of Education for an addition to our budget. Apparently the supervisor, who is a personal friend of Minister Sirkin, will be present during your talk, and we don't want to anger anyone now, of all times. You understand me, right?

———

My father warned me. I can't say he didn't.

*I took a course with your father at the university. What is he doing these days? Can you send him regards from Hanita Brodetsky? I hope he remembers me.*

My father still goes down to the beach on Saturdays at six in the morning, dear Hanita. He loves to swim in freezing water. I absolutely do not love to swim in freezing water, but when we spend a Saturday in Haifa, I go down to the beach with him because I like sitting in the Kadarim restaurant with him after his swim.

He had a heart attack when he was forty-nine. He survived and still plays basketball every Thursday, to this very day. But I still worry when he dives into the waves, and keep my eyes glued to him to make sure he doesn't have another sudden heart attack in the middle of the sea. If I lose sight of him for more than a minute, I get really stressed, and once, a few years ago, I sent the lifeguard and everyone on the beach to look for him because I was terrified he had drowned, but it turned out that he had just swum to another beach.

These days, the sea is filled with jellyfish, so he doesn't swim far out. And I can sit on the folding chair he always keeps in the car trunk—part of a full beach kit—and watch him snorkel in comfort. I have no idea why he swims in the Mediterranean Sea with a snorkel and mask, Dado Beach in Haifa isn't exactly Ras Burqa in the Sinai, but I've learned to accept this just the way I learned to accept and love his other quirks: The fact that he keeps a motorcycle in the building parking lot without ever riding it. The fact that he spends entire Saturdays playing chess with himself. That he refuses to learn how to use Word and writes all his articles with a fountain pen. That his favorite vacation spot is Tiberias.

There were years when I resented my father. Quietly and persistently, I nursed my anger toward him. And poured all that bitterness into the fathers I created in my books. But when I became a father myself, most of his anger-provoking behavior seemed suddenly understandable: He sometimes doesn't answer when you speak to him? That's only human, his head is filled with worry about making a living. He travels abroad for long periods of time? Obviously. A person needs to take a break. Sets a standard of integrity that is too high to live up to? Better than having a criminal for a father. Is unable to remain in the here and now, and always has to worry about his future and that of everyone around him? Okay, that's something about him that still drives me crazy.

People who knew him—former students, colleagues, or army buddies (not just you, Hanita)—always come up to me after lectures and say: You look so much like your father, you know? And I say: Thank you. Or: That's a real compliment. But I still wince slightly, an internal, imperceptible wince. A person wants to believe that he has free will. Then they ask how he is, and you can sense in their tone how much respect and affection they have for him. And I reply, He's great, thank you, and think to myself: I'm lucky to have him for a father.

My father comes out of the water now. His body looks like mine will look in thirty years. Only the scar on his chest from his surgery is still red, as if it were only yesterday that he was rushed to the hospital. He towels himself off. Puts on his glasses. Clips the sunshade on them. Gives me his wallet and says: Order us the regular?

When he comes back from the shower, the regular is already on the table: Two short espressos. Two soda waters. A plate of *labane*. A plate of hummus. A plate of pickled vegetables. A plate of sliced onions.

He sips his espresso and asks: So what do you hear from Shira'le?

I don't hear anything from her, I want to say. She hasn't spoken to me since she left, only to Dikla. But instead, I say: Everything's good. She's happy there at Sde Boker.

He wants to say: What kind of parents are you that your daughter ran away from you? What did you do to her? But instead, he says: That's wonderful. Really wonderful.

He takes another sip of his espresso and asks: And how is Arieh?

For some reason, he always calls Ari "Arieh." I don't correct him anymore. Once, when I still had a lot of things, they both helped me move, and after we finished unpacking the last carton in the new apartment, my father invited us to a restaurant and ordered a second steak and another shashlik for Ari, patted him on the shoulder, and said, Eat, eat, you deserve it, you're a good friend.

Not too great, I reply. I mean, the doctors aren't... optimistic.

It's a cruel disease, my father says with a sigh.

Yes, I say.

You visit him in the hospital, don't you?

Of course, I say, he's at home right now, so I visit him there.

It's important, because... he says, and stops. He pulls off a piece of pita and dips it into the hummus. Which is suspicious. Usually, the hummus is mine and the *labane* is his. And he adds sugar to his espresso, which he also never does. Only then does he continue: I had a friend, I don't know if I told you about him—

Mickey, I say his name to myself. And think: Grandpa told me, Grandma told me, Mom told me about your best friend who was killed in the Yom Kippur War—you're the only one who never did.

Mickey was in my high-school class. He . . . was killed in the Chinese Farm battle. The Saturday before he was killed, we both went home on leave . . . he lived on a street parallel to mine. And I said I'd stop by to see him in the evening.

Yes.

But I didn't.

Yes.

If you happened to hear this story from Grandma, she must have said that I fell asleep.

You didn't?

I was just feeling lazy.

Yes, Dad.

So what I'm saying is, visit Ari. Another espresso?

No thanks, Dad. I can't fall asleep at night as it is.

He called the waiter over and ordered another espresso. He never does that either, I think. He asks the waiter how he is. How it's going in the university. The waiter is one of the owner's sons, and since we started going there, he's always been the one to take our order. Now he tells my dad about a bureaucratic problem he's come up against at the university, and my dad gives him some advice. And writes down his phone number, in case he needs it. He's always eager to help, my dad. He's never nasty.

So why can't you fall asleep, son? he asks when the waiter leaves. My mother once told me that one of the reasons she fell in love with him was his remarkable ability to return to a conversation at the exact—and I mean exact—moment it was broken off.

No real reason. I'm a light sleeper, you know.

Like your mother.

You have to know which traits to inherit from whom. Color blindness from you, and from her—

So tell me, is everything with Dikla okay?

Yes, of course, why? Because she doesn't come to Haifa with us? You know Dikla, always busy.

That's true, he says, sounding a tiny bit dubious. But dubious nevertheless. And I know that he suspects something is very much not all right between me and Dikla. Because how much can you hide from your parents, especially if they're psychologists, and I know that now he'll turn around to face the sea, giving me the space I need to begin telling him what happened. I suspect that Mickey's story was a chess player's maneuver meant to leave me open to this moment, and I know I can tell him that I'm in trouble— yesterday I told Dikla that nothing actually happened in Colombia, that I had made up the story of cheating because I felt she was moving away from me and I wanted to shake her up, and she looked at me for a long time and said: You're screwed up, you know? All screwed up—and if I tell him that, I will have the benefit of his wisdom, his experience and kindness, his considered opinion, and all the qualities that put light in the eyes of the people who come up to me after my lectures—your eyes too, Hanita?—to speak about him. I know that he will be cautious and discreet about every intimate detail I reveal to him, he is very far from being a gossip. I also know that the window of opportunity here is narrow, because my Dad might be a psychologist but he is also a man of long silences, not a man who bulldozes, and in another minute, he'll turn around from the sea, signal the waiter to bring the bill, and say, Mom is waiting for us, we should go back. I know all this, but nonetheless, say nothing.

Why, starting from a certain age, can't we share anything important with our parents, Hanita? Is it because, as Genesis tells us "Therefore shall a man leave his father and his mother, and shall cleave unto his wife," or is it just because we don't want to worry or burden them? Or maybe we want to maintain the image of successful, thriving people we hope they see when they look at us? Then again, maybe I'm the only one who is silent with his father, Hanita, and as I write to you, millions of people in the world are sharing whatever is on their minds with their parents, without hesitation.

On the way back to the Carmel, we talked about Noam's bat mitzvah and about movies. My father loves to go to the movies and then criticize them as if he is, at the very least, a newspaper movie reviewer. Action movies are the only ones he really loves, and that's because they have no pretensions of being quality films.

In the end, I asked about you, Hanita. He doesn't remember you, but don't take offense. At home, my mother is responsible for the long-term memories, and when we got home and I asked her, she immediately said, Hanita Brodetsky, of course. She reminded him that you studied statistics with him and remembered who your boyfriend was, and she even remembered what you used to wear. In short, my parents send you their warm regards.

**When will they produce a film adaptation of your latest book? When I read it, I could actually imagine the movie.**

What a book! he said, shaking his head in disbelief. What a book!

Thank you.

I started reading it in the duty-free shop and couldn't put it down for the whole flight.

Thank you, thank you very much.

The minute I finished it, I said to my wife: This is a movie.

Really?

She didn't hear me, she fell asleep.

My wife sleeps on flights too.

Your writing is so ... visual. And the dialogue? Pure pleasure.

I'm glad you think so.

Between you and me, we could start filming tomorrow.

Great.

There's only one small thing.

Yes?

They'd probably have to move the story to Jerusalem.

Jerusalem?

Because of the Jerusalem Fund special grant for movies filmed in the city.

But—

And the heroine—would you object to her being German instead of Israeli?

Why?

It leaves the door open to a coproduction with the German company that worked with us on *Springtime in Sobibor*.

But—

Which, by the way, has just been accepted to the Cannes Film Festival.

Wonderful, but—

Do you have a suit and tie?

Yes, why?

You'll need it to walk on the red carpet in another two years.

But—

I get the impression that something's bothering you.

Actually, yes. How can the heroine be German if she meets the hero when they're both in the Israeli navy?

Everything is fixable.

What do you mean?

Why do they have screenwriters if not to fix things like that?

I don't see how scree—

Here's an example: Germany sells submarines to Israel, right?

Let's say it does.

So one day he's standing on the pier and her submarine emerges from the water. Like Bo Derek.

Didn't you say it takes place in Jerusalem?

Right, so there's no problem at all. She comes to the Western Wall. He's an army security guard there.

But—

And then we can get a development grant from the Cornucopia Fund.

The Cornucopia Fund?

They back films that have Jewish content.

But—

I hope it's okay with you that I've already called Gal Gadot's agents.

About what?

What do you mean, "about what"? About the lead role. I sent them the book.

But—

You know how much it will help market the movie if she agrees to star in it?

But . . . the heroine is . . . small and shy.

She was small and shy. In the book.

And in the movie?

She'll be Gal Gadot.

I don't know.

What is there not to know?

I feel that the connection between the book and the movie is getting weaker.

You want to drink something?

No thanks.

Excuse me for saying it like this, you know, straight out, but you have to loosen up.

Loosen up?

Cinema, it's a different kind of art. It has its own rules.

Yes, but—

We once worked with that kind of writer, faithful to the source. You don't want to know how it ended.

So what is it that you're actually proposing?

Go home, sleep on it, and come by tomorrow to sign a contract.

I'm not sure that—

Ah, yes, another thing.

What?

The title.

What's wrong with the title?

Would you buy a ticket to a movie called *Osmosis*?

What's wrong with *Osmosis*?

Half the people don't know what it means. And for the ones who do know, it sounds scary.

So what do you suggest?

I'm not suggesting anything, the focus group suggested it.

Focus group?

What's with you? You can't find a single movie in the market today that didn't have its title checked first by a focus group.

Okay—

*Operation Love.*

Excuse me?

That's the name they picked. The company that organizes focus groups for us said there wasn't a single objection. They haven't had such a unanimous focus-group decision for a long time.

But what's the connection between the title and the—

There's love in your book?

Yes.

There's a military operation in it?

An unsuccessful military operation.

What difference does it make?

Friendly fire. It's a . . . political statement.

Friendly fire during an operation or not during an operation?

During an operation.

I'm glad you're happy with the title.

But—

I want you to feel part of the process.

I—

And also, it's important that, when you're interviewed, you say how pleased you are.

Pleased?

That although a movie is not a book, it's a different art form with its own rules, but even so.

Even so?

The creators succeeded in preserving . . . the spirit of the book.

Listen—

You found yourself laughing, crying, falling in love with Gal Gadot.

How do I know what I'll feel? I haven't seen anything yet!

It doesn't matter what you feel. As far as I'm concerned, you can hate the movie. What counts is what you say in interviews.

But—

A writer who doesn't take part in public relations for the movie is sending critics the message that he's not happy with the adaptation. And if there's something the critics know how to sniff out, it's blood. You don't want to open the morning newspaper and see that they slaughtered us, right?

Right.

In the end, our success is your success. That's what I'm trying to explain to you.

I understand.

Flexibility is the name of the game.

Okay.

You're sure you don't want something to drink?

No thanks.

Coffee? Tea? Water? You look a little pale.

Maybe water.

Your book really is huge, I want you to know that.

Thank you.

I started reading it in the duty-free shop and couldn't put it down for the whole flight.

Thank you, thank you very much.

The minute I finished it, I said to my wife: This is a movie!

***Do you believe that, as a writer, you are obligated to be involved in politics?***

I meet with Michael Orbach, my American acquaintance. He's almost twenty years older than me, but he has fewer white hairs, and his gait, as we walk along the beach promenade toward Jaffa, is lighter. We met in another life, when I worked as a copywriter for an ad agency. Michael ran a workshop for us on social advertising, or as he called it, Meaningful Advertising, and when he lectured, I felt as if I were seeing the light. It turns out that it's possible to work in advertising without making a mockery of yourself. You can write slogans, radio spots, and scripts for worthy causes. You can use advertising techniques to encourage people to make significant changes in their lives instead of urging them to buy things they don't need.

I went up to him after the lecture. Mr. Orbach, I said, your words have inspired me.

I said, I'd like to join your company. Work with you. Maybe as a representative of Meaningful Advertising in Israel. What do you think?

He said I should send him my CV.

I sent it. He replied politely that, at the moment, he wasn't looking for new staff members, but he would keep my CV on file.

I wrote back that I know that what he said means is no in American, and asked if we could occasionally e-mail, because working in an ad agency had made me feel that my words were losing meaning.

We began to correspond. Exchange ideas. More accurately, I asked his advice on a series of subjects and he taught me a few things.

Every now and then, I would ask about the possibility of working with him. My days in the agency had become increasingly bleak during that period. As the municipal elections grew closer, a subsidiary company to handle political advertising was established in the office, and I was assigned to it for three months. We were supporting mayoral candidates throughout the country. Billboards. Radio spots. Party platforms.

One of the candidates was Yoram Sirkin. THE Yoram Sirkin.

I remember the first time I saw him. The ironic thing was that I wasn't supposed to be at that meeting at all. I had a deadline to produce a jingle for another campaign, but they took me off it and suddenly called me into the conference room. This is our copywriter, the big boss introduced me when I walked in, and then pointed to the other side of the table and said, Meet Yoram Sirkin, the next mayor. The three men sitting at the other side of the table were more or less the same age. None of them had the charismatic presence of a future mayor, so I didn't know which of them to look at, but I said to myself, It's definitely not the one on the left, because the minute the big boss said, the next mayor, the one on the left averted his eyes in embarrassment. Altogether, there was something saggy about him. His shoulders sagged, his shirt sagged, and so did his glasses.

But the guy on the left spoke first. His voice was slightly nasal and he paused in the wrong places between . . . words: I asked for you to come into . . . the room because it . . . was important to . . . me that you . . . join our campaign and see eye to eye with . . . us. No wisecracks, the kind ad . . . agency people like. You understand what I'm . . . saying?

Completely. What do you think about seeing heart to heart? I asked.

The room suddenly filled with a should-we-laugh-or-cry silence.

Good one, Yoram Sirkin said, touching the bridge of his glasses lightly. Taking their cue from him, his two escorts nodded.

The thing about a political campaign—I continued as if I were an expert on the subject—is to arouse the voters' emotions. To find the right buttons and press them. Over and over again.

What did you say your name was? Sirkin asked. And before I could reply, he turned to the boss and said, I want this kid to . . . be with us at every meeting from now . . . on. I like the way his mind . . . works.

---

The official purpose of the next few meetings was to learn our candidate's agenda, to find out what he wanted to promote, what he believed in, and what his plan of action would be—if he won the election. But Yoram Sirkin answered almost every question we asked with the same question: What do you think would go over well with the voters? I believe that, with the exception of his intense desire to be elected, he had no other clear aspirations. We replied cautiously that we should wait for the reports of the focus groups, and until we received them, anything we said about voters' preferences would be guesswork.

Yoram Sirkin nodded, and then, for the first time, made the gesture that would become the trademark of comedians imitating him in political satires on TV years later: rubbing his hands together as if he were performing the commandment of washing his hands before a meal.

The focus group concluded that the residents were quite satisfied with their city and more than anything, were afraid that a new mayor would change the way things were being done.

If that's the situation, I said at the next meeting, let's go all the way with it. Let's tell people to vote for our candidate because he's the only one who definitely won't change anything.

Good one, Yoram Sirkin said.

We flooded the streets with billboards that showed a large, nicely photoshopped picture of him—the glasses were gone and his evasive glance became an intense, direct stare—along with the fruit of my keyboard: Sirkin. Only he can preserve our city.

At the same time, we hired a language coach to teach him how to speak before an audience. We didn't delude ourselves that he would become a firebrand overnight, but we asked her to work with him on his ... pauses. Polls all over the world show that candidates who win elections are those who know how to pause in the right places.

When the campaign opened, the polls gave Sirkin four to five percent of the vote. But he was faithful to the list of messages prepared for him, and repeated them like a parrot in a cage: We love our city the way it is. Every change is risky. The risk is greater than the chance of success. If it's not broken, why fix it? If it's fixed, why break it?

Meanwhile, the candidate leading in the polls, a brigadier general in the reserves, was accused of sexual harassment and dropped out of the race.

We eliminated a third candidate with a negative campaign that placed in voters' minds the totally fabricated notion that he had ties with real estate sharks and would push for construction that would change the character of the city and lower property values.

From week to week, Sirkin's numbers rose another little bit in the polls. And another little bit. What is known in the professional jargon as gathering momentum. At the same time, and to our great surprise, his body language changed. Suddenly, he walked briskly, suddenly, his movements were sharp. Suddenly, he banged on the table: Get me the ultra-Orthodox!

And the ultra-Orthodox came to the office and closed a deal to support him in the election in exchange for future budget allotments.

On election night, at our headquarters and in the presence of a modest audience that included mostly members of his family, we celebrated Yoram Sirkin's victory in the mayoral race, never suspecting that it was only the first stop in his meteoric rise in politics.

The agency's subsidiary was dissolved immediately after the municipal elections.

A month later, I received a call on my personal phone from the new mayor.

Listen, kid, he said, I have to give a speech at the municipal education conference.

Okay.

I thought maybe you could . . . write a . . . few points for . . . me. A few killer sentences.

But . . . I thought our office doesn't handle your account anymore.

Tell me, kid, why should they make any money on me . . . or you? Work directly with me. As a consultant.

Let me think about it, Yoram, okay?

Okay. But the education conference is . . . tomorrow. Don't think too . . . much.

———

I always knew that copywriting was a hollow profession. Only when my path crossed Yoram Sirkin's did I understand that it was also corrupt. That I myself was already corrupt from so many years in the profession.

But I didn't know how to do anything else.

I hoped that Uncle Michael from America would rescue me from the predicament I was in. I waited for his e-mails the way children wait for the Independence Day fireworks. And he wrote the same reply every time: Of course, the minute I have a job to offer you, I will. Let's meet and talk about it the next time I'm in Israel.

———

We met when he came to Israel to run his workshops. We walked along the beach promenade from the InterContinental David, to the marina, and back through Jaffa. Always the same route. And he was always the one who spoke. I mean—lectured. About the mistakes in the last Labor Party election campaign. About the fact that the left wing in Israel didn't have to build its campaign around fear, like its right-wing opponents, but should base it on hope. About the fact that Herzl's dream was to establish a country for the Jews, and now that it has been established, we have to redefine Zionism, fill it with up-to-date content, otherwise it will remain hollow, and that hollowness will fill up with right-wing, Messianic elements.

Between one political prophecy and another, he also distracted me with advice in other areas: Start a family as quickly as possible, kiddo. Marriage isn't a prison, the way people mistakenly think, it's the freedom to stop searching for love. But you have to choose right, son, and the criterion is flexibility. A flexible partner is the key to happiness, and children—having children is the most creative thing a person can do in his life, children enrich your creativity, they don't damage it, trust me—

I trusted him. I felt I was learning so much from him.

On one of those walks, he told me in the same arrogant, know-it-all tone he typically used that he had closed his New York office and fired all the employees. Meaningful Advertising, the company, was not very profitable. And he was up to his ears in debt. So now he worked alone, mainly giving workshops in order to pay his debtors. A person needs to take responsibility for his failures, he said, otherwise there's no way he can succeed.

He didn't see any contradiction between his collapse and the fact that he continued to give others advice. There was something both ridiculous and impressive about that.

———

A few months later, I left the ad agency and began to write. I paid the rent by writing speeches for Yoram Sirkin. I no longer needed an uncle in America, and he didn't have any practical prospects for me anyway. Nevertheless, maybe out of habit or because we were both sociable people who, deep inside, felt chronically lonely, we kept meeting every once in a while to stroll along the beach promenade.

Now we're walking toward Jaffa once again. He has just finished giving a workshop for the directors of human rights organizations in Israel, and he's upset. It doesn't matter how crappy your governments have been, he says, the people were always optimistic. That's why I loved coming here. Your anthem is called "The Hope," and that's what there always was here: hope. But today—today I gave a workshop to a group of hopeless people. What happened to all of you?

Look, I begin—

And he interrupts me.

I read your last book, by the way. The translation is excellent. And the characters—they actually jump off the page. Forgive me for saying this, but I kept thinking, how can you write such a naïve love story that could take place anywhere, and be blind to the fact that the country you live in is causing so much suffering in the occupied territories? How can you write about a trivial love affair when women are giving birth at checkpoints?

Look, I try—

And he interrupts me.

You know what the problem is? That people like you go into art instead of politics. And people like—what's his name? Sirking? Sirkind?—are government ministers and legitimate candidates to lead the country. Do you get it? Your government lets you write books, make movies. What do they care? You can walk on the red carpet in Cannes. You can win at fucking Sundance. You can sell formats to HBO. It's all fine just as long as you don't get in the way of their building settlements and destroying the Zionist enterprise, right?

But—

A person like you, with your family background, has to ask himself at every moment whether he's doing the most meaningful thing he can. Write another best seller? Come on. You can do better.

I have an answer for him. But for the last few weeks, there's been so much tension at home between me and Dikla that I don't have the strength to argue with someone else now. And I think that, this time, there's something else underneath his typical heat-of-the-argument reversal. Something more personal he's going through.

———

It comes out as we pass Manta Ray restaurant.

His wife is leaving him.

They spent their lives waiting for this time to come. The kids left for college and now they would have time to make their dreams come true, the dreams they had to push aside in order to be parents. And now his wife does want to make those dreams come true. But not with him.

I nod in understanding. That was the first time in our history that he told me something really personal. I wonder whether I should put a hand on his shoulder. But I don't dare. And I wonder whether to tell him that, last week, Dikla stopped getting dressed when I'm in the room, and doubts every little thing I tell her. Whether I really sent the advance

payment to the hall we hired for the bat mitzvah, whether
I'm really starting to give the creative writing workshop on
Thursday evenings in Beit Shemesh, whether—

Right before Jaffa, he collapses totally.

On a bench.

I sit down next to him.

Surfers walk down to the sea with their boards.

Surfers come up from the sea with their boards.

Wild is the wind.

———

It happened so quickly, he says in bewilderment.

One evening—"We have to talk." Then a confession.
Well-phrased. As if she had polished it for weeks. Thank
you for all the good years, but I think that we should separate before it turns really ugly, she told him. The next day,
she took her things and moved into a rented apartment.
Which means she rented the apartment before she spoke to
him. Would you believe it?

A sixty-something American man is now leaving me
space to say something wise that will comfort him. Give him
some insight. But my life experience is so meager compared
to his that I feel all I can do for him is listen.

I'm completely lost, he says. There's a story I used to tell
myself about my life—and it turns out that it's wrong. And I
have no fucking idea where to go from here.

The three-card monte con man sets up next to us, this
is his regular place on the promenade. His cronies gather

around his box, but the fierce wind blows the three cards away—only one of them is the jack—and the con man and his cronies run after them to try and catch them.

How about eating at Dr. Shakshuka? I finally say.

My American friend laughs. He's crazy about shakshuka.

As long as a person keeps his sense of humor and his appetite, I think, there's a chance he can be saved. We head for the Clock Tower, the wind has died down a little, and I notice that he's slightly stooped and has slowed down. Usually I have a hard time keeping up with him when we walk, but now I have to slow down so we can stay close. Right before the entrance to Dr. Shakshuka, he stops, straightens up, and puts a hand on my shoulder. Partly patronizing. Partly to keep himself from falling. Think about what I said about politics, he says. If people like you continue to stay on the sidelines, you won't have a country left or sidelines you can stand on.

———

On the way back from my walk with my uncle from America, I see a billboard. It happens while I'm speeding along the Ayalon highway, so I have only a second to look. It's enough to register Yoram Sirkin's face and read my slogan: Sirkin. Only he can save our country.

**What doesn't the general public know about you?**

Not only the general public. Dikla doesn't know either that my relationship with Yoram Sirkin continued for years, and is continuing secretly to this day. My fingers tremble as I write this, and I'm not sure I'll have the courage to press Save after typing these lines, but it's the truth: I was there. At every step up Sirkin took. I'm the one who wrote the speech that propelled him into public consciousness, the one he delivered after a rocket hit a building in his city. The sentence "The best defense against a Quassam is the solidarity of our people"—it's mine. When, after the war, he decided to run in the national primaries, he hired an ad agency for the sake of appearances, but kept buying slogans from me on the side. I never believed that, with the help of my slogans, he would climb high enough on the list of candidates to win a Knesset seat. I never believed that you could lie to everyone, all the time. And I certainly never thought that, during his first term in the Knesset, they would begin talking about him as a candidate for the cabinet.

That was when I tried to end my dealings with him. I arranged an appointment with him. In a failing café in Kiryat Ono. I asked him to come alone. He said: You need money, kid? Is that what this is about? Because if you do, just say the word. That's not the issue, I said (money has never been the issue, the issue is having influence, the issue is hearing words I wrote echoing in the public space, the issue is that the influence and the echo are intoxicating).

Even in the failing café in Kiryat Ono, Yoram Sirkin's entrance caused a small commotion. The barman asked to shake his hand. The waitress wanted to take a selfie with him. And so did the stoned guy who worked in the adjacent kiosk. I watched him as he gave them his all. The last few years, I've seen him only on TV. We communicated only by well-coded e-mail. It turns out that there are things you can't see on TV. The small potbelly he'd grown, along with the suit he was wearing, gave him a more authoritative air. He really wasn't wearing glasses anymore, probably laser surgery, which enabled him to look directly at anyone speaking to him. He moved around nimbly, purposefully, and his face looked tan and healthy. As if he had been photoshopped.

In the end, it happened, I thought as he approached my table: Yoram Sirkin has stepped into the shoes of the image I created for him. The fiction had solidified into reality. The puppet had cut its strings. The parrot had spread its wings, broken out of its cage, and taken off.

What's up, kid? he said, sitting down and signaling for the waiter. What's happening in the world of literature? You're a disappearing world, believe me.

Listen, Yoram—I got straight to the point—I want to stop.

Stop what?

Working for you. Writing for you.

Okay. Can I ask why?

It doesn't work for me anymore. You and I really don't see eye to eye, ideologically, you know, recently—

But we're a great success, kid.

You are, Yoram. Maybe a little too great.

So the golem turns on its creator, eh?

Something like that.

Do I look like a golem to you?

No, Yoram, of course not, definitely not—

Waiter! he shouted suddenly.

The waiter hurried over, looking apologetic, and took our order.

When he left our table, Yoram said, Listen to me and listen well, and rubbed his hands together as if he were performing the hand-washing mitzvah. He spoke quietly, which is what made it so alarming.

Yoram Sirkin doesn't force anyone to work with him. But take into account that if you cut ties with me now, when I need you most, there will be a price.

A price?

I have all your e-mails, kid. One click on Forward, and you're finished.

Let me get this straight, you're threatening me?

Just the opposite, kid. I'm watching out for you. How do you think people in your milieu will react if they know you've been working for the other side? And with your family history? What will they write in that left-wing newspaper of yours? I can imagine the headline—

No need.

There's a Conference of Presidents, next week, kid. In New York.

I don't know, Yoram. Let me think about it.

I only need you to write the opening and closing of the speech. No one listens to the middle anyway.

In English?

Of course in English. Obama will be there. Bill Clinton. Members of Congress. Henry Kissinger. And...your faithful servant.

He's learned where to put the pauses, I thought.

Waiter! he shouted and rubbed his hands together once again. When the waiter arrived, he handed him his phone and asked him to snap a picture of us. "As a souvenir."

Only when the camera flashed did I realize: Our picture. Together. In a café. He'd send it to the media. A picture is worth a thousand e-mails.

————

I wrote the Conference of Presidents speech for him. The one that made the analysts begin to talk about him as candidate for party leader.

————

Dikla and I watched the live broadcast of the speech together. It was back in the days when she rested her feet on me when we watched TV.

Sirkin held the corners of the lectern, and occasionally, with remarkably perfect timing, raised his right hand in the air to emphasize a point he was making.

I don't believe a word he says, Dikla said, but he sure knows how to give a speech.

And he knows how to blackmail his speechwriters, I thought but didn't say.

Tell me, she asked, was he really such a nebbish when you helped him run for mayor? It's hard to believe that someone can change so totally.

He really was a nebbish, I said. But that was ten years ago and . . . he reinvented himself.

Now he'll say something about Jerusalem, Dikla said. Somehow, they always get around to that.

Bull's-eye, I thought but didn't say.

Sirkin delivered the closing sentence I wrote for him about the capital of Israel, that the link between it and the Jewish people is unbreakable, pause, a Siamese connection, pause. He banged his fist on the podium for greater emphasis. And in response, the American Jews stood up and cheered.

How about that? Dikla said and pulled her feet off my lap.

What?

That image, "Siamese connection," it's in one of your books, isn't it?

Wow, you're right.

Could it be that the bastard is stealing images from you?

I don't think so.

Sue him.

I don't know, Diki. Let's wait and see if it happens again. Otherwise, we don't have a case.

———

I could have confessed to her right then. There were many other times like that, when I could have confessed. I passed up all of them.

In recent years, not a morning went by when I didn't wake with a firm decision to stop it. Put an end to it once and for all.

But I don't know how to anymore.

**Could you live and write in another country?**

A trip to Arad to judge a local short-story contest. They don't pay me, but I have a soft spot in my heart for that city, and lately, the farther away I get from home, the less pain I have in my posterior heart. The hills are surprisingly green, the trip shorter than I remembered. There used to be a music festival here. Every year, I would take the five o'clock morning bus to my aunt and uncle's house a day before it and leave a day after, and the days in the middle were the happiest I ever had. After three nights of music and sleeping bags, my entire body pulsed with the beat of the bass, there was an on-the-verge-of-joy feeling in my throat, and everything seemed possible. I went to the festival for ten years straight (turn left at this traffic circle), once with a girl I was secretly in love with (I even kept it a secret from myself), once with Hagai Carmeli, who disappeared on me then, too, in the middle of the festival, and once with Dikla, who felt it was a little too much for her. That was where I first heard Brera Tivit and the band's electrifying drumming of Shlomo Barr, that was where I first heard the Friends of Natasha sing the words *"The ships of sorrow are drowning in the great sea of small hopes and wine."* That was where I jumped into the pool in the middle of a performance, slept in the middle of a performance, and kissed someone in the middle of a performance. That was where, after a performance, I walked to my aunt and uncle's house in torn sandals as the darkness turned slowly into light.

A disaster happened the first year I didn't go to the festival: The organizers had sold too many tickets, and in the beginning, two guys and a girl screamed because they were being crushed by the crowd. Then they had no more air at all. The festival ended that night, and ever since, any attempt to revive it has failed (here's the Oron Performance Hall, there's the place where the Black Israelites used to braid dreadlocks, and a bit farther, on the left, the head librarian is supposed to be waiting for me).

I make a desperate effort not to see what happened at the Arad music festival as a metaphor. Not to think about the fact that it happened three months before the Rabin assassination. Not to think that the avarice and the violence that brought about the disaster in Arad are exactly what is dragging us into the sinkhole now.

It's not that I don't have another country to go to. I do. To be honest about it, members of my generation have several other countries. But in none of them would I be asked to judge a short-story contest in a remote city, and on the way there, be flooded with sights and sounds and words. In none of them would the then and the now join together in such a way that it brings tears to my eyes. In none of them would the head librarian of that remote city, noticing the tears, be sensitive enough not to ask questions and offer me a glass of cold lemonade. Because the drive to Arad always leaves you thirsty.

How can you live and write in a place that summons up no memories ? That you don't care about? That doesn't infuriate you so much sometimes that you want to bang your head against the wall and your fingers on the keyboard?

**What is Israel for you?**

They had no furniture, only mattresses. The real estate agent whispered, the mortgage. The woman was pleasant. There were only mattresses, there was no furniture. The children looked hungry. What a view, the agent said. That was five years ago. We were looking for an apartment between Tel Aviv and Jerusalem, preferably with a balcony. I didn't say a word the entire time we were there. The agent whispered, the mortgage ate up all their money. The woman tried very hard to look pleasant. The view was spectacular.

**What is your earliest memory?**

It was the Yom Kippur War.

Of course, I didn't know it was the Yom Kippur War.

I was two and a half years old.

I know, people don't usually have memories from that age.

But I remember a house full of women. My mother's friends, apparently. Who came to help. And I was the center of attention, sitting in the living room, playing building blocks with them. Then there's a cut, and one of them carries me to Mom's room, where my mom picks up a simple recorder and plays something for me, until she suddenly starts to cry and one of the women carries me back to the living room. Again the building blocks. And that's it. That's where my memory ends. Anything I add would be a lie, or worse, an interpretation.

*How do you feel about the fact that one of your books is required reading in high schools?*

We'll arrange a taxi for you, the literature coordinator said.

Great.

Write down the driver's number, she said. His name is Mordecai. Call him tomorrow morning and tell him where to pick you up.

I wrote the number on a piece of paper and called it the next day.

A masculine voice answered. Hello. In a heavy Arabic accent. Must be a wrong number, I thought. I hung up and punched in the number again. The same voice again. This time, I tried anyway: Hello, can I speak to Mordecai?

A too-long silence, followed by: This is Mordecai speaking.

Hello, I said hesitantly. You're supposed to pick me up at noon today and take me to Jerusalem. Should I explain how to get to my place?

Yes, yes, the voice said. Too quickly. As if he sensed my hesitation and wanted to convince me that he really was Mordecai.

Are you writing this down? I asked. And he repeated: Yes, yes.

I gave him a full explanation, and he said he'd be there, I had nothing to worry about.

His Hebrew was okay, but the accent—totally Arabic. And that was a period of frequent terrorist attacks.

We ended the call, and I began to get ready to leave. I chose the books I wanted to read from and marked the passages with my usual bookmarks—business cards from Zarathustra, the intellectual café Hagai Carmeli had once tried to open in Jerusalem. And closed a month later. As I was inserting the bookmarks, a farfetched yet believable scenario began to take shape in my mind, explaining the conversation with "Mordecai": The number they gave me was wrong. I mistakenly reached a high-ranking member of Hamas who, after a few seconds of hesitation, realized that a golden opportunity had come his way and decided to play the game: pretend to be Mordecai, pick me up, kidnap me, and take me over the Green Line.

Though my suspicions seemed a little over the top, I still decided to be on the safe side and called the literature coordinator to make sure she had really given me the right number. There was no answer.

Having no choice, I put my nice shirt into the dryer to iron itself and got ready for Mordecai's arrival. I'll decide after I see what he looks like, I thought, calming myself. If he looks like a terrorist, I won't get into the taxi. And that's it.

But his appearance only confused me more.

When I walked out of the building, he was sitting on the hood of the car, smoking a cigarette. He didn't have a fanatic-Muslim beard, but he looked totally like an Arab. Mordecai my foot. But his handshake was gentle, and his eyes weren't hostile.

Ready to go? he asked.

Ready to go, I said, and got into the backseat.

We drove around the traffic circles on our way out of the city in silence. I waited for someone to call him on the two-way radio, so I could hear the name Mordecai spoken by someone else. But his radio was silent. No voice came out of it. No one asked who was available on Herzl Street. Maybe Mordecai doesn't work with a taxi station, I thought. But if that's true, why does he need a two-way radio? And why doesn't he talk to me? Since when are taxi drivers not talkative?

I began to think what would happen to the stories I still hadn't published. Would anyone bother to publish them after my death? Because that's when they might actually have commercial potential. People value artists more after they die. They hold tribute performances for them. They bring singers. Maybe even Ehud Banai would agree to sing at mine. But wait a minute, who would choose which of my stories to include in the anthology and which to leave out? And what about all the embarrassing stories, the ones buried deep in my computer hard drive with clever code names, the ones that, if published, might hurt my loved ones, or at the very least, shock them? Do their feelings still have to be taken into account even after I'm murdered in cold blood by a Hamas squad and my body is hacked into dozens of pieces, put in black plastic bags, and tossed into the sea near Gaza?

Mordecai turned onto Route 443. He had no reason to turn onto Route 443. If the school we were driving to was in Ramot or French Hill, it would make sense. A shortcut. But the school was in central Jerusalem, so the only reason he had for turning onto Route 443 was that it would be easier to get to Ramallah from there.

You'd rather drive this way? I asked suspiciously.

Yes, Mordecai replied. At this hour, there are traffic jams at the Sakharov Gardens. And this way, we bypass them in no time at all.

As far as I knew from my Jerusalem days, there were no traffic jams at the Sakharov Gardens after ten in the morning.

His two-way radio was still silent.

Minarets loomed on the hills that lined both sides of the road. Small villages. Area B? Area C? Not clear. After all, part of the road itself is located on the other side of the Green Line.

Tell me, I tried from a different direction, you're from Jerusalem?

Yes, Mordecai replied tersely.

Where exactly in Jerusalem?

There, next to French Hill, Mordecai replied, driving slightly faster now.

What's next to French Hill, Ramot Eshkol? Pisgat Ze'ev?

No, Mordecai said, pressing harder on the gas pedal. It's right next to French Hill. It's a village. Small.

Village? The only village next to French Hill is Isawiya. I once dated a girl who lived in the French Hill dorms, and when I slept at her place, the village muezzin used to accompany our lovemaking with his ululating call to prayer. Why didn't Mordecai say he was from Isawiya? If he didn't have something to hide, that's what he would have said. So apparently he does. In another minute, he'll probably turn onto a dirt road where the other members of the squad are waiting for him. If I'm going to die now, I suddenly thought, it definitely means that I won't sleep with that girl from the dorms again. Ever. Not that there was a chance it would happen anyway. Years had passed and she's already taken, and so am I. But damn it, that finality of death.

Suddenly, I was filled with the desire to live.

Stop here, I said.

What? Mordecai pretended not to hear.

Stop here, please, I said. I need to pee.

He gave me a small smile, and his soft eyes filled with scorn.

No problem, he said, pulled over to the side of the road, and stopped.

I got out of the taxi and walked over to a small bush past the shoulder. I looked right and left. If I'm going to take off, now's the time, I thought. I can make a run for the nearby intersection where soldiers are posted. I'd have to leave my wallet, my datebook, and a few Pilot pens in the car, but what are they compared to my life? On the other hand, I thought as I tried to look as if I were peeing, if Mordecai was planning to kidnap me, he wouldn't have stopped and given me the chance to run away. On yet another hand, maybe this is exactly how he builds trust so that later, when he veers onto a dirt road, I won't doubt him when he claims it's a shortcut?

I zipped up and turned back to the taxi. Mainly because Mordecai's eyes were too good and too amused to be the eyes of a killer. That's crap, there's no such thing as the eyes of a killer, I scoffed at myself as I pulled the seat belt around my waist. But let's say there is, how many have you seen that would qualify you to recognize them?

So Mordecai, I tried again to get him talking after he drove back onto the road, passengers have strange requests sometimes, eh?

Yes, he said with a smile. And added nothing.

What's the funniest request you've had from a passenger? I asked, sounding to myself like a talk-show host.

Ah, Mordecai laughed in embarrassment and touched his bald head like a religious guy straightening his yarmulke.

Come on, I urged him, tell me.

I don't know about a request, he said. But something funny once happened on the way to Tiberias.

There was a long line of cars at the improvised border guard checkpoint, and Mordecai slowed down. The thought crossed my mind that if he were a well-known Hamas activist, the soldiers at the checkpoint would recognize him.

So what happened on the trip to Tiberias?

When I went to pick up the man I was driving there, he was with a young woman, who put him into the taxi, gave me a piece of paper with the address he had to go to in Tiberias, and said, My dad's an old man, so be patient with him, okay? I didn't understand what she meant, but I said, Sure, no problem. And we drove off. So we're, you know, driving along, the old man and me. He was wearing glasses with thick black frames like people used to wear, and he had on a heavy brown jacket even though it was summer. At first we didn't talk, the only sound was the radio. But a while later, when we start to drive down to the Dead Sea, he asks me: Are we in Tiberias yet? And I tell him, not yet. And a few minutes later, he asks again: Are we in Tiberias yet? And I tell him no, soon. That's how it was, the whole way. Every five minutes he asks if we're in Tiberias yet and I say, patiently, like I promised his daughter: No, not yet.

The border guard soldier bent down, looked into the taxi, and signaled Mordecai with his head to drive on.

Until finally, he continued, two and a half hours later, we really did arrive in Tiberias. And then? As soon as we drive into the city and see the Sea of Galilee, he starts to ask: When are we going back to Jerusalem? When are we going back to Jerusalem? Soon, I tell him, soon, and I keep driving until we've reached the address his daughter wrote on the piece of paper. Then I helped him get out of the car and walked him to the door of the family he was going to visit. The truth is that I was afraid he'd get confused and lose his way if he was on his own.

Nice of you, I said.

People should be nice, Mordecai said.

His radio buzzed. Finally.

They called from the school to ask when the writer will be there, said a hoarse female voice.

We're already past the checkpoint, Mordecai said. In fifteen minutes, we're at the gate.

———

I relaxed in my seat. The story about Tiberias and the radio call had done their job. I still didn't understand why he called himself Mordecai, but I no longer feared for my life, which left room for the stage fright that always attacks me before these sessions but had been pushed aside this time by a much greater fear.

I rummaged around in my bag and took out the list of main points I'd written down. I read them again and again with blind eyes until we stopped in front of the school gate.

When should I expect you? Mordecai asked.

In about an hour and a half, I said. But keep your cell phone on so if it ends before that, I can let you know.

There was a good reason I left myself the option of cutting out early.

A week ago, a security guard had smuggled me out of a high school in Ramla in the middle of the question period. I had begun, as always, by telling them about my childhood, which included moving many times, and said the words that always create a link between me and them—you can really almost hear the click: "Once every year or two, I found myself being the new kid in class." I explained how my book, which they were studying for their matriculation exams, actually came from a personal place, as personal as possible: the attempt of an adult, soon to be a father, to find out for himself if there is a place in the world he can call home—and I saw their eyes open wide, wondering, "So is it all bullshit, everything our literature teacher told us about your book being a microcosm of Israeli society after the Rabin assassination?"

Then I opened the floor for questions.

The first question was a general one. About the rhymes in the book. A question that's pleasant to answer.

But the second question was, "Do you like Arabs?"

Just like that, right in your face.

The questioner was a teenager wearing glasses. People wearing glasses always look more vulnerable to me.

Silence in the room.

I told him that I gave a voice to an Arab character in the book because I felt that you can't write a book that takes place in the Castel and talk about the idea of home without hearing the voice of the people who once called that place, Al-Qastal, their home.

So you like Arabs, he said.

That's not what I said, I persisted. I said that it was important to me, is important to me, to listen to the story of the Palestinian worker in the book, who had been driven out of his village when he was a child.

They ran away, the teenager with the glasses corrected me. We didn't drive them away.

That's debatable, I said. In any case, I felt connected to that story because, as a child, I had to leave quite a few homes I wanted to stay in.

Didn't I tell you he likes Arabs? the teenager with the glasses asked another teenager sitting at the far end of the room, and explained to me: We had a bet. Now he owes me a combo at the Burger King.

Go fuck yourself, you didn't prove anything, the other teen said, stood up, and walked over to him. And pushed him.

Fists started flying. At first, it was just the two of them, then their friends joined in. The girls screamed. The teachers tried to separate them, and a security guard put a hand on my shoulder and said, Mr. Writer, I think I should escort you out.

————

This time, in the Jerusalem school, I decided not to get myself in trouble—and pass on the question period. But even so, a hand was raised when I finished telling them about my suitcase-childhood.

A delicate, female hand. Of a girl I would bet sang at school Memorial Day ceremonies.

I said, Yes, you want to ask something?

I wanted to say, she replied, that my favorite parts of your book are the white parts.

The white parts? I turned to look at the book in an effort to understand what she was talking about.

I think it's really nice, she went on, that in a book that has so many voices, you left room for silence.

Really, I said, as slowly as I could, thinking that maybe stretching out the word would bring me enlightenment.

For homework, she said, our teacher asked us to find an alternative name for the book, so I called it "Five Voices and Silence." Do you like it?

Very much. Tell me, can I take a peek at your book?

It's your book! she said, and all the kids in the room laughed.

She handed me the book, which was covered in the plastic book jackets that libraries use. When I opened it, I saw them almost immediately: white spaces. Wherever the voice of the Palestinian worker was heard in the original book, there was white space now. In the beginning, there were only a few white spaces, later on there were many, and toward the end of the book, after the Palestinian goes to jail, there was no longer any need for them.

Since I was looking through the white spaces in the book, I didn't notice that the literature coordinator had come over to me, and now she whispered in my ear: We had no choice.

In the current atmosphere of the city, with all the terrorist attacks, we couldn't take the chance that our discussion of the book would deteriorate into politics, you understand? And it would have been a pity to forgo the other good qualities it has, you see?

I think I nodded, a small nod that I regret to this day.

Then the student with the delicate hand asked if she could ask another question.

I said yes. Even though I felt that the right thing to do was to get up and leave.

She asked about the rhymes.

I told her that the rhymes appeared in the places that hurt me the most while I was writing.

Then she asked another question, I don't remember it anymore. And then applause. Yes, there was applause, and I bowed my head in false modesty.

Mordecai's taxi was double parked next to the school gate. Its lights flashed. I said goodbye to Sylvia, the teacher, who thanked me for the inspiring meeting, and sat down in the passenger seat.

Mordecai started the car. How was it? he asked.

So-so, I replied.

No kidding, Mordecai said.

We emerged from a small traffic jam at the exit to the city and began to glide down to Shaar Hagai. This time Mordecai chose Highway 1, which was not lined on both sides with Arab villages. Only rusty armored cars.

You still owe me a story, I said, turning to face him.

What do you mean, I owe you a story?

Why are you called Mordecai? Is that your real name?

Ah, Mordecai stretched his entire body on his seat—
even his bald spot stretched—it's a long story.

We have time, I reminded him.

My real name is Mustafa. But everyone calls me Mordecai. I'll explain why. In Jerusalem, on the license plates, there's
a special number for savages that come from the eastern part
of the city. Like, if you're from East Jerusalem and you have a
taxi, you have to have that number. Six-six-six. So what's the
problem? A Jew who sees six-six-six doesn't want to get into
the taxi and the Jewish taxi stands don't want to use a driver
with an Arab's number, so there won't be problems with the
passengers. Now—and this was something like twenty years
ago—I bought a taxi license from a Jew who left the profession
and became a journalist. Maybe you know him? Gadi Gidor?
You don't? He's famous, they show him a lot on TV. I bought
the license from him and went to the Armon Hanatziv taxi
stand and said, I want to work and I have a Jew's license plate.
The boss of that stand then was Mr. Shlomo. He's still a good
friend of mine. And what did he tell me? You look like a good
guy, I want you to work with us. But so there won't be any
problems, let's decide that on the radio, they call you Mordecai. I said okay, what do I care? And that's how it started. At
first they only called me Mordecai on that stand's two-way
radio network. And later, at another taxi stand where I also
started to work. Then my friends from the village started

calling me Mordecai, for fun. And today everyone calls me that. Even my wife and kids call me Mordecai.

Your kids really call you Mordecai?

Yes, sure, Mordecai said firmly. That's what they heard since they were little, so that's what they know.

And your mother?

Mordecai laughed. My mother is my mother. She won't accept anything but Mustafa. When we go to see her, I have to warn my wife not to call me Mordecai by mistake near her, or else she starts to yell so loudly that the whole village can hear her, What's this Mordecai, I don't have a son named Mordecai, and when she gets mad like that, my mother, she burps uncontrollably, it's really something. Mordecai-Mustafa roared with laughter. He must have been picturing his mother belching, and it made him laugh so hard that his shoulders shook.

It was weird—even though he was laughing, I wanted to put a hand on his shoulder to comfort him. But I kept my hand under my thigh.

———

All the way to the Tel Aviv area, we talked "soft politics" (terrorist attacks are not good, the occupation is not good, if only peace would come—we both chose our words carefully).

Every once in a while, we were silent and let the music fill the space.

When we reached my house, I asked Mordecai-Mustafa how I could contact him if I needed a taxi to Jerusalem again. He gave me his business card, which said MORDECAI QAUASMEH, and said, Call me, really. Even if you only need a ride to this area.

I shook his hand very hard. Then, as I walked to the front door, I took my keys out of the side pocket of my bag. I inserted the house key into the lock and turned it. The door didn't open. I checked to see if it was the right key and tried again.

Unfamiliar voices came from inside. The voices of strangers.

*One of your books was translated into Arabic. What responses, if any, did you get from the Arab world?*

I meet Jamal, my Palestinian friend, in Manchester. He's more or less my age. A businessman, always wearing a suit, likes to drink, likes soccer. And although we never talked about it explicitly, I suspect that he too has the tendency to harbor hopeless longings. Our friendship began when he came up to me after a sparsely attended event in the city, and it has developed cautiously over the last several years. Once he visits me and once I visit him. Once, we go to see a Manchester City match there, and once to see a Bnei Sakhnin match here. And today, he apparently feels secure enough to tell me about his parents, who had been driven out of Jaffa, then out of Lebanon, then out of Tunis, and then out of

Jordan. At the mention of each country they were driven out of, I sink lower in my chair.

I don't say a word and feel, to be precise, a combination of guilt along with a refusal to feel guilt. We are sitting in the best Italian restaurant in Manchester, where the waiters are solicitous, bring plates and remove plates, and he continues to describe to me the suffering of his family. There's also a cousin from Gaza who was killed in the last war, it turns out. A plane dropped a one-ton bomb on his home, killing not only him but also three women and seven children. One of them was a baby, he says, and I nod, thinking that it's not clear how we managed to postpone this conversation until now.

I try to make my nods empathetic, but I'm not willing to lower my head completely.

There are no good guys and bad guys in this story, I think, only strong ones and weak ones.

When dessert arrives, he tells me that—how had he not mentioned it before?—his father is a sculptor, one of a few Palestinian sculptors, and in the great escape from Lebanon to Tunis in '82, he had to leave all of his sculptures behind. He wasn't permitted to take even one of them. As an artist, he says, you can imagine the pain. The humiliation.

Yes, I say. That's the first word to come out of my mouth in the last half hour.

We speak English, although I suspect that Jamal knows Hebrew as well, and in his excellent English, he also asks for the check.

Let me pay, I offer, and he says, Of course not, *habibi*, you're my guest.

Yes, I object, but you paid last time, in Jaffa.

He smiles. But you were my guest then too.

I smile back, an automatic smile—

Until I understand what he means.

————

Later, when he drives me to my hotel, we are silent, which is unusual for us.

There's a security fence between the driver's and the passenger's seats.

The streets of Manchester are as empty as suburban streets, and we are the only car to stop at the red lights.

It's the responsibility of the winner to listen to the loser's story, I think to myself.

But something inside me rebels at the story he told me. More precisely, at the parts missing from it.

————

He stops in front of the hotel.

I thank him for dinner and ask when he plans to be in my area again.

I say "my area" so that I won't be forced to choose between "Israel" and "Palestine." He says he doesn't know, there's nothing concrete on the horizon at the moment. But *inshallah*.

So we'll talk, I say.

We'll talk, he repeats.

And, unusual for us, we part with a strong hug.

———

Several weeks later, in the middle of the night, the phone rings.

I fumble around for it in the dark. I'm afraid, almost know, that something has happened to Shira at Sde Boker.

Meanwhile, Dikla wakes up and rubs her eyes.

It's Amichai on the line. He introduces himself as the head of security at Ben Gurion Airport. Even his voice sounds like a head-of-security voice.

He says that, a few hours ago, at a routine security check, they stopped a Palestinian businessman who had flown in from London, and that "things got a bit out of hand." He doesn't say what "things" or how out of hand they got, but I can imagine.

He says that, when he was questioned, the man kept repeating my name. Claimed I was his friend and the purpose of his trip was to meet with me.

I remember that, in one of our conversations, Jamal told me about the seven circles of security he has to go through every time he comes to Israel. And I remember that I really did tell him, explicitly, that if they caused him problems again, he could mention my name.

Dikla, who is wide awake now, gives me a questioning look.

Amichai asks if I really do know Jamal Kanfani.

I say I do, and then he asks if I can come to the airport to clear up some doubts they have.

I ask if we can do it on the phone, and Amichai replies sharply, No.

I say, Wait a minute, and summarize the conversation for Dikla. She knows Jamal. One of the times we met to eat hummus in Jaffa, she joined us, and later said—she doesn't tend to say such things—that he's a guy after her own heart. She doesn't tell me what she thinks I should do now, but I see in her eyes what she thinks I should do.

———

When it's all over, I drive Jamal to his hotel. I want to ask what the real purpose of his trip to Israel is, but I'm afraid of sounding like another interrogator.

He asks how my kids are.

I ask how his kids are.

I tell him that my eldest daughter is very happy in the boarding school she moved to, but I still worry about her all the time.

He tells me that his eldest daughter is coming to Ramallah for a week this year as part of the Palestinian Diaspora's Return project. Like your Birthright project, he says.

He doesn't tell me what exactly happened in the side room the security people took him to.

And I don't tell him that, halfway to the airport, I almost made a U-turn because I suddenly began to be fearful and suspicious. And that the main reason I didn't make a U-turn in the end wasn't our friendship but the knowledge that Dikla would be contemptuous of me if I did.

I stop in front of his hotel.

He turns to me, his eyes shiny, and says, "Thank you." In Hebrew. For the first time.

I ask if he wants to meet tomorrow, in Jaffa, after my workshop.

*Inshallah*, he says, and from the tone of his voice, I understand that he has other plans.

So we'll talk, I say.

We'll talk, he repeats.

We part with a strong hug.

He gets out of the car, and I watch him through the side mirror, making sure he's walking to the hotel with his suitcase, that the doors really open for him, that he really goes inside.


**If heaven really exists, what would you want God to say to you at the pearly gates?**

That no one will ever ask me questions taken from the Bernard Pivot questionnaire.

That Ari isn't there yet. That at the last minute they'll discover a miracle drug for his illness and he'll live for years after taking it.

Last month, because of the painkillers, he shifted between totally groggy moments to totally sober moments.

I went to see him yesterday, and he suddenly said to me: Remember how angry you were at me when I didn't come to see you guys after Shira was born?

Of course I remember, I thought. How could I forget the only real argument we ever had? After she was born, everyone came to congratulate us. To give us gift cards for the best baby store in the country. He was the only one who didn't come. I waited a week. I waited a month. After four months, I was hurt to the core and began to block his calls. You should do the opposite, Dikla said. Call him. Tell him right to his face how unacceptable it is not to come to see us. Everyone deserves a hearing. Good friends definitely do.

Two hours after the conversation, Ari appeared at our place. With a bag of gifts, most of which were completely inappropriate for babies, a huge bouquet of flowers, and a pot of chili con carne for dinner. He volunteered immediately and without hesitation to hold Shira so we could eat, and while Dikla and I sat at the small kitchen table, he cradled her in his thick arms and sang to her: *La linda manita que tiene el bebé / Qué linda, qué bella, qué preciosa es.* He told us it was a song his mother used to sing to his brothers and sisters, and just imagine, until two minutes ago, he'd had no idea that he remembered it at all. Shira, who didn't take to strangers easily and usually reacted with piercing screams when she was held by unfamiliar hands, was completely calm in Ari's arms, and when we finished eating, he handed her to me, took a step back, studied me, and said, You were born to be a father, and to Dikla he said, That's what he always wanted, you know? Once, on a bus trip from Bolivia to Brazil, out of sheer boredom, I asked him what he dreamed of. And what did he say? Not being a writer and not books. Being a daddy.

I hope your turn comes soon, Dikla said.

He gave a bitter chuckle and said, I can't see it happening.

Then Dikla said she was going to rest for a while, and we sat down on the living-room couch, turned on the TV, and watched soccer. We didn't shout when there was a goal to keep from waking Shira, who was sleeping peacefully on my chest, and when the match was over, I walked Ari to the door. Only then, right before he left, did he say, Listen, I don't know why I didn't come until now. Something held me back, bro. I have no idea what. But bottom line, I was a shitty friend. And I'm sorry.

———

Now I get it, he told me yesterday in his apartment.

What?

I get what it was that held me back then.

When?

After your Shira was born.

Forget it, bro. That was a long time ago.

No, listen. There are people who see the future, right? All kinds of tea-leaf and coffee-grinds readers?

Yes.

So every time I tried to imagine myself as a father, my imagination got stuck. Like a computer that gets stuck and nothing comes onto the screen. Just like we have a reserve of pictures from the past in our memory, I think we also have pictures from the future. And if something isn't supposed to happen to you, you don't have an image of it in your mind.

Maybe. I mean, it's possible.

But I've been on strong drugs this last week. So it could be that . . . I'm talking crap.

It definitely could be. But bro, let's hope you get well. You know. And meet a girl.

Sure. And Hapoel will win the championship.

And maybe, in her pictures of the future, one will have kids in it.

Twins.

And maybe that will be enough.

Triplets.

And peace will come.

And the Sea of Galilee will overflow its banks.

And the Negev will bloom.

And hospitals will serve gourmet meals.

Are you hungry? Should I get you something from downstairs?

No. Go home. And give Dikla a big hug.

Okay.

Colombia or no Colombia—she's the love of your life. And the mother of your children.

You're right.

A few minutes later, he was asleep. Maybe, I thought on the way home, he's like Yaakov Shabtai, whose books were about the end of his life years before he had a heart attack.

Maybe Ari really knew in some hidden, prophetic corner of his heart that he would become ill at a young age before he could become a father. And maybe that was what kept him from coming to see us when Shira was born.

Maybe that was also the reason he could never give himself completely to any girl he dated, including a few who really, and I mean really, were keepers. Maybe he had guessed that there was no point. That it would cause only pain. And that when all is said and done, it's better to eat, drink, and be merry, because tomorrow...

Or maybe not, I thought. Maybe I'm letting him off easy here (apparently those are our true friends: the ones we're willing to let off easy).

———

When I walked into the house, Dikla was working on the computer. I went over to her and did what Ari said. I bent down and gave her a big hug. She hugged me back. A weak hug. Then patted me lightly on the back, with one hand.

What's with the pat on the back, I said, annoyed.

What?

What are we, pals?

What's the problem?

Once you used to hug me differently.

That's how I hug now. Besides, you're interrupting my work.

Well excuse me, really—

Maybe you should go and do some writing?

I haven't written for two years, Dikla.

So just go answer some of the questions in that interview—

### *Do you write on the computer or in a notebook?*

With a feather pen. And an inkstand. And when the pages fly off into the wind—I have no backup. I pick them up from the sidewalk one by one and, of course, pay for it with a slipped disk. You can't sit on a chair when you have a slipped disk, so I write standing up in front of an open window for several hours, like Agnon, until I come down with tuberculosis. Burning up with fever, unable to speak, lying on the shores of the Sea of Galilee, I dictate my books to Dikla with the movement of my eyelids. I blink Morse code and she writes it down. Or she writes whatever she feels like writing. I listen to the music of her laptop keyboard clicking and come to the conclusion that, yes, she's writing what she feels like writing. Bottom line, it doesn't suit her to be someone's assistant. Even in a fantasy. After all, at the few events she attended with me, she always said sarcastically that it seems a writer's wife exists only to allow her husband the freedom to write.

I try to change my dying pose so I can see what she's typing, but all I see is one word: liar.

———

Computer or notebook? I wouldn't dare to write without the Undo button, without the ability to retract, which frees me from the greatest fear of all: making a mistake.

If only we could click Undo for events in real life.

The literature coordinator in the Jerusalem school tells me that they cut the Palestinian worker's monologues out of my book—and instead of nodding in submission, I end my meeting with the students right there and then in protest.

Or I'm in the Subte, the subway in Buenos Aires, and see Hagai Carmeli—rust-colored hair, protruding elbows—walking away from the escalator, and instead of giving a damn about Carolina, the embassy's cultural attaché, and waiting for her to take her smartcard out of her bag, I jump over the barrier, shake off the guards, break into a frantic run, and manage to get on the same train he does before it pulls away from the platform and is drawn into a black hole.

Or I see the name Yoram Sirkin on my phone. A month after the municipal elections. And just block it.

Or Dikla. The night I come home from Colombia and she's in our bed, snuggled under the blanket, I still wake her with kisses, but instead of telling her a story, I carefully pull away a corner of the blanket, put my hand under her shirt, and move my finger to her spot, the tiny indentation between her buttocks and lower back, and gently draw little figure eights around it until she turns to me, the smell of her breath filling me with desire, and we make love. And even after our lovemaking, I don't tell her a story but ask how she is, because it takes more courage to listen than to make up stories, and she tells me snippets of what happened over the week I was gone, the successes and the failures, at work and with the kids, and doesn't ask how it was in Colombia, and I don't answer.

And there was the kid at camp. In the summer between the fifth and sixth grades. I think his name was Dan, but I'm not sure. His hair was parted on the side and his sports pants were too small for him.

We used to get off the bus at the same stop and talk constantly until we reached his house. But at camp itself, I ignored him. Barely spoke a word to him. At recess, I made sure to sit far away from him, and when the other kids started snubbing him, I joined in.

His only crime was not knowing how to play soccer. But he tried anyway. He wanted to participate. But on the field, he hurt our team in games against other teams.

Then it was decided—I really don't remember who suggested it, all the faces but his have been completely erased—not to speak to him anymore. At all. To make him leave the camp and by doing so, improve our team's chances of winning the championship.

It went on for four days. At first, he spoke to us and we just didn't answer. Then he stopped trying.

I remember the look on his face, the depth of the pain in his eyes.

I remember that the counselors didn't intervene. Even though it was a clear case of abuse.

I remember him sitting alone during breaks with his chocolate milk, his sandwich, and his hair parted on the side. Looking at me. Only me. For four days.

Camp finally ended, and the last bus ride home dropped us off at the same place.

In silence, we passed the house where the bulldog used to leap onto the fence, its teeth bared, and I never had the courage to walk past it without Dan at my side. We passed the Danish consulate, with its flag in front, and reached his house, which was the most beautiful one on the street.

There were a few seconds—maybe less, fractions of a second—before he turned to open the iron gate, when I could have said I was sorry.

Sorry for not doing anything. Sorry for not stopping it. After all, it only takes one to break a silence.

I didn't say anything. Not even bye. He didn't either, just opened the gate, went inside, and closed it behind him.

I kept walking, and when I reached my house, I burst into tears.

I remember my mom, alarmed, not understanding what had happened to me. Trying to get me to speak.

I remember myself saying, I don't want to go to that camp next year.

I remember her asking, What happened?

And I remember that I bit my lips. Ashamed to tell her.

———

I would Undo the way I acted with Dan. Or maybe, in fact, I would Cut and Paste. A Cut and Paste that would bring us together years later in a situation where he's the strong one—let's say, a couples' therapist Dikla's friends recommended to her. His hair would still be combed to the side, but his pants would no longer be too short. We go to him to find out if we can still be saved, and when we walk into his office, I see how, for a fraction of a second, before the professional curtain drops over his eyes, they light up with the same flash of admiration that lights up the eyes of men who see Dikla for the first time. That combination of her impressive height, her long, straight brown hair, and her look of boldness. Of seriousness.

In any case, Dan grants me only a quick glance, a seemingly I-don't-recognize-you look.

But later on, he unreservedly supports every claim Dikla makes against me, while he reacts to my claims with the thinnest of smiles and a meaningful raise of the eyebrow.

### Do you plan your books?

Do we plan our dreams?

### Do you have a recurring dream?

I have a recurring nightmare.

Someone hacks my hard drive and steals the terrible first versions of my books. And all the speeches I wrote for Yoram Sirkin.

Then he calls me from a cellar that looks like the ones in Tarantino movies and demands that I pay a ransom.

He has the voice of a pimple-faced teenager, but I agree.

Then he doubles the amount.

And I agree to that too.

But he doesn't show up at the meeting place he set, on a street lined with garages.

Like an idiot, I wait there with an envelope filled with dollars, and it becomes obvious to me that, in the meantime, he has sent all the files to the entire list of NATO nations, and I have been publicly exposed in all my nakedness.

*Is there such a thing as "writer's envy"? And if there is, does it motivate you to work harder at your craft?*

I do not envy writers. I envy Boaz Barzilai. He's the partner of one of Dikla's friends. And whenever he comes to our place, or we go to theirs, there's a moment when he and Dikla gravitate toward each other to talk. The companies they work for are more or less in the same field, data security, so the conversation always begins there, but the conversation is not the issue—I sit far enough away so it doesn't look like I'm eavesdropping but close enough to eavesdrop—the issue is her face as she speaks to him. I deliberately don't say her eyes, it isn't only her eyes, it's a performance in which her entire face, the eyebrows and lips and cheeks, is set in a small smile. Then her lips and eyes grow brighter again, and a finger always joins in, pushing away strands of hair that really don't need to be pushed away, and again the lips and the neck, that is, the place where the bottom of her neck meets her cleavage, where she places her long fingers, and then the show once again rises to her lips and cheeks, that are set in an even more generous smile, and the entire performance, in all its elements, is so familiar to me because once, not long ago, it was enacted for me.

*Will you encourage your children to follow in your footsteps and become writers?*

No, but if one of them does become a writer, it will probably be Yanai. The kid was born a fiction creator. When he was a baby and claimed that monsters came into his room at night, we figured it was his age and took turns sleeping on a mattress beside his bed to "protect him" from them. And at age five, when he told his day-care teacher that he had a twin brother his parents hid in the safe room, we laughed about it with her and said, Well, okay, it'll pass as he gets older.

It didn't pass. The older he became, the more stories he invented, and the more convinced he was that they were true when he told them to us or to people who happened to be visiting us: Superman stopped by his kindergarten and took a few kids for a short glide above the clouds. Ronaldo stepped out of the TV and played soccer with him, and he, my son, won. Today God made it snow only on his day-care center, and all the kids built a snowman. Why didn't your teacher take a picture and send it to the parents? Because snowmen don't like to have their picture taken. And he isn't the little brother of the family. Of course not. Apart from his twin in the safe room, he has an annoying little sister named Tali (why Tali, of all names?). And he wouldn't go to the first grade next year, he'd go straight into the second grade. Because he's so good at arithmetic.

Dikla thinks all those lies are cute.

I'm beginning to be a little disturbed by the sheer quantity of them. And am waiting to see whether there will be fewer of them when he starts school.

In any case, we definitely should take into account that he, our youngest child, will write a story about what has been happening in our house lately.

His opening sentence will be: At some point in his life, almost every kid is afraid he was adopted. Through my whole childhood, I was afraid that my parents would split up. And one autumn, after my sister left for boarding school, I was sure they would.

The hero of the story will be: Smarter than his age. Yet also very naïve.

The style: Poignant detective story. Yanush Korchuk meets Axel Wolff.

That is to say, the very naïve kid who is smarter than other kids his age will observe his parents carefully and look for signs.

He'll sit down and write a table of the signs.

In one column will be good signs like: Today Dad made Mom laugh.

After dinner, on the way to the sink, he put a hand on her shoulder. And she didn't push it away.

They didn't argue until after we went to sleep.

Next Saturday, they're taking us on a hike in the woods. I heard Mom talking to her friend about it. That means that they'll be together at least until Saturday.

And he'd write the bad signs in another column:

Dad slept in the studio he used to have. Instead of at home.

They don't sit on the balcony to talk anymore after they think we've fallen asleep.

Mom goes to the movies with her friend Gaia, instead of with Dad.

When I used to climb into their bed on Saturday morning, there was always a small space I had to squeeze into, and lately, the space between them is so large that I can almost spread my arms to the side when I'm between them.

On the way back from the hike in the woods, their song was on the radio. It starts with the word "sometimes," and the singer has a funny name: Johnny Shuali. I know that song because whenever it's on the radio, Dad makes it louder, Here's Mom's and my favorite song, but this time, Dad didn't make it louder and he didn't say that.

———

As the story progresses, there will be more bad things. And fewer good ones.

But what will really make my heart ache when I read it (he'll let me read it a week before the book is published, and he'll warn me not to look for myself in it: You know what that's like, Dad, he'll tell me, it's never one-to-one), what will really pain me is that the boy in the story believes he's responsible for the crisis between his parents. And he'll start to behave like a perfect little boy. He'll do his homework on the same day he receives it. And he'll make an effort to do better in English, even though it's difficult for him. Because he knows how important it is to his mother. And he'll give his father a big hug when he goes off to school in the morning so he'll remember the hug and won't feel like leaving. And one weekend, when his sister Noam is on a trip with the scouts, he'll tell his parents that he can stay home alone, without a babysitter, so they can go out, maybe to a movie? And he'll restrain himself from making a scene when they say he still isn't old enough, because he knows that his scenes always drive a wedge between Mom, who says that the first thing to do is to put him in his place when he behaves like that, and Dad, who says that first, they have to understand where it's coming from. He'll secretly read the Internet sites written by authorities on relationships, and realize that the most important thing is to keep the channels of communication between the couple open, and it all begins and ends with trust. On Friday, after their family dinner, he'll suggest a game of falling: every player in turn closes his eyes and falls back into the arms of the person standing behind him. He'll insist that not only the kids fall back into their parents' arms, or into each other's arms, but that Mom will fall into Dad's arms, and he'll ask her to try again, and again, after the first few times, when her foot pushes out in distrust. He'll applaud when Mom finally succeeds, and even lingers in Dad's arms for a second longer than necessary, as if she's resting for a moment from the effort of being angry at him—

But the bad signs will grow worse. And one night, when his dad is at work and his mom is sure he's sleeping, he'll hear her say to her friend Gaia, "I'm waiting until after Noam's bat mitzvah. I don't want to break the kids' hearts," and the next day, he'll get his hands on the phone number of the hall where the bat mitzvah is supposed to take place and ask to speak with Coral, who is organizing it. He'll explain the situation to her, all the signs and implications, and beg her to postpone the event, only for a few weeks, and maybe by then, Mom and Dad will make up, they always make up in the end. He won't accept Coral's explanation that the hall is very much in demand and dates are scheduled six months in advance, and they can't just shift an event at the last minute because, even with the best of intentions, it would be a violation of their contract—

A few hours before the bat mitzvah, he'll stop being a perfect little boy and eat twenty apricots, one after the other, and drink half a bottle of vinegar, and vomit it all up on the kitchen floor. He'll be disappointed to see that his parents don't cancel the party, don't even consider canceling it, but just call their neighbor's son, Ariel the babysitter, to sit beside his bed.

———

This is how the story will end: Later on in life, I learn that parting is a force of nature. Like falling. But that autumn, I believed with all my heart that I could stop it.

The name of the story will be: "The Perfect Little Boy."

### How do you combine family life and writing?

I wrote my first book when I was brokenhearted after a breakup. And single.

I thought: When I have love, I won't be able to write.

I wrote my second book when Dikla was pregnant.

I thought: When I have kids, I won't be able to write.

I wrote my third book when Dikla was pregnant again.

I thought: One daughter is okay, with two daughters, there's no chance I'll be able to write.

Now I have three kids. A house. A family.

And I think: If all this falls apart now, who gives a damn about writing?

———

We had a kind of ritual, Dikla and I. After the last kid fell asleep, we sat out on the balcony. Without phones. And drank red wine. One glass each. She finished hers quickly. I finished mine slowly. And as we drank, we talked about everything unrelated to the kids: A song she heard on the radio and liked. Insults one or the other of us had suffered. Places we wanted to visit. Clothes suitable for the change of seasons. Moral issues. The texts changed with the years, but not the rhythm: A sort of jazz. Unpredictable. Filled with leaps from subject to subject. We had rhythm, Dikla and I.

Now I'm waiting for her on the balcony. She's avoiding me.

Awake? (I text her. Even though we're both at home.)

Yes.

The men in my family die young.

Not funny.

Will you be joining me tonight?

No.

Because of Colombia? Because I told you that . . .

It's not because of Colombia.

So what's actually happened?

This isn't the life I wanted to live.

Want to come out to the balcony and talk about it?

No.

———

Then yesterday, suddenly—we had sex. After weeks
without any.

In the middle of the night, as if in our sleep, her body
began to caress mine.

Her hands undressed me.

Her hot mouth.

Her tongue.

But after she came, she didn't put her head on my chest.

She went to take a shower, came back, and burrowed
under the quilt, even though it was summer, and turned her
back to me.

I stayed awake for a long time, and when I finally
fell asleep in the early hours of the morning, I had a

lightning-quick dream of only one scene (or I remember only one scene): I'm climbing the stairs of Atarim Square in Tel Aviv, but instead of going up, I'm going down.

I think about the strange similarity between the beginning and the end of love. From the moment Ari introduced us, in the club on Kibbutz Cabri, I felt as if everything that would happen between Dikla and me from then on was inevitable, because the attraction drawing us together was stronger than both of us. And in fact, now too, I feel the same thing: That no matter what we do, this new force pulling us apart is stronger than both of us. And it's only a matter of time until—

———

We haven't been arguing at all these last few weeks, maybe because at the heart of every argument is the hope that something will change.

Yesterday, we walked quickly past each other in the house, and my shoulder bumped into hers as if we were strangers in the street.

She suddenly looks older to me.

And I must look old to her.

As if each of us had held on to our youth for the other, and all at once, it dropped away.

What crap. "Held on to our youth." "All at once, it dropped away." I escape to pretty sentences because I don't have the courage to tell the truth.

The truth is much more concrete.

**Cell phone.** Suddenly you need to punch in a code to get into her text messages.

**Subscription for two to the Cinematheque.** Not renewed.

**Melatonin pills.** Originally purchased to overcome jet lag when I came back from Colombia. Now I keep them beside my bed. To overcome insomnia.

**The 2014 Docaviv Film Festival.** Another way to overcome insomnia. My favorite summary: *The graffiti on the Berlin Wall, specifically the picture of East German leader Erich Honecker kissing Brezhnev, has become a symbol of the protest against the Communist regime. But who painted it? The film documents the search for the artist and the story behind the kiss. The results of the search are not only surprising but also scandalous, and raise the question: Who determines the significance of a work of art, the one who created it or the ones exposed to it?*

**Axel Wolff's book.** Another book by Axel Wolff. The fourth one she's read over the last few months. Spread open on her nightstand. From the back cover, Axel looks at me euphorically, as if he's the new man in her life.

**The living-room air conditioner.** Needs to be fixed. A pretty expensive repair. Maybe we should wait until the situation becomes clear (we both think but don't say, and no one calls the repairman).

**A stapler without staples.** (We are like...)

**Our wedding album.** Lying uselessly on a shelf in the living room, until the day Noam is asked to bring a family picture to school for her bat mitzvah project. She browses quietly through the album until she finally chooses a photo that was taken before the guests arrived (or after most of them had gone?). In the picture, Dikla and I are sitting at a table of friends. In one corner, you can see a piece of Hagai Carmeli's rusty mop of hair. But we have our backs to him, leaning completely into each other, deep in conversation, and you can see how very close we are. Noam shows us the picture, first Dikla, then me. And I suddenly suspect there is no class project and that the clever girl simply wants to remind us of us.

**Tax invoices/receipts.** Every month Dikla gives them to me to send to the tax consultant. I usually forward them automatically. This month, for the first time, I go over them carefully, searching for evidence of a secret affair. I find a receipt for a mediation course, and another receipt for a course in business English. She's been taking courses ever since I've known her. Always challenging herself. I find a receipt for three Watsu treatments. That's the only way she manages to let go of her ambition for a short while. I find a receipt for acupuncture, and for the monthly sum she contributes to ERAN, the emotional first aid NGO, because once, during a long stint of guard duty in the Arava desert when she was in the army, she almost went crazy, and a guy from ERAN spoke on the phone to her all night and saved her. I find another contribution to Shahal, a cardiac emergency service organization—her mother died of a heart attack— and three different receipts for CDs she bought. Because, single-handedly, she is keeping the dying CD industry alive all over the world.

I don't find any evidence of an affair, and strangely enough, I'm more disappointed than relieved.

**The gorgeous balcony table.** That we bought in the Moroccan Fantasy store up north. Who will keep it if we separate, Mom or Dad?

**Army shoes.** I once came home from reserve duty in the Gaza Strip, and she was in the middle of the Coen brothers' film *O Brother, Where Art Thou?* She barely looked over at me, and I was afraid that this would be like the time I came home from the Arad music festival and Tali Leshem didn't look at me, and two days later, I left our apartment. I was wrong. You can't infer anything about one love relationship from another one. *O Brother, Where Art Thou?* is a film you really can't take your eyes off. And Dikla and I had another ten good years after that time I was on reserve duty.

**Night shoes.** In movies, people always look at their kids when they're sleeping. When my kids are asleep, I look at their shoes: collect them after they fall asleep, pick them up from the living-room carpet, the bathroom, the shower. Then I arrange them in their rooms. In pairs. I look at them. And think about what I might lose.

**The carpet in the living room.** We made love on it once when we came home from seeing *Burnt by the Sun.* Or am I imagining it? Dikla is in charge of our couple memories, and now I can't ask her.

**The carpet on the wall.** My aunt Noa gave it to us as a gift. Shortly before her death. Framed. Rectangular pieces of somber, dark-hued fabric placed one on the other. Like a Band-Aid on a Band-Aid on a Band-Aid. Or like the wooden slats of a parquet floor. Meant to be impenetrable. Meant to imprison. Under those densely packed strips is the buzzing of protest, subversive activity: flowered fabric whose shape, before it was hidden, looked to me like someone dancing. And lately—like a demon.

**Alarm.** Installed during one of my trips, and since then, Dikla has no longer been afraid to sleep alone. Recently, she also sets it when I'm in the country and come home at night. I'm supposed to deactivate it when I come in, but sometimes I remember too late. Then it goes off. I hurriedly punch in our wedding date—18301—which stops the alarm but wakes the phone—the girl at the alarm company wants me to give her my password. To make sure I'm not a burglar. I feel like a burglar, but give her the password, and she says good night in a soft voice. After she hangs up, I'm sorry I didn't try to start a conversation with her. Once, before the alarm, Dikla couldn't fall asleep without me. During the day she was independent, active, a lone wolf. During the day she sometimes made me feel superfluous, an unneeded man. But at night she needed me. And waited for me in bed, awake, until I came home from the workshops. No matter how late. We didn't manage to do much. A hug. A few words. She didn't need more than that. I didn't need more than that. But now the house is silent and she's sleeping under the protection of the alarm. I walk through the rooms, gather the kids' shoes, and then read the program of the 2014 Docaviv Film Festival until I'm drowsy enough to fall asleep.

**Another summary from the Docaviv program.** *For the 65 residents of Maladhu Island in the Indian Ocean, global warming is not a theoretical problem. Barring unforeseen events, their small island is about to disappear because of the rising ocean waters. Inside their straw huts, Maladhu residents prepare to bid farewell to the place where they have lived their entire lives. But on nights when there is a full moon, they gather and pray to their gods in the hope that, at the last moment, there will be change in the plot.*

**Decaffeinated coffee.** (We are like...)

**Remote-controlled model airplane.** We bought one for Yanai. It cost a fortune. We took it to the park, and on its maiden flight, it got entangled in a treetop. A city worker with a ladder managed to get it down and return it to the boy, but the wings were broken.

**Dikla's screensaver.** A photo from a family trip to the Black Forest. From three years ago. The photographer, a German who happened to pass by, chided us: Smile, why aren't you smiling? After the picture, we got into our rented Opel, and during the drive to the campsite, all the kids fell asleep, even Noam, who never does, and the car filled with the kind of quiet that comes after a great effort. Dikla put her hand on my thigh, I covered her hand with mine and looked at her. Eyes on the road, she said, and I said, That's a problem, you're too beautiful. Then she said, I think I've figured out this whole business of family trips. So tell me, I said. You shouldn't expect to enjoy yourself all the time, she said, the thing is to collect the good moments, the moments of quiet joy.

**A red Hapoel Jerusalem basketball scarf.** Hanging on the wall in the den. It moved with me to all the apartments I've lived in since I left my parents' house. The only permanent element in my life. On the scarf is the team logo and the sentence "Love conquers all." I bought it with Ari after a game. We split the cost and agreed on a custody schedule, a year with me and a year with him. In the end, somehow, it stayed with me. Lately, Dikla has stopped saying that the scarf makes the room ugly. On one of my recent visits to Ari in the hospital, he told me, to my surprise, that she'd left a few minutes before I arrived and he laughed at us, saying that we were the most mismatched married couple he knew. He said, You know, she looks sad, your wife. Don't tell me that, now that I finally understand why you married her, you're going to split? No way, amigo. You know, he said, that if she came to see me, she hasn't given up on you, right?

**Megaphone.** White. Signed by all the workers in the NGO Dikla ran. A memento of the period of demonstrations. She led the march, used the megaphone to call out slogans we'd made up the night before in the kitchen. She explained the message she wanted to get across and I tightened and rhymed. She trusted me. I was proud of her. And even if I didn't have the passion she had, I joined the demonstration the next day and, as we walked through the throngs,

I thought to myself: This woman in the front, the tall one with the megaphone? I sleep with her.

**Sticker.** From her campaign to be elected leader of the apolitical-but-clearly-political movement she helped run. "Definitely Dikla" was written on the sticker pasted on the computer that was once hers and had been passed on to Noam. She lost by five votes. It turned out that behind her back, a deal had been made for the sole purpose of preventing her election. The movement's old guard was uneasy about her controversial and uncompromising views. Her extreme independence. And made sure she wouldn't be elected. She was even more disappointed by the betrayal by people she thought were her friends than by the failure. Then Noam was born, and she was offered a job she couldn't refuse in the private sector.

She won't admit it, but the thought of what-might-have-been-if haunts her to this day.

**Picture of Barack Obama.** Taken during his 2008 campaign. Pinned onto the corkboard above her desk. On the night of the US elections she watched CNN until the morning and cried during his victory speech in Chicago. I don't know why, she said, he's not going to be my president, and after everything I went through, I should be immune to politicians. But he has something . . . I don't know. When he speaks, you feel the person he is . . . behind the words. Besides, don't be insulted, but he's the best-looking man I've ever seen.

**The brown dress.** She hasn't worn it for years. But sometimes, when she's not home, I open her closet, riffle through her dresses until I reach it, touch the fabric, and remember.

**Hangers.** There were always a few empty ones in her closet that I could steal. There haven't been any recently because she's been buying a lot of new clothes. The style is more restrained. Tailored pants and button-down shirts. And yet, it's impossible not to notice that, these days, she opens one more button.

**Thermometer.** Once we both got sick at the same time. We only had Shira then. My mother came and took her, and we remained alone in the house. Surrounded by tissues. Coughing. Burning with fever. Making tea with lemon for each other. Telling each other our strange dreams. Laughing. Coughing some more. Happy.

**Dream notebook.** She's crazy about the poet Agi Mishol. I buy her every new Agi Mishol book. I browse through it while I'm still in the bookstore until I find a poem that I can use as a dedication, and only then do I ask for it to be wrapped as a gift. A few years ago, I bought her Agi Mishol's *Dream Notebook*, and since then, influenced by the book, she began to write down her dreams in a notebook she keeps on her nightstand. I'm not allowed to look at it. She said that explicitly: My dreams are none of your business. I respected her wishes. I never looked inside the notebook. Until yesterday.

I read quickly, afraid I'd be caught, although she wasn't home and wasn't expected back until the afternoon. This is what was written there (more or less—I read it once and immediately closed it with the intention of never opening it again, so I remember the plot more than the wording):

*I'm in a hotel, not in Israel. There's a knock on the door and a man's voice says, "Yes, we can." I open the door even though I'm wearing only a bra and underpants. Barack Obama enters the room dressed in a writer's jacket, places his book on the table, and leaves before I can say anything. I'm hungry. I didn't know I was hungry before Obama and the book arrived, but now I'm really starving. I open the book and see that there's a huge butterfly between the pages. There's something written on its enormous wings that I can't read. The butterfly spreads its wings and tries to get out of the room, but keeps banging against the window. I open the window and, both sad and relieved, I see my dinner fly away from me.*

**Speakers.** Huge, in the living room. That she bought. On Saturdays she plays CDs and dances with the kids. For the last few weeks, she's been raising the volume as high as it will go.

**Letter on the kitchen table.** She would leave it for me. And go. If we didn't have kids. (Parents simply can't get up and leave. That theatrical, unambiguous movement is not something they can usually do. So they are doomed to a slow death.)

This is what she would write in the letter she would leave on the table before she went, if we didn't have kids.

*I've changed my mind about what I told you on one of our first dates—that I want to marry a writer. Turns out that it's not such a great thing after all. When a writer isn't writing, he's lost and troubled, and when he is writing, he's focused on*

*himself and troubled. Not to mention the fact that everything
that happens is material for him. Everything is exploited,
immediately. You sprained your foot? So does his heroine. You
had an ugly argument about money at six in the morning? The
couple in his story will argue about money. But there's no connection. Of course not. He lets you read the manuscript and
you see everything there, including intimate details about your
eldest daughter's life, which he tells himself he has disguised
well, and you have to pretend it's not transparent. And pretend you didn't notice that as the years have passed, he can't
make small talk anymore, he always has to tell you a story
with a beginning, a middle, and an end, even when he con-
fesses to supposedly cheating on you in Colombia, the description is so vibrant and imaginative that you're afraid it's South
American magical realism meant to catch your attention and
arouse your jealousy. But it succeeds in doing the opposite.
Then there's the self-importance if his book succeeds. And the
total collapse if, heaven forbid, it doesn't. And the interviews
to the media. The slips of the tongue that give away more than
he thinks. And the compassionate looks of your co-workers
after those interviews. And the women who come up to him in
cafés as if you're not sitting there. And flutter their lashes. And
say how much his book touched them. And the fact that it's
legitimate not to listen to you when you're sitting together in a
café on Friday morning because he can't decide how to move
the plot forward, which keeps him from sleeping. And the fact
that it's legitimate to do research on strippers. Because there's
a stripper in the story. And traveling to Argentina for a week*

*because, what choice does he have, the most important scene in the book takes place in Argentina. And of course, without actually being in Argentina, he can't write about Argentina.*

*Really, Mr. Writer? I have no problem with your trips as such. Terminals and hotels are, after all, pretty sad places. So I don't envy you. And sometimes, to be honest, I'm happy for the chance to have a short vacation from you. Especially since you started with that dysthymia, which has made you even more self-involved, because that's one of the symptoms. The real problem is that you keep on telling yourself you're a great husband, a wonderful father, and a man of principle. So I have news for you: A great husband feels it when his wife is on the edge and doesn't push her over it. And a wonderful father doesn't steal details from his eldest daughter's life to put in his book. And a man of principle doesn't still secretly write speeches for that fraud Yoram Sirkin.*

*Of course I know. You really think you can hide something from the woman who's been living with you for twenty years? I swear, I don't understand why you keep on doing that. Money? Power? Or are you jealous of your characters and do you want some action in your own life? Tell me, aren't writers supposed to concentrate on writing? To sit at home every day and write, and pick up the kids from day care at noon like Garp in* The World According to Garp? *And then, when their wives come home—late!—from their important and interesting jobs, to welcome them with dinner and anecdotes they've collected for them—and only for them!—from the many hours they've spent with the kids?*

*That's the movie I had in mind when I told you that I wanted to marry a writer. But you apparently imagined a different movie. Or you changed the screenplay. Or adapted it. I don't know. Imagery is your field.*

*It's not that I don't love you anymore, I want you to understand that. Still hidden under the depressed, totally self-involved writer you have become is the sensitive, upbeat man I fell in love with—I just don't love being with you anymore, that's all there is to it.*

*I feel oppressed by you. I need some rest from you.*

*I need to distance myself from you now so I can remember who I am.*

*If you want, you can call this an investigative trip.*

**Rust.** On one of the legs of the beautiful balcony table we bought at Moroccan Fantasy in the north. (That's what we're like. Or am I wrong? Maybe it's just because of Ari and the long hours at his bedside, along with my uncontrollable tendency to connect various details into a weighty structure, that everything in my life and surroundings, in my home and my homeland seems to be rusty, eroded, portending their end, when actually—)

———

Maybe I should stop here. I've gone too far as it is.

You have to understand, it's no accident that Dikla works in an information security company. In Ma'alot—she once explained to me—if you smoke with a girlfriend behind Ben-Naim's grocery store, your parents know about it half an hour later. And that's why, since she left the city, she's been super-protective of her privacy. For example, she never allows photographers in the house. And here I am, letting the word-camera into the house.

She always claimed: The book is important. Not you.

And also: You don't have to satisfy their voyeuristic urges. Leave them curious. Leave some things secret.

And also: The kids and I are not to blame that you chose this profession.

Before every interview, I check with her about what I can and cannot say. She would be horrified to read what I'm writing here.

She would be horrified, even though I'm doing a good job of using fabrications to conceal the real reason for our crisis.

She would be horrified, even though, for the time being, the kids are barely mentioned in this interview. (Actually, they are my entire world, my kids. And I dash around among them like a waiter serving love. My life is in their hands. And my happiness. It's clearly no accident that the dysthymia intensified after Shira, my eldest daughter, the apple of my eye, went away to school at Sde Boker.)

I should, I must stop answering this question. It's too dangerous. I might even describe my embarrassing night trip to Sde Boker. How I hid in the bushes to get a glimpse of a sixteen-year-old without her seeing me.

The truth is that I ought to end this entire interview.

But I can't. I have nothing else to hold on to these days.

*It seems like the love affairs in your books never work out. Why? And do you think you'll ever write a love story that has a happy end?*

Later, it turned out that she followed me from the ZOA House to the parking lot. She hid behind cars and kept a steady distance from me, like she saw in the movies. As I was about to open the car door, she closed the distance quickly, came up to me from the side, and asked urgently: Can you give me a ride?

I didn't recognize her. I lecture to large groups participating in the Birthright project. Two hundred people each time. Four times a day. Who can remember a face, even if it's beautiful?

Where to? I asked.

The city you mentioned in your talk, the one you live in? Yes?

That's where I need to go.

Wait a minute, do you belong to the Birthright group?

I don't belong to anyone.

Okay . . . But as far as I know, you're not allowed to wander around on your own.

So?

You can get into trouble.

I want to get into trouble.

———

I'd been lecturing to Birthright groups for a few years. It pays well, but that's not the point. Those American kids are between eighteen and twenty-something years old, and I like to talk to people that age. You can reach them. Everything's still possible. That must be the reason they bring them here at that age. For ten days, they sell them a kind of imaginary Israel. Just. Exciting. They take them to Masada, to Ben Gurion's grave in Sde Boker, and to organized fun nights in Tel Aviv pubs. And then—on the last day—I meet them and ask them to write about the moment they felt a contradiction between what their guides told them about Israel and what they saw on the streets with their own eyes.

I'm not naïve. I know that inviting me to speak at the end as a subversive, challenging voice is also part of the campaign. But I have my own aims.

———

Is there a specific place you need to reach? I asked as we approached the entrance to the city. She took a lipstick out of her bag and, looking in the mirror, applied it to her lips.

Not really.

Okay, so why this city, of all places?

I'm looking for somebody.

Can you give me . . . a few more details? So I'll have something to work with?

I still haven't decided if I trust you.

Okay, so listen for a minute—by the way, what's your name?

Rachel.

Listen, Rachel, in another second we'll be in the city and I have no idea where to go from here. Do you happen to know the address of the person you're looking for?

No.

So...

Just... drive a little ways.

Okay, but the chances of finding him this way, by accident, are pretty slim, so maybe...

Keep driving, my heart tells me we'll find the person I'm looking for.

———

I drove randomly through the streets while she strummed on the tight strands of fabric above the tear in her jeans, humming an unrecognizable song, her eyes searching for somebody. So I wouldn't feel like a complete idiot, I began crisscrossing the network of streets that connect the only two main drags in the city. The last time I drove that way was a year ago, when Luna, our dog, got lost. She was sixteen, which is a hundred and something in dog years, and we had already stopped letting her out of the house without a leash, the way we used to when she was young. Her hearing had deteriorated and she was going blind, and we were afraid that, without supervision, she would be run over. But her passion for open spaces was stronger than any prohibition, and one day, when we opened the door for a delivery guy, she took advantage of a moment when we weren't paying attention and ran off. I drove up and down the streets with my second daughter, the one who had apparently inherited my thin skin, and we whistled Luna's whistle through the open windows as we searched for her.

———

Why did you stop?

Look, Rachel, I don't have all day and . . . I think it would help if you gave me a few more details about your somebody. Then, at least you'll have another pair of eyes.

She has a brown hat, from the army . . .

Aah . . . so we're looking for a girl soldier?

Yes.

With a brown beret?

Yes.

From the Golani Brigade?

Yes, Golani!

Okay. Where did you meet her?

First promise me you won't put us in one of your books.

What? Why should I . . .

You said in your talk that you're a "story hunter." And this is a bad time for you to hunt my story. And it's an even worse time for you to hunt Adi's story.

Okay. I promise not to put either of you in one of my books.

And you'll keep driving.

Look, I'm driving.

We met at Masada.

On the snake path?

No, on the top. On the mountain. You see, my father committed suicide. So when the guide started . . . to glorify the fact that everyone killed themselves there so they wouldn't be taken prisoner by the Romans, I couldn't keep quiet.

I can . . . imagine.

So I raised my hand and asked if there were women and children who killed themselves too. He said yes. So I said, well excuse me, but it was a stupid decision, and it's a horrible story.

Wow.

What wow? It's a horrible story and it's a fucking chauvinist myth. Don't you think so?

How did the guide react?

Everyone attacked me. Not just him. They all started throwing the Birthright propaganda at me.

And . . . wait a minute, that soldier . . . Adi . . . she was there too?

She was with a completely different group. But she was standing next to us and heard everything. Later, she came up to me, put a hand on my shoulder, and asked if I was okay. She handed me her bottle of water so I could take a drink. That was the first time anyone on this trip was nice to me, they're all such children and I've almost finished my master's in gender studies. We're worlds apart. Understand?

Of course.

Then she asked to transfer to our group, and we spent the next two days together. Constantly together. I told her about my dad—and you need to understand, I don't talk to anyone about my dad—and she told me what it's really like to be in the army. It turned out that she served three months in the territories. And the things that happened there freaked her out. But she had no one to talk to about it until she met me.

It sounds like—

I'm such a jerk, you know? She had these huge eyes and a big body. Exactly my taste. And on the last day, when we said goodbye, she looked at me and I looked at her and I knew that she . . . and she knew that I . . . but neither of us had the courage . . . you know, to make the move. And we each went to our bus. And then, at the lecture, you suddenly said that you live . . . here, in the same suburb she does, so I thought, maybe it's a sign . . . do you believe in signs?

———

The clerk at the city emergency center asked us for identifying marks. I remember her tone. Matter-of-fact. Tinged with impatience. The end-of-shift tone. I said, Small body, light brown. White paws. A white stripe on her forehead. A long white tail. Uncombed. Then I asked Noam if she wanted to add anything. Yes, she said, she's really smart, our dog, whenever I'm sad, she feels it even if I don't say anything, and she comes to sit near me.

Okay, the clerk said. I'll get in touch with the city animal shelter and check if anyone picked up a dog that looks like her.

I remember the long minute that passed until she came back to us. I remember that my daughter bit her nails down to the flesh. And I remember forcing myself not to say anything about her biting her nails down to the flesh.

———

Tell me, didn't we pass that ugly building already?

It's possible. We've been driving for an hour already. And this is a small city.

"A city without a libido."

What?

That's what Adi said about your city.

Wow. And do you also happen to remember Adi's last name?

No.

Or . . . other things she told you about herself?

Like what?

I don't know. Things she likes to do, let's say. Does she play tennis? Basketball? Buy secondhand clothes? Like hummus. Every bit of information can move us forward here.

She likes to read, I think.

Okay, that's good! Explain.

I told her that we were going to meet an Israeli writer. You, I mean. So she told me that she had read all your books.

Great.

No offense, but she said that the first one was the best, and everything after that went downhill.

You don't say.

Hey man, I have no idea, I didn't read any of them. I'm more into Scandinavian writers. I'm crazy about their sick minds. You know Axel Wolff?

Unfortunately, yes.

Never mind. What I said before . . . does it point you in any direction?

Look, we can try to go to all the bookstores in the city, but that would take a lot of time. Aren't you supposed to go back to your family? Isn't your flight tomorrow?

So?

———

Then, too, when we were looking for Luna, I almost gave up. I remember saying to my daughter: It's dark already, what are the chances we'll find her now? But that daughter who, unlike her older sister and her younger brother, almost never asked for things for herself, wanted to try a little more. Just a tiny bit more. And she lowered her lashes as if she were about to cry. I took a deep breath and started to drive in the general direction of the house, but very slowly. The speed of a bicycle. And then—we saw her. I mean, first we heard her. A whimper. Familiar. Heartbreaking.

We found her behind the monument for the soldiers who fell in the Second Lebanon War. Licking herself. When she saw us, her whimpering turned into short barks of joy. She tried to run to us, but collapsed to the ground when she tried to stand up. Only then did we notice the large, bleeding wound that had opened slightly above her left leg.

Wait a minute!

What?

I just remembered something else Adi liked. Apart from reading books.

What?

Ice cream! She always said how much she feels like eating ice cream.

Okay...Ice cream's a little general. Did she say what kind of ice cream?

Yes, she did, the soft kind. You know, like they sell at McDonald's for a dollar?

American ice cream?

Yes, she really told me you call it that. I don't get it. What's American about soft-serve ice cream?

The truth is that—

Why are you driving slowly again?

So you can enjoy my city. When we drive quickly, you miss out on its unique charm.

Cut the crap. Why are you driving slowly?

Because I have an idea. And I'm turning it around in my mind. Slowly.

What? Tell me!

Don't get too excited. It's pretty much...a long shot.

Come on, tell me already!

There's only one shopping center in the city that has both a bookshop and a McDonald's.

We drove cautiously with Luna on the backseat. She kept licking herself and bleeding on the upholstery. My daughter sat beside her, stroked her head, and spoke to her like a mother comforting her child. We drove to an all-night veterinary clinic in our old neighborhood. Luna was happy when we lived there, in a not-so-new house that was neither symmetrical nor entirely legal, on the edge of the city, adjacent to the fields. She had so much space: A small jump over the low stone fence, and she was free to run in any direction and bark at the moon. When I think about it, it was only when we moved to the new house, trapped between other houses, with no view to speak of, that she began to deteriorate. As if old age had assaulted her all at once.

The vet we knew wasn't in his clinic. The night-shift vet was there instead.

Usually, we went to the clinic with Luna to get her vaccinated, and she used to bark and try to run away. This time, she didn't have the strength even to protest.

We placed her on the examination table, with her wound facing up.

The vet said: Wow. And asked: Did you see the car that hit her?

We said no.

She lightly touched the area close to the wound and Luna whimpered. My daughter's voice broke as she asked: Can you . . . bandage it?

I can, but . . . the vet replied in an ominous tone.

———

How do I look? Rachel asked.

She had been checking herself in the mirror for a few minutes now, rummaging through a small makeup case, and at some point, she even took out a hairbrush. And brushed her hair.

Sorry, Rachel, I'm driving now. I can't look.

So look when we get to a light. Please.

I looked when we got to a light.

Straight black hair with one blond streak. An eyebrow ring. Large dark eyes. A Jewish nose. Thin lips covered in very red lipstick. A blush of excitement on her cheeks.

You're lovely, Rachel, I said truthfully. But—

You think Adi will be glad to see me?

Rachel, listen, for years I've been looking all over the world for a friend who disappeared on me, and the chances that—

My heart tells me she'll be there, Rachel said with conviction.

"My heart tells me." I repeated her words silently, sarcastically. And thought: These Americans. They think that life is Hollywood.

———

Then I called Dikla and told her to meet us. I knew that when it came to Luna, I didn't have the right to decide alone.

After all, she was originally Dikla's dog. She'd found her wandering around the streets during one of our separations, and when we got back together, she said: I won't go back to living with you without the dog.

I couldn't stand dogs until Luna. The first dog I ever knew in my life was the crazy bulldog in Haifa that used to leap onto the fence with bared teeth whenever anyone passed. And once, on a path below the house on Einstein Street, it bit me, not to mention that an army tracker dog on weekend leave that, mistaking me for a terrorist, tore a piece of flesh off my back. Years later, I would still get chills on the back of my neck every time a dog barked near me. But Luna was small and pacifistic, and never jumped on anyone with her teeth bared. Just the opposite: Our first night together, she climbed onto the bed and put her head on my chest. Slowly. As if asking for permission. And so she and I became bosom buddies, as she did with the kids.

———

Dikla arrived and listened to the vet's detailed explanation, one we had already received. I knew that slow nod of hers very well, the "digesting bad news" nod. She had nodded exactly that way when she was told that, even after a recount, she hadn't been elected head of the movement.

———

There she is, man!
No way. Where?

There! And, in fact, standing on the sidewalk in front of McDonald's was a girl soldier. With an American ice-cream cone in her hand. And a Golani Brigade beret under her epaulette.

You're sure that—

Yes, stop the car already.

I stopped the car already. Rachel hurried out, leaving her bag behind. I watched what was happening through the window. Her back was to me, so I didn't see her face, but I did see the girl soldier. Her first reaction was to tense up. Almost recoil. She even put a hand on her rifle stock. It took her a fraction of a second to realize who was approaching her. And then—there was a lovely moment of recognition. Her face was illuminated by a new light and her large body, which had been slightly stooped, straightened up. They hugged briefly. The soldier was still holding the American ice cream, so she hugged Rachel with only one hand. Then they moved away from each other and Rachel spoke. I didn't hear a word, but I saw her embarrassed, excited hand movements, and I saw the effect of her words on the soldier. I saw her eyes soften and her lips open slightly, in amazement. I saw the ice cream fall from her hand and land upside down on the sidewalk. Then they hugged again. And the hug was so warm and intimate that I should have looked away. But I couldn't.

After a long moment, they broke away from each other and walked hand in hand toward my car.

I thought: What a tender sight it is, two women walking hand in hand.

Before I realized what was happening, Rachel bent down quickly and, through the window, planted a warm kiss on my cheek.

Thank you for everything you did for me, she said, and gestured for me to give her her bag. I'll read all your books! Even the awful ones! I promise!

A moment before the two girls disappeared into the bookstore, my phone rang.

It was Ron, from Birthright. The Project with a Purpose.

I wanted to thank you for the lecture, he said. I had good feedback on it.

Great, I said. I enjoyed it too.

We'll talk longer next week, he said. Right now, I have to cut it short, the truth is that we're in a bit of a mess here, one of the girls is missing. And their flight is leaving tomorrow morning.

Wow.

A problematic kind of girl, a little unstable. With a family history of . . . we're afraid she might . . .

Of course.

We're scouring Tel Aviv. The police are on the lookout too. We can't allow a hair on her head to be hurt!

| | |

I didn't go right home after that. I knew what was waiting for me there. Or, more accurately, what wasn't waiting for me.

I drove up and down the streets of the city for another hour, with the window open.

Whistling Luna's whistle. In the wind.

*If you could relive a moment in your life, what moment would you choose?*

We said we'd meet on the beach in Beit Yanai. She already had a new boyfriend, I had a girlfriend. We hadn't seen each other for almost a year, since the split. Out of the blue, she left me a voice mail: Want to meet up? Her teenage voice.

I had a haircut first thing in the morning. Even though I didn't think there was a chance. She was waiting for me on the bluff, wearing the brown dress she knew I couldn't resist. I kissed her on the cheek. The scent of her body lotion. I didn't notice that she was carrying a leash until she said, Meet Luna.

Nice to meet you, Luna—I bent down and petted the dog's head.

I thought you didn't like dogs.

I don't, I said.

Should we go down to the beach for a while? she said, taking off her shoes. Her feet. I took mine off too. We walked along the waterline until there were no more people. Luna walked at our side, occasionally barking at the waves.

You still live in Givatayim? she asked.

You still make shakshuka with feta cheese?

She laughed. The small snort she makes when she laughs wholeheartedly.

Let's sit down for a while, she said, and took a large towel out of her bag.

We sat down. Close. Shoulders almost touching. Luna circled around us, agitated. We didn't speak for a few minutes as we watched the sunset. And then Dikla put her head on my shoulder. At first I felt her soft hair. Then her cheek. I put my arm around her naked shoulder and pulled her toward me.

I'm tired of it, she said into my neck.

Of what?

Of fighting against it, she said.

I sighed and rested my cheek on her head, as if to say, So am I.

Suddenly, Luna climbed onto me and began licking my face. I was startled. I drew back. Her wet tongue. Her piercing paws. I tried to pry her off me gently.

Dikla laughed. You might not like dogs, but Luna likes you!

The pleasure is all mine, I said.

The pleasure is all mine? Since when do you say that?

People change, I said.

It grew dark, the first stars came out. Dikla lay back on the towel. Luna stretched out beside her, suddenly calm. I lay down too. My elbow touched hers, our faces to the stars. Then we turned to each other at exactly the same second, as if the same metronome were ticking in both of us. Her face, so close. Her wide mouth.

I can't kiss you, she said, I have a boyfriend.

I can't kiss you, I said, I have a girlfriend.

We kissed. A gentle kiss. Hesitant. I began to lift her dress and she caught my hand in hers and said: No. I stopped. Our fingers intertwined. I was still breathing quickly.

Maybe it's a sign, I said.

What sign?

It was clear to me that she knew, but wanted me to say it out loud. So I said: If we can't forget each other for such a long time, maybe it's a sign.

Maybe, she said, uneasily.

Luna jumped over her and squeezed between us. Don't be afraid, she doesn't bite, you can pet her. She had a long white stripe in the middle of her forehead. I petted it gingerly.

She loves being petted there, Dikla encouraged me.

Where did you find her?

In front of the vehicle licensing bureau in Holon. Someone abandoned her there.

She's sweet, I admitted.

So are you, Dikla said, looking at me warmly.

We kissed again. A long, hungry kiss this time. A prelude kiss—that we had to stop because Luna started kicking sand on us with her hind legs.

Sometimes she wants attention, Dikla apologized and pulled her over to us with her leash.

I tried to get my breath back, calm my hungry heart.

You have sand on your lashes, Dikla said. Close your eyes for a second.

I closed my eyes. She came very close and blew on my face, gently. Once, then again.

Chills ran up and down my spine.

I have to get back, she finally said.

Me too, I said.

She stood up. So did I. We brushed the sand off our clothes and, in the light of the moon, walked toward the parking lot. On the way, I boasted that my first book was coming out. In two months.

That's great, she said, I'm really proud of you. I always wanted to marry a writer.

I remember, I said.

She described her new job enthusiastically. Those dramatic hand gestures of hers. I thought: She has finally found what she was meant to do, and I have found writing. Maybe now, when we're happier with ourselves, we can stop screwing things up between us. I thought: Don't say anything now. Absolutely not. You haven't seen each other for a full year and it might freak her out. Let it ripen for a while.

I said: Is September okay for you?

Okay for what? she said, stopping suddenly. We were already fairly close to our cars.

For the wedding. Cyprus. Just you and me. And a month later, a party for family and friends.

You're saying that just because you're hot for me, she said teasingly.

I'm saying it because I love you.

I love you too, she said, suddenly serious. But . . . are you sure that's enough?

A week later, she moved in with me and brought Luna with her. As a condition.

In September of that year, we got married. In Cyprus.

Two years later, Shira was born.

| | |

The only memento we had of Luna was a framed picture in the living room. It had been taken in the Ein Hod Artists' Village—Luna with her leash tied to a stone sculpture of a lion. To the stone tail of the lion. Her own tail is wagging in the air like a mane.

I was the one who opened the door for the pizza-delivery guy. I'm the one who forgot to close it behind him when I went to get my wallet, which enabled Luna to slip through the opening onto the dangerous streets. Dikla was still at work, the kids were in their rooms. There were no witnesses. After the vet, after the injection, after Noam went to sleep, when Dikla asked me, But how did it happen? How did she get out?—I rearranged the details of the story to show myself in a more positive light. The delivery guy came in, I told her, and before I could close the door, she...just...squeezed behind it and ran away.

Dikla didn't ask anything else. Didn't speak. All she did was give me a look that said: We both know that Luna couldn't move fast enough to do something like that. And it also said: I know you're lying to me. And I'm embarrassed for you. But we won't get into that now.

### Who do you draw inspiration from?

On my way back from Kiryat Shmona, Robbie Williams is singing that he wants to feel real love. The taxi driver's phone rings and he apologizes. It's his daughter, he has to answer it.

Robbie Williams continues singing, at a lower volume, that he wants to feel real love and the driver's daughter says, I don't feel well.

You don't have to go to school, he calms her down.

And she says, I'll go anyway, Daddy.

Whatever you decide, my love, he says. And I think: Maybe if I had said to Shira, "Whatever you decide, my love," more often, she wouldn't have left us.

It starts to rain. Drops splat diagonally across the windshield of the taxi. There's a new hotel at the Koach intersection, and next to it is a grounded hot air balloon. And Robbie Williams sings that he wants to feel real love. Wants to feel the home he lives in.

*Do your children read your books?*

For years, I had this scene in my head of Shira on her post-army trip to South America. She's finished reading all the books she took from home, and after two weeks of not speaking Hebrew—because, if I know her, she deliberately planned her trip to avoid the Hummus Trail—she boards a bus. I always imagine her walking down the aisle, her matchstick legs stuck in stiff hiker's boots, looking for an empty seat. She has put her large backpack on the roof of the bus, so she only has a small purple (her favorite color) bag on her shoulder. And a guitar, of course, on her back. On purpose, she lets her curls—still light brown? maybe already dark brown?—fall onto her face, the way she always does when she's embarrassed, and apologizes in beginners' Spanish when the neck of the guitar bangs into the shoulder of one of the passengers. She sits down, her head tilted back, her eyes closed. Small white earbuds are stuck in her ears. What is she listening to? Salsa. At the beginning of the trip, she hated it, then she became addicted. Her right knee rises and falls to the beat of the music, that knee has had a beat of its own since she was a child, and when the never-ending song finally ends, her knee stops moving, and in the ensuing silence, she suddenly hears Hebrew. She opens her eyes. A group of Israelis is sitting in the last row of seats. Though she's a bit put off by their loudness, she has no choice but to go over to them because she needs a book desperately. After a brief discussion, one of them says that he has a book he's willing to exchange. He takes it out of his bag and she sees that it's one of her father's books. Even as a child, she was embarrassed when people made the connection. And as she grew older and more rebellious, the embarrassment actually caused her to cringe. She doesn't say anything about it to them and thinks to herself that the last thing she wants to read is one of her father's books, but the alternative is to remain bookless. And who knows when she'll have another opportunity. So she takes the book, gives the guy one of hers, and goes back to her seat. She doesn't like to read when she's in a moving vehicle, it makes her nauseous—she's been that way since she was a child—so it isn't until that night, in the hostel, wearing a now faded sweat suit I bought her years ago, that she opens the book. I've always hoped it would be my first book she starts reading in the hostel. It's my most innocent book. In my mind's eye, I see her finishing the first page, touching her tongue with her finger—something her mother does—and turning the page. And another one. She keeps reading page after page, feeling slightly disconcerted. Or she puts the book down, uninterested. I created several detailed options in my mind for this scene. But sometimes, reality beats out imagination. And Shira, being Shira, had plans of her own.

*I myself have tried my hand at writing, and the hardest thing for me is developing a plot. Do you have a tip for me?*

Tell your kid bedtime stories, or borrow someone else's kid and tell him. I've been doing it for more than a decade.

And if my plot-developing skills have improved slightly, it's thanks to my kids. It has always been true that if the story I make up doesn't interest them enough, they stop listening. Their eyes wander. Their bodies move restlessly. And sometimes, they tell me to my face: Dad, it's boring. Or even more embarrassing: Forget it, Dad, read us something from Dr. Seuss. So I had no choice, and very slowly, from failure to failure, I learned how to dance out a plot. How to move a story so deftly that the next step is never predictable.

These days, only Yanai still asks me to make up a story. After his bath, I wrap him in two towels and carry him to his bed. We call it "Yanai in a pita."

Carefully, I carve out a path for us through the Lego pieces scattered on the floor of his room, put him on the bed wrapped in the towels, and take his superhero pajamas out of the closet.

He asks to stay wrapped in the towels for a little while longer. I say okay. And rub his body through the towels to warm him up. Then I peel them off him, slowly, and help him into his pajamas. When he lies down, I cover him with his blanket and take a quick sniff of the wonderful smell of his scalp. Then I sit on the large quilt on the side of his bed.

He already knows that the story is about to begin and looks at me.

His eyes are identical to his mother's, brown and large, with beautiful long lashes.

But the way he looks at me—is so different. Free of disappointment. Free of anger. Shining with pure love.

I begin telling the story. He looks at me, eager to devour every word, and his face reacts with great emotion to every turn of the plot.

Those are the best moments of my day. No dysthymia. No dying Ari. No evasive looks from Dikla. Just Yanai and me and the stories about the intrepid boy, Eelai (he needs the name change in order to believe it can all happen: a bird that carries a child in its beak when the child is unable to get down from the tree he's climbed; a boy who's bitten by the mix-up mosquito at night and, in the morning, instead of going to kindergarten, goes to his mother's office, and his mother, who was bitten by the same mosquito, goes to his kindergarten).

When I leave the room, Dikla goes in.

Well, actually, she waits a few seconds so we won't accidentally brush against each other in the hallway and then goes in to lie down next to him. Her hair spreads out on the blanket. Her long legs hang slightly off the edge of the bed. She kisses him. Hugs him. Often falls asleep beside him.

If she does fall asleep there, I go inside again and look at the two of them wound around each other. So alike that it's funny. Yanai also has long legs. And a defiant, rebellious curl to his upper lip. His hair is very dark and his skin very light. Like hers.

I think Yanai is too young to understand that we have been taking comfort in him recently, each in our own way. Or maybe I'm wrong.

Yesterday, on the way to school, he told me that his classmate, Guy, is really living it up because he has two homes, his dad's and his mom's. And each has a whole drawer full of candy just for him.

It's because his parents split up, Noam explained to him in her big-sister voice, what's so great about that?

It is too great! Yanai insisted. In his little-brother-has-an-opinion-too voice.

I didn't say a word.

I dropped Noam off at her school, and continued to his. "Kiss and go" or "walk and hug"? I let him choose, as I did every morning. Walk and hug, he said. I was glad. That meant we'd have more time together.

I parked far away. We got out of the car and walked hand in hand. When we reached the gate, I hugged him. Too hard. You're crushing me, he said. I let go. I watched him as he went on his way, and didn't walk to the car until he disappeared. On the way, I called Oranit from the after-school program and told her he wouldn't be staying that day.

I waited for him at the gate at 12:45. He was surprised. What are you doing here?

(What could I say? "Your mom is growing more distant from me and if it keeps on this way, you and I might end up seeing each other only twice a week, which would destroy me, so while I still have a say in this, I want to be with you and Noam as much as possible"?)

I thought we'd go out and have a fun day, I said. What do you say?

**There are quite a few mentions of photographs in your books. Are you a photography buff?**

I can't stand photography. I don't want to take pictures. Don't want to have my picture taken. I'm like the witches in the Bolivian Witches' Market—when someone takes my picture, I feel as if they're stealing part of my soul.

Even more—that desire to document, to freeze a moment, is alien to me. And goes against the Taoist approach on which I have been trying to base my life since I read *The Book of Tao* when I was twenty-three, in South America: everything passes, everything is in motion, life is a powerful stream you should give yourself over to instead of trying to stop it. Or in the words of Lao Tzu: "Where Taoism acts, people say—it happened of itself."

I try to adopt that approach in my writing as well, by the way. I was supposed to be writing a novel this year. Instead, I'm writing answers to this interview, which is based on "a selection of our surfers' questions" that the editor of an Internet site passed on to me. I was supposed to prepare standard answers to those questions, but I decided to answer truthfully. It was supposed to be only an interview, nothing else, but slowly—it seems I can't do it any other way—I've been turning it into a story. I was supposed to leave Dikla and the kids and the dysthymia out of it. And all of them are in it. Occasionally, in the middle of the night, I drive to see Ari, in oncology, to get his blessing. If he's awake, we watch repeats of Champions League games and talk about this and that. If he's asleep, I straighten his blanket, fill his empty glass, and listen to him breathing. Being with him, for some reason, confirms my feeling that I have to keep writing this text, even though I have no idea—really no idea—what's going to happen as I go on.

**Would you agree to appear on the other side of the Green Line?**

I didn't hesitate to meet with readers in Ma'ale Meir. If what I try to do in my books is deny that there is only one truth and challenge every narrator who claims to be omniscient, how can I refuse the opportunity to get to know people who think and live so differently from me?

In addition, they asked me so nicely. I mean, she asked. Iris. The librarian. Everyone here loves your books, she wrote, adding, and so do I, very much. And added a smiley face.

It's almost impossible not to return love to people who love you.

So we set a date. All I asked was for them to provide a bulletproof car to pick me up at the checkpoint. After all, we were in the middle of what was turning out to be another intifada.

I can't promise bulletproof, she wrote. But my Fiat is rock-proof. Is that good enough?

I was already trapped in my agreement-in-principle to go there, and I was ashamed to admit that what was safe enough for her wasn't safe enough for me. So I said, yes. Of course.

| | |

You expected to see an ultra-Orthodox lady, eh? she said when I got into her car.

The truth is . . . yes.

With an ugly hat and a crazy look in her eyes. And an American accent that's almost, but not quite, undetectable.

More or less.

Nice to meet you, I'm Iris, she said, extending her hand. And she gave me a smile which, at that particular moment, I mistakenly thought was distracted.

You don't . . . ?

Don't avoid touching? She left her hand in mine—after only the first handshake!

Her tone was cheerful, but her handshake was limp, almost melancholy.

| | |

On the drive from the checkpoint to Ma'ale Meir, she gave me a rundown of the terrorist attacks that had taken place in the area.

You see that monument on the right? Iris asked as she pointed at it. The Arzi family. A Molotov cocktail, their car went up in flames, the father, the mother, and the children died.

The pile of stones lit up on both sides by spotlights? In memory of Aharon Goldschmit, the military security coordinator of Elisha G. Two bullets in the chest—an ambush. Died before the ambulance arrived.

And a bit farther, there, on the hill after the curve, you can see the caravans of the Lior outpost. His friends from the yeshiva built it after he was run over and killed at the Tapuach intersection. A kid, twenty years old.

———

With each passing minute, I cowered lower in my seat. I tried to reduce my surface area in case someone decided to shoot at Iris's car with me sitting in it. Unconsciously, I locked my hands behind my head to protect it. Looking out of the window, I tried to see figures lying in wait in the dark.

Isn't it hard, living in constant fear? I finally asked. And to my shame, I felt the quiver in my voice.

It depends when, Iris said, her voice firm. Now, specifically, is not a great time. But here we are, almost at our destination, she added. By the way, ten meters ahead, on the left, you can see the Boaz Memorial.

Don't tell me—I tried to ease the tension with a joke— the stones hit the windshield. He lost control of his car. Forty-five years old.

Almost, Iris smiled that distracted smile. Stabbed in the chest. At the gate. Thirty-four years old. Left behind three sons, and me.

I stopped short.

I mean, the car kept moving, but inside me, something suddenly braked.

Oh, I didn't know. I'm really sorry for—

It's okay.

No, really, it was so insensitive of me.

Never mind. You didn't know.

But still . . . I'm sorry for your loss. It must have been . . . for you . . . how long ago did he . . .

Two years, she said, and ran a finger over her right eyebrow. After a brief pause, she added, But it feels like it happened this morning.

Maybe we should stop for a minute near the memorial? I suggested, trying to make up for being so tactless. And you can tell me a little bit about Boaz?

Some other time, she said, and kept driving, smiling that smile I had mistakenly thought was distracted and now knew was sad—they're waiting for us in the library.

————

Half of the community is here, Iris said when we entered.

I noticed that most of those present were women. Seated next to one another on plastic chairs that were crowded together in the small space between the reception counter and the bookshelves.

Two of the women—probably Iris's assistants—stood up, welcomed me warmly, and asked if I wanted something to drink. Tea? Coffee?

Just water, please, I said. I took the books out of my bag, walked over to the non-stage, and arranged them on the table. Near the vase of flowers. There is always a vase of flowers.

Iris turned on the microphone and introduced me. She mentioned that my grandfather was once prime minister. Listed the names of my books. Said how much they appreciated my coming at a time when even their relatives were afraid to visit.

Then she turned to me and said, I've spoken enough. We've come to hear you.

| | |

The meeting went smoothly. At least at the beginning.

I deliberately chose to read passages that weren't directly political, but even so, they had at least one moment when a character unexpectedly identifies with "the other": A man suddenly realizes why his wife is not happy with him. The father of a little boy forgives his own father, in retrospect, for his flaws.

During the question period, I was asked very cautiously about the writing process. What time of day do you write?

What happens if you have nothing to write about? What is the role of your editor?

Neutral questions you can answer with humor that seems spontaneous but is actually well planned and timed.

Then Iris raised her hand.

I recognized the raised hand and riding on the wave of the earlier laughter, I said to the audience: Like in the International Bible Contest, when it's time for the prime minister's question? So now we have the library director's question!

This is nothing like that, Iris said so quietly that her words were almost inaudible. I have to ask you something. How is it . . . why did you agree to come here today?

What do you mean, why? Why not?

None of the other . . . left-wing writers agreed to come. I try to invite them every year. And don't say you're not left-wing. I googled you. I read your articles. It's pretty clear which side you're on.

I thought before replying.

I drank some water.

I weighed my words.

Curiosity, I finally said, I'm curious about you. About settlers in general. The fact that you choose to live in this place . . . it affects the future of our country. If affects my life. I personally think that settlements like yours are an obstacle to peace. Frankly? I think you're destroying the chances that my children and I will ever have a normal existence here. But I think that from a distance. The last time I crossed the Green Line was in the army. And out of curiosity, I wanted to come here and see things with my own eyes. With me, curiosity usually conquers any force that stands in its way. Including ideology.

How much can you really see in an hour and a half? The complaint came from the last row.

It's better than nothing, another voice said from the other side of the room.

Let him come here for Shabbat, and then we'll talk, said a woman sitting right in front of me who nonetheless used the third person.

Why here? asked a male voice, let him spend Shabbat with our Arab neighbors in Ein Tor. And let him bring his children with him. Then we'll see if you talk about peace after the welcome they give you there.

Angry mutterings of agreement rose from the audience.

I drank some more water from the glass, which was almost empty. I tilted it desperately to trap the last few drops. And the truth is, I drank air.

I picked up my last book. There's a passage in it that I always read at the end of these meetings to send people home feeling pleasantly comforted. But what, what would be comforting? I put the book down and considered telling them about Jamal's father and that final moment before he left Beirut, when he stood at the door of his room, looked at the sculptures he had worked on all his life, and parted from them. With a look. Maybe he went up to one of them and ran his hand over the cool marble. A caress. Or maybe not, maybe there hadn't been time—

But I wasn't sure it was an appropriate story for this audience. Or even whether a story was what should happen now between me and them. But what instead? And what am I doing here anyway? I'm a writer. I'm supposed to write books that end with a few blank pages on which the reader can argue with me in his imagination.

That's where I should meet my readers. In our imaginations. Person to person. Not person to audience.

Okay—Iris rescued me, people were already moving around in embarrassment on their plastic chairs—our time is up. I want to thank you sincerely for coming. You are not the only curious one, as you can see from the number of people who have come to hear you and the number of questions. I hope this won't be the last time we see you here. And that many other writers follow you.

| | |

The audience dispersed quickly to their homes. I put my books in my bag. I took another drink of air from the glass.

No one came up to ask a personal question. No one asked me to write a dedication.

Only Iris came over and said it was fascinating.

I appreciated the fact that she didn't say "lovely." People who say "it was lovely" are usually hiding a different thought.

Shall I drive you down to the checkpoint, she half said, half asked.

But then the beep of an incoming message came from her phone.

She looked at it for a long time.

And said: Oh dear.

What happened?

The road is blocked off. There's a targeted warning that a small gang of terrorists is in the area.

So what do we do?

Wait.

How long can it take?

At least four or five hours.

That long?

Yes, I'm sorry, but it looks like you'll have to spend the night here.

Oh boy. Are there any B and B's here?

B and B's? Now it was no longer a sad smile. It was a broad smile, which turned into real laughter.

Iris was roaring with laughter, and it was a spectacular sight. Large dimples deepened in her cheeks and her entire, slim body shook with glee.

Okay—I felt a blush climb from my neck the way it always does when I blurt out something totally stupid—I realize there are no B and B's, so where . . .

You're invited to my house.

Really? That won't be a problem for you here? After all, I'm . . . a man.

I noticed.

| | |

B and B's—she repeated on the way to the car and put a hand on her stomach—fantastic! I haven't laughed that hard in a long time.

| | |

When we lived on Hatishbi Street in Haifa, a family that lost their father in the First Lebanon War lived across from us. Their son played cops and robbers with me, so I spent all my waking hours at his house. I remember how, after the father died in the Tyre disaster, their living room became a shrine to him: Memorial candles were lit every hour. Pictures of him, in color and black-and-white, with the family and alone, lined the sideboard, beside the honorary shields he received from the units he had commanded. You couldn't go into that friend's house without mourning.

| | |

I looked around Iris's living room while she went to get linens from the bedroom.

No candles. No pictures. No honorary shields.

A hammock stretched from one side of the room to the other. A phonograph. With a long row of records beside it. The record at the end of the row, the one whose cover showed an ashtray with a cigarette butt in it, was visible, and I recognized it right away: Shalom Hanoch's *Waiting for the Messiah*. There were large cushions on the floor, and on the walls hung unsophisticated, highly emotional paintings. Some of them quite sensual. Hers?

| | |

She came back to the living room and spread a single child's sheet on the couch. She added a blanket and a pillow. And placed a man's tracksuit on the pillow, along with a Golani Brigade end-of-course T-shirt.

I said thank you. And the chills of an on-the-verge-of-a-mistake passed through my body.

Coffee? she offered. Or do you always drink "only water"?

| | |

She came back from the kitchen with two steaming cups of coffee and said in the tone of a squad commander: Follow me!

We climbed the stairs that led to the second floor of the house. For a moment, I was afraid she was taking me to her bedroom, but she kept climbing even after the second floor until we reached a small ladder. Which led to a kind of opening in the roof that had an iron cover.

Come on, she said, lifting the cover, we can see the Tel Aviv Azrieli Tower from here.

| | |

On the roof, between the solar water tanks, stood two red-and-white-striped deck chairs. We sat down on them and looked at the lights of Tel Aviv and the surrounding cities.

I sipped my coffee and remained silent. I had spoken so much during the meeting with my readers that I had no words left.

When there's silence, you notice things. So I noticed that the steam rising from my cup blended with the steam rising from hers.

And that she gave off a light fragrance of body lotion, which wafted in my direction with the wind.

And that her jeans ended slightly before her socks began.

And that all the houses in the settlement were completely illuminated. As if no one here was planning to go to sleep, ever.

| | |

That's where I met Boaz, she said after several moments, pointing toward the towers of Tel Aviv.

In Azrieli?

Not far. I was studying literature and teaching in the Kibbutzim College of Education. One of the girls in my class was giving an Independence Day party. And he walked in. Our eyes met. He didn't look away. And I said to myself, He's wearing a kippah, so cool it. Then he came over and just started talking to me, no clever opening line, he simply began a conversation. I said to myself, Iris, stop with the pounding heart, nothing will come of it, he's wearing a kippah. And then he offered to drive me home, and I said to myself, If there was a chance that something serious might come of this, then there's a reason to play hard to get, but there is no chance, so let him drive me home, and come up for coffee, and kiss me more gently than I've ever been kissed before, and have sex with me as if he knew instinctively what turns me on, and he'll sleep over and hug me all night, a protective kind of embrace, and he'll make breakfast for me—what difference will it make? He's wearing a kippah.

She spoke very quickly, without taking a breath between one word and the next, between one sentence and another. As if the words were already fixed in her heart, and she had been waiting a long time for the chance to bring them out into the light.

And that was it? I asked. You stayed together until he passed away?

Of course not. Over the course of four years, we broke up and got back together again and again. Each of us tried to impose our lifestyle on the other, and naturally, it didn't work. So we distanced ourselves from each other and tried to go out with other people, and of course, that didn't work either. Finally, I went to him and said, Listen, I'll say this in the kind of religious language you understand, we can waste our whole lives trying to avoid each other, or we can accept the situation. For a start, I'll tell you that I'm prepared to live with you wherever you want. On the condition that inside the house, I can live the way I want.

Wow.

How did you put it at the meeting? When your curiosity wins out, no force can stand in its way, including ideology. So in our case, love won out over every force that stood in the way.

Including ideology.

Ah-ha.

And that's how you ended up in Ma'ale Meir?

The truth is that we wanted to rent an apartment in Jerusalem, but it was too expensive. Do you see? That's how we became "settlers." And there are other people like us here, each with their own story. You wanted to see things close up? No problem. Just take into account that when you see things close up, you notice the small details. And afterward, it's harder to make generalizations. In articles published in the newspaper, for example.

Which means, I'm done for, that's what you're saying. My curiosity has gotten me into trouble.

Exactly!

There's just one thing I don't understand, I said after a brief silence.

Feel free to ask, Iris said.

| | |

I sipped my coffee to keep from saying the words that were on the tip of my tongue. I knew what I wanted to ask, but not how to word it in a way that wouldn't offend her. Something about the way she described her dead husband was so alive.

I'll tell you what you want to know, she said.

What do I want to know?

What's keeping me here now that Boaz is gone? Why don't I take the kids and just leave? Right? I'll tell you why. In your opinion, how long does the official mourning period last?

Ah . . . seven days, no?

In Ma'ale Meir, it continues for three hundred and sixty-five days. You are surrounded on all sides by love and caring for a whole year.

That's very nice.

In my case, it wasn't just nice, it was crucial.

Why?

For the first month or two, my body reacted as if Boaz and I had just separated again. My body knew how to deal with that. It was kid stuff. But then, after about three months, it hit me. I couldn't drag myself out of bed in the morning. It would take time for the antidepressants to kick in, and meanwhile, someone had to take care of the kids. People here took turns around the clock. And they didn't care that I didn't wear a head covering. They took the children home from school. They brought me a doctor. They shopped for me. They gave me reflexology treatments. There's someone here who does Watsu in a huge tub he has on his lawn. Everyone gave what they could, do you see? After that year, an unbreakable bond was forged between me and this settlement.

I can imagine.

No, you can't. Because you don't know what a community is. I can see that in your books, too. Everyone is always alone. And if you created those characters, then you must be a loner as well. So imagine that there is no loneliness in your life anymore. That people never let you feel alone. Because you are always surrounded by warmth and support. Do you understand how much that gives you?

| | |

We sat on the roof a while longer, until even the lights of Tel Aviv began to dim. And the coffee grew cold. And the wind shifted from cool to cold.

Shall we go inside? she asked.

I nodded. And stood up after her.

When we passed her bedroom, she lingered briefly, as if trying to decide whether to invite me in or not, and then shook her head, seeming to shake off the thought, and continued walking down the stairs.

I followed her down. We reached the living room.

We stood facing each other. As if we were about to part. Or embrace. I clasped my hands together, behind my back. Like a diligent student. Or someone afraid that his hands might move of their own accord.

Do you have kids? she asked.

Two girls, I replied, and told her their names and ages.

And these are yours? I asked, pointing to the paintings.

Yes, and don't say they're beautiful. First of all, they're not. Second, I don't care whether other people think they're beautiful or not. I started painting them for myself. A month after Boaz died. Does it . . . happen to you, sometimes? Just writing something for yourself?

Less and less.

You should.

I nodded.

She took a step back.

If that's the case, I thought to myself, then a parting, not an embrace. It's better this way. I leaned back and put a hand on the back of the couch.

Do you want another blanket?

No thanks.

Great—she reached out suddenly (it really was sudden, there was no sign that it was about to happen) and stroked my cheek slowly, gently, the way you caress a child. And brushed her fingers across my chin.

And then, all at once, she pulled her hand back and said: I'll wake you at six and we'll drive to the checkpoint. The alert will definitely be over by then.

| | |

I tried to sleep in my pants and button-down shirt. But after an hour of tossing and turning in an effort to get comfortable, I gave up. I undressed in the dark and put on Boaz's tracksuit and shirt. They fit me really well. But sleep continued to evade me. I could still feel the touch of Iris's hand stroking my cheek. And fragments of all kinds of memories began to run through my mind, searching restlessly for meaning.

Then I heard footsteps, a sort of light patter.

I didn't move. I kept my eyes closed. I was afraid that if I made a movement that was too sharp or too eager, she might be alarmed and change her mind.

The footsteps came closer.

I deliberately breathed slowly. As if I were sleeping.

I maintained that rhythm of breathing even after I felt a hand supporting a body on the mattress close to my waist.

But the body that spooned against my back a moment later was not Iris's but a smaller one, with smaller arms.

I remained facing the wall. The small arms tightened around my body.

We lay like that for a while until I could no longer restrain myself and turned around slowly to see. The boy moved slightly but didn't wake up, and now I could see his face. He didn't look like Iris. He must have gotten those features from his father: A dominant nose. Long lashes. Lips that turned downward a bit. Giving him a slightly offended look.

He put his arms around me again. He was absolutely not willing to end our embrace.

I gave him a little more room on the couch, turned him slightly. And now I could hug him from the back, pull him close to me.

I thought: I've never hugged a little boy. It's difficult to explain. More muscular? Not exactly. And no less clinging. Maybe an echo of the memory of holding your own body when you were little.

We fell asleep, clinging to each other.

| | |

I woke up to the gentle touch of a hand on my shoulder. Iris was standing at the head of the couch, watching us with glistening eyes, and she whispered: The alert has been lifted.

I was afraid to move, I didn't want to wake the boy to discover that he had slept with the enemy.

I whispered to her: I don't want to wake him.

And she whispered: So stay for Shabbat.

After a very brief silence, during which she might have been waiting for my response to her invitation—she smiled her melancholy smile, and explained what to do in whispers and gestures, careful not to touch me: Yes. First remove your arms from around his waist. Then slide your body away. Exactly like that. And be careful when you move your leg over him.

———

Nimrod—not Yanai—was the name we had planned to give to a boy if we had one. And since writing is also, perhaps mainly, compensation for what didn't happen, or still hadn't happened, I named the children in various books Nimrod.

And now a real Nimrod had slept in my arms. For a whole night.

Reluctantly, I withdrew my arm from around his body. Very slowly. To prolong the moment. His long lashes quivered slightly, as if his eyes were about to open, but a few seconds later, the quivering stopped, and he continued to sleep.

———

The sun rose over the Shomron hills. Iris slowed down a bit and put her sunglasses on as she drove.

It's amazing, she said. On the surface, Nimrod handled Boaz's death better than the other kids. His siblings cried constantly. Clung to me. He was the only one who went to his room to play on his PlayStation with his friends. From the sidelines, it seemed like he cared less. At first I thought that maybe it was because he was the youngest and had had very few years with Boaz, but later, he began to act out in different ways.

For example?

Fighting in school, Iris said. I mean, he hit other kids. And at the same time, he suddenly became very devout. Scolded me for all the small liberties I allow myself to take on Shabbat. He rebuked me for naming him Nimrod, which is a slightly . . . unusual name for religious people. For a while, he went back to wetting his bed at night. Then he started sleepwalking all over the house.

Actual sleepwalking, with his hands held out in front of him?

No, that's only in movies. In reality, they walk with their hands at their sides and their eyes closed.

No kidding!

Apparently . . . that's how he got to you on the couch.

| | |

I retained the memory of his touch the way I would the memory of a night of lovemaking. During the drive to the checkpoint, I felt the warmth pulsing in my body. In my stomach as it pressed up against his back. In my arms as they held him.

| | |

I wonder if he'll remember anything when he wakes up, I thought out loud.

Usually he completely forgets what happened at night, Iris said. Once he ate half a pot of soup that was in the fridge. Just like that. From the pot straight to his mouth. As if it were a water canteen. And he didn't remember a thing in the morning. But if he says anything, I'll let you know. I have your e-mail address, right?

| | |

No one would dare to admit it publicly. Even I find my fingers blushing as I type this now. But when the victims of a terrorist attack live beyond the Green Line, it matters less to those who live on this side of the Green Line. Our minds hear the news, and from the names of the victims, we know whether they are members of the tribe or not, and often, we decide to push aside the pain and anxiety: "They chose to live there and endanger themselves and their children? So let them pay the price."

———

I didn't receive an e-mail from Iris. Nor did I send one.

But after the night I spent in Ma'ale Meir, the Green Line was no longer the line where compassion stopped.

On the contrary, for years after that, I still tensed up when I heard a report about a Molotov cocktail, a car that overturned after being stoned, infiltration into a settlement. I moved my radio dial from a music station to the IDF station, I listened to news bulletins. And when the names were announced in the papers the next day, I scanned the article with a pounding heart: Just not Nimrod just not Nimrod just not Nimrod just not Nimrod.

Maybe it was also the way she described him that made him seem like a kid who was asking for trouble.

| | |

"Four teenagers entered a Palestinian village, apparently to spray hate slogans on the wall of the local mosque. From the information we have received, it appears that a group of masked men were waiting for them, and now the boys are trapped in the mosque. The army is operating in the village. The situation is not completely clear at this time, but we can already say that there have been some injuries."

I sat in front of the TV and listened to the reports.

Dikla said, Look at how they drive the whole army crazy, those settlers.

And she also said, I hope they learn their lesson.

I didn't reply. I didn't argue. I didn't say that love conquers everything that stands in its way, including ideology. Or that love is the ideology. I kept watching TV all night. Waiting for the names.

I had a gut feeling. Like mothers have before the army representatives knock on the door.

It came right before dawn: "Our military correspondent reports that the boys were rescued alive. One of them, Nimrod Sali, is moderately to seriously injured, and has been taken to Tel Hashomer hospital."

| | |

I waited for the right moment. I didn't want anyone in the hospital to stop me and say that visiting hours were over. I didn't want Iris or anyone from Nimrod's family to see me. I sat beside Ari's bed in oncology and we played the game we'd regularly played since he had started drifting in and out of consciousness: He closes his eyes and dozes off for a while, and when he opens them, he asks if Ronnie visited him while he was asleep. I say yes, sure, and he smiles in satisfaction, closes his eyes again, opens them after a while and asks if Lihi visited him while he was asleep. I say yes, sure. We continue like that, visited by more and more girls who had disappeared since he'd become ill.

———

When Ari fell asleep for the night, I walked around other departments for hours. I pretended to be a waiting relative and tried to find the path that would take me to Nimrod's room, with zero exposure and a minimum of doors that opened only from the inside.

At four in the morning, I reached my destination.

When I entered the room, I saw Iris sprawled on a chair, sound asleep.

Her hair was speckled with gray. Her brow plowed with wrinkles. After all, the passing years had left their mark. On her and on me.

I walked over to the bed. The machines beside Nimrod gave off a dim light, illuminating his face. The stubble on his cheeks. His slightly drooping lips, giving him that old, offended look.

Gingerly, I climbed onto the bed and hugged him from behind, the way I had then. His body curved, abandoning itself to the embrace as if it remembered. His long lashes quivered slightly, as if he were about to wake up. But he continued to sleep.

I listened to his breathing to make sure it didn't stop and waited for first light to appear in the window. Then I got out of his bed and headed home. I drove through the deserted streets and switched stations on the radio, maybe one of them would broadcast an update or at least play "Waiting for the Messiah." But the Messiah didn't come.

I waited in my living room for some news, occasionally getting up and patrolling the other rooms. Sunbeams had begun to penetrate the shutters in my kids' rooms, illuminating their delicate faces, the dreamcatchers that guarded their sleep, and the furniture in their rooms, painted pink or blue.

*Your grandfather, Levi Eshkol, may he rest in peace, was the second president of the State of Israel. How does it feel to be named after him?*

Not the president, the prime minister.

*Your grandfather, Levi Eshkol, may he rest in peace, was the second prime minister of the State of Israel. What memories do you have of him?*

Not the second. The third. And he died before I was born.

*Your grandfather, Levi Eshkol, was the third prime minister of the State of Israel. What legacy did he leave you?*

Sugar cubes.

During the official memorial service in the Har Herzl cemetery, the family would stand in the first row facing the black marble headstone. After the chief military cantor chanted the final prayer—which always filled me with a general sense of deep sorrow that was unrelated to my grandfather, who died before I was born, and no matter how hard I tried, I couldn't mourn for him personally—each of the politicians would place a small stone on the grave and then stand in line to shake hands with the entire family. I remember that Shimon Peres's handshake was limp, that Gad Yacobi was handsome, that one of the last people to shake my hand was a thin-haired man named Shalhevet Freier. Then everyone—by that, I mean all the members of the Mapai party, friends of the family, and Shalhevet Freier—would drive to Ramban Street, to my step-grandmother Miriam's house, and stand in the small living room holding glasses of soda, analyzing the situation of the country as if it, the country, was their private possession, even though, in the years I'm writing about, Menachem Begin, the head of the opposition party, was already the prime minister.

We children, cousins, would retreat into a side room where there were thick files we were not allowed to open, and on the table that had once been his desk was a Scattergories game. For the letter *L*, in the category Famous People, it was obvious what everyone would write. So I chose Lincoln or Leonardo da Vinci to score more points, and every few rounds, my cousins—who were all older than me—would send me on a mission to the rear, which was the living room, to grab a handful of sugar cubes from the silver bowl and bring them, without incident, to the children's room. I remember the taste of those sugar cubes in my mouth: First they were hard, like sucking candy, and after a few small bites, they softened on the tongue and crumbled into tiny bits. I remember that Doron, my eldest cousin, taught us how to drink tea, holding a sugar cube between our teeth and letting the hot liquid flow through it. And I remember that once, Shalhevet Freier caught me red-handed in the living room. He intercepted my hand on its way to the silver bowl, held on to it, and said in a heavy German accent: It's not candy, son. I must have looked very frightened, because he quickly let go of my hand, offered me a box of bitter chocolate, and said, Take this instead. I hated bitter chocolate, but I took it. Something in Shalhevet Freier's tone told me not to argue.

He died a few years ago, and the obituary that appeared alongside his picture in the newspaper mentioned that he had been the chairman of the Atomic Energy Commission. And so, after a certain delay, I realized where the force of his deterrence came from.

Over the years, sugar cubes disappeared from the world. Like fireflies. Every once in a while, mainly in the Carmel Center and in the cafés populated by German Jews, they still put a bowl of sugar cubes in the middle of the table, and I take a few, suck them as slowly as possible to keep them from crumbling right away, and think about the grandfather I'd never known, saddened that I had never known him. They told me that he would compromise until he got what he wanted. That he had a warm, wise Jewish sense of humor.

That not only his supporters but also his opponents loved him. That he was not a member of the conservative party, made up of people who had only one great love in their lives. That he stuttered at the wrong moment. That he was responsible for the Six-Day War victory but was never given credit for it. That he died before he understood how much trouble that victory would cause us. That even though he was almost never home, he managed to instill in my mother, it's not clear how, a strong sense of his presence as a father. That, the older I get, the more I resemble him physically, so much so that, over the last few years, I avoid looking at pictures of him, because more and more they seem like a prophesy.

### Does your grandfather's political legacy influence you as a writer?

I had a real grandmother. Not famous. On my father's side. Who lived in Holon.

She was an almost-Holocaust-survivor, having emigrated from Poland to Israel alone right before World War II broke out.

When I was fifteen, my grandfather died and there was no one left to argue with her in Yiddish.

She had two or three close friends, but most of the time she watched TV, went to the clinic, and cooked.

In her house, lunch was at eleven thirty. Dinner at six. And there was an entire shelf for medicines in her fridge.

When I was twenty-three, I split from Tali Leshem for good.

Since I was the one who left the apartment we lived in together, it was clear that I needed a new place.

It was 11:30 at night, and I had nowhere to go with the two garbage bags I had filled with my clothes.

I caught the last bus to Holon. I knocked on my grandmother's door, where my grandfather's name still appeared on the nameplate, and when she opened it and saw me, she asked in alarm: What happened, *sheyne punim*?

I told her.

She made me a cup of tea with three teaspoons of sugar and added a metal straw that had a small teaspoon on one end for mixing it. As I sipped, she opened the sofa bed in the small room near the bathroom and spread a flowered sheet on it. Although she was a very small woman, her arms seemed to grow miraculously long when she spread a sheet. I had already noticed that when I was a child.

When we went back to the kitchen, she didn't say a word about Tali. Or the breakup. Nor did she mention what had happened when Tali babysat at my sister's place. All she asked was whether I wanted a piece of cake with my tea. When I shook my head, she sat down across from me and remained silent in solidarity until I finished drinking.

In the morning, she woke me too early because she was afraid I'd be late for work.

I lived with her for three months. The longest stay of a grandson at his grandmother's house in the history of the family.

I ate a lot of compote, sweet carrot salad, and instant tomato soup she enriched with real, home-cooked rice.

Every time I paid attention to a particular food on the table, she asked why I was ignoring the other food.

Every time I left a light on in the house, she turned it off.

Every time I wanted to watch soccer on TV, she gave up her programs without my asking.

Only when I lived with her did I realize what a sad person she was. A deep, fundamental sadness, like another organ in her body. And that somehow, that sadness of hers had transformed into concern for others.

Only when I lived with her could I see in her face the young girl who left her parents and siblings to move to Israel without knowing that it would be the last time she saw them.

Only when I lived with her did I understand how attached she had been to Grandpa Itzhak, and that when he died, a kind of countdown had begun inside her.

———

Two years ago, I went to Warsaw on a book tour.

My father gave me the address of the house my grandmother had lived in as a child, and I asked my hosts to take me to the Praga district. On the way, we passed bare trees and huge apartment complexes that reminded me of Kieślowski movies, and my mind was already arching to close the circle.

I didn't know that Warsaw had been totally destroyed in the war, that not a single building had been left standing in the Praga district after the Allied bombing, and that it was so cold in that city that even gloves couldn't save your fingers from numbness when you got out of a vehicle. I wandered the streets of the district for a while, trying hard to ask for help from the few people I saw, but the address written on the slip of paper no longer existed, and a man wearing a high hat, who, for a fraction of a second, I thought might be Hagai Carmeli, claimed that the street I was looking for had been in a different district altogether and no longer existed. Hailstones began to fall, hard as rocks. My pinkie turned to ice. So I decided to close the circle in a different way: to send my grandmother a post-card from Warsaw.

I sent her a postcard from every place in the world I'd been.

She never understood why I traveled so much—now that the Jews finally have a country of their own!—but she was always glad to receive a sign of life from me.

Near the ghetto, I found a small souvenir shop that still sold old-fashioned postcards and chose one with a picture of the reconstructed royal castle. I wrote to my grandmother that in the lobby of my hotel, they serve cremeschnitte and tea. And that yesterday, in a gourmet restaurant, the first course was chicken soup and kreplach. And that, though I didn't find her house, everything in Warsaw reminded me of her. Even the concern of my hosts.

I sent the postcard to her old address, 164 Arlozorov Street, even though I had no idea who lived there now.

———

Whenever someone asks me about my famous grand-father, I want to tell them about my grandmother, may she rest in peace, but no one wants to hear.

**Which artists and works of art influenced you when you were young?**

On Arlozorov Street, one hundred meters from my grandmother, lived my aunt Noa Eshkol. A choreographer, the creator of movement notation. A guru with a group of believers who worshipped the ground she danced on. A woman who chose to oppose. Prizes. Clichés. Falseness. Hair-dying. Instead of children and grandchildren, she had cats and dogs. Instead of serving refreshments to her guests, she served beer. Instead of an upper floor in her house, there was a large, unfurnished space where you could run wild while the adults argued politics down below. She liked to argue, Aunt Noa. And express opinions so bizarre that they were infuriating. And now, as I write this, I suddenly see a fragmented line I never saw before, con-necting her and Shira, my eldest child. Aunt Noa gave me the first record in my life—Stevie Wonder's *Hotter Than July*. I smoked my first cigarette in her house. She didn't come to my wedding because she didn't like formal events, but when Dikla and I went to visit her a few weeks later, she was very excited and kept saying how much Dikla im-pressed her. Two minutes after we arrived, she was already

stroking Dikla's hair and saying how soft it was. When
Dikla tried to share a few anecdotes from our wedding, she
stopped her in the middle and said: You know, it's amazing,
the difference between the tone of your voice, so reasonable
and moderate, like a metronome, and the movements of
your hands. They have . . . a private choreography of their
own . . . full of passion . . . do you dance? she asked. I danced
in a group in high school, Dikla said, but nowadays, only at
parties. Aunt Noa nodded slowly, as if considering asking
her to join her group, which had broken up years earlier.
Then she took us to her studio on the third floor, showed
us some new wall carpets, and said, Choose one, a gift.
While I almost swallowed my tongue from shock—it was
well-known in the family that Aunt Noa didn't give or
sell her carpets to anyone—Dikla walked around silently
looking at them for a few minutes until she chose the one
with the hidden wound, and Aunt Noa said, You have good
taste. Then we went downstairs, opened more and more
beer bottles, and talked, that is, it was mostly Dikla and
Aunt Noa who talked, and occasionally Aunt Noa stopped
to compliment Dikla on her original opinions, or on her
eloquence, or on the way the color of her skirt matched
the color of her tights. When Dikla went to the bathroom,
Aunt Noa lit a cigarette, gave me a long look, sighed, and
said, Oh, how much it will hurt. What will hurt, I asked.
Aunt Noa took a drag of her cigarette and said, When she
leaves. But seeing my grimace, she exhaled and added: I
didn't say it isn't worth it, kid. She's really something, your

wife. It isn't every day that you see such a beautiful combination of pride and delicacy.

She loved beautiful things, Aunt Noa. And since she rarely left the house—in fact, why didn't she? what was she so afraid of?—she wanted beautiful things to be brought to her.

Those Saturday visits to my grandmother and then my aunt were intertwined with my childhood: We went from Poland to bohemia in five minutes. We left my grandmother's house with large bags of secondhand clothes and walked up the street to Aunt Noa, who afterward, would cut those fabrics into pieces that would be sewn into her brightly colored wall carpets. She had begun making those carpets during the Yom Kippur War because she couldn't dance when friends were being killed every day, and since then, she had created more than a thousand. She didn't receive pieces of fabric only from us; they flowed to her from factories and sewing workshops all over the country. She blocked out designs on large sheets of cloth and then sent them, along with the pieces of fabric, to her dancers-admirers to do the menial work of sewing. The breathtaking results hung on the walls of the studio as if it were a gallery, and as a kid, when I finished jumping around to the sounds of Stevie Wonder, I would stand in front of those carpets and try to understand them. Then I'd give that up and try to dance to them.

Aunt Noa never agreed to show her wall carpets in a real gallery. Nor did she agree to be interviewed or receive an award from Tel Aviv University. And she didn't agree to die.

She suffered great physical pain during her final years—slowly, before our eyes, she turned from thin to skeletal—but still clung stubbornly to life so she could finish yet another carpet. Yet another dance.

| | |

After Aunt Noa's death, my father collected materials that could serve anyone who wanted to write her biography. Among those materials, I found love letters she had written in her youth from London to someone named Robert who lived in Israel. When I read them, it occurred to me that there is a gene that makes the people who possess it feel a more intense sense of longing than other people. And that gene is hereditary.

They sent the material to publishing companies that rejected it, claiming that the name wasn't well-known enough to the public at large for her biography to sell. I'm writing about her now so that others will remember that there had been such an Aunt Noa in the world, and that she gave many people the courage to be what they wanted to be. Including me.

**Are you involved in creating the covers for your books?**

I choose from various options I'm given, not to mention that I drive the designers crazy until there's an option I like. But in the unlikely event that this interview is turned into a book, I wouldn't need options. And I wouldn't drive anyone crazy. A photo of my aunt Noa Eshkol's wall carpet, the one in our living room, will appear on the cover: layer upon layer upon layer. And under them, a wound.

On the first inside page will be a warning completely opposite to the usual one:

> The plot of this book, the characters mentioned in it and their names have been taken from the life of the writer. Any resemblance between the plot of the book and real events is not the slightest bit coincidental. Any resemblance between the characters and their names, and real people, living or dead, and their names is not the slightest bit coincidental either. Nevertheless, given that the writer is a compulsive storyteller, every statement made in his name, including this one, should be taken with a grain of salt.

Only one word will appear on the dedication page: Dikla.

(This will be either a gift of love or a memorial to love. It's too early to tell. Yesterday, she packed a small bag and drove off. To an ashram in the desert. She said she needed time to think. She didn't say for how long.)

*There are a lot of dreams in your books. What role do dreams play in your real life?*

My dreams are embarrassingly simple. Sometimes, when I wake up and remember how crude and direct my dream was, I say to myself: From you I would expect more.

Dikla's dreams, on the other hand—

She forgot to take her notebook with her when she went to the ashram.

She left it on her bedside table.

A stronger person might have withstood the temptation.

———

*My mother calls me. In the dream, it's clear that she has found a technological solution that enables the dead to have a direct phone connection with the living, and such conversations are routine. She tells me, I'm proud of you, Dikla, and I ask, Why didn't you tell me that before? That's what's good about dying, she replies, you get perspective. What exactly is it that makes you proud of me? I insist on knowing, I manage to hear her sigh, and then the call is cut off, leaving the rhythmic sound of dialing that grows louder and turns out to be his alarm clock.*

———

*No one comes to Noam's bat mitzvah. Which, for some reason, takes place in the school gym in Ma'alot. We sit in the gym and wait and wait, but no one comes. The deejay keeps playing songs to get people dancing, but there's no one there to dance. Yanai bursts the balloons with a pin. I cancel the pizza order. Noam is too shocked even to cry. We leave the empty gym and walk to the huge parking lot where there are only two carriages. He goes to one and we go to the other. When we start driving, Shira says: Couldn't you control yourselves?*

———

*I'm in Colombia, in the city called Cartagena, looking for that woman. I follow a smell that leads me to a club I'm sure she's in and as soon as I see her, I'll ask her, yes or no, a story or reality, but the music in the club is really good. There's an Enrique Iglesias song, "Duele el Corazón" ("My Heart Aches"), so instead of looking for her, I start dancing, and in the dream, I know that it's only a dream and I'm sorry it's only a dream because I feel so so so good, and then there's a cut. And I'm in a desert, maybe in Colombia, maybe in Israel. The sun is so strong that my shadow looks completely different from me, as if it's someone else's shadow.*

———

*I win the Man Booker Prize in the "writer's wife" category and refuse to accept it. They call me up to the stage in English, and I stand up and answer in Hebrew, No thanks, and only after I sit down again do I see that the man sitting beside me isn't the man I'm married to but Eran, our assistant director of marketing.*

———

*I perform Watsu with the baby, Shira, not at the pool I usually go to but in the moshav Beit Zayit pool, which I have never been to. I cradle her in my arms and glide her through the water the way Gaia does with me, singing the melody of Billy Joel's "Honesty" to her without the words, but then*

suddenly there's a kind of hole in the pool like there is sometimes in rubber pools, and the water drips out slowly until
we're left sitting on the exposed bottom surrounded by coins
that people threw into it when they made a wish.

---

I forgot to dye my hair and all the cats in the neighborhood
come to me to be fed.

---

I'm in that damn sentry booth in the Arava desert. But I'm
at the age I am now. And I'm not wearing a uniform. Darkness, howling jackals, and again that terrible fear rises up
in me that I have no one and I'm alone. Completely alone in
the world. My heart races with the all-alone anxiety. I try to
tell myself that I'm already a mother and I have the kids, but
that doesn't help the pounding of my heart, which is growing
stronger, so I call ERAN, the suicide hotline, like I did then,
ashamed that after twenty years, I'm back to where I was
then, but instead of ERAN, the suicide hotline, Eran, the assistant marketing director with the broad shoulders, answers,
and in the dream, I wonder what dreaming about him for the
second time means.

---

We're in the office of the deputy mayor of Lefkara, the
city in Cyprus where we were married. This time we're there
to separate, but it turns out there's a problem: My right arm

*is attached to his left one. The deputy mayor examines the connection with a magnifying glass and says he's sorry, but surgery is not possible.*

———

*I go to visit Ari in Ichilov hospital and wander from room to room with a bouquet of flowers trying to find him, but all the rooms are occupied by bald women who look like my mother, even though my mother actually died of a heart attack. When I go to the reception desk to ask where Ari is, the nurse checks the computer and tells me that he's in Tel Hashomer hospital. How can you not know where your husband's best friend is hospitalized? she scolds me and takes the flowers from me as if I had failed an exam and now all was lost. I drive to Tel Hashomer, and I even have the number of his room, twelve, but when I go inside, it's my husband lying in the bed, hooked up to an IV, his eyes closed, and Ari is sitting at his bedside saying to me: I'm sorry, you arrived too late. I cry hysterically in the dream, not understanding how they had managed to hide the truth from me all that time.*

### Is there any biblical character that is especially close to your heart?

Every now and then, I look for a pit in which I can hide from the world for a while. Like Joseph, Jacob's favorite son, who was hated and shunned by his brothers. First, he withdrew from harsh reality into dreams, and when he could no longer dream, he withdrew into the pit. I know that isn't the accepted interpretation of the events in that chapter, but that's only because people don't notice that the pit is dug between the verse "And Judah said unto his brethren: What profit is it if we slay our brother, and conceal his blood? Come and let us sell him to the Ishmaelites..." and the verse that comes right after it: "And there passed by Midianites merchantmen; and they drew and lifted up Joseph out of the pit, and sold Joseph to the Ishmaelites for twenty pieces of silver: and they brought Joseph into Egypt." How can you explain the fact that Judah persuades his brothers to sell Joseph, but the ones who actually sell Joseph in the next verse—and earn twenty pieces of silver!—are in fact Midianites? There is only one satisfactory explanation: In the middle, between the verses, Joseph refuses to get out of the pit. He didn't take hold of the rope his brothers threw down to him, so how could they pull him up? With his keen senses, Joseph realized that only there, in the darkness of the pit, could he dream without interruption, where his brothers couldn't mock him for being a dreamer and no one could criticize him for the contents of his dreams.

For seven days and seven nights, Joseph dreamed about gold coins and many gods and a beautiful hand brushing a stalk of grain across his collarbone, dreams that the Bible didn't dare, couldn't dare, to include in the official story. During that time, Canaanites passed close to the pit he was hidden in, Jebusites and Hittites, but even though Joseph was very hungry, he didn't call out to them. Absolutely not. He still didn't miss real life and its pain enough.

In his last dream, on the final night, his brother, little Benjamin, was torn to pieces by a wild beast, and Joseph could not restrain himself and cried at his grave—

And only after he woke up from that dream, only after he wiped away the real tears on his cheeks—

He called to the Midianites that passed by the pit. He caught the rope they threw down to him. Used it to climb out into the dazzling light. And returned, his heart fluttering, to his role in the Bible.

———

Sometimes, books are—for their readers and writers—a pit to burrow into.

This interview is that kind of pit as well.

You can't imagine what is going on outside.

———

Dikla called from the ashram on Saturday evening and said: I need a little more time with myself. Her voice was different. Politer. Sure, I said. Of course. Then she asked to talk to the kids. Then she texted me a list of chores related to the bat mitzvah that had to be done that week. I knew them all, but I still texted her back: Received. Will do. Enjoy. Love. She didn't text me back. Or answer my calls over the next few days. I read on the Ashram in the Desert site that a Tantra festival would be held there the coming week, and the guests were invited to participate in workshops called "Unleash Your Inner Goddess," "Dance of the Heart," and "Until the Next

Pleasure." That did nothing to increase my peace of mind, but what could I do? I drove the kids to their afternoon classes. I drove them back from their afternoon classes. I drove them to birthday parties. I drove them back from birthday parties. I nurtured and nourished, explained and restrained, and after they went to sleep, I looked at Mayan's picture for a while and watched TV until I fell asleep. I never fall asleep in front of the TV when Dikla is home.

On the third night, I remembered the moment when the boy in the movie *The Life Before Us* asks the old man, Hamil: Can we live without love? But I couldn't remember Hamil's reply.

On the fourth night without Dikla, it crossed my mind that maybe this week was her experimental dry run to find out what it was like for her to live apart. On the fifth night, I reached the conclusion that she wouldn't come back. There are stories like that, about mothers who one fine day simply get up and go, leaving behind a brokenhearted husband and children who are screwed up for life—that kind of mother is always tall and beautiful, like Dikla. And she always has another man in the wings.

She wouldn't really do that, I tried to calm myself down, she's not the type, but then I remembered small moments from our life together, when something suddenly exploded inside her, without warning, and I watched in amazement as my noble wife slapped someone who had blocked her car on Ibn Gevirol Street; stood up in the middle of a premiere at the Jerusalem Film Festival and shouted at Lars von Trier that he's mentally disturbed; stopped the car in the middle of Geha Highway and got out because I had the nerve to say something critical about her sister; drove off the road into an olive grove in Crete, stopped the car, and put her hand between my legs.

On the sixth night without Dikla, I could already imagine what kind of man she was dallying with in the ashram. A widower. That was obvious. Her eyes always cloud over when she talks about widowers. The wife of that widower died from an illness less than a year ago and he's alone with their two sons now. That short stay in the ashram is the first time he has allowed himself to leave them. He brought a guitar. So he could play around the campfire at night. With that guitar, the sharwal, and the rasta braids, he looks a little like Lenny Kravitz, if you think about it. Lenny Kravitz with a sorrowful look in his eyes. A combination that Dikla would find hard to resist for long. While I was making sandwiches, they were most likely talking together in the ashram. She and her sorrowful widower Lenny. While I was helping Noam with her homework, she was most likely inviting him to continue the conversation in her mud hut. Or he was inviting her to continue the foot massage in his mud hut. Or they were splashing around together in a small pool. Half naked. Or not just half. She tried not to look but still saw that every man has his good points, and he tried to look, discovering the secret known only to me, that Dikla is even more beautiful without clothes than she is with, and then, after he leaned toward her and she leaned toward him and they reached the point of no return, she decided not to return. And when she does return a few months or years later, he is with her, holding her hand, and when I try to object, he shakes his rasta braids from side to side as if I'm disappointing him personally, places his free hand on my shoulder, and says, That's how it is, bro. I'm sorry your situation has let you down.

### How did the idea for your last book come into being?

The messenger from the Transportation Ministry said sign here, here, and here. After I signed, he informed me that I had accumulated too many points for traffic violations and therefore, in accordance with the law, my driver's license was being revoked as of that moment. The next day I went to the vehicle registry office. I tried to argue. To plead. To finagle my way out of it.

No license. For three months.

The first few days, I stayed home, mortified. Who would drive the kids to school? To their after-school classes? What was I supposed to do? So, having no choice, I went back to using public transportation, and after a week of riding trains and buses, I realized that a miracle had happened to me. Nothing less. Israelis in the public space, how can I put it delicately, are not exactly Brits in the public space. They don't read books or evening newspapers. They talk on their cells. Loudly. And I sit there, eavesdropping. From moment to moment, conversation to conversation, I understand that I have stumbled upon a gold mine.

During my three license-less months, I heard: Men being dumped live. Inheritance conflicts dripping with bad blood. Financial manipulations that, if exposed, would send those involved to prison. Military secrets—when the operation would begin, what the targets were, and which troops would take part.

And just when I thought that I'd heard everything, there came the crowning glory.

She boarded the train at Binyamina. And about a minute later, she began to speak. She sat down behind me and I deliberately didn't turn my head so she wouldn't suspect I was eavesdropping. Her voice was gentle and ingenuous.

From what she said, I understood that she was speaking to her sister.

I also deduced the following details:

She was supposed to get married in two days.

She was canceling the wedding.

The groom didn't know.

The only one she'd told was her sister (and everyone sitting in the train car).

Then came the really fascinating part, the part that granted the conversation an indisputable place in the pantheon. From Hadera northward, they spoke only about the dress. She was very concerned about it and wanted her sister's advice. What the hell do you do with a wedding dress? Sell it? Rent it? Keep it and remake it into an evening dress?

She got off at Acre. I couldn't quite catch a glimpse of her, and maybe that was a good thing, it left room for the imagination. That, after all, is the important thing about the moment a book is born: It needs to have something unknown. A gap you will want to bridge with your writing. And of course, it should relate to some pain you have suffered. So that you are linked to the moment by an invisible tunnel, like the ones you dig in wet sand on the seashore until your hands finally come together—

———

When I woke up on the morning of our civil wedding in Lefkara, Cyprus, Dikla wasn't in bed.

There was a note on her pillow: I went out to take a short walk.

The marriage ceremony in the deputy mayor's office was scheduled for one o'clock in the afternoon.

And at twelve thirty, Dikla still hadn't returned.

There were no cell phones then, and I was forced to wait for four hours, during which I moved from euphoria to fear to anxiety to total realization, based on many clear indications from the weeks preceding our trip, that she was about to cancel everything.

It was so clear to me that I didn't even put on my groom's clothes. I stayed in my tracksuit. And every once in a while,

I went to the window to look, just in case. But all I saw were the famous lady embroiderers of Lefkara sitting at the doors of their shops, embroidering. And embroidering. And embroidering.

At twelve thirty-one, Dikla came into the room. And along with her, an unfamiliar smell.

She kissed me on the mouth.

What happened? I asked, trying to keep my voice steady.

I had to think for a while, she replied, her expression serious.

About what?

For the last few weeks, I've felt like I was being swept away by a strong current and I never stopped to think: Is this what I really want?

Okay. So what did you decide?

Yes.

Oh, great.

Are you angry?

Very. But we don't have time for that. The ceremony is in half an hour. Do you want to change into your dress?

Of course. And you? You're going to stay in your track-suit? Actually, you look good in it.

Then we went to the deputy mayor's office and read aloud the vows we had written in advance and kissed and wandered around the village of Lefkara and bought a few pieces of embroidery to cheer up the famous, dejected-looking embroiderers and drank lots of red wine and made love again and again in the large white hotel bed and flew back to Israel and had a party for family and friends and those four hours of her disappearance were swept far under our shared consciousness, along with the unfamiliar smell that had risen from her and that we have never spoken of. It wasn't until the time she stayed at the desert ashram that all sorts of brief, discomfiting images from Cyprus flashed through my mind. How I stood at the hotel-room window, muttering to myself, Come back, come back, please come back.

———

She came home yesterday. Took off her backpack and propped it up against the wall.

I stood up from the couch and hugged her, unburdening myself of a full week of longing, but her entire bearing reminded me of a line from the Shmulik Kraus song: *Give me a minute to get used to you again.*

So I went into the kitchen.

Want something to drink? I asked. I'm boiling water.

I'll make it myself, she said.

We stood close together in the kitchen. Not touching. Not looking directly at each other. Taking a quick glance, I noticed that her face was relaxed, the way it is when she comes home from water therapy with Gaia, and she was suntanned, which looked good on her. But I knew that compliments would not be well received now.

We took our cups of tea into the living room. There's one long couch there that can seat several people, and perpendicular to it is an armchair. She sat down on the armchair and wrapped her hands around her cup without sipping from it. Which left me no choice but to sit on the long couch alone.

So how was the Tantra festival? I asked, and added a forced smile, like someone adding a smiley face to a text.

I didn't go to the Tantra festival, she said.

But on the ashram site, it said—

Is that how well you know me? I was there for the weekend, but the minute the place started filling up with all kinds of huggers with rasta braids, I took off.

Really?

Aha.

So where...?

I went to see Shira.

Shira?

She nodded.

At Sde Boker?

Yes. I called her and asked if I could come.

And she agreed?

On the spot. One of her roommates had gone to see her parents in Metulla, and the teachers gave me special permission to sleep in her bed. Where are you going?

Ah... to... to get cookies. Want some?

No thanks.

———

I didn't really want cookies. But like Effi, the graduate of the anger management workshop from Minneapolis, I preferred to cut off contact and move away from the situation before I said things I would regret. He had stepped out of the car into a snowstorm, and I—I went into the kitchen and pretended to look for cookies. I opened and closed a cabinet and a drawer and another cabinet, although I knew exactly where the box was, and meanwhile, tried to absorb:

Not a sorrowful widower Dikla met in the desert but our eldest daughter.

But still, betrayal.

When that daughter learned to talk, she used to tell me five times a day: I love you. And draw red hearts on slips of paper that she put on my keyboard. When she learned how to write, she would draw a heart with an arrow piercing it: On one side of the arrow she wrote "Shirush" and on the other, "Daddy." For years, we had a silent bond that sometimes upset Dikla, who remained outside it, and now—

When I returned from the kitchen, I was already two people. One sat straight and continued speaking with Dikla, and the other withdrew into himself.

So you were with Shira for three days? I asked as I placed the plate of cookies on the table.

Yes, with her and Nadav.

Nadav?

Her boyfriend.

She has a boyfriend?

She has a boyfriend.

I don't believe it.

One of those nature types. With curls and sandals.

But Shira... she's so...

So what?

I don't know. Vulnerable. She...

She's absolutely fine. And so is he. You should see how he looks at her.

But... I don't want him... to use her.

Forget it. He's madly in love with her.

Shira has a boyfriend. Wow.

Yes. And she... asked me not to tell you.

Why?

You know why.

But—

Listen, she's happy. She's really found her place there. I never saw her like that.

What... you really talked? You had a conversation?

Not just a conversation. A heart-to-heart conversation.

No kidding. I mean... it's great that you talked.

It's that Nadav, he's a good influence on her, she suddenly opened up to me. Like those flowers in the desert that open at night.

She didn't ask you why you suddenly showed up.

She did.

And what did you say?

That I needed some time away.

Which is true.

Which is true.

I can't believe she has a boyfriend.

She has a boyfriend.

And I can't believe she told you not to tell me.

You should see them. They walk down the paths of Sde Boker hand in hand.

I really should see them, because I can't imagine Shira with—

One night he brought a pot of soup to the room. He made it himself. He added all kinds of herbs he picked in the herb garden. And he requisitioned bowls and tablespoons from the dining hall.

Are you sure it's your daughter who's in love and not you?

Come on, really. It's just so awfully nice to be near it. Love... in fact, it's a beautiful thing.

At their age.

At every age.

Yes. At every age.

And it's such a relief... that she's happy. We've wished for it for so long.

I don't know, I said. I don't feel relief.

Why?

Maybe because... I wasn't with the two of you.

But—

And I don't want to be happy too soon.

I picked up the plate of cookies. I offered her some again. She shook her head and hugged herself.

Are you cold? Do you want to come and sit next to me? I asked. You're so far away over there.

I feel good here, she replied, and took a long drink from her cup of tea.

Okay, I said, and drank from mine.

We didn't speak for a long while.

There was a time when our silences were relaxed, I thought.

In the end, it's simple mathematics, I thought. The number of thoughts you have during a conversation with your wife that you don't share with her, divided by the total number of thoughts that pass through your mind during the conversation, equals the chances you will split up soon.

———

How are the kids? Dikla finally asked.

Fine, I replied. They had a good week. And I wanted to add: But I had a bad one.

I missed them.

We missed you, too, and every night, when—

But I needed that time. I've been chasing my tail ever since Shira was born, and if at any time during those years a doubt slipped into my mind, I told it to go away, I have no time for you. And then . . . then Shira left for boarding school and you . . . you came back with that story from . . . Colombia, that you made up or didn't make up, I don't know anymore which is worse, and that forced me to say to myself "Stand still!" And think. That's what's happening now. I'm standing still. Thinking.

Okay. So . . . did you reach any conclusions?

I've had a few insights.

Want to share?

No. They stay with me for the time being. Tell me, how's Ari?

They're trying some new drug on him now. Developed in Canada.

You don't say.

Yes. The chances are slim. I'm even afraid to hope. But imagine if he gets well?

I hope so. We'll keep our fingers crossed.

Are you coming to bed? I asked.

In a little while.

Okay, I said, stood up, kissed her on the forehead as if she were my sister, and went to the bedroom. I waited a few minutes in the hope she would join me, but when I heard voices coming from the TV in the living room I understood that she wouldn't. I felt both disappointment and relief, because as much as I wanted her, I was afraid of being rejected.

I texted her father: She's back. (He didn't understand why she hadn't answered his calls all week, so I had to make up stories to calm him down.)

And to her, I texted a line from our song, Johnny Shuali's "Sometimes."

**Is there a meeting with readers that you remember in particular?**

It was before the civil war in Syria, but even so, I knew no one would believe me when I said I was going to a meeting with readers in Damascus. So I told everyone that I was going to eastern Turkey. Which was true, because that's where I would be smuggled across the border. Everything was arranged through e-mails with a British go-between, Jeremy. He was the first to contact me and say that a reading group in Damascus was discussing the Arabic translation of my book and the members wanted to know if I was willing to meet with them there. I replied that it sounded a bit problematic, technically, and he e-mailed back that most of the technical problems were solvable if I happened to have a foreign passport. I wrote him that, as it happened, I did. I was born in Bern when my parents were there on a sabbatical, so in principle, I had a Swiss passport. Which had expired. I traveled to Basel, where I received the next e-mail from the head of the Damascus reading group. Jeremy forwarded it to me. He wrote in fluent English that the group was very excited to hear that I had agreed to visit them and explained that I need not concern myself about security measures. Among the members of the reading group were high-level officers who would guarantee my safety throughout the visit. All that remained was to set the date and time of the meeting and book my flight to Turkey. They would pay for it, of course, and also take me on a tour of the city. The only thing I had to do was make sure my Swiss passport was valid.

In the following weeks, we tried to set the time for the meeting, which turned out to be a complicated business. Their holidays did not coincide with ours, their Sabbath was on Friday, and the smuggler's trail from eastern Turkey to Syria was open only a few days a month. In the end, with

Jeremy's active mediation, we found a time convenient for everyone.

I wrote in my diary: Izmir. Eight o'clock in the evening. Meeting with readers.

I didn't want to write "Damascus," in case someone saw it, was alarmed, and either tried to talk me out of the escapade, using valid, logical arguments, or else accused me of being a traitor.

At dinner at Dikla's father's house in Ma'alot, I had to really control myself. Her father was born in Damascus, grew up in Damascus, and was imprisoned for one year in Damascus for wanting to immigrate to Israel. Dikla says that he never talked about Damascus. When they were kids and asked him what it was like there, he said he didn't remember anything. That all of it had been erased from his mind.

Then, two days before my trip, he suddenly remembered. In a Damascus open market, there were artichokes the size of watermelons, he said, and everyone at the table was struck dumb with astonishment. There were spice stalls there, he said, that made you sneeze when you just walked past them.

Is it large, that market in Damascus? I asked him. The others were too stunned to speak.

Twenty times larger than the Machane Yehuda market in Jerusalem. And I'm not exaggerating.

What are some other places worth visiting in Damascus? I asked.

Why, you're planning to go there in the near future? he chuckled.

I have a trip to Izmir and thought I'd pop over afterward, I said (the truth is sometimes the best lie).

Everyone at the table laughed. But their attention didn't waver. Even the young grandchildren leaned forward to hear more about their grandpa's forgotten childhood. And he spoke—looking at me but speaking to everyone—about the Barada River that crosses the city, about the Great Mosque and the Jewish quarter, as lucid and detailed as a tour guide. Then, as suddenly as the window of his memories had opened, it closed. *Khalas*, he said in Arabic, enough. I talked so much that it made me tired. Who wants fruit salad for dessert?

At the end of the evening I went over to him and asked if he happened to remember the address of his childhood home.

The house behind the synagogue, he said. That's the address.

No numbers?

Not in the Jewish quarter. But why are you so interested in Damascus all of a sudden?

I'm thinking of writing about something that happened there, I said (sometimes time transforms a lie into the truth).

Ah, he sighed. Writing. Deep down, he never understood why his daughter had chosen to marry someone who didn't have a real profession, but he knew her and her semi-Syrian stubbornness, and he knew that objecting would not help. Just the opposite.

———

I left on Sunday. I knew I was doing something irresponsible, but eight years of suburban living can drive a person so crazy that all he wants is for something interesting to finally happen, for God's sake.

The driver of the van that waited for me on the smuggler's trail played a Zohar Argov cassette. His best hits. I knew that under no circumstances should I let it slip that I knew that Israeli singer, but still, melodies have hidden power, and in a moment of inattention, I hummed along with the song "Elinor." The driver looked at me in surprise through the rearview mirror. A beautiful melody, I explained quickly in English, and he stared at me suspiciously but continued driving.

I moved from the first van into another vehicle, but not before I was blindfolded with a handkerchief. I tried to sharpen my other senses so I could pick up what was going on around me, and based on the voices, I decided that there were three other people in the vehicle with me.

There was no music in that vehicle, and only occasionally ululating songs drifted through the windows from the street. An eternity later, my co-passengers offered me water. I drank without seeing and a bit of the water spilled on my shirt. I heard more and more sounds of the city: horns, drilling, street vendors. Okay, I didn't really hear the street vendors, but after my father-in-law's stories about the Damascus market, I imagined I was hearing them.

When they removed the blindfold, I was on a small stage in a dark cellar that reminded me a bit of a club in Tel Aviv, the Left Bank. There were around twenty people in the audience. Bassel came over, shook my hand, and apologized for the blindfolding. I'm sure you understand the sensitive nature of your presence here, he said, and I nodded. He picked up the microphone and introduced me. From the little I understood, I could tell that his introduction was based on my Internet biography, which was filled with minor inaccuracies. I used to correct anyone who introduced me using that Internet biography. But as time passed, I began to believe that it really was my biography.

While he was speaking, I looked at the audience. One of the men in the last row looked like Ron Arad, the missing-in-action airman, in his last photo, with the thick beard and sunken eyes, taken more than thirty years ago.

The stage is yours, Bassel said.

I began to speak, and when I finished, I stayed for a long time answering questions. Unlike what I might have expected, the questions did not focus on the political aspects of the book. I think that more than anything, my Syrian readers wanted to know what was "real" in the book and what wasn't. They weren't the first to ask that, of course, readers in general are determined to get to the biographical core of the book, based on the erroneous assumption that it will help them understand it. But my Syrian readers were more than determined, they were obsessed. For hours, I answered as patiently as I could, and in the end, I concluded by saying that, usually, the more I "lie" in biographical terms, the closer I actually get to the deep truth that is beyond the facts.

Finally, they gave me a mild round of applause.

Bassel came onto the stage, asked me to sign his copy, and then introduced me to the man I thought was Ron Arad. This is Ghalib, he said. He will be happy to show you the city in the brief time you still have here.

———

I asked Ghalib to take me to the Jewish quarter, to the house behind the synagogue. We drove there, and on the way, I examined his profile, trying to decide if he was him.

When we arrived, I asked for and received permission to take a picture of the building that now stood on the ruins of my father-in-law's childhood home.

Ghalib remained a short distance away from me, stroking his beard slowly and looking around with visible discomfort. Finally, he approached me, pointed to his watch, and said in fluent English that the van was already waiting to take me back home. And that I mustn't be late.

During the drive, I looked at his profile again. From a certain angle, he still looked like Ron Arad, but from a different angle, he suddenly looked like Hagai Carmeli. Hagai Carmeli with a beard.

Tell me please, aren't you . . . ? I asked him in English a moment before we parted.

No, he replied in Hebrew, and shoved me into the van.

———

I knew that no one would believe I took the picture of the house behind the synagogue in Damascus myself. So at Friday dinner in Ma'alot, I made up a story about a Kurd who came up to me in Izmir, reprimanded me for my mistakes about the descriptions of kubeh in my book, and pulled out a picture he had taken a few years earlier on a visit to relatives in Damascus, who told him that the building they lived in was built on the ruins of a house in the Jewish quarter.

I didn't think anyone would buy the ridiculous story, but guess what, they swallowed it whole (sometimes it's much easier to believe a lie than the truth).

Dikla's father, in any case, held the picture for a long time. He shed a single tear that detached from his eye like a space shuttle separating from the mother ship, and then he put the picture down and asked, Who wants fruit salad?

### How is the younger generation of writers different from the older generation?

Among the photos of family trips to Eshtaol Forest is one—as if it didn't belong—of a man with gray hair and a small paunch, leaning on a slide and looking off into the distance, his expression melancholy. I looked at that picture for quite a few seconds until I realized—

When I was thirteen, my voice started to change. I remember how estranged we became, my voice and I. I felt as if someone else was speaking from my throat.

For the past year, I've been taking off my glasses before I look in the mirror. I'd rather not see the changes. But I can see them in other people's eyes. In women's eyes.

Only in the world of literature am I still considered a member of the younger generation.

Before we grew distant from each other, Dikla used to say: You look better now than you did when we met.

We both knew it was a lie. That we were going downhill. But that wasn't the issue—

The issue was the incongruity. Inside, I'm twenty-five, just back from my trip to South America, and outside, I'm this man with the graying hair and the paunch, in a picture taken on a trip to Eshtaol Forest.

**What embarrasses you?**

Walking into a meeting hall and discovering that projected on the large screen behind the stage is a huge picture of me taken fifteen years ago, in which I look the way I looked fifteen years ago.

**When was the last time you wanted to cry?**

The tests showed that the Canadian drug wasn't working. Ari didn't tell me.

But his mother called. Said that the tests had come back and the results were unequivocal.

She said: Get over to his apartment quickly, *corazón*. So someone will be with him now.

I said: *Claro*. Of course.

When I arrived, he acted as if everything was as usual. I kept waiting for him to tell me about the test results, but he talked about Hapoel Jerusalem. Said he felt like there was hope this year. That the team is in synch. And there's the new arena too. He watches the games on TV, and aside from all the statistics, he's noticed that the team finally has character. We have Yotam and Lior, who are winners, he said, and they'll pull the others up with them.

I played along with the conversation. I offered my opinion. I even argued with him about whether new players should be brought in or whether they would throw their great teamwork out of synch. And the entire time, I was thinking: In the end, he'll talk about the tests.

In the end, he said, I'm a little tired, bro. Thanks for coming.

And he pulled the blanket up to his neck and closed his eyes.

I knew he was pretending to sleep.

So I controlled myself and didn't cry.

———

All the way home, I pictured myself collapsing in Dikla's arms. How I would open the door and say, I need you, Diki. Can you please love me again? At least for one night?

Sitting in the living room was Ariel, the babysitter, and waiting for me on the kitchen table was a note: I'm at a party with Gaia. Home late. Don't wait up.

The difference between faint hope and no hope is infinite.

I asked Ariel, Do you have a minute?

What?

I need to talk to someone, I said, do you have a minute?

He looked at me in horror and said, They're expecting me at—

Sure, I said. Of course. Here, take—how much do we owe you?

———

I went into Yanai's room. He has a convertible bed, so I opened it and lay down next to him. I imagined a life in which I was allowed to see him and Noam only twice a week, and I thought to myself: I'll never survive it. It wasn't exactly a thought. More like asphyxiation. Then I said the word "enough" to myself. And three more times out loud: Enough. Enough. Enough.

I stood up and went to Shira's room. That is, the room that had been Shira's and now was a kind of playroom no one played in. When Shira lived at home, she never went to sleep. At night, after I came home from my talks, I used to go into her room, sit on the edge of her bed, and listen to the dramas she had lived through during the day. She said she wanted me to "advise her," but I knew that if I really dared to give her advice, she'd throw me out. So I would nod. And nod again. And sometimes even share with her the victories and defeats I had experienced when I was her age. I noticed that knowing that I too had wondered and blundered calmed her down. Now I sat on the edge of the bed. I stroked the blanket for a while. And nodded into the darkness.

Dikla woke me when she came home and said to me: Come to bed, sleep normally. I followed her. In bed, I told her about Ari. She was silent and groped for my hand. I stayed awake all night, holding her hand. I didn't want morning to come.

### When was the last time you cried?

It was in the seventh grade. Or the eleventh. I'm not sure.

There was a grammar test. Before the class, I went through the textbook and memorized the exceptions to the rule for the last time, and when the teacher walked in, I forgot to put the book back in my bag.

She handed out the test papers and when everyone began to write, she walked around from desk to desk. I remember the clack of her high heels. Her Farrah Fawcett hairdo. The smell of her perfume. Older women's perfume. When she reached my desk, she stopped, picked up the book, and shouted: What is this supposed to be? She waved the book around in front of my eyes and I said: Sorry, I forgot it was on the desk. Oh come on, she said, you think I'm stupid? No, I replied, adding: Please believe me, it was an accident, I just forgot to put it in my bag. Her answer was to take my test, tear it in half, and put it back on my desk. Other kids giggled. Obviously at me. At my far-fetched explanation. I stood up, walked out of the classroom, and slammed the door behind me. Hard.

There are moments in life when you're bursting with love or mortification, and all you can do is walk and keep walking. So I left school and kept walking, and in Haifa in the eighties, if you walked long enough, you would reach the Carmel forest.

I leaned against a tree, slipped down into a sitting position, and wept.

There is nothing more humiliating than when someone doesn't believe you. Even if you're not telling the truth.

Actually, there was another time I cried after that.

I had come back from Ari's place. It was before he got sick. We watched Barcelona play Chelsea. But there was another reason I'd gone to see him that evening. One of my books had just come out, and those few weeks before the first reviews appear are pretty much a nightmare. What has been internal for so long has suddenly become external, and you feel like you're exposed. Like you've shown more than you intended to show. And no attempt to cover yourself with your hands can ever hide it.

I knew that, at Ari's place, there was no chance we'd talk about it, for one simple reason: He wasn't crazy about my books. He tried to read the first one. Two months later, he returned it to me and said: I tried, bro. I really did. But I just couldn't get into it. You're not angry, are you? When I gave him the second one, which I had signed with a very personal dedication, he complimented the beautiful front cover, read the blurb on the back cover, and said, It's pretty much like the first book, right? The same mindset?

———

Aren't you a little offended? Dikla asked when I told her.
Just the opposite, I said, it's great.
What's great about it?
Everyone I've met since I started writing books treats me too much like a writer. He just treats me like me.

———

That evening, he made chili con carne with black beans that he bought especially in a Mexican store in the central bus station. After Iniesta scored the winning goal for Barcelona at the last minute, we ate. I mean I ate. He devoured. And we drank, I mean I drank and he emptied one and a half bottles of Bitter Lemon.

We talked about the decision of the district attorney's office not to indict Yoram Sirkin for fraud and breach of trust. Ari, who had just become a partner in the law firm where he worked, said more than once that the decision didn't prove that Sirkin hadn't defrauded, only that they hadn't found a smoking gun. Then we talked about the girl Ari was dating at the time, and there was a feeling in the air that maybe this time it would finally happen.

The drive home from Tel Aviv was short and relaxed. No traffic jams, twenty minutes tops. There was happy music on the radio and a spring breeze drifting through the window, so nothing prepared me for what happened when I tried to get out of the car.

Moving from sitting to standing is something you do a hundred times a day without thinking about it.

The pain was so sharp that I almost fainted. I grabbed the side mirror with both hands to keep myself from collapsing on the street, and I closed my eyes until the dizziness passed. Then I took a few deep breaths and tried to straighten up—but my body refused to obey the command. I tried again. Nothing. Then I realized that I had left my phone in the car, on the passenger seat, and that I wasn't able to bend toward it. And that I had no way to call for help. I kept my grip on the side mirror and looked around. At that time of night, all the tenants in our building were already asleep, and the parking area was totally silent, except for an owl that occasionally hooted from the treetops.

I don't know how long that humiliation lasted. Ten minutes. Maybe less. At some point, I began to cry. I hadn't cried since that language test. Twenty years. Not that there hadn't been reasons. My heart was broken at least three times. I wasn't accepted into the military unit I wanted to join. My grandmother died. Dikla lost by five votes. Not a single tear.

And suddenly, out of the blue, in the middle of the parking area. Alone, betrayed, clutching a side mirror.

Luckily for me, a neighbor finally came out to throw her garbage into the bin. I called to her and she got Dikla, who somehow managed to push me into the backseat of the car and take me to the emergency room. Later, I did physical therapy for three months. I learned a series of preventive exercises, and also that each vertebra of the spine has a number.

But to this very day, I haven't forgiven my body.

It's so difficult to build trust after it has been betrayed.

### When was the last time you had a broken heart?

I can't write it. I shouldn't. But I have to.

We took Shira to the boarding school at Sde Boker.

Her suitcases were in the trunk and she was in the backseat with her earbuds. I couldn't catch a glimpse of her face in the rearview mirror. But I kept trying.

Dikla and I were silent. We both knew that every sentence spoken now might be interpreted as an accusation.

I remembered our drive from the maternity hospital, sixteen years ago. It was pouring. I drove slowly, people honked. I didn't care. In the backseat—our first daughter, wrapped in a blanket. So small. The rain stopped when we reached our street. The wipers kept working. We sat in the car for a few seconds. We didn't speak.

We had the feeling that when we stepped out of the car, we would be stepping into a totally different life.

Of Shira's first year, I remember only her. Writing didn't interest me. Teaching didn't interest me. I wanted to be her father all the time. And she wanted to be my daughter. She wanted to be held in my arms. On my shoulders. She wanted to be hugged. Kissed. Rocked. When she was a bit older, she used to clutch my waist in desperation when I went to work and ran to me when I came home as if we hadn't seen each other for a week. She would put her small hand in my large one even if we were only going from the living room to the kitchen. I told people: From the day she was born I stopped being sad. I told myself: The wandering is over. Until a few years ago, along with the high-speed metamorphosis from little girl to teenager, she began to cut herself off from me. All at once, there were no more words of love. Or hugs. All at once, she didn't want to talk to me. Spend time with me. Do her homework with me. All at once, she had this enormous anger about a list of wrongs committed against her, first and foremost among them that we judge her all the time and don't accept her as she is. Welcome to adolescence, people with experience nodded at me sympathetically. But I went through several years feeling like a man who had been tossed away. And then, just as the storm was dying down a bit and she was even doing better in school, she told us that she wanted to register in Sde Boker for high school. A residential high school in the desert. Apparently without our knowledge, she had already attended their open house, where she met a few girls she clicked with immediately.

We drove down there, Dikla and I, to Sde Boker. To have a look around. I hoped we'd be disappointed. But at the end of our visit, I had to admit to myself and to Dikla that I completely understood what Shira saw in the place. Open spaces. The feeling there is that it's all open spaces. Totally unlike her high school here, which looks like a prison and treats its students like prisoners. Besides, the latest graduating class had written quotes from Meir Ariel songs on the walls of the dormitories as a parting gift. How can you not like a place that welcomes you with *"And it's all about drinking something cold in the middle of the desert"*?

When we came back from Sde Boker, we sat on the balcony to talk. I mean, she and Dikla talked and I mostly listened and thought: How beautifully she expresses herself. And how smart she is. And why haven't we been able to gain her trust?

Later, Dikla went to bed and only I, my daughter, and the mosquitoes remained.

So what do you say, Dad? she asked.

I wanted to tell her that it was too soon for me. I wanted to tell her that we had stopped arguing only a few months ago and I wanted to enjoy this golden age a bit more before she went. I wanted to tell her that we hadn't been careful enough with her and that I was sorry.

But instead, I said: I trust you, little girl. If you feel you'd be happier there—go for it.

Thank you, Daddy, she said. And for the first time in four years, she hugged me.

A quick hug. Hesitant. Reserved.

| | |

I drove to Sde Boker slowly.

Dikla was engrossed in her phone, texting busily to someone.

Shira fell asleep. Or pretended to be asleep. Which dealt a death blow to any chance I could catch a glimpse of her face.

When we arrived, she wanted to say goodbye at the gate.

But the suitcases, I said.

I'll manage, she said, putting an end to the conversation.

Then there were another few seconds of silence. And desert wind. And the wait for a divine voice to come from the heavens as it did when Abraham was about to sacrifice Isaac: Lay not thy hand upon—

Then she kissed us both on the cheek.

And said to Dikla, Mom, don't cry. It doesn't suit you.

We remained standing in front of the gate for a few seconds. Watching as she walked away. Then we got into the car and sat there in silence. Not speaking. Not moving. For quite a while.

You'll definitely write about this trip, won't you, Dikla finally said.

What? Where is that coming from now? I said.

But she chuckled and said, I hope you'll at least write the truth.

The truth?

I know you. You'll add a quote from some poet. Describe the desert. Do everything not to incriminate yourself. Oops, sorry—not to incriminate "the character of the father" in the story.

Incriminate myself? In what, exactly?

Are you serious?

Explain it to me, incriminate myself in what?

When, in your opinion, did we begin to lose Shira?

It wasn't a specific moment, Diki, it was an ongoing—

I'll tell you exactly when it was. When you wrote about her in that book.

It wasn't about her—

You think she's stupid?

But she never—

Read it? I know that in your fantasy, she's only supposed to read your books on her future trip to South America. But reality doesn't always line up with your fantasies.

How do you know?

I read it in her blog.

What blog?

*Ophelia's Blog.* A friend sent me a link, and after the third post, I realized it was her. Here. Read it.

From *Ophelia's Blog*:

## My Dad

*My dad tells stories. That's his profession. He tells*
*stories to other people. And sometimes to himself.*
*Let's say he really loves to tell himself that he's a good*
*person. And a good dad. And if something doesn't fit*
*that image, he ignores it. For example, if he takes*
*things from his daughter's private life and puts them*
*in his book without asking her permission, he'll tell*
*himself that he's disguised it enough so that no one will*
*notice. He really loves that word "disguised," my dad,*
*and he's right. When the book came out, no one really*
*noticed that he stole from his daughter's soul. Except*
*for his daughter, who read a passage from the book on*
*the Internet. And didn't say anything about it to him*
*because the moment she realized that anything she tells*
*him might appear later in one of his books, she doesn't*
*want to share anything with him anymore.*

## My Mom

*Mysterious. I wish I could be as mysterious as my*
*mom. And regal. I have a kind of ordinary walk, and*
*she always moves like a dancer, straight and tall.*
*I can't hide my feelings. If I love someone, I have*
*hearts in my eyes. But she—she doesn't give of herself*
*easily. Only in small doses. And only to someone she*
*really likes. Let's say, I have about ten girlfriends and*

*though I divide bits of me among them, I actually*
*feel alone most of the time. My mother only has two*
*friends, Gaia and Hagit, but they are really close. In*
*any case, she's fine with being alone. She's not afraid*
*of it. And she always seems to be holding on to a secret.*
*That's probably why Dad and other men are crazy*
*about her. I think her secret is that she doesn't know*
*how to be happy. But I'm not sure.*

### My Mom and my Dad

*They once loved each other very much. I tell that to my*
*sister, Noam, and she doesn't believe it. So I tell her that I'm*
*the oldest and I've been in the house the longest, so she has*
*to believe me. There used to be things like this too: Dad and*
*Mom do a slow dance in the living room after Friday-night*
*dinner. Dad and Mom laugh their heads off in the middle of*
*the night. Dad and Mom go on vacation alone and leave us in*
*Ma'alot with Grandpa. They don't go on vacation alone any-*
*more. And there's always a kind of tension in the house, mostly*
*in the area of the kitchen and the living room. As if, any min-*
*ute, something's going to fall and break. That's another reason*
*I want to move to Sde Boker.*

———

I don't remember anything about the drive back. Only
that, at some point, it started to pour. And all at once, it
stopped completely when we reached our street. The wipers
kept working. Of all the songs in the world, David Bowie's

"Absolute Beginners" was playing on the radio. We stayed in the car for another few seconds. We didn't speak. We had the feeling that when we stepped out of the car, we would be stepping into a totally different life.

*Why are there no Japanese in your books?*

Because of what they did to David Bowie in *Merry Christmas, Mr. Lawrence.*

Writing is sometimes (perhaps always?) an attempt (destined to fail?) to get even.

———

Dikla was the one who introduced me to Bowie.

A few weeks after we started dating, we reached that moment when you feel secure enough about the future to ask about the past. So I asked who her first had been. David, she said.

David? I wondered. It sounded like the name of a volunteer on a kibbutz.

Bowie, she explained. Some people call him Ziggy Stardust.

Wow, I smiled, that's a pretty high standard.

I had no choice, she said, and I didn't smile. Boys in Ma'alot never gave me a second glance.

They probably wanted you but were scared, I said.

No they didn't, she said. They just wanted other girls. More easygoing ones.

So . . . You hung a lot of David Bowie posters on your bedroom walls?

Posters? Are you kidding? We had a relationship, David and I.

You don't say.

I used to talk to him. Tell him things. And he opened up to me too.

What did he tell you?

I'm not sure I can say. It feels like a betrayal of David.

Are you serious?

———

Later, she gave me a quick course on David Bowie. She played all his records for me and read aloud passages from interviews with him that she kept in a special folder. People think he's a cold person, she explained, but that's absolutely not true! It's just that, people who were . . . unusual or not accepted when they were kids never forget it and always feel a little Major Tom.

———

We watched *Merry Christmas, Mr. Lawrence* the way people watch *The Rocky Horror Picture Show*. Again and again and again. And again. And at every viewing, we added another private ritual, another small interjection. Some were meant to slam the Japanese characters (Yes, commit hara-kiri! It's exactly what you deserve!), others were meant to praise Bowie (You look great in the scarf with the holes!), but most were emotional and pointless calls to Bowie and Ryuichi Sakamoto to do the impossible and act on the suppressed homoerotic attraction between them (Come on, kiss already!).

This morning, after I dropped Noam off at school, they played "The Man Who Sold the World" on the radio, and when the song ended, the announcer said that Bowie had died.

I hurried home to Dikla. I thought I'd find her crying and pictured how I would console her. But when I got there, the house was empty. She'd gone to work. I waited a few hours so as not to be the bearer of bad news, and then I texted her: Sorry for your loss. She replied: Sad. And when she came home in the evening, she said she'd bought tickets for Yoav Kutner's lecture on Bowie at the Eretz Israel Museum on Friday morning. She didn't think Kutner would have much to tell her that she didn't already know, but maybe it would do her good to be in the same room with other people who loved David. Maybe she'd be able to cry. I'd be happy to go with you, I said. She replied that she had already asked Gaia, her hydro-therapist, to go with her. But we could find out if tickets were still available. There was nothing malicious in her tone, she's not like that. She wouldn't deliberately say something to hurt me. It was just the situation at the time: I wasn't the first option on her list.

In the end, Gaia stood her up. I swallowed my pride and went with her. Friday morning. The Eretz Israel Museum. A talk in the lecture-series style. The tickets were waiting for us at the box office. We went into the auditorium expecting to see people our age. But it was mainly pensioners sitting in the seats. What did they have to do with my David—I knew that Dikla was thinking the same thing and I saw that small, familiar wrinkle of disappointment that went from her mouth downward. Actually, we're not much younger than they are, I thought. Kutner came onto the stage. Showed us the album cover of *Space Oddity* and played the title song for us. The sound was good. I put my hand on Dikla's. She didn't return the caress or the pressure, but she didn't move her hand either. Kutner played "Jean Genie" and talked about the differences between psychedelic folk and rock-and-roll blues. For whoever cares, I thought. Then he showed us the cover of *Hunky Dory*, the album that has "Life on Mars?" on it, and played "Changes," saying that changes was a motto for Bowie. Never repeat yourself as an artist. Always do the opposite of what people expect from you. Dikla nodded slightly at his words. And she's not a nodding sort of person. A lecturer can evoke a nod from her only if he says something super-exact. After *Ziggy Stardust*, Kutner talked about Bowie's film career, told the audience that in another minute, he would be screening a scene from *Merry Christmas, Mr. Lawrence*, and said a few words about the behind-the-scenes of the movie. Dikla's hand moved almost imperceptibly under mine. Of all the scenes in the world, he had chosen the one we loved most, the one we used to rewind to see again and again. The parade ground. All the prisoners are standing in groups of three. Sakamoto, the camp commander, is about to vent his anger on them. His long sword is ready. Then Bowie steps out from the line. Walks up to him, his head held high. Stops in front of him—and touches his shoulder gently. The startled Sakamoto pushes him to the ground, but Bowie is not defeated. He stands up again, takes hold of Sakamoto's shoulder, but this time moves his face close to his—eyes to eyes, lips to lips.

Come on, kiss him already!—Dikla and I shouted in the middle of Kutner's lecture, part of a series, in the Eretz Israel Museum on a Friday morning—Kiss him!

Heads turned toward us. Mouths shushed us. Dikla took my hand and said to me, Come on. We stood up to leave. The entire row grumbled and stuck their feet out to trip us. To slow us up. In the background, Kutner kept talking about Bowie's transformation into a pop star in the eighties, and we heard the opening, slightly clichéd notes of "Modern Love."

We escaped from the auditorium. Out onto the lawn. The open air. Laughing. Laughing hysterically. Dikla's laughter slowly turned into tears. Her shoulders shook. I hugged her. I held her close to my chest. Every spot on her body had a sister spot on mine. Everything was touching. She said, Enough, it's pathetic, crying for someone I didn't know. It's pathetic. I didn't cry for my mother like this, she said. I didn't say anything to her. I just kept stroking her hair. Then we walked to the car with our arms around each other, feeling as if we were inside a bubble. I hoped it was a sign of the future. I feared it was only a flashback.

### Why don't you write about the Holocaust?

He came up to me at the end of the lecture. A dignified-looking man. In a tuxedo. The head of the Jewish community in a large German city. He held it in both hands, not one.

As a token of our esteem—he said, as if he were giving a speech, though he was speaking only to me—we would like to present you with the autobiography of a member of our community, Marcus Rosner.

Thank you, I said.

He handed me the book and added, in a different, more tentative tone: Marcus is . . . a survivor.

Thank you very much, I said and bowed my head. I am most grateful.

———

Hardcover. Very hardcover. Nine hundred and thirty-six pages. In German. Here and there, an old black-and-white photo. Here and there, a drawing. Ugly. Distorted. Repellent. His handiwork, apparently. On the back cover, a brief text and small photo of him taken on his wedding day in the ghetto. There was no bride in the frame, not even a veil, but from the poles of the wedding canopy being held by three unsmiling men, you could tell it was a wedding. Marcus Rosner himself stood in the center, wearing a gray cap, glancing at the person who looked nothing like a rabbi but was apparently presiding over the ceremony. Maybe the head of the Judenrat?

The next morning, I tried to get Marcus Rosner's huge volume into my suitcase but couldn't manage it. I swear, I just couldn't manage it. The zipper wouldn't close, really.

Then the phone in my room rang and it was Thomas, who had been sent by the publisher to escort me, calling from reception to say that the taxi was waiting, we had a train to catch and we already missed one train because of me.

I don't like saying it, but I write really well on German trains.

There's room under each pair of seats, the German countryside at the end of winter—bare trees—isn't spectacular enough to distract me, no one speaks loudly on his cell, no one recognizes me from reserve duty, from the university, from my ad agency days, there's no one to greet me with hi bro, what's happening, what's up, what's new, man.

———

I was in the middle of a letter to Dikla when the phone rang. The head of the Jewish community was on the line.

We enjoyed your lecture very much yesterday, he said.

Thank you, I replied in my most modest voice.

To tell you the truth, he continued, when you sent us the title, "How and Why I Discovered I Was a Jewish Writer," we were a bit surprised. After all, you were born Jewish, so what was there to discover? And yet . . . you opened our eyes.

Thank you very much.

I'm calling you about a different matter.

Yes.

The reception desk in the hotel called us.

I see.

It seems that you forgot Marcus Rosner's book in your room.

Oh my God.

Oh my God if he finds out. Imagine the insult.

Of course.

I sent a messenger posthaste to the hotel you will be staying at tonight.

Thank you very much, thank you from the bottom of my heart.

Naturally, I won't tell Marcus. Just confirm by return e-mail that you have received the book.

———

I swear that this time, I fully intended to cram the book into my suitcase after it arrived with a messenger as promised, but the next day was Saturday, and all the stores in the city are closed on Sunday, so I had to buy all the presents for the kids, I had no choice, each one wanted something else, and Noam asked for high, pink boots, which barely fit into the suitcase, so it was either the pink boots or Marcus Rosner's autobiography, and the phone in my room rang, and I knew it was Thomas, sent by the publisher to escort me, calling from reception to tell me that the taxi was waiting, and we'd already missed two trains because of me, and Noam was going through a difficult period anyway, what was happening between me and Dikla had affected her, even though she didn't talk about it, and girls that age can be so

cruel to each other, and the whole business of outward appearances is critical to their self-esteem, and if I come home
without the boots, she'll be so disappointed—

Having no choice, and with a heavy heart, I made a
*selektzia*. I shoved Marcus Rosner's autobiography way
under the bed and left.

———

The train had almost reached the final station and I was
close to finishing the letter to Dikla—when the phone rang.

The tone of the head of the Jewish community was
hostile this time, even threatening, but the content remained
matter-of-fact.

The book. You forgot it again. Luckily, the hotel owner
is Jewish, so he had the sense to call me. Marcus called as
well, by the way. To ask what you said about his book. I
didn't tell him. Of course not. As it is, his health is failing. A
thing like this could finish him off. You writers, your minds
are always somewhere else, aren't they? I sent another messenger to the next hotel you will be at. At my own expense.
Certainly at my own expense. But this time, if you will
forgive me, will be the last, yes?

———

The next morning, I didn't give up. There was no way
I could get the book into my suitcase without taking something out, so I removed two shirts, a pair of socks, a slimmer

volume I had brought with me, and also a raincoat I especially loved, and left them in the hotel room. I put Marcus inside. He had suffered enough.

In his wedding picture, he had actually tried to smile, but the corners of his smile drooped. And the men holding the poles of his wedding canopy looked terrified. As if standing outside the frame were armed Germans making sure that the head of the Judenrat didn't deviate from the rules of the ceremony. As if, when the event was over, they shot everyone and didn't notice that under the pile of corpses, the groom was still breathing.

––––––

With a clear conscience, I reached the airport check-in with Marcus Rosner's autobiography safely tucked in my suitcase. But my suitcase turned out to be overweight. By four kilos.

It's only four kilos, I pleaded with the Aryan clerk.

That's a three hundred Euro fine, she persisted.

Look, I said, pulling the book out in front of her, the only reason I'm over the limit is this book, I received it as a gift, I explained, and added, in a different, more subdued tone, the writer is ... a survivor. The only one in his family to survive his wedding. They shot all of them right after the ceremony.

A three hundred Euro fine, sir, she repeated, or one of the following two options: Leave the book in the airport or board the plane with it.

From that moment on, Marcus Rosner's autobiography was my constant companion. Although the security check separated us briefly—the autobiography slid under the scanner while I went through the physical check—we reunited immediately after that. Together, we wandered through the duty-free shops, only looking, not buying, and finally, we sat down together for a cup of coffee at one of the airport cafés. I put Marcus Rosner's autobiography on the table, next to my cup. I thought I would browse through it a bit, maybe find some clue to the identity of the bride, who was absent from the wedding photo on the back cover, after all, Marcus Rosner couldn't have married the head of the Judenrat, but the book was so heavy that the table began to wobble and I didn't want the coffee to spill, God forbid, and stain the drawings inside—twisted limbs, twisted faces, piles of ears—so having no other option, I put the book on the floor, next to my right foot.

I drank my coffee and thought about the letter I was writing to Dikla. About its final paragraph. I knew it would surprise her to receive a real letter from me, with an envelope and a stamp—that hadn't happened since South America—but I also knew it would not be enough by itself, that the final paragraph was crucial if I wanted that letter to be not a requiem but a turnabout. And finally, it began to play in my mind—after all those days, I realized how I wanted to end that letter. Not with lines from an Agi Mishol poem. With lines from a Jacques Brel song. *"I will invent meaningless words for you, which you will understand."*

I could claim that that's why I forgot the book.

But the truth is that I remembered Marcus Rosner's autobiography the minute I walked out of the café.

The truth is that I still could have turned around, gone back inside, bent down, and picked it up from the floor. Five steps at the most, a quick bend of my knees—

But something inside me protested. One of my spite muscles stretched and made me leave. (Apparently the same muscle that had been at work in my senior year in high school when I had to write an essay entitled "My Thoughts on Joining the Army," causing me to write that I wasn't exactly thrilled about it. That I would go, naturally, but like a sheep to the slaughter. The literature teacher was shocked by my choice of words, justifiably so, and I was called down to the assistant principal's office for an urgent talk.)

Several days after I returned to Israel, the doorbell rang. At the time, whenever that happened, I was afraid there was a messenger with divorce papers on the other side of the door. It's true that Dikla isn't like that, but ever since I answered a question in this interview by making up the story about a messenger with divorce papers appearing at the studio in Givat Chen, I've been afraid that it would become the sort of self-fulfilling prophecy that terrifies writers.

Standing at the door was a FedEx messenger.

He was holding a package with both hands.

Inside the package, along with Marcus Rosner's autobiography, was a letter from the head of the Jewish community. Please note, he wrote, how exciting and unique is the fate of our people. A Jewish man forgets a book in an airport and boards a plane. What are the chances that the book will return to him from its exile? But lo and behold, another Jewish man sits down at precisely the same table. And it turns out that this Jew is a relative of the head of the community that had given the book as a gift. The relative reads the dedication, puts two and two together, and calls me. And so messengers and the angels of FedEx leave here and arrive there, and in the words of Jeremiah, the sons have returned home. The book has been returned to its owner in the Holy Land. Tell me—is it not clearly a miracle? Proof that our people are able survive the most terrible catastrophes and will endure for all of eternity?

I carried the book to the shelves that held my Israeli books.

There was no room for even a pamphlet on the shelf that held Holocaust books, second-generation Holocaust books, and third-generation Holocaust books. But then, with the imposing image of the head of the Jewish community looming large in my mind, I shoved some books on the shelf below it to the right, and a few Scandinavian thrillers to the left, and lost Marcus Rosner's autobiography among them. For all eternity.

*In recent years, there has been a rash of thrillers, mainly Scandinavian, but not only. Are you tempted to write a thriller?*

No. In a thriller, it's clear that someone has sinned, and the only question is when he will be caught. The real suspense—which I find fascinating to write about—is whether our sins are in fact sins. And how the hell can we tell?

The Scandinavian thriller writer Axel Wolff did not stop drinking during our meal together in Jerusalem. His face flushed, his eyes grew red, and when dessert arrived, he began to cry, really sob. Between one sob and the next, he managed to say that he was going through a crisis. With his wife. Since what-happened-in-Colombia-and-didn't-stay-in-Colombia, she didn't want to read his manuscripts. And he was totally dependent on her opinion. Between the lines, I understood that she was also the one who rescued him from writer's block with the help of brilliant plot ideas that only someone free to advise from the sidelines can come up with.

I poured him a glass of water.

He drank, and then suddenly began to speak to me in Swedish.

I should have known that was not a good sign, but I kept nodding as if I understood and tried to follow the music of the words in an effort to get a sense of the content.

It continued for several minutes: He spoke to me in Swedish and beat his chest in self-righteousness, or anger, and I did a free translation in my mind.

Then he collapsed.

I hadn't seen anyone's body go so quickly from upright to prone since Haim Huri fell onto the grass in the middle of the Memorial Day ceremony our senior year in high school.

I hurried over to him and tried to pick him up from the floor, but he was too heavy. A real Viking. Waiters rushed over to help me, and together we managed to carry him to the couch in the restaurant foyer. Someone unbuttoned the top button of his shirt, someone else lifted his legs. In response, his eyes still closed, he mumbled the same sentence in Swedish over and over again, "*Yag dödade honom, yag dödade honom, yag dödade honom . . .*" I asked the waiters to call an ambulance, but before it arrived, he had already opened his eyes, buttoned his shirt so that it was still about to burst open on his huge chest, and began speaking English again. He insisted that there was no need to take him to the hospital. That's how he is, he explained. Sometimes his body has to shut down totally before it can restart. And look, he can stand up, even walk a straight line. Okay, not ruler-straight but quite straight, he said. And he has a colleague from Israel with him who will make sure he gets to his hotel and into bed. That's all he needs now, a good bed with clean white sheets, and tomorrow morning, a short espresso. Two at the most. And he's all set. Really. Believe him.

In the taxi, he stretched his legs comfortably and fell asleep, so I couldn't ask him what the hell *Yag dödade honom* meant.

I called Dikla to tell her I'd be home late.

She didn't answer. My wife has been screening my calls for the last few weeks. My wife. Screening my calls. And she no longer dresses in front of me. Or tells me anything about what's going on at work. Only by accident did I find out that she'd been promoted. So gifted. My wife. So distant.

I supported Axel all the way from the lobby to his room, until he fell onto the bed, fully dressed. There were three bottles of liquor from the minibar on the bedside table. All empty. Right after I made sure that his snores were just snores and not death rattles, I went over to his laptop, which was open on the desk, and typed *Yag dödade honom* into Google Translate.

No results.

Then it occurred to me to write *yag* with a *j* instead of a *y*.

The translation appeared immediately: I killed him.

A moment later, there was a knock on the door. Not on the front door. On the other, hardly ever used door that connects a hotel room to the adjacent one.

### How long did it take you to write your last book?

Actual writing time—three months.

Total time—three years.

In the middle, many other things stole my attention: Yanai's entrance into first grade, trips to Sde Boker with night-vision equipment to make sure Shira was all right, Sirkin's run for party head that required a new catchphrase almost every day, long testimony I was forced to give in the police investigation in Sweden, and of course, the search for Hagai Carmeli in the Rosh Pina area.

It began with Ari, who said that someone who visited him in the hospital said he saw Hagai wandering around Rosh Pina. Ari couldn't remember who the person was and apologized: It's those painkillers. They space me out.

Could you have dreamed it? I asked.

Anything's possible, Ari said, and scratched his bald head. A bit embarrassed.

Still, because there was a small chance, because I have a deep respect for dreams, and because the air in my house smelled of separation anyway—the invitations to the bat mitzvah had already been sent—I enlarged a photo of Hagai Carmeli from our high-school yearbook ("Our Hagai / he's a real blast / took his driving test seven times / and still hasn't passed"), raced along the winding road between Acre and Safed, rented a cheap room in Rosh Pina, and began my search. I started in the town itself. I asked people, showed them the picture. On the trees in the area of the Ja'uni café I hung a few photos of him, along with detachable tabs showing my phone number. I went down to the mall, the gas station, the minimarket next to the gas station. No one recognized Hagai, but I had a gut feeling. If I were playing the hot/cold game, I just knew the other players would be saying, "Getting hotter . . . getting hotter."

On the second day, I drove up to the hills above Rosh Pina with a tent, a sleeping bag, and a one-piece snowsuit that Ari once filched during reserve duty. It was freezing cold, but that didn't stop me. I kept searching for Hagai in crevices and tunnels and forests as, above me, a flock of cranes migrated south. I waited for his rust-colored hair to suddenly appear among the fallen leaves. For a sunbeam to reflect off the thick lenses of his glasses. I imagined us sitting beside a campfire and talking. Unplugged. Like we used to.

———

*Dysthymia?* he asks.

I explain it to him. *It's kind of like a permanent sadness, on a low flame, that lasts for a long time without sliding into real depression.*

*Or maybe it's the opposite?*

*What do you mean?* I ask.

*That starting at a certain age, it's harder to feel joy.*

———

*You know what the problem is about living with the same woman for years, Carmeli?*

*I have no idea, man, I never have.*

*That her expression when she looks at you gets wearier. And dimmer.*

*I don't understand, what do you want, to be admired?* he asks.

*A little. Why not?*

———

*Nothing happened in Colombia.*

*No?*

*That journalist really did come to the hotel with me. And we went up to the room, and I poured wine from the minibar for us. But then, Yanai, my youngest, called and asked what kind of present I was bringing back for him, and after I spoke to him, I couldn't do it. I couldn't get hard.*

*I don't understand, so why did you tell Dikla that something happened?*

*I was hoping it would shake her up a little. That it would make her look at me the way she used to.*

*Or you hoped to bring things to a rapid end.*

*How I've missed your way with language, Carmeli—*

*In any case, you're an idiot.*

*I know.*

———

*Or maybe there was another reason—*

*A reason for what?*

*For confessing to something that didn't happen.*

*Okay, what?*

*It's just a better story. More dramatic. Look, now you have a crisis to be stressed about, something you've always liked.*

———

At night, I walked along the goat paths above Rosh Pina and looked for campfires that Hagai Carmeli might have sat beside. My nostrils searched for the smell, my eyes for the flames, and my ears for the sound of crackling twigs.

---

I didn't shave for a few days. I washed in springs but I didn't shave. My beard grew wild and I enjoyed running my hand through the soft stubble.

So many years had passed since I allowed myself to not shave. So many years of being too smooth. It was clear to me that Hagai Carmeli, if he were alive, had a beard. I have no explanation for that, I just knew it. A reddish, pointed beard, better-groomed than mine. I imagined our meeting, beard to beard. We probably wouldn't hug, he's unhuggable, Hagai Carmeli, but I would see the happiness in his eyes and he would see the relief in mine. Then we would gather firewood and twigs, place a piece of tissue under the twigs, and use a flint to light the fire, and when the flames were steady, we'd talk, without any stupid attempts to tell each other everything that had happened in the time that had passed, we would go straight to the burning issues.

---

*And if Dikla were telling the story?*

*What do you mean?*

*Let's say it's her story and you're the character of the husband. How does it feel from her vantage point?*

*What is this, Carmeli, an exercise in a writing workshop?*

*No, idiot, it's an exercise in love.*

*Okay . . . so I think she feels . . . exhaustion.*

*Exhaustion.*

*Yes, she has no more strength.*

*For you?*

*Not just for me. If it weren't for the kids, she would go to India for a year.*

---

*Go on. What else do you see from her vantage point?*

*Something happened when she went to the desert ashram and Sde Boker. She came back different.*

*A man?*

*I don't think so.*

*A woman?*

*No, no. More like a decision. Something that became clear to her.*

| | |

*It's too bad we can't take a break.*

*A break?*

*If not for the kids, that's what we should do now. A separation of forces. Each of us should go our separate ways for a year. She should really go to India, and I should go to the Sinai, despite, or maybe because of, the warnings.*

*So do it.*

*Don't be offended, Hagai, but it's obvious you're not a father.*

———

*Will you come with me to visit Ari?*
*Of course.*
*No one but Dikla and I go to see him anymore. Would you believe it?*
*No one, no one at all?*
*At first it was an endless stream. Lots of girls. Now there's death in the air. Death has a real smell, you know?*
*Does Ari say anything about it? Does he notice?*
*You know him, he turns it into a joke. Every time I see him, he tells me about another girl he's "taking out of his will" because she stopped coming.*

———

During my second week of searching, on a night with a full moon, at the entrance to a wadi, I saw a small campfire in the distance. And someone sitting beside it.

I approached with a pounding heart.

Sitting alone near the campfire was none other than Ehud Banai, one of my favorite singers. He was wearing an Ehud Banai hat. And he had Ehud Banai stubble. And Ehud Banai glasses. He had a harmonica on his chest, Dylan-style, and he was quietly strumming his guitar.

With a look, I asked if I could sit down next to him, and he responded with a glance that I could.

I listened to him play for a long time.

We didn't exchange a word. It seemed inappropriate.

He didn't play familiar songs that I could sing along to, only instrumental passages, without plots. One of them reminded me of the opening sounds of "You Touched the Treetops," but it quickly dispersed into a different melody. More random.

I made an assumption: Maybe he'd come back here after years to remind himself how it all began, to commune once again with that innocent place before the applause began.

But I had no way to verify that assumption.

The ground groaned.

Time traveled.

I was filled with a sense of deep serenity as Ehud Banai strummed his guitar.

Flocks of cranes continued to migrate south, even at night. But a bit more quietly.

Finding Hagai Carmeli is not the most important thing, I thought. The most important thing is to keep searching.


*In your opinion, will people continue to read books in the future?*

People will continue to need stories.

And storytellers like me will continue to need people.

It's possible that books in the form we're familiar with now will disappear from the world. But who knows? Maybe the new form will be cooler?

Soundtracks, for example. It drives me crazy that I can't add soundtracks to my texts.

This interview, let's say? I'd begin with a bold beat. In a loop. To be slowly joined and enriched by sadder instruments. In the paragraph about Ehud Banai, I would simply put the sound of him playing in the background. Because no matter how I describe Ehud Banai's strumming, it will never be like hearing Ehud Banai's strumming.

The same thing with dancing.

I can write many pages describing the way Dikla dances. I can look for totally original phrases and juggle super-ingenious images. But if there were a way now, this minute, to add a short clip, thirty seconds, no more, of her dancing, eyes closed, to the sounds of "Come on Eileen" at the Kibbutz Cabri club in 1995, everyone would understand immediately why I began dancing beside her in the hope she would open her eyes at the end of the song. And if there were a technology that enabled readers to smell while reading, they would be able to sniff the nape of her neck when I press up against her from the back at night as she sleeps. I can write that it's similar to the smell of challah being baked for the Sabbath. But it wouldn't be like actually sniffing the nape of her neck.

Readers say, "I really got into the book." But what if it were possible, virtually, to enter into the reality of a book? To be a fly on the wall, a dog lying on the floor, a smoke detector in the light fixture—

In the bedroom that Dikla and I share. The night I came home from Colombia, let's say. Oh, then the reader could see whether my lower lip really trembled slightly, signaling a lie, when I told her what happened in Colombia. Whether the look in her eyes showed that she believed me. Whether she threw me out of the house or we stayed in the same house and the same bed, awake all night, without touching each other. Without exchanging a word.

**Do you write in the morning or at night?**

I try—but don't always succeed—to write in the morning.

At night, I'm with Yanai and Noam. And once a week, I get into the car, supposedly to drive to a lecture, but actually to drive to Sde Boker to observe Shira.

I take along Ari's military snowsuit and the night-vision equipment he forgot to return when he was in basic training. He's the only person who knows that I drive to Sde Boker to spy on my daughter. He thinks I'm totally screwed up, and that instead of hiding in the bushes, I should just knock on her door and tell her I want to speak to her. I tell him that he doesn't understand anything because he's not a dad, and that children sometimes need to distance themselves from their parents so they can find themselves. Especially if they had a strong, maybe too strong, connection to him. To them, I mean. He doesn't comment on my Freudian slip. But he rolls his Indian eyes at me. I have to respect her boundaries,

I try to convince him, and he says, Great, bro, so why do you always drive down there? Ah, no, I explain, that's because I miss her.

———

I have a permanent observation point. That I can't reveal here.

A bit after seven in the evening, the kids leave the dining hall and head for the living quarters. Then I have a little more than a minute to watch her through Ari's binoculars, and guess how she is from the way she walks, from the movement of her hands as she speaks—strong, like her mother's—from the responses of the people walking beside her.

In a bit more than a minute of walking, she smiles more than she did during her entire last year at home. Her clothes are much lighter, airier. She has switched from painfully tight jeans to sharwals. From leather jackets to T-shirts with sayings printed on them. All in all, she looks good. I mean, she seems happy. I'd like to think that it's the desert that's making her bloom. But it's probably the distance from us.

———

Yesterday, I became anxious when she didn't come out of the dining hall. Her girlfriends did. Her boyfriend, Nadav, did. But she didn't.

I watched Nadav through the binoculars to see if he was using her absence as an excuse to flirt with other girls.

The kids walked off to their rooms, and ten minutes later, all the lights in the dining hall were turned off. What happened to my little girl? Why didn't she go to eat? Where is she? In her room? And maybe not? Maybe she's already left the school and I'm the only idiot who doesn't know it? Bottom line, if she asked Dikla not to tell me about Nadav, how can I be sure that there aren't other things she asked Dikla to hide?

I couldn't call Dikla. Because then I'd have to explain what I was doing there in the dark.

I couldn't knock on the door of her room. Because I wasn't wanted.

I couldn't question her friends either. Obviously, they would tell her immediately that her father was wandering around, bothering them with questions. And that would be the end of me.

A cold wind penetrated my snowsuit and I decided to risk walking in the direction of her room. Maybe I'll be lucky and no one will see me, I thought. Maybe I'll be lucky and her curtain will be open. That way, I can look inside and at least see if she's there. If she's alive.

I sprinted from building to building, from bush to bush, and trying to show myself as little as possible, I crossed an area filled with junk and picnic tables. Finally, I reached my destination. I circled the building and the yard it shared with other buildings to get to the window, but when I did, the curtain was closed. I couldn't see what was happening inside from any angle.

Then she came out. When I heard the door open, I moved cautiously toward the path in the front yard. She was holding her cell phone close to her ear, but when she saw me, she said, Just a minute, I'll get right back to you, then opened her eyes wide and asked: Dad, what are you doing here?

Instead of replying, I knelt down and said: I'm sorry, Shira, please forgive me. She looked around and then said, Dad, get up, don't embarrass me. I asked if I could come in. She nodded slowly and we went into her room and talked. Finally, we talked.

———

All that happened in my imagination. In reality, I retreated through the shadows to my car and drove home with a heavy heart. When I walked in, Dikla was on the phone. From her tone, I could tell it was Shira on the other end, and from the content, I understood that she wasn't feeling too well. She had a cold. Nothing serious. Nadav was taking good care of her.

**_Do you ever feel like changing or correcting your books after they've been published?_**

Usually, after a book comes out, I regret not having deleted more. Sometimes, when I read from my books to an audience, I edit them: take out a word here, a paragraph there.

But there's one story I would cut completely. All of it. The one that Shira came across on the Internet.

It takes place in Haifa, in the eighties, and the protagonist is a sixteen-year-old girl who is in love with a boy a year ahead of her in school. That boy is tall and handsome and popular and doesn't notice her at all. So, under the influence of the romantic movies she watches with her mother on pirated cable channels, she decides to do something about it. Her mother tries to dissuade her, tells her that men don't like that kind of woman, but one night, she stands under the boy's window with a guitar and serenades him with the cover of the Smiths' song "Last Night I Dreamt That Somebody Loved Me," over and over again. Neighbors open their shutters and shout at her, Enough! But she keeps singing. People walking their dogs so they can do their business stop near her. And she keeps singing. A dog pees on her, and she keeps singing. Until a kid who lives in the building begins to feel sorry for her and wakes up the father of the boy she's in love with, who goes out onto the balcony and tells her that the boy isn't in, he's at his girlfriend's place. So shut it down and go home, he says. She doesn't go home. She continues to sit in the street and play until the kid who shouted to the boy's father calls her mother. When she arrives, wearing an Adidas tracksuit and an old-man's undershirt, she doesn't reprimand her, doesn't say "I told you so." She just sits down next to her until the sun rises over Haifa Bay and the stench from the oil refineries fills their nostrils, as the kid from the building looks longingly at the girl.

---

If Shira agreed to talk to me, this is what I would tell her:

I'm sorry I hurt you. I'm sorry I published that story. But I just want you to know—

That girl standing under the window is me.

You and I are alike. More alike than you think.

That's why you saw yourself in the story, and it infuriated you.

And that's apparently why you have to distance yourself from me now.

And that's okay. I mean, it hurts, but it's okay—

### *What kind of father are you?*

So what brings you to me?

Our son, Yanai.

Tell me a little about him. How old is he?

Seven.

Second grade?

First. We kept him in kindergarten another year. He was born in December. We thought he wasn't mature enough yet.

I understand.

We were wrong, of course. I am a parent, therefore I err. But that's not why we're here.

So why are you here today?

The boy—how can I put it nicely—is a liar.

I understand.

No, you don't. You can't believe a word he says.

Children sometimes tend to blur the boundaries between truth and imagination. You must certainly be aware of that.

No blurring and no boundaries. The kid's a liar. You want an example?

You can give an example, but I'm asking myself—

I ask him whether he did his homework, okay? So he says yes, and it turns out that he didn't. I ask him whether he saw the TV remote, and he says no, but it turns out that he hid it in the crack between the couch cushions.

I understand. Is it possible that what you call "lies" are, in fact, means—age-appropriate means, by the way—of bypassing or denying the difficulties life poses for him?

Terrific interpretation. Really, hats off to you. And how does that explain the fact that in the shoe store, he insists that he wears size thirty-seven, when he barely fills a size thirty-five? That he tells his teacher he was born in America and came to Israel when he was two years old? That he tells the kids in the playground his name is Nimrod? That his surname is Ben-Yochna? We don't know anyone whose surname is Ben-Yochna. The kid just can't stop lying. He was always like that, but this last year, it's gotten completely out of control.

And is that so . . . bad?

Excuse me?

I'm asking myself why you, both of you, experience as a tragedy the fact that your son isn't always faithful to the truth?

What do you mean? What if his sister learns from him? What if we all start lying? What would life in our home be like? There's a kind of contract between people in the world that they will try—they don't always succeed, but they try—to tell the truth. Our ability to trust each other is built on that foundation. If you pull that card out, the entire tower falls.

I understand. If that's the situation, I have to ask you if the tendency to lie . . . has appeared in the family before.

What? No. Of course not.

Why are you smiling, Dikla?

Because it's amusing how a person who likes to think he's self-aware can be so totally clueless about himself.

Meaning?

My husband is a writer. So when it comes to everything related to habitual lying—

Hold on, Diki, that's not fair—

You're addicted. You think of your life as a story. You think of me as a story. A character in a story. Once, your words had value. Today, they have as much value as Yoram Sirkin's words.

That's enough.

But it's true.

Your truth . . .

The objecti—

I'm stopping you for a moment. Even though I am getting the impression that there is definitely room here . . . for couples therapy. But this is neither the time nor the place.

And also . . . the price is different. Therefore, I suggest that we go back to focusing on Yanai. I'd like to know, Dikla, if Yanai already reads books on his own.

The child is a bookworm. Since he learned to read, he finishes two or three books a day. And add to that the stories his father tells him.

How many stories a day do you tell Yanai?

Let's see. There's the waking-up story. Otherwise he can't wake up. There's the daily toothbrush story. I mean, the toothbrush is a kind of creature that talks to Yanai. Then, in the car on the way to school, instead of playing a boring CD of children's songs, I tell him another story. But a short one. And another very short one on the way home from school. Then, in the early evening, there's a hammock story.

Hammock story?

We both lie in a hammock and look at the clouds. He tells me what shapes he sees, and together we make up a story based on them. Then supper, a bath, and a bedtime story.

And that's it?

The truth is that there's also "Where Is Mr. Marshmallow."

Mr. Marshmallow?

It's not really a story, more like a musical detective rhyme. Right before he falls asleep. We're walking down the street. The light is yellow. There's no time to think. Where oh where is Mr. Marshmallow?

I understand.

In the end, the kid in the story—excuse me, the musical—always finds Mr. Marshmallow, and then I pretend to eat him. Yanai, I mean. And he giggles hysterically. He's crazy about it.

So altogether—correct me if I'm wrong—you tell him seven stories a day.

The hammock song is only in the summer.

That's all he does with him, do you see?

That's not true, Dikla. And it's not fair. We also go to the supermarket together on Fridays.

When you tell him a story about the little pepper that lives inside the big pepper.

If I don't, he gets bored and drives me nuts. It doesn't count.

I ask myself—

Tell me, why do psychologists always "ask themselves"? After all, you ask us, not yourself. Why skirt around it? And what is that saxophone in the background? Your neighbors? Aren't they going a little over the top with the volume?

I wonder . . . Look, on the one hand, the picture you describe is heartwarming. It seems that you and Yanai have a lively and . . . creative bond. On the other hand, you can't dismiss out of hand the possibility that there is a line that joins the abnormal number of stories the child is exposed to and his tendency to offer his own subjective interpretations of the variegated aspects of reality.

Can you repeat that in people speak?

She's just telling you what I tell you all the time. That seven stories a day—

Six, in winter. One is only a rhymed musical detective story, so—

Five and a rhymed musical detective story—is too many. Yanai can't tell the difference between truth and fiction anymore.

Am I to blame for that too, Dikla?

It's not a question of blame.

Yes it is.

It's—

I'm stopping you. Look, I still need to meet with Yanai in order to verify my gut feeling, but it may very well be that what you call lies are, for him, only small stories. He takes pleasure in inventing those stories and in the fact that they allow him to effectuate an independent inner world—

You know, it sounds kind of cute when you say it. "Small stories." "An independent inner world." But it's not. It's not cute. It's worrying. The boy is already seven years old.

What exactly is worrying you? In developmental terms, it's still age-appropriate.

What do you mean, what's worrying me?

Look here. I realize that you're both in distress, and I'm not taking that lightly. I merely want us to be precise about the essence of that distress. What exactly is it that worries you?

We're not preparing him for the world. In the end, his lying will get him in trouble. Children will see that he's lying. Teachers will stop thinking it's charming. I want to spare him the humiliation.

And how . . . do you see it, Dikla?

I don't know. I think about it a lot. If we're seriously considering Yoram Sirkin as a candidate for prime minister—that says it all. Maybe there is no more reality. Just Photoshop. And maybe, in an upside-down kind of way, we're preparing our son extremely well for the true reality of life. Because apparently only liars can survive in a fake world and in a country where you can't believe what anyone says about anything. But then again, speaking as a mother, daily life becomes very difficult when you can't trust your own child. When you need to be suspicious of everything he says.

I can imagine.

I don't know how to react, whether to pretend I'm not paying attention, or . . . I see how the flicker of suspicion in my eyes hurts him, and that . . . makes me sad. A few weeks ago—you went to lecture in Eilat—he didn't say anything all weekend, and only when I pleaded with him to tell me why he wasn't speaking to me, did he say . . . in a small voice . . . that he was afraid . . . that if he opened his mouth . . . lies would come out.

You didn't tell me that, Dikla.

What do you want, you weren't home.

Why didn't you tell me that?

I would like to suggest something. Let's conduct an experiment that may or may not succeed. But let's try, in the coming weeks, to reduce the number of stories you tell Yanai from seven to . . . let's say three. And report to me whether it has an effect. Again, this is an experiment. I'm not promising that it will succeed. Certainly not right away. But . . . do you think you can manage it?

I don't know . . .

I understand.

I'm not really sure you do.

Then explain it to me.

I don't know anymore . . . how to be with him. Not only with him. In general, I don't know how to be in the world anymore. With Dikla too. Instead of telling her that I feel her slipping away from me, I made up a story I thought would bring her back to me. But it pushed her even farther away.

I understand.

Do you have a tissue? Isn't a psychologist supposed to have a box of tissues on her desk?

I have one.

Thank you, Dikla.

Thanks, Dikla. Sorry I'm like this, Ms. Psychologist.

It's all right. And my name is Ayala.

It's that kind of time.

I understand.

No, you don't.

Then explain it to me.

Everything . . . everything's falling apart. Tell me, am I the only one that saxophone is driving crazy? Sorry for nagging, but it sounds really close . . . is someone in the house playing the saxophone now?

To be honest, yes. My son. He's practicing.

To tell the truth, he's not bad at all.

Thank you.

It's not a compliment for you, it's a compliment for him.

I'll pass it on to him. Can I ask how old you are?

Me? Forty-two. Ah...three.

That's...age-appropriate.

What is?

That feeling that everything is destabilizing. Many people suffer from it at your age.

You know, that's exactly why I stopped studying psychology. What you just did is inexcusable.

What did I do?

You put my personal experience into a paradigm. It's offensive. It makes me feel like a statistic.

I'm sorry you feel that way. It wasn't intentional.

So what was your intention?

I believe that—

Tell me, can your son hear our conversation?

Of course not, he has no way of—

Because when I started to get angry at you, his playing got livelier. As if he were creating a suitable soundtrack.

It's purely accidental.

Let's say.

In any case, what I wanted to say is that the realization that we are not as unique as we think we are, that other people experience similar difficulties—similar, not identical—to ours, that realization can be liberating. Can perhaps even inspire us to change.

Inspire us? In what way?

I would like to remind you how we ended up having this discussion. I asked you whether you could change your routine and tell Yanai fewer stories, and you replied that you're no longer sure you know how to experience the world directly, without the intermediary of stories, right?

More or less.

When I look at the life stories of my patients, I often find that yours is the age when they are at a turning point. Amid the crisis and uncertainty, people begin again. Differently. You can find other ways to reach Yanai. There are other things you can do together as father and son. There is an opportunity here.

I'm crazy about the kid. I want him to be happy. I want him to not be lonely and sad the way I was as a child.

That's clear to me. It's clear to all of us here in the room.

Have you noticed that the saxophone sounds melancholy again? I advise you very strongly to check whether your son hasn't somehow found a way to eavesdrop on what's going on in this room.

I suggest you concentrate on your son. Both of you. Dikla, you've been rather quiet during our conversation, and I ask myself, that is, I wonder where it touches you, this discussion.

In a slightly different place.

Meaning?

Meaning, I'm not sure that the fact that he tells Yanai stories is the source of the boy's problem. It feels a bit superficial. Even dishonest.

Dishonest?

Patients also lie to their psychologists, don't they? Tell a story in which they're the bad guy to hide a story in which they're even worse.

I understand.

No you don't. Our daughter has already run away from us to a boarding school. And with the situation at home this last year . . . it's no wonder that another child of ours runs away into his imagination. How did you put it? That he uses "age-appropriate methods to bypass or deny the difficulties that reality poses for him." It's exactly that.

Can you give details?

What's the point? Whatever I tell you will be my manipulative version of reality. That's why I stopped believing in verbal therapy. I do water therapy. Once every two weeks. Gaia, my therapist, and I barely exchange a word, but my body tells her everything.

So what are you saying, Dikla, that's the reason you don't sleep with me?

I don't think this is the time or the place to—

It never is the time or the place—

I'm stopping you.

Why do you keep stopping us? Shouldn't it be the opposite, that the psychologist frees us from our inhibitions?

Perhaps, but our time is up, friends. We'll let the things that have been said here sink in. I would like to remind you that next week, I'm meeting with Yanai. Would you like to pay by check or bank transfer?

That's not what the psychologist said at the end.

Or before the end.

I can't tell the story of that session—or other events that took place in my life last year—the way they really happened. And yet—

Once out of the psychologist's building, we stopped for a moment, adjusting to being in the street. We were supposed to go our own ways—I to pick up the kids, Dikla to work. But then Dikla said, I feel like ice cream.

I think there's a good ice-cream parlor on the corner.

We walked there together, close, but not touching. We pretended to be undecided about the flavors we wanted. Until she chose tiramisu in a cup and I French vanilla in a cone. I didn't have to say "Do you remember when..." because I was sure that we both remembered when. That we both understood we were reliving a moment that had occurred at the very beginning of our relationship. A true moment, not the ones I've scattered throughout this interview to protect her privacy—

Her mother had died suddenly. A heart attack. A little while after we started dating. On the fifth day of the seven days of mourning, I drove to Ma'alot.

I wasn't sure whether she was even into me. Or whether, after a few dates, I should go to the shivah.

The house was filled with people who had come to pay their respects. She was sitting in a separate room, wearing jeans and a Bart Simpson sweatshirt. I bent down and hugged her, and she hugged me back, limply. There was no place to sit next to her, so I sat down at the far end of the room. Her friends kept coming in. I didn't know she had so many friends. The girls cried on her shoulder. The boys all seemed to be secretly in love with her. I didn't know what to do or say. I couldn't even recognize her in the photo albums that were passed from hand to hand. From a few things she had mentioned casually during our two dates, such as the fact that her father was the chef in all the factories owned by Stef Wertheimer, and that the food he cooked at home was incredibly delicious, I had gathered that she was more of a daddy's girl. But I wasn't sure.

After about an hour, I stood up to go. At the front door, I felt a hand on my shoulder. Thanks for coming, she said. And then she shook my hand, a long, lingering handshake that allowed her to place a slip of paper in my palm.

I was in the car before I had the courage to open it.

*Drive to the end of the block.*

*Wait for me at the monument.*

*I'll find an excuse and go there.*

Half an hour later, she finally appeared. Riding a bike that had a little girl's seat.

My heart went out to her. Maybe because she pedaled so slowly. So mournfully. Her pedaling was mournful.

Maybe because the wind tousled her hair.

Suddenly, I could imagine her at seven years old, at ten, a miniature of herself, a lonely kind of child. Riding her bike with no one at her side.

She reached the monument, swung an extremely long leg over the crossbar, leaned the bike against the structure without chaining it, and turned to me. She was breathing hard, her chest rising and falling, as we moved closer to each other. I didn't know if it was because of the bike riding or me. She was still so unknown to me. I had no idea whether I could hug her then. If I was allowed. She stood on tiptoe and kissed me—a quick kiss, on the corner of my mouth—and said, I feel like ice cream. It turned out that there was an ice-cream parlor in Nahariya called Penguin that she and her mother used to go to when she was a kid. It's not a little too far, Nahariya? I asked. A little, she said, but I need some air. We got there in less than twenty minutes. We barely spoke on the way, apparently words were more than she could manage. She ordered two scoops of tiramisu and I ordered one scoop of French vanilla. We stood on the street, in front of the ice-cream parlor and licked our ice cream. I took small, careful licks, and she—almost full bites. Her tongue moved quickly, greedily, shaving off one side of the cone, then switching right over to the other side.

When we finished, she asked me to take her back to her bike.

During the drive, my hand rested in hers, and when we reached the monument and got out of the car, I thought she would go straight to her bike, but then she came around the car to where I was standing and hugged me tightly for a very long time. I had never before hugged a girl who was exactly my height. I felt how every spot on my body had a sister spot on hers. Everything touched. It made me press her even closer to me. When we finally moved apart, she asked if I could come again tomorrow. I said yes. Of course. At that moment, I would have done whatever she asked me to do.

———

We hugged after the psychologist too. We finished our ice cream and, without saying a word, turned to each other all at once and hugged. Tightly. For a very long time. At that moment, I would have done whatever she asked me to do— but she didn't ask me to do anything.

### Do you believe that literature still has an influence in our world?

He walked beside me from the minute I left the auditorium. At first, I didn't notice. I was busy beating myself up about a few insipid remarks I'd made during the meeting, trying too hard to be liked. Then, when I noticed him, I thought he was walking with me because he needed to go in the same direction. When I stepped out of the school gate and he followed me, I began to realize that he was sticking close to me intentionally, like a bodyguard.

Did you want to ask me something? I asked, stopping and turning to him.

He choked. He must have thought we would walk in silence.

I studied him. A short boy. Short even relative to that age when boys come up to the waists of the girls in their class.

Black hair clipped short. Thick eyebrows. And something foreign in his face. Not from here.

I write stories too, he said, looking left and right.

Great, I said. It's wonderful that you write.

I wanted to know something, he said, looking left and right again.

Yes?

But let's keep walking, he said. I can ask you while we walk.

I thought it was a bit strange, his insistence that we keep walking. But I couldn't find a reason to refuse. So we began to walk again, I taking long steps in my black leather shoes, and he taking small ones in his dirty white sneakers, trying to keep as close to me as he could.

So what do you want to know? I asked when I saw that he was silent again.

I wanted to ask, he said, how to create the end of a story. I mean, there are a lot of beginnings in the stories I write...but I never manage to end them.

What's your name?

Yehuda.

Look, Yehuda. There are several kinds of endings, I told him. And the end is really very important, because it gives meaning to the story, and that's why endings are so hard. They're hard for everyone who writes, not only for you. I talked and talked, very passionately, until I realized he wasn't listening. His eyes were searching frantically for something I couldn't see.

I stopped talking.

We kept walking down the long path from the school gate to the parking lot. Tall bushes grew wild on both sides of the path. Suddenly a vague sense ran through me, like chills, that someone was watching us through them, but I dismissed it.

Tell me, Yehuda asked quickly, as if he were trying to get rid of the words, when you write, do you decide on the subject of the story in advance?

My suspicion, that he wasn't really interested in a reply, grew stronger. That question had already been asked during the meeting with the students, so why was he asking it again? I answered anyway. On the slim chance that it really was important to him. I told him that in stories, as opposed to essays, there is no real subject, it's more like a question that preoccupies the writer, and sometimes, while he's writing, that question turns into a different question, and he doesn't usually get answers.

Yehuda didn't even bother to mumble ah-ha. Or nod. He just didn't listen. His eyes were focused on the bushes, and then on the large dumpster we were passing.

We kept walking in silence. His shoelaces became untied, but he didn't stop to retie them. His shoulders were hunched, his hands clenched into fists, and he bit his lower lip hard. As if he's preparing for something, I thought.

When we reached the car, he stopped and said—avoiding my eyes—Thank you.

You're welcome, I said, and before he started to leave, I said: Wait.

He put his hands on his hips. And his gaze on his shoes.

Now I have a question, I said.

A question? His thick eyebrows rose in puzzlement.

Yes. I want you to explain why you walked with me. You're not really interested in my answers, so why did you ask all those questions?

No reason, he said.

I don't think it was for no reason.

You don't want to know.

But I do, I said. And thought that there was something too knowing about the phrase "You don't want to know." Too bitter for a boy.

They . . . bully me, he said quickly.

Who?

A gang of kids. From the ninth grade. They wait for me in the bushes. Every day after school, he said. I remembered our walk and his frantic eyes.

Are you the only one they bully?

Yes.

What do they want from you?

I don't know. Once, at recess, I looked at one of them and he told me not to look at him like a faggot, and that's when it started.

What do they do to you?

They drag me into the bushes and hit me.

And what do you do?

At first, I tried to hit them back, but now I lie on the ground and wait for them to get tired of it.

I leaned on the car and took a deep, heavy breath. I surveyed the bushes in the hope of seeing one of the bullies. Those chickenshits. Taking advantage of someone weaker than them. I could feel my anger rising, and I clenched my fists.

Tell me, does your dad know about this?

My dad doesn't live with us.

And your mom? She can't come to pick you up?

She works.

Do you have older brothers?

I'm the oldest.

And the principal, she knows the whole story?

Yehuda looked up at me and chuckled. She knows, but she's afraid to say anything. So she won't get a chair smashed on her head, like the last one did.

So what can be done? I asked him, and actually, myself.

Nothing. In the end, they'll get tired of it and move on to another kid.

I thought again of one of the trying-to-be-wise remarks I'd made at the meeting. "Someone who writes stories does not have the privilege of being hopeless. He has to believe that things can be changed, because there is no story without change."

But wait a minute, I said angrily. It isn't possible that nothing can be done about this. What if we go to the principal right now and talk to her?

Yehuda looked at me, disappointed.

I already told you she won't do anything. And besides, today is Tuesday.

So?

It's her day off.

Okay, so we'll go to see her tomorrow, I wanted to say. But I remembered that tomorrow I would be home, far from here.

Yehuda kicked a stray pinecone. It slid along the asphalt until it was caught under the wheels of a car.

Where do you live? I asked.

Why? he replied, looking at me suspiciously.

Will it help if I give you a ride home?

You don't have to. From here on, it's all main streets and they won't do anything to me when there are people around.

You're sure?

Yes, he said, and bent down to tie his shoelaces. Then he stood up to go.

I didn't know what else to say. Or do.

Take care of yourself, I called to him, and immediately regretted the words. I mean, that's what it was all about. He couldn't.

He kept walking, but after a few meters, he stopped and turned back to me.

I really do write stories, he said. Don't think I lied to you.

**How do you cope with the loneliness involved in writing?**

I think I've already answered that question. It seems that basic issues tend to keep bothering you.

But if there is a way to escape from the hall of mirrors, it's to devote yourself totally to others. Or in my case, to teach. To be a teacher.

For three hours, twice a week, I have the opportunity
to be with other people and *their* stories. To listen to them,
stimulate their imaginations, help them free themselves and
blossom. At this point in my life, it's my true salvation.

*What exactly do you teach in your writing workshop?*

**What is beauty**

The wife of the hostel owner

In Puerto Viejo

Sweeps the area in front of the hammocks every
morning.

———

**What is conflict**

The wife of the hostel owner

In Puerto Viejo

Where we're staying on our honeymoon

Sweeps the area in front of the hammocks every
morning.

———

**What is conflict development**

The wife of the hostel owner

In Puerto Viejo

Where we're staying on our honeymoon

Sweeps the area in front of the hammocks every
morning.

She gives me a look.

## What is plot

The wife of the hostel owner

In Puerto Viejo

Where we're staying on our honeymoon

Sweeps the area in front of the hammocks every morning.

She gives me a look and signals me to follow her.

---

## What is a turning point in the plot

The wife of the hostel owner

In Puerto Viejo

Where we're spending our honeymoon

Sweeps the area in front of the hammocks every morning.

She gives me a look and signals me to follow her.

In one of the hostel rooms she shows me black-and-blue marks and asks if we can help her get away.

### *Is it really possible to teach someone to write?*

He died a day before the last meeting of the workshop. I'm already saying this now, so there won't be any illusions. I don't remember who spoke before him when the members of the group took turns introducing themselves. I think it was a retired teacher who said something about how much she loved to read. In any case, his turn came after hers. His bald head was tanned, crisscrossed by veins and capillaries. Later I thought that men have it easier as far as that's concerned. He said: Good evening, my name is Shmuel. I have cancer and the doctors give me another few months to live. A month ago, my daughter said I should try to write. And that was the best piece of advice anyone ever gave me. I've been writing constantly for a month already. I write day and night. I write with one hand and hold the IV with the other. I just can't put my pen down.

And what do you expect from the workshop? I stuck to the routine question.

I want to finish at least one story here, he said. A story with a beginning, a middle, and an end.

| | |

He did all the homework exercises I gave. And came to every meeting. Since that workshop in a northern town was funded by the State Lottery, the participants didn't have to pay a penny. Which meant that no one felt obligated to attend regularly. Except for Shmuel. Who appeared every week, five minutes early, with a pad of yellow paper, a blue Pilot pen, an extra Pilot pen, and a dusty tape recorder to tape the session.

Most of the time, I felt I was speaking mainly to him. And he came up to me at the end of every class, leaned on his cane, and asked me to explain a point that wasn't clear enough to him. Or he came to disagree with me. It was especially difficult for him to accept that it was possible, sometimes even desirable, to use colloquial language in a literary text. Forgive me, but what you suggest means forcing the language into prostitution, he claimed. But your characters don't speak a language that was natural to them, they all sound just like the narrator, I persisted. Who said that was bad? he persisted right back. Isn't it like that in Agnon? And Amos Oz?

In the end, we reached a compromise. I suggested to him that when young people—only young people—in his stories speak to each other, he would allow them to speak the Hebrew that is natural to them. Fine, he said, but without words like . . . like . . . I can't even say them aloud!

At the end of the eighth lesson, I reminded him that he'd wanted to complete one story during the workshop and asked whether he wanted us to focus on one of the homework exercises he had already done and work on it.

He ran his hand over his bald head, slowly, as if there were still hair on it, and said that it was difficult for him to give up on a story. There are so many to tell and so little time, and whenever he's drawn to a new story, he always abandons the one he's already begun.

That's perfectly all right, I told him. But if you change your mind and decide to choose a text and develop it . . . you should hurry, because the workshop ends after two more meetings.

———

At the beginning of the ninth session, he handed me some pages and said: This is what I'd like to develop.

While the others were busy with an exercise I gave them, I couldn't resist and read the pages. It was a short story about a father helping his beloved only daughter with the final preparations for her wedding. I don't remember specific sentences. All I remember is that he managed to convey beautifully the ambivalence of the situation. And that something about the daughter's speech still wasn't natural.

When I finished reading and looked up, his chair was empty.

He returned several minutes later. But left the room again at least three more times during the lesson. His face was pale and his eyes sunken. He rested his elbows on the desk and put his head in his hands. The cane, which always stood tall at the side of the desk, fell noisily to the floor, and he didn't bend down to pick it up.

I'm sorry, he said when he approached me at the end of the lesson. I didn't feel well today. That's why I had to go out. But I recorded everything and will listen to what I missed at home.

I read your story, I said, gathering the pages that were scattered on my desk.

Well, what do you say? he asked. His voice shook. The veins on the top of his head bulged.

A very good story, I said, and handed him the pages. I'm proud of you.

Don't let me off easy—he refused to take the pages and waved his finger at me—I know you have comments. You always have comments. So tell me what they are. Don't take pity on me because I'm sick.

Look . . . I hesitated. The story is constructed well . . . but if you want to polish it . . . if it's important to you—

Of course it's important to me, he interrupted me angrily, what do you think?

It needs a bit of tweaking, just a tiny bit, in . . . the daughter's speech.

I knew it! Shmuel said—almost happily. I had a feeling that I didn't get that right. But what can I do? I just can't cope with that language, young people's language.

So maybe you should record them, I said, pointing to the tape recorder in his hand. Record young people talking and then weave the words you've recorded into the story.

Now there's an idea! Shmuel said, as if a lightbulb had gone on over his head. Not a bad idea at all!

Work on the story during the week, give it to me again at the beginning of the last session and I'll read it while you're doing your final exercises, I promised him.

It's a deal, Shmuel said.

His daughter called me a few hours before the last class and said, This is Shmuel's daughter. Dad . . . won't be coming to class today.

I asked, How does he feel?

Dad passed away, she said, this morning.

I was silent. We were silent.

Then she said, I want to thank you, in my father's name, for the workshop.

And I . . . I want to thank you . . . for encouraging him to
come.

He just needed a little push, you know.

Yes, I said, and asked, Where will you be sitting shivah?

She gave me the address.

—————

I didn't go. Ari's condition worsened that week, the doctors couldn't say whether he had a few months or a few days
left and I didn't want to take the risk. I hardly moved from
his bedside.

We met when we were fifteen, Ari and I, in the stands
behind the basket at Malcha Stadium. Hapoel was losing by
a large margin and the game was so lost that we could talk. I
mean, he imitated one of the sportscasters calling the game,
and I roared with laughter.

He taught me how to laugh, and that was one of the
greatest gifts I have ever received. Not that I didn't laugh
before that, but the basic approach to life in my home was
terribly serious and critical. It wasn't that my basic approach to life changed completely because of Ari—but
thanks to him, it took on another aspect. Suddenly, I could
find the comic side of certain situations. When I failed the
theory part of my driving test the second time—I imagined describing to him all the ridiculous questions I got
wrong. And as they were crushing my free will during basic
training in the Armored Corps on the Ovda cliffs, I collected golden moments for him: When Velkstein couldn't

stand at a ninety-degree angle because he didn't know what ninety degrees was. When the squad commander dozed off during the platoon commander's speech. I knew that on Friday night, no matter what, Ari and I would go out to the Octopus or some other bar in Jerusalem. On the way, he would drink in my little stories about the army, and when we left the bar to go to his father's car—I was the designated driver—he was totally shit-faced and would hug strangers in the street, zigzagging in that drunken walk of his. My God, how much I miss that walk now that he's bedridden, a happy walk, as if he's dribbling a basketball or as if he himself is a bouncing basketball—

————

In his hospital room, I told him about my student, Shmuel, who died before he could complete the first story he ever wrote. He listened, as always, with deep curiosity—he was curious about everything—and when I finished, he shifted in his bed and said, It beats me, all that writing stuff you people do. You, for example, since you started writing, you've become even sadder, isn't that true?

Yes.

Even Dikla has no more patience for your moods, isn't that true?

Yes.

So here's the thing. It's not the Colombian girl, because from what I know about you—and I know quite a bit—there's no way it really happened.

Apparently.

All that writing has put you in a funk. Dikla too. Because between you and me, she's no ray of sunshine either. So something in the balance between you is fucked up, isn't that true?

A nurse came in with a tray of hospital food and put it on the night table beside his bed.

No way I'm touching that, he said.

Should I get you something from downstairs? I asked.

Thanks, amigo, Ari said.

What should I get?

You know what.

Bitter Lemon?

And a roast beef sandwich.

Are you even allowed to eat roast beef?

Fuck what I'm allowed.

————

When I came back with the roast beef and the Bitter Lemon, he wasn't in his bed.

That's it, grief crash-landed inside me. It's over. They took him. And I didn't get to tell him he was a brother to me.

A second later, he emerged from the bathroom, his IV pole connected to one hand and the sports sections in the other, and said, I thought about it.

I breathed a sigh of relief. Silently. So he wouldn't feel that I was breathing a sigh of relief. Shoot, I said.

I also have something I want to finish before I go, he said. Like that Shmuel of yours in the workshop.

What?

I want to see Hapoel in the arena. After all the years of standing like ushers in Malcha, don't we deserve it?

*Yalla*, let's go.

*Yalla*, let's go.

I'm serious, but Ari—

What?

It's a bit of a cliché, isn't it? Taking a sick friend to a game?

Fuck clichés.

Okay. Can you even leave here?

Hell no.

So what . . . how?

Smuggle me out.

———

I thought he was kidding, but he called me the next day and sounded as strong and sly as the old Ari. He'd thought about it. There was a window of opportunity when the nurses changed shifts, around six in the evening. We'll pretend we're taking a stroll and then vanish into the service elevator. You, he told me, have to get two tickets to the next game. And find a car large enough to hold the wheelchair. Ah, yes, and if you can arrange direct access to the field with the wheelchair—that would be huge.

I called my former boss at the ad agency. We hadn't spoken for almost fifteen years, but I read in the papers that he sat on Hapoel's board of directors now. I told him the story and he immediately said there was no problem and I didn't have to buy tickets either. Park in the lot and call me, he said. In the same tone he once used to give me instructions.

————

Halfway up to Jerusalem, Ari talked constantly about other journeys we'd made together. Remember how we ran after the plane in Ecuador? Remember that crazy girl who bit my ear in Bolivia? Remember Oren from Hadera? But when we hit the turns on the road before the entrance to Jerusalem, he turned pale and withdrew into himself. I asked him what was wrong, and he asked whose car it was. When I told him it was rented, he said, Then there's no problem if I vomit on the upholstery, right? That scared me, and I asked whether he wanted to go back to the hospital, but he shook his head and said in a weak voice, Drive, just drive.

My former boss turned out to be a real prince. One of the managing directors was waiting for us at the gate and took us through the side entrances directly to the court, not far from Hapoel's basket. Hand over the scarf, you jerk, Ari said with a smile. I unwound if from my neck and wound it around his. We have love, and love conquers all. We looked at the stands, which were filling up. The die-hard fans sat together at one of the gates and I saw some familiar faces among them. I didn't recognize anyone else in the stands. TVs hung from the ceiling like in America, broadcasting pictures and commercials. There were more stands higher up than the others, and people—incredibly—rode an escalator to reach them. It's like Yad Eliayhu here, I said. And Ari shook his head and said, Much more beautiful.

———

Hapoel played badly. Lost balls, missed shots, scandalous defense. Everything they're famous for. That was the only thing I hadn't taken care of, I thought. I should have gone into the locker room and told the players to give it their all. For Ari. Actually, they're all Americans, or British. Please, I should have said in English, put the ball in the hoop. Do it for my friend. Maybe it's his last chance.

Ari himself waved his hands and cursed every missed shot in Spanish. He always curses in his native language when he's really pissed off. *Hijo de puta. La concha de tu madre. Burro.* And then suddenly, he said to me in Hebrew: I haven't been this angry in ages. What a blast!

His bald head glistened with sweat.

We were so close to the parquet that we could hear the players' shoes squeaking. And so close to Hapoel's bench that we could hear the coach spurring his players on during the time-out.

The management guy suddenly appeared with two bottles of water, looked at Ari, and asked him if everything was okay.

I remember that when Ari drank his water, some spilled on his red shirt. And I remember, right before halftime, Yotam Halperin scored a three-pointer out of nowhere, which made Ari rise out of his wheelchair and stretch the scarf between his hands, in the air, and the speakers blared out at the spectators: Now's the time, let's make some NOISE! And I remember that I knew, though we hadn't said a word to each other, that the announcement annoyed Ari too and made him miss the mumbled announcements at Malcha as much as I did.

After the halftime whistle, I put my hand on his shoulder and asked if he wanted anything from the cafeteria. He said, No, let's split, bro.

Are you sure? I asked, Hapoel is always better after the break—

I don't feel well, he said, putting his hand on his stomach.

———

The enormous, silent parking lot looked like a field planted with cars.

We were silent on the way back. Ari closed his eyes, but it was obvious to me that he was awake. Every once in a while, he grimaced in pain. And his hands clenched into fists.

We listened to radio updates on the game.

Hapoel lost. And the analysts agreed it was clear now that this was a crisis.

Then suddenly, Ari opened his eyes and said: This is a humiliating disease, you know? A damn humiliating disease.

After we drove into the hospital parking lot, he turned his entire body around to me and said, Thanks for taking me to the arena. Now I can close up shop.

What? I said, alarmed.

He pulled the scarf from around his neck, put it on mine, and said, You keep it.

But—I tried to object—

He ignored me and said, I have to ask you for something.

I said, Of course, anything—

And he said, Bro, I need you to help me die.


**When was the last time you lied?**

I drove back from the hospital. The last things Ari said were: "We'll do it at my place. It's safer"; "There's a nurse here who likes me. She'll get the stuff for us. I made arrangements with a private doctor who'll come afterward and sign the death certificate"; "All you have to do is give me the injection."

Those words had upset me so much that I took a wrong turn on the way home and suddenly found myself in Kiryat Ono. In the middle of a neighborhood of high-rises. At the first traffic light, I tried to type in my home address. But Waze warned me that I'm not supposed to type while driving. "I'm not the driver," I lied to it. "I'm not the driver."

(Then I thought, This whole fucking year. I haven't been the driver this whole fucking year.)

*Your books are pretty sad. Why?*

There are people whose wounds don't scab over and heal. There's a medical term for it, but right now, I don't remember it.

Those people should never cut themselves, not even once. Because there's a good chance they'll die. From the bleeding.

I'm that way—with partings.

None of them scab over. I'm still in mourning over Rakefet Kovacs, my girlfriend in the fifth grade.

The tissue of my mind doesn't close over the wound and heal it.

So it remains open, bleeding.

And new partings are added every year. More wounds bleeding sadness. There's no way to avoid them. Because, what's the alternative, to not love?

| | |

Before I started writing, that's how I lived my life, bleeding sadness from the inside. All the time.

When I began to write, I found myself dividing my pain among the characters in the books I created. Each one received its dose of sadness, to be administered when needed. And in real life, I had some room left for happiness.

Once, people used to say things to me like: You're pretty suntanned for a writer. Or: Where do you get your optimism from?

It worked for almost fifteen years.

And then, out of nowhere, or maybe out of everywhere, the dysthymia made an appearance.

I've already mentioned the bitch more than once in this interview, in response to other questions. So maybe it's time to distinguish between it and its more famous older brother: depression.

In contrast to a depressed person, who has no desire to live in general, or to have sex in particular, a person with dysthymia sometimes displays the opposite symptoms: It's actually the ongoing despondency and his difficulty in experiencing happiness in ways he had experienced it so easily in the past that lead him to search actively, sometimes even intensively, for new stimuli which, like sunbeams, might disperse the black clouds enveloping his consciousness.

In other words, a depressive person has already given up the hope of feeling and is already steeped in the darkness of submission. A dysthymic person, on the other hand, searches desperately, even in his dreams, for deliverance.

**What is the best advice you ever received, and who gave it to you?**

My mother.

Summer vacation, 1979. We had just moved to a new city again. And again, I had no friends. She saw me sprawled on the living-room couch and said: Go out to play.

*What book influenced you in particular in your youth?*

I took it out of my parents' bookcase during the summer vacation between the ninth and tenth grades: An ugly cover. Yellowed, crumbling pages. And the text on the back cover wasn't particularly enticing either. Nonetheless, on the first page I found a dedication written in a woman's hand: To the Zorba in Eshkol.

Signed: N.

Beneath the signature she quoted: "I knew that over and above the truth there is another duty, much more important and much more human."

Now that made me curious.

Who is the mysterious N who gave *Zorba the Greek* to my grandfather? (None of the names of his three official wives began with N.)

Moreover, what does "To the Zorba in Eshkol" mean? And what human duty is more important than the truth?

I began to read.

The protagonist, a writer by profession, comes to Crete and hires the services of a crude-spoken peasant named Zorba, who teaches him through mime and dance that joy is first of all physical. For me, as someone who grew up in a family that sanctified education and the written word, that idea was nothing less than revolutionary. Zorba advised me to dance and not hang back, to devour food and not poke at it with a fork, and to know a woman and not fantasize about her. I found myself underlining the strong sentences in the book. As if I wanted them to be guiding principles of my future life as a man: "Make a pile of all your books and burn them in a fire, then you will be able to understand." "Have you ever scolded a fig tree for not bearing cherries?" "What would an intellectual say to a dragon?" "To be alive is to look for trouble!" "I do everything as if I am going to die any minute." "There is a devil inside me and he's shouting. And I do what he says."

There's a devil inside me too. Mischievous, sometimes wicked. And he shouted too. But until I met Zorba, I didn't really listen to him.

| | |

Then, as an undergraduate, I took a course called Physiological Psychology.

We learned that high levels of dopamine and serotonin generate a feeling of happiness. And lower levels of dopamine and serotonin generate a feeling of depression. We learned about neurotransmitters and synapses and cortexes and amygdalae, and I wrote in the margin of my notebook: Zorba was right.

Occasionally, at various crossroads in my life, I asked for his advice.

Obviously, you can ask a literary character for advice. It's just a question of how willing you are to suspend disbelief.

———

It was Zorba who encouraged me to propose to Dikla: The sexual attraction has been so strong, for so many years—he claimed—I never heard a better reason to get married.

He also urged me to leave the world of advertising. Look at the skin of your face, he said. That rash. What does it look like to you? Not like a delayed allergic reaction to the campaign you ran for that nothing, what's his name?

———

I recently consulted with Zorba again.

We were sitting in the port. Drinking rum.

I gulped it down to get high. He sipped—held the liquid in his mouth to enjoy its taste, and only then let it slide down slowly and warm his insides.

His eyes glowed through his suntan: Disparaging, sad, restless. Ablaze with passion.

I told him what Ari had asked me to do. And I told him that ever since he'd asked me to do it, I'd been spending my nights tossing and turning: On the one hand, I knew that doing what Ari had asked would really be a kindness. On the other hand, every time I tried to imagine the situation, I couldn't. On the third hand, it was a criminal offense, and even if Ari claimed it was all arranged, no loose ends—

Excuse me, Boss, Zorba growled at me in response, what is all this crap?

But, Zorba—

Why are you thinking so much? He shook his large, heavy head. You keep a scale in your head all day. You weigh things to the last gram. Hey, *habibi*, fuck the scale.

But—

Pardon me, but I once killed a man. Fifty years back. And I can't get that bastard's face out of my mind. A Turkish shell exploded on him. His whole stomach... was spread all over the ground. And he... he pointed to my gun and asked me to help him.

So you simply shot him?

I said it was simple, Boss? You heard me say it was simple?

No.

My heart broke when I pulled the trigger. It split into two parts, my heart.

Okay.

But sometimes you have to do something for someone else. You understand that, Boss?

Yes.

Criminal offense or not, a friend is a friend!

Okay, Zorba, don't be angry.

Why should I be angry? Zorba said. And sipped some more rum. Then he smiled broadly and said, Otherwise, Boss, how are you?

As I was reading him the definition of dysthymia from my cell phone, he stopped me and said, Enough with all those big words, tell me in words a person can understand!

Okay, so... you know the kind of chills that make your scalp tingle when someone surprises you from behind, covers your eyes with his hands, and asks, "Who am I?"

So?

So dysthymia is the same thing. Only instead of a few seconds, it lasts for a few years. Excited anticipation combined with inevitable disappointment. Usually, people are excited with anticipation when they're starting out on some kind of mission, but here, you have no desire or ability to carry out a mission, you anticipate nothing, maybe death, maybe your body smells the danger inherent in despair or the potential of jumping off a roof—

Stop, man. Give me some feelings. Not all this bullshit.

Okay. The mornings are usually the hardest. The chills I talked about are absorbed into your scalp and drip down from your neck to your back, and around noon, they solidify into a motherfucking anchor between your shoulders. Then some invisible hand starts to pull at that motherfucking anchor as if it wants to tear it out, but it actually cuts into your flesh and anchors the pain once and for all in your posterior heart—

"Posterior heart"? What is all this crap?

No one talks about it, but we have two hearts, one in the front and another behind it, in our back.

Let's say that's true. Go on.

So you go everywhere with that constant pain in your posterior heart, no rest, no moments of relief, not during the day and not at night, not after two glasses of rum and not after ten. After everything you try to do to ease the pain, you check to see if it's still there, in your posterior heart, and fuck, it's still there, and that's what causes the most frightening chills of all, the knowledge that it won't pass, it will never pass—

It will pass, of course it will—

And the worst thing is that you have no idea what started it all. There are a lot of obvious reasons, but you keep thinking that the real, deep reason, invis—

So go out to play.

What?

Go out to play, like your mother said. I don't understand how you can whine to me here about pain in your posterior heart and still keep yourself closed up in a room all day.

But—

No buts. You won't get over this until you go outside into the sun. To people. Fight with them. Hug them. Look them in the eye. Do what the devil shouts at you to do.

But for twenty years, Zorba . . . for twenty years I've been writing instead of living. I'm not sure I still have a devil—

So keep whining. No problem. Just don't be surprised if your wife really leaves you after the bat mitzvah. Women want men with balls. That's just how it is. It's nature.

Wow.

Now take your last drink of rum—and get up. Do you dance?

No.

No! His hands fell in shock. Okay, so I'll dance, Boss. Get out of the way, so I don't run you down, eh? He leapt up, broke through the fences, threw off his shoes, his coat, his undershirt, rolled his pants up to his knees, and began to dance, his face still smeared with coal, blacker than black, the whites of his eyes glittering. Totally swept away by the dance, he clapped, skipped, spun in the air and landed on his knees, then skipped and glided in the air as if he'd been shot out of a cannon, then he suddenly leapt in the air again, as if determined to defeat the laws of nature, spread wings, and fly.

***Is there anything you refuse to write about under any circumstances?***

Later on, I discovered who it was that wrote that dedication to my grandfather. But I'll keep that to myself. Maybe because, as N quoted, "over and above the truth there is another duty, much more important and much more human."

***I am a devoted reader of yours. I e-mailed you a year ago and you didn't answer. Why?***

I don't want to answer your question now either. Because what can I write? That receiving compliments on previous books when you're suffering from writer's block only underscores how much you've deteriorated? That the dysthymia diminishes my strength and the only things I was able to write this year were speeches for Yoram Sirkin and answers to interview questions? That dejection combined with compliments produces tears? That yesterday, my best friend asked me again to help him die and I can't bring myself to do it for him, even though he deserves my help?

That my eldest daughter, the apple of my eye, left for the Sde Boker boarding school, and although she has no problem letting her mother sleep at her place for three nights, she absolutely refuses to let her father visit her for a single afternoon?

That her boycott of me is so utterly devastating that nothing else in the world seems important to me?

That her leaving for boarding school destroyed the fragile balance we had at home, and since then, Dikla and I have been on shaky ground?

That I wish I was sure there isn't a much simpler reason why we're on shaky ground?

That my son, who usually has no problem leaving me in front of the school gate, asked me to walk him to his classroom this morning, and I told him that I didn't have time because I had to send Yoram Sirkin a draft of his speech before the Herzliya Global Policy Conference by nine in the morning?

That my other daughter's bat mitzvah is next month, and all the signs indicate that right after it, Dikla plans to tell me that she wants to separate—and then who will have time to answer readers' e-mails, what with all the lawyers and mediators we'll have to see?

But of course I won't tell you all that. I'll want to be the good guy and it'll be important for me not to disappoint you. Readers create an image of a writer in their minds, and my readers, I've noticed, imagine me to be a good guy. You too, according to your e-mail (obviously I received it, and even read it, over and over again), imagine that I'm a great guy. The kind you can send an e-mail to, inviting him to have a beer with you sometime.

Sure, bro, anytime. Sorry I didn't answer before. Your e-mail landed in my junk-mail folder by mistake. I just now fished it out and read it. Thank you for the kind words. They arrived at exactly, and I mean exactly, the right moment.

### Did you ever decide not to publish a book you wrote?

The elevator opened straight into an empty office. I walked through the corridors, my book under my arm, and called out a few times: Is anyone here?

No answer.

Finally, about to give up and turn back, a bare foot emerged from one of the offices. Followed by an entire leg. Followed by the body of a man. Followed by the words: May I help you?

Yes, I'm the lecturer. We set a date, I mean. For a lecture.

You don't say? On what subject?

Secrets from the writer's desk.

The guy scratched the right side of his receding hairline and said, Wait a minute. And disappeared back into the room he'd come out of.

Long minutes passed. Once again, I thought about leaving. And then I reminded myself how much I would get paid for that lecture. I decided to stay.

The guy with the receding hairline finally returned, with another guy. Also barefoot. Both were unshaven and wearing athletic shorts.

I see that they didn't update you, the second guy said.

Apparently not.

When did they ask you to lecture?

Around December.

No kidding, he said.

We shut down the company on May first, the first guy said. There was no sorrow in his voice. On the contrary, he said it almost cheerfully.

They fired the human resources girl, so there was no one to let you know, the second guy said.

Wait a minute, I said, if they shut down the company, then . . . what are you doing here?

The day-after crew, they said in unison.

The day-after crew?

It's like when you split with a girl, the first man explained, and he seemed to be experienced at it—there's the end, the actual split, and then the little things left to take care of after the end: bank accounts, joint property, that kind of stuff.

And why—I asked cautiously—did they shut down the company?

A Canadian firm developed the same technology at the same time and went on the market before us, the first guy said.

There's a race to release, and we lost it, the second guy explained.

Ninety-five percent of start-ups fail, the first guy said. This is the fourth start-up I've worked for that closed down.

Maybe it's because of you, the second guy said, chuckling, you're the curse!

No, it's you, the first guy said, and pushed the other guy lightly with his hand.

No, it's you, the second retorted.

Then only you two are left? I asked, trying to pull them out of the loop.

No, of course not, the first guy said, there's Ravit too. The administrative director. Should I wake her up?

Whatever you want.

She'll be angry at us if she finds out there was a lecture and we didn't wake her up.

Careful, bro, she might fire us, the second guy said. And they both started laughing wildly, too wildly.

They didn't see Ravit come out. On her head, surprisingly, she wore the crown of feathers of an Indian shaman. It was weird, no question about it. But at that point, I still wasn't a nonbeliever.

Do you have a presentation? she asked.

No.

She asked whether I needed a bottle of water and I nodded. She went to the drinks machine in the corner, plugged it in, dropped a coin into it, and came back with a bottle of red wine.

I pulled a chair over from one of the empty rooms, turned it around, and sat down, a leg on either side.

The two guys, Ravit, and the crown of feathers sat in a semicircle in front of me.

I took a long drink of wine.

The first guy looked at his watch and said: You have twenty minutes, tops. We have to wrap up by two.

Two is indoor soccer time, the second guy explained.

Our indoor soccer game is top priority, Ravit explained.

I placed my books on the floor. Arranged them in front of me in chronological order of publication, from right to left, then reconsidered, moved them aside, took another swig of wine, and began to tell them about the book I wrote that was never published. The one I had never told anyone about.

I worked on that book for more than a year, I told them. I had already reached page two hundred on the computer, which is about three hundred pages in a book.

The book was called *Accounts*, and it was based on the powerful sexual tension between a man and a woman. They live in the same apartment and are very attracted to each other, but for various reasons, they're forbidden from acting on the attraction. In my original plan, they're supposed to overcome the prohibition on the last few pages of the book. But after a year's work, I couldn't take the sexual tension between the characters anymore. They wanted each other so much, and I had more and more difficulty stopping them, so I decided to do something about it: to write the final scene before the actual end, to free myself and my characters from all that frustration and then put the scene aside until it was time to insert it. And that's what I did: I wrote fifteen pages of wild sexual abandon, a long, detailed, erotic scene, and really, I had a truly pleasurable week at work, except that the moment I finished, something super-problematic happened: I lost interest in the book. Totally. I tried to force myself to fight it, to shake it off, to keep writing. But the efforts exhausted me so profoundly that once or twice I even nodded off while writing and my face actually fell onto the keyboard. Finally, a month later, I had to concede that the book would not be finished. More than a year of work down the drain.

Did you at least save it? Ravit asked, shaking her feathers.

The truth is that I deleted it. If I had already decided to shelve it, then why not go all the way.

But what was the bug? the first guy wanted to know.

The bug?

What was the real glitch in the book?

Yes, the second guy joined in, like... the way you tell it, it sounds like if you hadn't written that sex scene in advance, everything would have been fantastic. But that's crap, bro. It's like when we tell people the reason the company folded is that the Canadians beat us to it.

And that's not true?

Of course not, our user interface was complicated and clumsy, and theirs was more user-friendly. That's why they were able to attract paying customers. And we weren't. That's the real story. That's why eighty people went home.

You should always ask yourself—the first guy clarified—what's concealed behind the official explanation. I mean, why did you really shelve that book? Otherwise, how will you learn for the next time?

Every crisis is an opportunity, Ravit said. Then she pulled a feather out of her crown and stuck it between her teeth as if it were a knife.

When one door closes, another door opens, the first guy said.

Soccer time! the second guy said.

They stood up and stacked their chairs on the side. I did too.

The first guy put a miniature soccer ball the size of a tennis ball on the floor and signaled the second guy to stand at the other end of the corridor. The game was about to begin, and it seemed as if they were no longer interested in secrets from the writer's desk.

Ravit walked me to the elevator along the yellow brick road and said, Thanks, the guys received a lot of added value. I haven't read your books, but now I will totally consider reading them.

The elevator began its slow descent to the lobby. On the twentieth floor, it suddenly stopped.

And a huge crab entered. If a regular seashore crab is a ten-point font, then this one was a seventy-two-point font.

Its red claws spread along the length of the elevator walls and I had a feeling that it was looking at me through its antennae. I glanced in the mirror to keep from creating eye contact between us, God forbid. And for the first time, I began to suspect that I wasn't real.

The elevator stopped at the eighteenth floor (only later did I figure out what the numbers meant), the crab went on its way in its crablike sideways walk, and Yoram Sirkin, along with a few suits, took its place in the elevator. They spoke English to each other, and one of them, who looked like Ari before his illness and was holding a small hypodermic needle in his hand, kept repeating in the same tone in which Ari after his illness asked me to help him end his suffering: Start-up nation. Start-up nation. Start-up nation.

He said "start-up nation" eight times until the elevator reached the twelfth floor. Each time he said it, he sounded more desperate. And the eighth time it really sounded like a cry of anguish.

They got out at the twelfth floor (the bat mitzvah floor), and Dikla entered, wearing her brown dress.

She came over and gave me a long kiss on the mouth, the way she used to. Then she opened the zipper of my pants and reached inside, but before we could do anything, the elevator stopped. And she exited without a word. No one entered in her place.

The elevator shook wildly, as if it couldn't recover from her departure. And then it continued to descend. To plummet.

For a long time.

Too long.

When I finally reached the lobby, the doors opened directly into a white abyss. Standing on the bottom, waving at me, was Mayan from Death Road.

***Do you believe in God?***

No, but I tend to believe in karma, that if you do something bad, it has repercussions, and if you do something good, it comes back to you. It's never one-to-one, of course. Fate is more circuitous. And most of its boomerangs are invisible. Take, for example, a story. Not mine, but one written by R (a pseudo-letter), who came up to me after a readers' meeting in Kfar Saba and said: You said you were a story hunter, right? So I have a story for you. Want to listen to it? She was wearing a sweater that was several sizes too large for her, thick glasses, and black New Balance running shoes. Her tone was matter-of-fact. Almost businesslike. And she looked a bit tired. Nothing in her appearance even hinted at scandal. Nonetheless, I liked that she said "listen" instead of "hear," so I asked her to sit on the bench outside the library.

———

It turned out that R had once had an affair.

And not just a run-of-the-mill affair. A sadomasochistic affair.

Twice a week she used to meet with a square-chinned guy on the bottom floor of the Beit Silver parking garage near the Ramat Gan Diamond Exchange, and there they would hurt each other until they swooned in pleasure or one of them would say the word "suburbia." That was their code word. To signal the other that the pain had passed the point where it was arousing, and to calm things down, they said "suburbia."

At first, R thought she was succeeding in living her dangerous life on the bottom floor of the parking garage and her normal life on the third floor of the building in suburban Kfar Saba without either of them affecting the other.

In addition, she sometimes felt that one complemented the other. That one enabled the other to exist.

But then R's husband began to have pain.

He couldn't pinpoint its specific location. Sometimes he thought it was in his stomach. Sometimes his back. Sometimes it climbed to his throat.

In any case, it was very strong. So much so that he couldn't fall asleep at night. He tried painkillers—starting with over-the-counter medications and moving to prescription drugs—but nothing helped.

She had no choice but to take him for tests. Which showed nothing. There was no finding that could explain the pain. No unusual blood test results. No growth. No damage to any of his internal organs.

Each doctor sent him to another doctor, and at first, each new one was loudly skeptical of the professionalism and judgment of the previous one, but ultimately was forced to admit that he too had no idea what the source of the problem was.

And then—the tough square-chinned guy went abroad. To a work conference. During the two weeks they didn't meet, her husband's condition showed a marked improvement.

R didn't notice the connection right away.

It took another few visits to the Beit Silver parking garage, after Square Chin returned from abroad, and another few visits to the emergency room, when her husband's pain grew worse again—for her to understand: It was her. She was hurting her husband.

Something in his subconscious felt it. The poisonous substance of her infidelity was seeping into him.

From the moment she realized it, she had no doubt about what she had to do.

She made a date to see Square Chin outside of their regular meeting times in the parking garage, told him what she had discovered, and said that was it, it was over.

He grabbed her ass, slammed her against his car, and said, Nothing is over.

She pushed his hand away and said, I'm serious, it's over.

He grabbed her by the back of the neck, yanked her head closer, tore at her hair painfully, and said, Don't play games with me.

She tried to push him away, and said, I'm not playing.

He pressed his pelvis against hers, locked her arms behind her back with his huge hand, and began to grind against her.

She said, Suburbia.

And he kept going.

She said, Suburbia!

And he kept going.

So she kicked him in the testicles.

He shuddered for a moment, recovered immediately, and punched her a few times. Real punches. The bones in the back of his hand crashed into the bones of her nose. And then into her stomach.

She fell onto the filthy ground next to her car, and he, as if waking from a daydream, bent over her quickly. I'm sorry, sweetie, he said.

I said suburbia.

I'm sorry, I didn't mean it. I got carried away.

Take me to the emergency room, she said, clutching her stomach. No, don't take me to the emergency room. Just go.

Your nose is bleeding. I can't leave you like this.

Please . . . go.

Go?

Yes, I'm begging you. I'll manage. Go. Enough. It's over.

R called her husband, told him that a car had hit her in the parking garage and taken off, and asked him to pick her up. He came with his soft, vulnerable chin and, horrified, hurried her off to the emergency room. He sat beside her for hours, the way only someone who loves can. He held her hand and didn't let go. He brought her decaf with soy milk and a not-too-warm chocolate croissant from the shopping center. He walked alongside her bed when they moved her from one department to another. He brought her another blanket from a different department when she was cold. He slept all night on two chairs joined together at her bedside, and talked with the doctors in the morning, his voice trembling and his eyes wide with worry.

One of the doctors, young and not yet burned out, recognized him from his own visit to the same department several weeks earlier, and asked how he was. It's strange, he replied, since my wife has been hospitalized, I have no pain at all. Nothing. As if someone cut-and-pasted: pulled it all out of me and shifted it to her. Did you ever hear of anything like that?

I've heard stranger things, the young doctor said. Medicine has made great advances, but between us, as far as the mind-body relationship is concerned, we're still groping in the dark.

―――――

I asked R whether it would be okay if, in the future, I put her story into one of my books. She thought for a moment and then said: Let me sleep on it.

Only on the way home did I realize that I didn't have her e-mail address or phone number.

I could have made a greater effort to get hold of them. I didn't.

By any criteria, it would be obscene to use R's personal story here word for word, without checking that it's okay with her.

And someday, the karma police will probably punish me for it.

*Are the characters in your books based directly on real people, from life?*

Not usually. Writing about real people is limiting. What I know about them distracts me from imagining what I don't know about them. And adding stories about people who are close to me to my books is morally complicated. They can be offended. Or—if they happened to have studied law—they could sue the pants off me.

My characters are made like salad. I chop an ingredient from each real person and mix all the ingredients into a new person: one woman's hair flows onto another woman's shoulders, which are joined to the body of a singer who didn't pass the audition for *The Voice*—and that body ends in the small feet of one of Ari's girlfriends.

Except in one instance.

Of a major character, in fact.

Gili Arazi was part of our crew in high school. But he was closer to Hagai Carmeli. Gili and I were never really close. There was a period when we trained together before the army. We ran along the seashore to the hill and back, but that didn't make us friends either.

I pictured him constantly while writing my last novel. The physical description of the character was almost identical to his. The family background too. And other things, small, specific, and not necessarily flattering, which I won't mention here. I've already ruined his life once.

In any case, I saw him last week.

He'd gone off to San Francisco to do a postdoc, and I assumed that, like most people who go to San Francisco on the bay from Haifa on the bay, he wouldn't feel far away. And he wouldn't come back.

But there he was, walking toward me on the street, and I couldn't turn back because he was already waving, and when he reached me, he greeted me happily with a hug, exactly the way I had described the character in my book hugging his friends. A limp hug, the bare outline of a hug.

So tell me, he says, still holding my shoulders lightly, you became a writer?

Yes, I avert my eyes suspiciously.

Honestly? I didn't see that coming, he says. I mean, I thought you'd be a psychologist.

Me too.

But it's great. I'm proud of you.

Thanks.

Don't be offended, but I still haven't had a chance to read your books. It's not you, academe has dried up my brain. I haven't read a book for ten years already.

No rush—I breathe in relief and try not to let him see how relieved I am—really, there's no rush.

Maybe we can get together, he says, the whole gang, I'm in the country until the weekend. My brother is getting married.

Sure, I say, we really should.

Tell me, he asks, have you heard anything from Hagai Carmeli?

No. Have you?

I thought I saw him at a conference in Singapore. In the end, it was some other redheaded guy.

No kidding.

So, see you, eh? Give me a call?

———

Wait just a minute. There was, in fact, another instance apart from Gili Arazi: the girl from the train.

Okay, it's no wonder I didn't think of her from the first minute. Our memory tends to edit out humiliating scenes.

———

Gili Arazi, that is, the character in my book based on him, was desperately in love with a female character whose motivations I understood, but I couldn't imagine what the hell she looked like.

I searched for her in cafés, in workshops, in meetings with readers but couldn't find her. I tried to keep writing the book with no picture of her in my mind—to no avail. My male protagonist was obsessed with a woman, and I still didn't understand what there was about her to justify it.

So I went to Berlin to visit a couple of friends who had been living there for years on a grant from the Heinrich Böll Foundation. The three of us tried to drown my writer's block with beer, zigzagging along the city sidewalks, trying not to step on the black tiles on which the names of Jews had been written in gold letters.

A few days later, we boarded a train heading for another city to visit another couple of friends from Israel who lived on the guilt feelings of the Germans. We were three people sitting in a space designed for four, and I placed my bag on the empty seat next to me. The train was already leaving the station, but the last passengers looking for seats were still moving through the packed cars.

Even before I really saw her, I felt the gust of energy that arrived with her.

I took my bag off the seat, and she sat down.

I looked at her and knew immediately: She is the one I have been looking for this entire year. The blond bangs, the glasses, the stiff pants with the pockets on the sides, and the soft, thin blouse above them.

I've never been good at beginnings. There's an abyss there that I usually can't jump over.

But in this case—I had a goal.

So I asked. And she named the same city we were going to.

And I asked again. She replied that she had a readers' meeting at the Literaturhaus to discuss her book.

What a coincidence, I'm a writer too.

I don't believe you.

I only lie in books, I said.

I don't believe you, she repeated. You're too suntanned to be a writer.

So I suggested that we google each other.

While she was googling me, I googled her.

It turned out that she writes about vampires, and that her bloody books are huge best sellers in Germany and outside it. On one site, there was a picture of her lying on a piano, wearing a slit-to-the-thigh wine-colored dress, her expression simultaneously defiant and shy.

She looked up from her phone, examined me skeptically, then looked down at her phone again, then looked up again—

It's all fiction, I wanted to tell her. Don't believe a single word written there—

But before I could say anything, she spoke: You're pretty photogenic, eh?

Coming from her mouth, it sounded like an insult. But I didn't have time to waste on that. I was in the middle of a mission: to find out the small, specific things she does that so enthrall Gili Arazi.

I asked about her books. And while she answered, I observed her hand movements, which told a different story, and sometimes actually undermined her words; I observed her bangs, which moved slightly when she spoke; I observed the rare moments when something embarrassed her. She seemed anxious to project the image of a strong, liberated woman whom nothing could embarrass, and that was why, when she suddenly bit the nail of her pinkie finger, there was something moving about it.

When we got off the train at the station—how lovely it was, the way she hopped off the step onto the platform—I felt that I needed a bit more time with her. A bit more information.

So I suggested that we meet for a drink after her lecture. You must know all about it, I said, the better the lecture is, the lonelier you feel after it.

I don't remember what we talked about in the bar. I mean, there was a text, but I remember the subtext better. And I remember that I said to myself while we were sitting there, No no no, absolutely not, she's definitely not your type, Dikla is your type and you don't want to risk what you have with her—

But when she pushed her blond bangs aside, leaned over, and whispered in my ear, My hotel . . . it's right around the corner—

She was definitely Gili Arazi's type. And there are things you can know about a character only if you sleep with her. So I went to the hotel with her. Which was much more luxurious than the dumps they put me up in. I followed her into her room, her suite. Before I could do anything, she pushed me up against the wall.

She grabbed my arms with both hands. And held them over my head in an iron grip. Her pelvis trapped mine so that I couldn't move, and her mouth headed toward my neck.

I fought to free myself. But she was stronger than me. I must have cried out, which only caused her teeth to dig deeper into my neck. Then the pain lessened. My resistance weakened, my neck abandoned itself to her mouth, and she sucked my blood and everything that flows in it. I actually felt how she sucked out entire memories: the bag of apricot pits I'd collected in fourth grade that left me deep in debt at the end of recess when I lost the game; the kid from camp we ostracized because he didn't play soccer well enough; the squad exercise during the officer training course when an accidentally discharged bullet scratched Gal Miller's left ear; Tali Leshem standing very close to me on the Stella Maris promenade and I didn't have the courage to kiss her; Dikla and I throwing eggs at each other in a no-holds-barred fight in the apartment on Raban Street, and then making passionate love on the floor, mixing yolks with whites; Dikla saying hurtful things to me during an argument in the apartment on Yaldei Teheran Street, and then waiting hours for her to apologize, which she didn't, because she doesn't believe in apologizing—

After the German writer removed her teeth from my neck and released my hands, I thought it would be natural for us to continue to the large bed in the middle of the room.

But she thought differently. She called reception. To order me a taxi.

———

Sitting in the backseat, I closed my eyes and felt empty. Not empty. Hollow.

The driver drove with the window open, and the freezing wind blew into the taxi, but I didn't have the strength even to ask him to close it. I didn't have the strength even to open my mouth.

That bitch had sucked the life-force right out of me. All of it.

And didn't deign look in my direction when I left the room.

———

Six months later, she sent me her book. In German. The gold letters on the cover were embossed, as befits a book meant to be a best seller, and in the neat handwriting of a perfect little girl, she had written me a dedication on the first page:

*To the suntanned writer from Israel*
*Thank you for helping my investigation.*

**There are a lot of extramarital affairs in your last books. Do you think all married people are ultimately destined to have affairs?**

I think that all married people are ultimately destined to imagine an affair.

**How much of you is in your characters?**

They are melded into me and I into them. So much so that sometimes it's hard, in all that amalgam, to see who is who. In this interview as well, it's time to admit:

Some of the things I supposedly revealed really happened to me.

Some I am terrified will happen to me.

Some I desperately hope will happen to me.

And some happened to Ari, or to Axel Wolff, the Scandinavian writer.

If you google him, you'll get a series of pictures of him in almost chronological order. In the first few shots, from the beginning of his career, he's an arrogant Viking giant, his blond hair pulled back, holding various award statuettes, a different statuette on a different stage each time. In pictures taken the last few months, he's slightly stooped, his hair is thinner, his eyes haunted. Under the pictures you'll find a link to the huge scandal connected to his name—several days after returning from the Jerusalem International Book Fair, he found three documents from his wife on the kitchen table: a farewell letter filled with Swedish curses, a statement of claim for divorce, and one for ten million kronor owed her for being the actual writer of all the best sellers in the Scar series. She and her husband had made a quiet agreement, according to which she would write the books, and he, with his blond hair, towering height, and blue eyes, would be their PR image. It worked beautifully, sales doubled every quarter, until what happened in Colombia happened. And she decided to put an end to the sham.

---

That affair didn't surprise me at all.

Right after I heard the knocking at the door that separated Axel Wolff's hotel room in Jerusalem from the adjacent room, I heard a thick female voice. Open the door, please, it asked. The tone was proper. Matter-of-fact. Like the tone of voice of the woman on Waze. I didn't sense that I was in any danger, and even after I opened the door, no alarm bells rang for me. The owner of that proper voice was properly attired, and her hair was pulled into a proper bun on the top of her head. She introduced herself as Camilla, the writer's wife, thanked me for taking care of him, and said she wanted to check that Axel hadn't spoken too much nonsense that evening. Because he sometimes did that when he drank.

Truthfully, I confessed, there was one sentence he kept repeating the entire time.

*Jag dödade honom*, Camilla asked.

How did you know?

I am his wife, after all.

Do you have any idea why he claimed that he murdered someone?

If I tell you, I'll have to kill you.

I was sure she said that with a smile. Her lips spread and curved upward until the left corner of her mouth almost merged with the small scar on her left cheek. It was clear that smiling did not come naturally to her, and her effort to seem as breezy and affable as a TV personality made it even sadder. And therefore, intriguing.

That's why I said, I'll risk it.

She and Axel met at a party, she told me. And immediately fell wildly in love. They left their spouses and children to be together. Three months of wild passion, just the two of them, cut off from the world like prisoners. And then came his confession: "One night, a few years ago, I killed a young man who abused my daughter. I strangled him with a rope and tossed his body into a river. Everyone thought he had committed suicide by jumping off a bridge. I made sure they would think that. I left clues. I forged his suicide note. I planned it in advance, down to the smallest detail. The police never suspected. No one knew. Not my daughter. Not my ex-wife. But with you, I want to be completely honest from the beginning. To build our relationship on a foundation of trust. Do you think you can live with a murderer? Because if not, better to say it now."

What could she do? Her heart was already his. But that secret he told her—

Secrets in general—they metastasize all through your body.

In the end, she had no choice but to write it. Of course, she didn't write it. We, the storytellers, she said, giving me a piercing look, never tell the real secret, the dark one. That remains ours alone. Sometimes we don't even fully admit its existence, as we transform it, remove evidence, and turn it into art.

When she completed the manuscript, she told me, she gave it to Axel to read and said, You're its first and last reader. She had intended to turn the secret he told her into a story only to free herself of it. She had no intention, desire, or ability to deal with readers and criticism.

But Axel, realizing immediately that what she'd written had the potential to be a series, manipulated her emotionally, after manipulating her sexually, into the binding arrangement that was the basis for their joint success: She would write books, he would be "the writer."

She straightened the blanket around Axel's body, which was sprawled on the bed, and looked up at me.

And that's how it's been ever since, she said. Five years. Ten books in the Scar series. Thirty million copies sold throughout the world.

What a story, I said.

And now that I've told it, I have to kill you, she said.

I laughed.

She took out a gun she'd hidden in the hem of her corduroy pants.

I've been looking for someone like you for a long time, she said with a sigh. A random stranger to whom I could momentarily, but only momentarily, entrust the real, dark secret that could not be written. But I warned you in advance: There are too many considerations involved here. We can't allow ourselves to let you leave this room and spread rumors that would damage the Axel Wolff brand. Sorry.

From the moment she cocked the pistol until I opened my mouth to speak, I managed to think the following thoughts: What do I care if I die, my life lately has been on the brink anyway, and the effort to not fall into the abyss is so exhausting, but what will happen to my children, who will help them through the next stages of their lives, who will be there when they fall into their own abysses, and what will happen to Ari, what if there is the smallest chance that, at the last second, a new drug is developed for his disease, and what about the slim chance that Dikla will start loving me again?

Apparently everyone occasionally needs to have a loaded gun pointed at them.

A fiercely passionate desire to live surged inside me like a geyser and broke through the dysthymia's layer of ice, to be or not to be? To be! To be! To be! the reply rose from deep inside me.

Go ahead, shoot me, I said to Camilla. Just do me one favor, afterward, when Axel wakes up, ask him what else happened in Colombia, something he didn't tell you about.

Something else? she said, looking at me in confusion. The barrel of her gun dropped slightly. Just a hair or two.

I took advantage of that to slap it out of her hand to the other side of the room and ran out of there while I still could. The elevator didn't come, hotel elevators never come when you need them, so I ran down the stairs from the thirteenth floor to the lobby, pushed aside the guard who tried to stop me, and kept running through Sacher Park to the Valley of the Cross. I ran among the olive trees from which Christ's cross was made, I fell on stones and was scratched by branches, but I didn't stop until I reached the entrance to the monastery and the church inside it. I broke through the confessional door and dropped into a sitting position. While I waited for a priest to come, I caught my breath and licked the blood pooling from a deep cut that ran the length of my arm.

After Camilla petitioned for divorce, Axel Wolff tried to kill himself. Without success. The bullet that was supposed to kill him grazed his left earlobe. When he was in the hospital, fans all over the world held their breath. From my TV chair, I watched the reports from the front of the Stockholm hospital enviously—there, in minus twenty degrees, a huge crowd of people had gathered to light candles. Only two days later, he was released with a small bandage on his ear, which provoked a wave of rumors that the entire story was about a petition for divorce and a suit for royalties and the attempted suicide was only a public relations ploy designed to increase interest in his/her new book.

While I was watching TV, my phone rang.

I asked Noam, who was closer, to answer it for me.

Daddy, she said, handing me the phone, someone from the Stockholm police wants to talk to you.


*Where is the most special place you've ever met readers?*

The meeting was supposed to take place in a small hall in the basement of a culture, leisure, and sports complex in the town of Re'ut. The organizer had arranged forty or fifty white plastic chairs in straight rows, and left several more stacks on both sides of the hall because "You can never know, some people don't sign up in advance."

There were light refreshments laid out on a white plastic table outside the hall. A store-bought cake. Pretzels. Tea. Coffee. And many dozens of paper cups.

Three people came. A man and two women, one of whom reminded me a bit of Hagai Carmeli. I mean, if Hagai Carmeli had surgically altered his sex, he would have looked like her.

It turned out that a musical reality show finale was being broadcast at the same time, and since one of the contestants was a resident of the town, everyone was glued to their TV screens, texting votes for him.

What a waste of chairs, said the woman who looked like Hagai Carmeli as she pointed to them, we could have had the meeting in the Jacuzzi.

Jacuzzi! What a fantastic idea! The other woman laughed in delight.

The truth is that I just happen to have my bathing suit with me, the man said.

I have no objections, the organizer said, her expression serious.

The four of them turned to me. In anticipation.

I went with the flow.

And it's not that I'm much of a goer with the flow. Dikla always says I'm so sure about what I want and don't want that there's not much room left for maneuvering in life with me. But that evening in Re'ut, I didn't have the strength to protest.

(Years ago, on the very day I left the apartment on Hess Street, where I lived with Tali, I had an interview with the army liaison officer. I arrived unshaven, I remember, and distracted, and he said there weren't enough people with my training in the Gaza Division. Instead of protesting and saying, "Gaza? You've got to be kidding!" or "I'm heartbroken. Gaza? You've got to be kidding!" I nodded apathetically and found myself under torrents of mortar shells in the winters that followed.)

My three readers and I stepped into the Jacuzzi beside the pool.

I was in my underwear, they in their bathing suits.

The man reached behind him, pressed the button, and everything between us began to bubble.

———

"There's a catch inherent in a meeting with readers," I always begin my lectures, "and right at the outset, I want to put it on the table. After all, the most important meeting has already taken place. And if it hasn't, it will—and I hope it turns out to be an intimate, unique meeting with the book itself—"

But that introduction didn't seem appropriate to the situation. Even on the literal level. At most meetings, when I say that I want to put the catch "on the table," there is an actual table in front of me. With a vase of flowers on it. But here, only currents and bubbles, bubbles and currents, and, occasionally, a foot touching another foot under the water. By accident.

The man leaned forward slightly and shook some water out of his ear. The two women cut off their mumbled conversation. And the three of them turned their wet eyes to me.

It was clear that they were expecting something to begin.

I reached behind me and took one of my books out of my bag. Perhaps I would read them a passage? My fingers were wet, making it difficult for me to turn pages, and I couldn't find the bathtub scene in my last book. Too bad, I thought, because it would have been a perfect fit for this meeting. I put the book back in the bag. Then I closed my eyes, spread my arms to the side, leaned my head on the rim of the Jacuzzi, and slid down a bit so my lower spine would be directly in front of the jet.

I remained like that for a few seconds, inhaled the chlorine smell, and then opened my eyes and began to tell them. The truth.

I said, Sunday is my younger daughter's bat mitzvah.

I said, Apparently right after it, my wife is going to tell me that she wants us to separate.

I said, Not a difference of opinion, a crisis.

I said, I still love her.

I said, I've loved her from the age of twenty-three.

I said, She has the most wonderful smell, I don't think there's another woman in the world who smells so good.

I said, Her collarbones.

I said, I don't know how I can live without her.

I said, I felt that she was moving away from me and tried the wrong way to bring her back.

I said, Our eldest daughter went off to boarding school, and that . . . shifted the balance at home.

I said, I probably won't understand the real reason for years.

I said, In any case, it's not something that couples therapy can solve.

I said, Maybe there was a moment when our marriage could have been saved, but I let it pass.

I double-clicked on the moment: A Friday morning, several months ago. The children were already at school. She woke up first and began working on her computer. But I could see without looking—after all, we'd been together for twenty years—that she was only answering e-mails. I could have said: Let's eat breakfast together. I'll make you an omelet with mushrooms and onions, cherry tomatoes on the side, and after we eat, we'll start to unravel the tangle, thread by thread. But instead, I went to my computer. She made herself toast and coffee. And didn't ask if she should make some for me. Once, we solved problems like that with sex. Once, I used to kiss her neck and all was forgotten in our passion. Maybe on that morning, I should have simply gone to her and kissed her neck.

In any case, she's in another place, I said.

And emphasized: Not another man—another place.

And said: These are not normal days for me. These are the final days of a period in my life that lasted for more than twenty years. I'm walking through my life, and at the same time, observing it from the sidelines.

Summing up, I said: But it also has advantages. In normal times, you never could have persuaded me to have a meeting in a Jacuzzi.

When I finished speaking, there was a long silence broken only by the music coming from the lifeguard's transistor.

The man spoke first. A nice story, he said. Although a little too sad for my taste.

The part I liked best was when he almost made her breakfast—said the woman who looked like Hagai Carmeli—but in the end, they both ended up in front of their computers. That's exactly how it is.

I didn't think it was believable at all, the other woman said. That whole scene with the computers and the toast. Who has time for things like that on Friday morning, when you have to prepare for Shabbat? It would have been much more convincing if it all happened in the supermarket, let's say.

I don't understand what you want, girls, the man said, it's a story, it doesn't have to be exactly like life.

———

I didn't correct them. I didn't explain that there wasn't the slightest bit of fiction in what I told them. I let them continue arguing and touching each other and me with their feet, under the water, accidentally or not accidentally.

I closed my eyes, pressed my hands to the sides of my body, leaned my head back, and slid down a bit, to place my lower spine in the flow of water.

I remained that way for a few seconds, and then opened my eyes.

And began to cry.

None of my three readers noticed.

The salty drops falling from my eyes blended into the spray of the Jacuzzi.

———

On the drive home, Johnny Shuali's "Sometimes" was on the radio. I didn't want to remember, but I did. The first time Dikla and I heard it together was in the Kiryat Yuval dormitory. Dikla had heard it before and drew my attention to it. We were in her room—she had a roommate who left the university in the middle of the year—lying on her bed, brushing against each other, and the song began.

She said, Listen to how beautiful it is, and reached out to raise the volume.

*Sometimes you don't realize that I'm with you,*
*There's no one else for me,*
*I love you more each passing day . . .*

Johnny Shuali's voice was borne on the surging sounds of his guitar.

And when he reached *"And the autumn winds have stripped me as bare as the day I was born,"* I felt Dikla's hand reach for mine. Spreading my fingers to lace hers between them.

———

When I reached home, a note from her was waiting on the dining room table: I'm going to sleep. Don't forget to go to the bakery tomorrow morning to order a cake for the bat mitzvah.

***Is it possible to live without love?***

At five in the morning, I decide to surrender to my insomnia instead of fighting it. I get out of bed quietly to keep from waking Dikla, walk to the living room, open the shutters, and wait for the dawn. All the women I've been with in my life enter the room, one after the other. And caress me. Each in her own way. All of them still love me. At least the way I love them. Making it difficult to reject the possibility that I might still be lovable. At six, the darkness turns into almost-light. All the women I've been with in my life leave the room one after the other, and a moment before they do, they bend down and kiss me on the mouth, each in her own way.

Soon, light will flood the living room. Soon, I will go to the bakery. Soon, the bat mitzvah will take place. Soon, it seems, my life will collapse.

But for a rare moment, I manage to see the big picture.


***What is the most unique response you've ever received from a reader?***

He came up to me after an event in Germany, in a provincial town whose name I don't remember. Nor do I remember what the auditorium looked like. Or whether there was a vase of flowers on the table or not.

He waited on the side until the last of those who wanted an autograph had gone, and only then did he approach and say "Shalom" in Hebrew. Eighty years old, at least. Tall but not stooped. A brown jacket. Watery blue eyes behind glasses. Life-experience blemishes on his cheeks.

After the "shalom," he switched to German-accented English.

He said: I read your book and just bought another copy.

He said: I wanted to ask you to write a dedication to Paul in the new copy.

He said: Paul and I were together in the war.

My pen stopped in the middle of writing: Wait a minute, did he really expect me to write a dedication to his Wehrmacht buddy?

But he—perhaps understanding why I froze—added hurriedly: The War of Independence. Paul and I fought together for the entire war, and in the Battle of Latrun, he was wounded by grenade shrapnel and I did my part to help evacuate him. He kept saying he was going to die, and I calmed him down and told him that he had nothing to worry about, because in another week, we'd be drinking whiskey together. It continued like that until we finally reached the medic, he talked about the next world and I held his hand and promised him whiskey. In this world. Ever since, we meet once a week, he comes from Israel, and we drink a glass of whiskey together. Paul says I saved his life. I'm not sure it's true. But I don't argue with him.

So... he should be arriving soon? I asked, opening the book to the dedication page.

No, this time I'm going to him. He's... very sick. In a hospital in Jerusalem, for a few weeks already. I'm not sure he'll even be able to hold the glass of whiskey. But it's okay. If I have to, I'll hold it, bring it to his lips so he can take a sip, and then I'll read him something from your book. Can you write the dedication in Hebrew?

Of course. What should I write?

I don't know. You're the writer. Maybe something about friendship?

**Do you use drugs or alcohol to help you write?**

Twenty years have passed since then.

Many things have grown dim. Not that.

I never wrote about it directly, perhaps because I'm afraid I won't be able to convey it in words. That instead of writing it, I should give each reader a bit of the potion the Israeli girls had brought from home and say: Taste it, you'll understand.

There were two girls with us, I don't remember their names. I met the curly-haired one years later at the photocopier in the Gilman Building at Tel Aviv University. We exchanged a few words and a glance—the deep, lingering glance of two people who had once been entwined in each other's dreams.

She was the one who suggested bringing us a small pouch. I had just read *The Book of Tao*, which had imbued me with a spirit of adventure. And I didn't have children at the time.

So I said, Great.

I had no idea what I was getting into.

The next day, they put the pouch on the threshold of the cabin I shared with Ari and went to eat breakfast.

Inside the pouch was a green liquid. Cactus juice. That was all I knew.

Later I found out that Indians use it to commune with their gods.

Later I read Carlos Castaneda.

Only later.

Ari slept late that morning. If one of us drank it, the other probably shouldn't, he'd said when I told him the night before that the girls were going to bring us a small pouch. I knew that if he woke up, he would be the one to drink it and I would be the sober one, as usual. So I grabbed the pouch and my travel journal and hurried down to the creek. The small bridge that spanned it was made of wooden planks, with one missing.

It's incredible how I remember everything.

I sat down on the damp ground beside the small bridge. The water flowed beneath me. The first sunbeams filtered through the huge leaves on the branches above me. I made a large hole in a corner of the small bag, like I used to do with the corner of the plastic bag of chocolate milk in camp, and sucked out a bit.

It was bitter. Terribly bitter. So I drank the rest in one gulp. Without stopping.

There were no usage directions on the small pouch. I had no way of knowing it shouldn't be done that way.

———

A minute later, I vomited. I hate when characters vomit in stories, but that's what happened.

I threw up some of the green liquid I'd drunk, and then came the first sign that my consciousness was changing. The green color of the vomit looked beautiful to me. I stared at it in astonishment, almost elation, while it was still spilling out of my mouth onto the ground.

The ground also looked beautiful to me. Brown and blazing. And those were the first words I wrote in my journal: Brown and blazing ground.

Then I heard voices approaching from the direction of the cabins. I didn't want to be around people. More accurately, I didn't feel the need to be around people. The trees, the branches, the sunbeams, the birds—supplied all my needs.

Then I straightened up, crossed the bridge to the other bank, and began to walk down the path beside the river.

———

Ari told me later that it took a long time to find me. The girls woke him up after they themselves had drunk from a small pouch. Straight Hair told him they saw me walking away on the path, and in her opinion, the stuff they had been sold was spoiled.

Curly Hair didn't say anything. Only occasionally, as they walked, she pointed to a flower and said: How beautiful.

———

While they were searching for me, I lay shirtless on an exposed hill above the river and looked at the clouds.

Actually, first there was the donkey. I want to be accurate. I won't always have such a detailed, vibrant memory of what happened, and at some point, I'll need these words to keep from forgetting:

The donkey was far from me and close to me. The two possibilities didn't cancel each other out. At some point, I remember, the thought passed through my mind that it was part of a painting. That it wasn't real, that it was part of a two-dimensional painting I was looking at. Every time I closed my eyes and opened them, it was a different distance from me, but even when it was really close, I wasn't scared. All in all, at that stage, I still wasn't scared. Was the man who came and took the donkey away real, or a product of my imagination? It's difficult for me to say for sure. I only remember thinking that just because the man was made of cardboard, like a figure in a shooting range, it didn't rule out the possibility that he was human.

After the donkey was taken away, I watched the clouds.

Pages of my travel journal are filled with descriptions of the shapes I saw in them: crabs, monkeys, cats, and then crabs again.

And from behind the clouds—the city of the gods sparkled at me.

I remember thinking: Behind the clouds is an ancient city where the gods live, and now I've been given the once-in-a-lifetime opportunity to see it and maybe even talk to the gods. I believed that if I focused hard enough, I would be able to communicate with the gods through the power of thought alone. Without words.

I even wrote in my journal: I tasted the fruit of the tree of knowledge.

Then Ari and the girls appeared.

We had a dialogue, some words were exchanged, I don't remember them.

I do remember that the two girls lay down on either side of me and Ari stood above us.

Curly Hair was right beside me. Straight Hair was farther away.

Curly Hair asked, What are you looking at?

The clouds.

She looked up and said, They're so beautiful.

Do you see the crabs?

Sure, she said, and then again, they're so beautiful.

I felt that Curly Hair and I had a deep understanding of each other.

Straight Hair, on the other hand, really pissed me off. She kept complaining that nothing was happening to her. That they'd been sold spoiled stuff. And she warned us over and over again that it was about to rain. As if it mattered.

I thought, I could kill her. If she doesn't shut up, I'm capable of getting up, grabbing a rock, and smashing her head in. And then I panicked that maybe they'd heard my thought.

I want to be accurate: I wasn't afraid that I'd spoken the thought out loud, I was afraid that, in the world I inhabited then, thoughts could be heard.

Ari stood above us the entire time. I asked him to come closer to me and I whispered in his ear: Can you hear my thoughts?

No, bro, he said.

I think you should take her back to the restaurant, I said. I was sure he would know which one of the girls I meant.

I think everyone should go back to the restaurant, Ari said.

It's going to start raining any minute, Straight Hair said.

In response, my hand clenched into a fist.

Rain is so beautiful, Curly Hair said.

I always wanted a big brother, I said.

Me too, Curly Hair said.

I want to go back, Straight Hair said.

I'm not moving from here, Curly Hair said.

I'll take her to the restaurant and come back as fast as I can, Ari said.

---

The rain started a minute later—or an hour later, my sense of time had leaked away.

Long rows of small drops fell on us from the clouds. I'd never seen rain fall from that angle, lying down, and it was so—

Beautiful, said Curly Hair.

So much it makes me want to cry.

The ground beneath our bodies became damper and damper, and looser. Our bodies sank into it.

The ground will swallow us up, Curly Hair said.

I don't care.

Neither do I.

We lay next to each other, our faces to the clouds.

We didn't turn to each other or touch. There was no need. We had the sense that, effortlessly, we had become connected to each other and to the nature around us. That there was a certain harmony between all the elements of the moment we were living in.

I even wrote the word "harmony" in my journal. But that was later, in the cabin.

I didn't write anything while it was raining, and I wasn't bothered that my journal was getting wet.

Nothing bothered me. Nothing. There was nothing that I longed for. Nothing I missed.

| | |

Ari returned and suggested we go back with him because it would be dark soon.

I didn't say anything. As far as I was concerned, darkness wasn't a reasonable possibility. It was just morning.

Curly Hair didn't say anything either.

He sat down beside us. Silently. Wrapped in a poncho.

I thought to myself, What an amazing person that Ari is.
And he said, Thanks.
I thought to myself, How patient he is.
And he said, Not patient. Just worried about you.

———

The rain finally weakened. And daylight died. From behind the clouds, the lights of the city of the gods turned on.

Curly Hair said, I'm hungry. And sat up. As soon as she said that, I also felt hungry. Very hungry. And terribly thirsty.

Let's go to the restaurant, Ari said. You can keep looking at things there too.

I think now about how much wisdom there was in those words. About his ability to understand that our true desire in those moments was to look. About the patience needed to sit there beside us in the pouring rain—who knows how much time really passed—until we agreed to leave. About the fact that he didn't ridicule us even once. Despite his tendency to turn everything into a joke. Even though I'm sure we looked ridiculous.

The change came in the restaurant. It's hard to pinpoint the precise moment. I'm not sure there was a precise moment.

I remember that the four of us were sitting at one table. That in fluent Spanish, his native language, Ari ordered soup that was like a stew. He took pictures of us. From several angles. And I couldn't follow the conversation.

I managed to hear the beginnings of sentences, but then my attention wandered and I couldn't hear their ends.

I remember that Curly Hair said, I think it's starting to pass—

And Straight Hair said, It's supposed to pass after—

I remember thinking: It's not passing for me. It's not passing for me. And as Ari's conversation with the girls grew more relaxed and logical, my thought changed: It won't pass for me. It will never pass for me.

I felt that something wasn't right with me, that everyone in the restaurant could see it and they were all sending pitying, get-him-to-a-hospital looks in my direction.

In the four pictures Ari took in the restaurant, I really do look like someone to worry about. My hair is plastered to my forehead as if I've just finished a triathlon. My head is tilted, as if my neck can't hold it up. And something in my eyes is totally shattered.

I can't look at those pictures. I saw them only once, after we'd returned from the trip, and I asked Ari to keep them and never show them to anyone. I didn't have to explain why. He'd been there when everything went out of control.

———

I said, My head hurts, I'm going to the cabin.

Curly Hair said, Feel better.

Straight Hair said, I told you that stuff was spoiled.

And Ari asked, Should I come with you, bro?

He came, even though I didn't ask him to, and lay down on his bed.

I said, It's not passing for me, Ari.

He said there was nothing to worry about. It was because I drank the whole bag without eating first, and that's probably why the effects were lasting longer. That's all.

I wanted to believe him. But the fear, which had been on a low flame in the restaurant, turned into real anxiety as the minutes passed. It'll never go away, I thought. I'll never be able to have conversations with people. Or continue the trip. They'll have to fly me home. Hospitalize me in the cuckoo's nest. They'll inject me with sedatives that will screw me up even more.

But my greatest fear was sleep, I was afraid to go to sleep. And then wake up and not know whether I was in a dream or in reality. That was my feeling: that falling asleep was an enormous danger.

---

So I won't sleep, I decided. A day, two days, a week, however long it took.

But what'll happen if I fall asleep for even a few seconds without realizing it?

When I open my eyes, how will I know where I am?

---

Years later, during one of the first interviews I gave, the journalist told me—maybe as a way to create intimacy—that he was bisexual.

That's great, I said, you can enjoy both worlds.

Enjoy? he grimaced. You don't understand how disconcerting it is not to be sure about something that should be axiomatic.

That night in the cabin, I wasn't sure about one of the axioms of our existence: That everything that happens really does happen. And not only in my imagination.

Were the clouds gathering on the cabin ceiling real?

Were crab claws actually emerging from them?

Was the cabin even real?

Did the bed I was lying on exist?

I closed my eyes so I wouldn't see the claws and tried to think about Dikla. About my mom. About my sister. I tried to hold on to them. But picturing them allowed my mind to do weird things to them. Exchange their faces. Connect one's limbs to the body of the other. Make them shorter. Make them taller. Distort them.

Like an ATM telling you that it's not working, my long-term memory was saying, to my horror: Don't trust me now.

My heart was pounding. My awareness of that only made it pound faster. The crab claws were coming for me. They descended and moved slowly closer, threatening to sink into my throat.

The only sure point of reference in all that chaos was Ari.

He was clearly lying on his bed. Two meters from me. Wearing the striped sharwal he'd bought in the Indian market in Otavalo. One arm was tucked under the back of his neck, as usual. He hadn't taken off his socks. As usual. He clearly smelled like Ari. And his voice, when he spoke to me, sounded like Ari's voice.

With a heart threatening to explode, I explained to him that I was like a strand of hair. And that he was holding the end of it.

I asked him to stay awake. And every time I called out, Ari! he should reply, Here!

He didn't laugh at me or hesitate. He just said that if he should happen to fall asleep anyway, I should shout louder or throw a shoe at him.

———

Shoes were not needed. He stayed awake all night.

I shouted: Ari!

He replied: Here!

I shouted: Ari.

And he replied: That's me.

———

My struggle to maintain my sanity—I'm not exaggerating, that's how I felt that entire night, that I was struggling to maintain my sanity and might lose it if I fell asleep—lasted until the first rays of sun drove the crabs and the clouds from the cabin, and I heard the real, familiar sound of birdsong.

Half an hour later, we got on the first van leaving the farm and drove away from there. I knew that Ari would have been happy to remain, but he didn't say a word. I mean—if I reproduce the exact dialogue—I said, Listen, I don't feel it would be a good thing for me to stay in that cabin. And he said, So let's get the hell out of here.

———

I remember the trip. The first minutes of the trip. We leaned against our backpacks in the back of the van and didn't speak. It was weird: Instead of being relieved that my fear of losing my mind had passed, I felt as if I'd been cast out of Eden.

The cities of the gods no longer glittered beyond the clouds. The clouds themselves were just clouds. And everything that had looked so magnificent when I was under the influence of the cactus juice, now looked ordinary. Banal.

The flow of the river seemed much slower. The sunbeams that had filtered through the branches looked dimmer. The birds weren't singing. Only chirping blandly.

To be accurate, I felt as if I had shifted from a state of overwhelming, boundless awareness to one that was narrow. Limited. Painfully sparse. The world had returned to being merely the world. Nothing more.

I remember thinking: The high point of the trip is behind us. Anything that happens from now on will never match what happened to me yesterday. For better or for worse.

I remember that Ari asked: What's happening, amigo? And that after that last night, I felt we were close enough for him to understand the abrupt switch from the fear of insanity to the sorrow of constricting rationality. So I explained it to him.

He was silent for a few seconds, then said: Okay, you have two choices. Choice number one—get ahold of more cactus juice. But you should take into account that this time, you might not survive it.

And the second choice?

Write, he said.

———

How could he have been so sure, I wonder now. How could he have predicted the future that way?

———

I took my journal out of my backpack and opened it. There were a few phrases I'd written under the influence of the cactus juice, and like most of what is written under the influence of drugs or alcohol, they were worthless. So I turned to a new page and began to write something else. On the top of the page, I wrote "To Dikla" out of habit, but it ended up being a short story. About Curly Hair. Her family in Israel. The broken heart she'd suffered a few weeks before leaving for South America. The son-of-a-bitch musician who broke it. It was all made up, of course. The only thing I knew about her was that she'd always wanted a big brother. And that was my starting point.

I threw all of myself into that story. My eyes never left the pages.

The van kept moving, but I no longer saw the world that had become so faded and flat after the fall.

I saw Curly Hair's life. It spread out before me in its entirety, an Eden of possibilities.

———

The van reached its destination that evening. Only then did I return the journal to my backpack. But in many senses, that trip has continued to this day.

———

And my bond with Ari has as well.

His condition has deteriorated these last few days. They sent him home because none of the medical treatments helped. Then they hospitalized him again to administer painkillers directly into his vein.

He was groggy most of the time, and only sometimes did he open his eyes for a few seconds and speak. Sometimes he sounded totally lucid, and other times his mind would stumble around like a drunken sailor.

Yesterday, for example—we were alone in his room—he asked me again to help him die. My parents flatly refused to do it, he said. I mean, my mother. All of a sudden, she re-membered that her grandfather was a rabbi, can you believe it? And my father doesn't want to do it without a green light from her. Those two, with that togetherness of theirs. In short, that's it, there's no one but you.

I didn't say anything.

Ari gave me a pleading look.

I had never seen him plead.

I kept silent and he kept looking at me. For long seconds. Or minutes.

Time moves differently in the oncology department.

And then, suddenly, he clutched my hand and said: Thank you.

I wanted to tell him that I'd thought about it, but it was too much for me, I mean, Zorba is right, it's probably the right thing to do, but still, I'm sorry, I'm not sure I'm capable of it—

But he went on: That night . . . in Ecuador . . . if you hadn't been with me in that cabin, I would have gone crazy.

It's the other way around, I wanted to correct him.

But his eyes were closing. And there was no point.

I kept holding his hand and looking at the monitor, which showed dot after dot, and I begged the gods, the ones behind the clouds, please, please make him stop hurting.

Then I had an idea.

I went down to the café next door to the hospital. I opened my computer. I foraged around old e-mails and found the list of phone numbers of the members of that workshop, the one the guy who'd written the subversive story about euthanasia had attended. I called him. He answered. How are you, he said, how's your back? Still hurting? I told him about Ari: I need that kind of angel urgently, like the one in your story. Someone willing to give the injection.

There was a silence. A long one.

A long silence was what I was hoping for.

Finally, he said: This conversation never happened. Text me your friend's number. Not by WhatsApp. Then immediately delete it. He and I will make all the arrangements. Don't talk to me. Don't ask me what's happening or what's going to happen. You won't have any way of knowing exactly when the angel will visit. There's no way of predicting. It could happen tomorrow or in another month. Depending on the circumstances. In any case, from now on, you're out of the picture. Is that clear?

***Forgive the technical question, but what is your record? What is the largest number of pages you wrote in one sitting?***

Sometimes, one exactly right sentence is preferable to dozens of ineffective pages. That, by the way, is why I suffer from poet envy. It's like the famous bridge scene in *Indiana Jones*: While I'm scrambling around in the ruins of characters and plot for so many pages, poets, in one good line, fire a shot and hit the bull's-eye.

Nonetheless—once, on the roof of a hostel in Peru, I wrote for two straight days. Twenty-five pages of a single letter to Dikla. The night before, I'd called her from the pay phone in the local post office. We spoke, and for the first time since I'd left for South America without her, she sounded distant. Trying hard to show an interest she didn't really feel. Also, the name of a guy from the university, Mickey, came up twice in the conversation, and something about the way she said it... I don't know. It stressed me out. In those days, there was no texting or WhatsApp you could use to allay your fears. So I told Ari that I needed a little time for myself and wrote Dikla a letter. I told her about the cactus juice and what happened to me when the effects of it didn't pass. I described how, when the crab claws came down from the ceiling and threatened to close around my neck, I shut my eyes and tried to think of her. Only her. I knew that if I could focus on her hugging me, it would stop the claws, but I couldn't. Her image faded in my mind every time I tried to stabilize it. And of all the things that happened to me that day and night, that was the most frightening.

Don't fade away from me, I wrote her. I love you. I'll propose to you as many times as it takes, with helicopters and billboards and everything, but you should know right now that I want to have children with you.

For many pages, I continued to imagine what our children would look like. Two boys and a girl, of course, I described each one and the relationships between them, and what a happy pandemonium our family meals would be in our home in the Galilee. I described that home. The herb garden. The hammock hung between two grapefruit trees.

The small soccer goals. The hanging speakers playing Meir Ariel and Alona Daniel alternately.

———

We had two girls and a boy. And we didn't move to the Galilee.

But I was right about one thing: That was the perfect moment to send Dikla a love letter.

———

Months after I came back to Israel—we were living together by then—she confessed: I was just about to crack. That guy Mickey called and asked me to go with him to the Student Day celebration at the Dead Sea. And I almost said yes. But then an envelope from you arrived. It was so thick. As if you'd sent me dollars. I had to open it.

———

I wrote another letter to Dikla during these past few months. More accurately, I tried to write. By hand. On the computer. Dozens of drafts. All beginning with "Don't fade away from me." And they all faded away. I didn't know how to continue. I tried switching to poems. To songs. I tried quoting from Agi Mishol and Jacques Brel. But I couldn't find the passionate, stirring words that could really tip her inner scales in my favor. Maybe because there was too much past between us that didn't promise her a future. Maybe because I'd become too much of a writer to write something from my heart that would go directly into hers. Or maybe because the real story here is not about a man who has to mollify the wife he's afraid he's losing but about a man who understands too late that he has already lost her.

In any case, tomorrow is the bat mitzvah. All the preparations have been made. The album of her photographs is ready. The deejay has been given the official list of the definitely-yes songs and the definitely-no songs. Her dress has been bought. Tried on at home. Removed with bitter weeping. And tried on again. The cake has been ordered and I only need to pick it up from the bakery in the morning. The final visit to the hairdresser is planned for tomorrow at noon, and tomorrow night, the five of us will get into the car and drive to the hall. When it's over, we'll drive home, and after the kids have gone to sleep, Dikla will say, I want to talk to you about something.

### How do you know when you've reached the end of a book?

In my workshop, I teach a lesson called "The Body and Erotica." First, I ask my students to cover their eyes with a handkerchief, then I spray perfume in the room and ask them to imagine the woman wearing that scent. Then I spray aftershave around the room and ask them to imagine the man wearing that scent. After they remove their blindfolds, they have to write about the man and the woman sitting in a room, longing to touch each other but unable to.

The period of time the students are blindfolded is the only time in the ten meetings of the workshop that the instructor can look at his cell phone unashamedly.

I had intended to check my e-mails to make sure the Stockholm police had received the written testimony I'd sent them about Axel Wolff—and that's how I found out.

In the middle of a class. His mother had sent me a short text.

You don't need many words for the really important things.

I love you: three words.

Ari died, funeral tomorrow. Four words. You can't walk out in the middle of a session and leave an entire class without a teacher. I listened to erotic texts and thought that Ari would have said that the situation was hysterically funny, and I thought, That's it, I have no one to collect situations for. I wanted to cry, but crying in front of students is like crying in front of children, so I restrained myself until the last student, who'd forgotten her cardigan in the classroom, came back to get it, and then left. I turned off the lights and played a song he was crazy about on my phone (Ari didn't just like songs, he was crazy about them).

*She's gone on her way. Oh Oh Oh Oh.*
*She's gone on her way.*
*In large planes above the sea.*
*Where is she headed?*
*Where is she headed?*

Then I locked up, turned on the alarm, and began to wander the streets of Jaffa. I couldn't go back to my too-new apartment feeling like that. I had to find someone. Something. I stopped at a kiosk. Bought a bottle of Bitter Lemon in Ari's memory and drank the bitterness down to the last drop. I thought, Maybe the guy behind the counter? We occasionally talked as Hapoel fans. But he was busy with customers who wanted to give him their betting forms for the British horse races, and I didn't see how I could manage it. I crossed the street. The pitiful homeless guy was in his regular place near the trash cans. When I sometimes offer him leftover refreshments from the workshop, he takes them and says, Bless you. I threw the empty Bitter Lemon bottle into the trash and began walking toward him, really, I wanted to, but his head suddenly dropped to his chest. He'd fallen asleep. And I didn't have the heart to wake him up. So I continued toward the area of bars. On the way, a charming couple passed me. He looked charming and she looked charming, and the way they walked beside each other—almost, but not really, touching—was charming. Even the way they looked at me seemed to say, "We have enough love. Want some leftovers?" So how could I interrupt them? And on a Thursday, no less. A second before they left for a weekend at a country B and B. I walked faster and went into an unpopular bar where I sometimes drink after the workshop. On Thursdays, in an attempt to attract more customers, the unpopular bar features a deejay, who plays hip-hop classics from the nineties. He plays them so loudly that if you want to order, you have to hold up the menu for Elad, the bar-man, and point to the drink you want, because there's no way he can hear you. I pointed to Arak and grapefruit juice, and Elad brought me the tall glass. I took out the straw and drank it down in one swallow, caught his glance, and finally said—quietly, so he wouldn't hear—My only friend is dead.

———

Dikla came to the funeral with me.

A few days after the bat mitzvah, we agreed—that is, she asked and I had no choice but to agree—that I would leave the house. I rented an apartment on a nearby street. I moved the few things that were "mine" and not "ours" into it. Mainly books. Nonetheless, Dikla came to the funeral with me. She didn't just come with me. She picked me up in her company car and walked at my side as the coffin was taken to the grave. I thought it was a nice gesture on her part. And that if we hadn't known each other and I was seeing her for the first time there, in the cemetery, with her button-down white blouse and her hair pinned back, I would have been turned on.

I thought that I didn't regret a single one of the thousands of days we'd been together. It had been good. We'd been good. And even if our temporary separation becomes permanent, and a real, not imagined, messenger with divorce papers knocks on my door this week, she will always be the love of my life.

———

After I read my eulogy and went back to stand at her side, she groped for my hand and held it for the duration of the ceremony.

It had been clear to everyone, including me, that I would be the one to write the eulogy. But it took me long hours to write even a single word. Reading through the e-mails we'd written each other over the last few years, I came across something I'd written to him from London, a few months before they found the tumor.

————

*Twenty-five years later, the major subjects of debate at the Speakers' Corner in Hyde Park are still the same: Muhammad, Jesus, the banks, it's not easy to be a homosexual. And the grass is exactly the same color: English green. And it's cold. But not cold enough to chill you to the bone.*

*Remember how we started arguing loudly then, about nothing, just to get people to gather around us?*

*Meanwhile, you've become a lawyer who argues cases in court. And I've found my own way to give voice to what was silent inside me.*

*I no longer need to stand on a bench to attract attention. And in the free time I have on my work trips, I'd rather watch. Do you feel that way too?*

*I don't know why I'm writing you now.*

*Maybe because I miss you and the time when we had time to travel together to far-off places.*

*Maybe because you told me on the phone before I went to London that you feel stuck. That you're dying to leave the firm now, of all times, after you made partner.*

*I've been feeling like that for about five years already. Even though I manage to hide it from everyone. Even you.*

*And suddenly, here in the park, I had a kind of lucid moment, you know? For a second, I could see the inner reel of my life. The one that is usually hidden from me.*

*I don't know if I can explain myself. But for a second, I could see that, despite everything, we managed to move out of square one, you and I. And if we did it once, there's no reason we can't to do it again. Right?*

————

I couldn't imagine getting through that entire letter without choking up in the middle.

So in the end, at the grave, I just talked about how Ari and I met. Not the story of the basketball court in Malcha Stadium. The real story.

Our Memorial Day ceremony in high school included a parade that ended in the soccer field. We marched in threes, in the blazing sun, as the names of the fallen were read. The list grew longer every year, and every year, a few students who couldn't take the heat fainted and dropped onto the grass during the ceremony. Since the fainting was as age-old as the ceremony itself, "evacuation monitors" were appointed every year to silently and unemotionally carry the unconscious on a stretcher to the side of the field, where a medical crew waited.

Ari and I were monitors that year. On the days preceding the parade, we practiced opening the stretchers and carrying them, over and over again. But none of the teachers who taught us how to do it could have prepared us for the fact that Haim Huri was the first to fall.

Haim Huri was a head taller than us. And ten inches wider. Captain of the basketball team. Arm-wrestling champion of the class. But the year was 1985, the Israeli Army was still mired in Lebanon, many new names had been added to the list, and there wasn't a single cloud in the sky to soften the sun. Haim Huri fell like a twig in the brief pause between the letters *L* and *M*.

Haim fell, Ari whispered to me.

We ran over to him with the stretcher, dutifully rolled his huge body onto it, and panting so much we could hardly breathe, raised the stretcher onto our shoulders and began walking.

The first aid station was about one hundred meters away. After about ten meters—we collapsed. The stretcher was too small, and Haim Huri slipped off. We tried to catch him— and we fell too. We picked ourselves up, put Haim back on the stretcher, and after another ten meters, my knees started to shake and I fell—and the stretcher, Haim Huri, and Ari fell on top of me.

Forget it, Ari said, I'll take him and you take the stretcher.

To this day, I haven't been able to figure out where he got the strength to carry Haim Huri piggyback.

But that's what happened. He put him on his shoulders and started walking. I skipped after them with the stretcher. When we reached the first aid station, I was sure Ari would be angry at me. Or make fun of me. We were at the age when you elevate your own status by putting down others. Instead, Ari lay down on the grass, exhausted, and laughed at me. He laughed quietly—after all, we were in the middle of a Memorial Day ceremony—but there was no mistaking it: Ari thought that all of it had been more amusing than humiliating.

————

You gave me another pair of eyes, friend, I told him.

And I ended my eulogy with three lines from "Fall and Get Up," by Shabak Samech, his favorite band.

*Because there's another place so sweet,*
*Where you have more time,*
*As much as you need.*

————

After the funeral, we went to his parents' house. I say "we," in the plural, out of habit, even though Dikla apologized for not joining us, saying she had to go home and make supper for the kids. We stood at her car, in the dirt parking lot, and the embarrassment in the air strangely resembled the embarrassment that comes at the end of a first date.

Thank you for coming, I said.

What do you mean, of course I came.

I don't know, I said. You were never crazy about Ari.

He introduced us, she said. He was a part of my life for twenty years.

Right.

What you said was nice, she said, and then quickly corrected herself. Not just nice. True.

Yes, true. I looked down.

I brought you this, she said and took the new Docaviv Film Festival program out of her bag. It came in the mail and—

Thank you for . . . thinking of me, I said.

And then, suddenly, she crossed the time that separated us and hugged me. She wrapped me in her two long, delicate arms. In the middle of the cemetery parking lot.

It had been weeks since a woman had hugged me.

We remained immersed in each other for a long time. Body inside body inside body.

Memory inside memory inside memory.

Finally, she broke away from me. Slowly. First her breasts. Then her neck. Then her arms.

Will you be okay? she asked. From a safe distance.

I nodded. And she got into her car.

———

The next day, I went to the shivah.

And also the day after that.

The pain of Ari's death was too great for me to remain alone with it, so I found myself spending an entire week with the Strelin family. I didn't sleep over. There was a limit. But I would come early in the morning and leave at night with the last of the visitors, carrying away with me the many trash bags that accumulated each day.

———

My thoughts that week were surprisingly lucid.

The dysthymia disappeared almost completely. Pills hadn't made it go away. Sessions with psychologists hadn't made it go away. Training for the triathlon hadn't made it go away. Falling in love hadn't made it go away. It just went away by itself.

I remembered how, every time we moved from city to city when I was a kid—and we did it often—I would be sad for months before the move, and when it finally happened, I was actually relieved.

I think that deep inside, I mourned the inevitable separation from Ari and from Dikla before it happened, I passed through all five stages of grief in advance, and now a kind of energy that had been trapped inside me was released.

I felt no weight on my shoulders, as if I'd taken off a backpack after a trek.

Being cut off from everyday demands—from text messages, e-mails, students who want to know when I'd finish reading their texts, the Stockholm police. (Who weren't satisfied with my written testimony that I had indeed heard Axel Wolff say he was the murderer, and in endless phone calls, demanded more trust-inspiring details from that

damned night in Jerusalem. You're a writer, the chief investi-
gator said, what reason do we have to believe you?)

That total break gave me something I hadn't had for a
long time.

Perspective.

I could look at my life and its collapse over this past year
from the sidelines. And understand what it was all about.

How it happened. What led to what. How I was caught
in the web of lies I myself had spun.

———

On the sixth day of the shivah, Sirkin called. I blocked
him. He called again. And again. I went outside with the
phone. He wanted me to write an outline for the debate.
I told him that I was sitting shivah for a friend. He said it
was urgent. I told him to go to hell. He threatened again to
expose our relationship. Without hesitation, without clear-
ing my throat, I said, Do whatever you want, Yoram. I have
nothing to lose anymore.

———

On the last day of the shivah, Hagai Carmeli showed up.

He walked into the living room. With that puzzled
expression of his. And a red beard.

At first glance, he looked the same. He hadn't faded at
all.

I was surprised he'd come. And at the same time, it was
the most natural thing in the world.

I went over to him. I could see in his face that at first, he didn't recognize me. And then he did.

We hugged. That surprised me. Hugs were never his thing. You could barely get a high five out of him.

After the hug, we still held each other's shoulders loosely. Now I could see the small wrinkles on the sides of his eyes. And the sunspots on his cheeks. If we were women, that would have been the moment one of us would say that the other looked absolutely wonderful. But instead of playing fast and loose with the truth, we walked over to a corner of the living room.

I said, Bro, where have you been? I looked high and low for you! Far and wide! Up and down!

He didn't reply. He just smiled that minimal smile of his.

———

Ari's father came over to us. Stooped. So stooped.

Hagai, he said in a gloomy voice. It's good to see you.

I'm so sorry for your loss, Hagai said as he stood to greet him.

No one could feel more sorrow than we do, but thank you. There are empanadas on the table if you're hungry. Don't be embarrassed to take some.

Thank you, Hagai said.

Ari's father tilted forward at a sharp angle, and, for a moment, I thought he would fall onto Hagai. But then he straightened and turned to go back to the kitchen.

Hagai sat down again and said, I'm sorry that . . . I disappeared on you like that.

What happened?

He rubbed his beard for a while.

And then said: A girl.

And was silent for another three beats.

———

I remembered that the pace of Hagai's speech used to drive Ari crazy. I like people you can have a ping-pong conversation with, he once explained to me, and that Carmeli talks tennis. Two hours between sentences.

I think it's because he wants to be precise, I defended him. And I didn't rush him now either.

I saw her reading your book, Hagai finally said. In Buenos Aires. In the El Ateneo. That bookstore in the opera house?

I knew it! I knew you were in Buenos Aires! I ran after you there, in the subway, but—

I went up to her and said that you and I were close friends. She was curious about that. So she agreed to have a drink with me when she finished the chapter.

Wait a minute. What was she doing there?

A trip after she finished her degree.

A kid, eh?

A cloud passed over Hagai Carmeli's eyes. Something about the word "kid" grated on him and he gave me a disappointed look. On the verge of scorn. A look that, in high school, he reserved for those who preferred Queen over the Smiths.

A few seconds later, he looked away and spoke quietly. Almost to himself.

I didn't feel any gap between us. We were together for a month, more than a month, in Buenos Aires. It was ... the happiest time of my life. Maybe the only happy time of my life. One night, I drank enough to ... propose. She said no, she was young ... and needed time to take it all in. To get her thoughts in order. Then she went to Bolivia with her girlfriends. They rode in a van to La Paz—

Don't tell me. Death Road.

Yes.

Was her name Mayan?

No. Nirit.

Describe her to me.

He described the girl standing beside Mayan in the picture. Holding a surfboard. Black curls. A straight part between them. Huge eyes. A slightly arrogant stance.

Then he was silent for a few beats.

He touched the corner of his eye with his pinkie finger. And wiped away a tear. A single tear.

He was silent for another three beats. Withdrew into himself.

Then suddenly, he came out of his reverie and asked: Wait a minute, who's Mayan?

———

I told him about the meeting in Ganei Tikvah. And about Mayan's mother, who came up to me with the picture when it was over.

I hesitated for a moment before telling him about the relationship that developed between me and Mayan after she died. But then I thought, if anyone could understand—

He nodded occasionally and looked at me nonjudgmentally, and when I finished telling him, he asked: Want something to drink?

He went and got some Zero for me and real Coke for himself.

He handed me the plastic cup and asked: Do you still have the picture?

Sure, I said. In my workroom.

He rubbed his beard, looking as if he'd just thought of something, and said, Remember how we used to go to the beach and I didn't go into the water?

Of course I do, I said, you used to bring a chessboard with you. And play against yourself.

She taught me how to surf, Nirit, he said. Can you picture me surfing?

Then, in a choked voice, he said, She called me "Carmeli" and I called her "Cheeks," because her cheeks were kind of plump. When I was with her, it felt like everything would work out.

The place they went to, he said, had no hope or loss, no regret or sorrow, not even pain, the place they were in had everything. It was a perfect place.

He didn't have to say he was quoting a poem by Natan Zach.

We were silent for a while. All around us, people continued to talk about Ari and about Yoram Sirkin's upsurge in the latest polls. Someone said that Sirkin couldn't speak a single word of truth, someone else replied that there's no such thing as truth anymore. Truth is passé. Trays of empanadas kept coming out of the kitchen. Ari's photo album was passed around, and when it reached me, I couldn't browse through it, not yet, it was too soon for me, so I handed it to Hagai, who, to my relief, also passed it on. Every now and then, I could hear Spanish break through the Hebrew. Outside the building, someone turned on a lawn mower. Hagai got up and came back with two empanadas, one for him and one for me. I remembered that, even when we used to sleep over in the basement of his house, he would always fuss around us, bring drinks, food, pillows to put under our sleeping bags, rekindle the embers of the conversation with a new subject, the neckline of our history teacher, Doreen Schwartz, black holes, *The Hobbit*, Maradona. When our eyelids had almost dropped, he would keep us awake by suggesting that each of us talk about his favorite masturbation fantasies. He would begin, and the others would follow. Their fantasies were always as bare-bones as a mug shot, and my turn came quickly. With me, there were obstacles, conflicts, rounded-out characters, and plots, so that by the time I finished speaking, everyone was fast asleep—except Ari. Before zipping up his sleeping bag for the night, he would say in a sleepy voice: Bro, I think you're going to be a writer. But you have to learn when to stop.

———

I'm not going to write anymore, I told Hagai after the last sip.

Why not? he asked. There was no shock in his voice. And no reproach. Only pure interest. I remembered why I loved talking to him so much.

It doesn't make me happy anymore.

So stop, he said.

I've become a liar, I said. An obsessive storyteller and a cannibal. Everything that happens is food for my stories, even when Dikla said, I'm leaving you not because I don't love you anymore but because I don't believe a word you say anymore—even then, I thought, that's a powerful sentence, I should put it into a story—

If that's the case—

And the world is overflowing with lies now, lies are the global currency these days.

There's something in—

I feel like going out to play, man, to do something real, something concrete. Establish an NGO, run for the Knesset, castrate a pedophile—

Okay, you've convinced me. Maybe you really do need to stop writing for a while.

There's only one text I have to finish, I said. And that's it. Questions that some Internet site sent me a year ago.

Maybe they've already forgotten the whole business, but I've been hanging on to it as if it were a lifesaver, because I had nothing else to hang on to this year. I always lie in those interviews, you know, give a writer's answers. This time, I tried to answer honestly, or at least to move in the direction of honesty, and there was something liberating about it. In any case, I only have a few lines to finish, and then I'll start a totally different life.

### Is there anything you want to add?

When the shivah was over, I went to do some things in the apartment.

I began with the kids' rooms. I repainted the walls in bright colors. I filled them with light wooden furniture. I put surprises on each one's pillow to make them happy on their coming visit: white chocolate for Yanai, *The Guinness World Records* for Noam, and an Adidas hat for Shira. Who, surprisingly, had said she wanted to come. I didn't think it mattered what I did, there would be sadness in the air when they arrived. I didn't think it mattered how much sadness there would be in the air when they arrived, I was going to fight for them. For them and for everything else that still isn't lost here, in my home and my country. Dikla texted me: Is it okay if I bring them a little early? I have something at work. I thought she probably had a date and was lying to keep from hurting me. I texted her back: It'll be fine. I was bitterly jealous of her date. I imagined what he looked like. I could guess what he looked like. A combination of Eran, the deputy director of marketing in her company, and Barack Obama. I unpacked the few things I'd brought, arranged them in the living room and the bedroom, put up a small shelf in the work corner, and placed *Zorba the Greek, The Book of Tao*, and the picture of Mayan on it. There's a hint of a smile in the corner of her mouth. Not an actual smile. Definitely not laughter. More an inclination of the mouth that hints at an inclination of the soul toward goodness. I said to her: Now it's just you and me, I asked her: Don't leave me. I took out my laptop, plugged it in, and opened the document that contained my answers to the surfers' questions. I thought to myself that this would probably be my last interview, and that's good. I pushed the little square on the side of the screen all the way up to reach the beginning so I could go over what I'd written. Then I changed my mind.

No. I won't rewrite, won't rethink, won't embellish. Not this time.

I attached the document to an e-mail and addressed it to the site editor.

I took a long, deep breath, the way you do before jumping off a roof—and sent it.

CREDITS

ESHKOL NEVO, born in Jerusalem in 1971, is one of Israel's most successful living writers. His novels have all been bestsellers in Israel and published widely in translation. His novel *Homesick* was long-listed for the 2009 Independent Foreign Fiction Prize; *World Cup Wishes* was a finalist for the 2011 Kritikerpreis der Jury der Jungen Kritiker (Austria); *Neuland* was included in the *Independent*'s 2014 Books of the Year in Translation; and *Three Floors Up* (Other Press, 2017) will be adapted for film by the acclaimed Italian director Nanni Moretti in 2020. Nevo owns and co-manages the largest private creative writing school in Israel and is a mentor to many up-and-coming young Israeli writers.

SONDRA SILVERSTON has translated the work of Israeli fiction writers such as Etgar Keret, Ayelet Gundar-Goshen, Zeruya Shalev, and Savyon Liebrecht. Her translation of Amos Oz's *Between Friends* won the National Jewish Book Award for fiction in 2013. Born in the United States, she has lived in Israel since 1970.